PENGUIN BOOKS

Father Brown

G. K. Chesterton was born in London in 1874. He was educated at St Paul's School and studied art at the Slade School. He converted to Roman Catholicism in 1922. Chesterton began a career in journalism, writing with Hilaire Belloc for the *Speaker*. He wrote for *Eye Witness* (later the *New Witness*), which he transformed into *G. K.'s Weekly* in 1925 and edited it until his death in 1936.

Chesterton's first novel, *The Napoleon of Notting Hill*, was published in 1904. His most famous stories are those of Father Brown, who first appeared in *The Innocence of Father Brown* in 1911 and brought Chesterton a wider audience. His prolific writings on a wide variety of subjects include the fantasy novel *The Man who was Thursday* (1908); literary studies of Robert Browning (1903), Dickens (1906), Robert Louis Stevenson (1907) and Shaw (1910); biographies of Francis of Assisi (1923) and Thomas Aquinas (1933); collections of essays on political and social subjects; several volumes of poems; as well as works of apologetics including *Orthodoxy* (1909) and *The Everlasting Man* (1925). He also wrote his *Autobiography*, which was published posthumously in 1936.

Ian Ker taught English Literature at York University before being ordained a Roman Catholic priest. Subsequently, he has taught both English and theology at universities in the USA and Britain, where he now teaches in the theology faculty at Oxford. Like Father Brown, he is also a parish priest who is often away from his parish, as he lectures all over the world on John Henry Newman, on whom he is the author and editor of twenty books, including the definitive *John Henry Newman: A Biography* (1988).

G. K. CHESTERTON

Father Brown

Selected and Introduced by Ian Ker

PENGUIN BOOKS

PENGUIN BOOKS

Published by the Penguin Group
Penguin Books Ltd, 80 Strand, London WC2R ORL, England
Penguin Putnam Inc., 375 Hudson Street, New York, New York 10014, USA
Penguin Books Australia Ltd, Ringwood, Victoria, Australia
Penguin Books Canada Ltd, 10 Alcorn Avenue, Toronto, Ontario, Canada M4V 3B2
Penguin Books India (P) Ltd, 11 Community Centre, Panchsheel Park, New Delhi – 110 017, India
Penguin Books (NZ) Ltd, Cnr Rosedale and Airborne Roads, Albany, Auckland, New Zealand
Penguin Books (South Africa) (Pty) Ltd, 24 Sturdee Avenue, Rosebank 2196, South Africa

Penguin Books Ltd, Registered Offices: 80 Strand, London WC2R ORL, England

First published in Great Britain as *The Father Brown Stories* by Cassell 1929
Published in Penguin Books in the United States of America
by arrangement with Dodd, Mead & Company, Inc.
Published as *The Penguin Complete Father Brown* in Penguin Books 1981
A selection from *The Penguin Complete Father Brown* reprinted
with a new Introduction in Penguin Classics 2001
1

Set in 9.5/12 pt New Caledonia
Typeset by Rowland Phototypesetting Ltd, Bury St Edmunds, Suffolk
Printed in England by Clays Ltd, St Ives plc

Contents

Introduction

In his *Autobiography* (1936), G. K. Chesterton explained how he came
to create the character of Father Brown, with his blend of 'external
simplicity and internal subtlety'; pointing out the fallacy of supposing
that, because a novelist may derive the idea of a character from a person
in real life, that created character must *be* that person. Chesterton
acknowledged that Father Brown did have 'an original in real life' –
even though he turned out to be very different from the actual priest
who first suggested the clerical detective to the author.

For while Father Brown 'did take some of his inner intellectual
qualities from my friend, Father John O'Connor of Bradford', in every
other respect he was quite different. The point about the character was
that he should be 'pointless', in the sense that 'his conspicuous quality
was not being conspicuous', as it was his 'chief feature to be featureless'.
Because his 'commonplace exterior was meant to contrast with his
unsuspected vigilance and intelligence', his creator had 'made his
appearance shabby and shapeless, his face round and expressionless,
his manners clumsy, and so on'. The real-life Father O'Connor did not
have 'any of these external qualities'. Quite the opposite; he was 'not
shabby, but rather neat', 'not clumsy, but very delicate and dexterous',
and he not only was, but looked, 'amusing and amused'. He wasn't even
the same nationality, being 'a sensitive and quick-witted Irishman',
whereas Father Brown was 'a Suffolk dumpling from East Anglia'.

Still, Chesterton explained, there was 'a very real sense in which
Father O'Connor was the intellectual inspiration of these stories'. He
had first met him while giving a lecture at Keighley in the West Riding
of Yorkshire. The Irish priest had impressed him by the 'tact and
humour with which he mingled with his very Yorkshire and very Protestant company.' Like them, Chesterton soon discovered that the real

Father Brown was also 'a character'. However, if anybody had told him that ten years later he would be 'a Mormon Missionary in the Cannibal Islands', Chesterton would 'not have been more surprised than at the suggestion that, fully fifteen years' on, he would be making his confession to Father O'Connor upon becoming a Roman Catholic.'

That meeting was to be the first of many, and it was on one of these that 'the incident occurred, which led me to take the liberty of putting him, or rather part of him', into the Father Brown stories. Chesterton had mentioned that he was intending to take a certain line in print about 'some rather sordid social questions of vice and crime'. O'Connor replied that he thought he was wrong, or rather misinformed; and 'he told me certain facts he knew about perverted practices'. Earlier in the *Autobiography*, Chesterton had confessed to having imagined to himself 'any amount of iniquity' in his younger days. It was therefore 'a curious experience to find that this quiet and pleasant celibate had plumbed those abysses far deeper' than he ever had. Indeed, he 'had not imagined that the world could hold such horrors'. On returning to the house where they were visiting they met two Cambridge undergraduates. One of them, having expressed admiration for Father O'Connor's cultured and knowledgeable conversation, nevertheless remarked that being 'shut up in a sort of cloister', he couldn't 'know anything about the real evil in the world'.

The 'colossal and crushing irony' of this comment caused Chesterton, 'still almost shivering with the appallingly practical facts of which the priest had warned me', 'nearly' to 'burst into a loud harsh laugh in the drawing room'. For he 'knew perfectly well that, as regards all the solid Satanism which the priest knew and warred with all his life, these two Cambridge gentlemen (luckily for them) knew about as much of real evil as two babies in the same perambulator'. At any rate the world of detective fiction is in debt to that naive undergraduate, since it was at that moment that 'there sprang up' in Chesterton's 'mind the vague idea of making some artistic use of this comic yet tragic cross-purposes; and constructing a comedy in which a priest should appear to know nothing and in fact know more about crime than the criminals'. Accordingly, Chesterton records, he 'permitted' himself 'the grave liberty of taking my friend and knocking him about; beating his hat and umbrella shapeless, untidying his clothes, punching his intelligent countenance into a condition of pudding-faced fatuity, and generally disguising Father O'Connor as Father Brown'. For the 'disguise . . . was a deliberate piece of fiction, meant to bring out or accentuate the contrast that was the point of the comedy'.[1]

The Father Brown stories first appeared in magazines before being collected into five books: *The Innocence of Father Brown* (1911), *The Wisdom of Father Brown* (1914), *The Incredulity of Father Brown* (1926), *The Secret of Father Brown* (1927), and *The Scandal of Father Brown* (1935). If not the most important of Chesterton's writings, they have remained the most popular and widely read. Chesterton certainly didn't regard them as of any great importance. His faithful secretary, Dorothy Collins, has recorded how some of them were written for purely financial reasons, particularly to help pay for his newspaper, *G. K.'s Weekly*. On being informed of his precarious bank balance, Chesterton would reply: '"Oh, well. We must write another Father Brown story", and this would be done at lightning speed a day or two later from a few notes on the back of an envelope.'[2]

Father Brown's commonplace, ordinary exterior is not only intended as a disguise for his extraordinary powers of observation and insight. It also reflects Chesterton's own love of ordinariness. And just as his creator delighted in depicting the most commonplace and familiar things with a vivid freshness as though they were entirely new and strange, so too Father Brown is able to detect a vital significance in the most unremarkable things; what everyone else fails to notice because of its apparent insignificance, he sees. Nobody noticed that somebody *did* actually enter the building: namely, the postman, or somebody who purported to be the postman, but who was ignored precisely because he looked like a postman. Or it may be, as in another story, a completely unsuspicious remark, as when the murdered admiral's solicitor is told that he has been drowned, and instead of assuming that it was at sea – as anybody else would – he asks *where* he was drowned. The identity of another murderer is spotted by Father Brown when he fails to start or look round at his victim screaming as she crashes to her death. In the story of the postman, Father Brown makes the shrewd observation that people don't answer what you ask but what they think you mean.

Ronald Knox commented that the Father Brown stories could not really be graded among mystery stories. In the first place, Father Brown is not really a detective at all, in the sense of being the expert who solves crimes which no one else can – such as Sherlock Holmes, for example. The only expertise that Father Brown possesses is his intimate knowledge of the human heart. And this knowledge he acquires from his religion, in two ways. To begin with, there is his belief in original sin and the human capacity for evil. It is precisely because of his own sins as a human being that he can understand another's. He rejects the science of criminology because it treats human beings as though they were external objects for study, whereas he knows that criminals are friends, not strangers, because they are fellow human beings. Instead of trying to observe the criminal, Father Brown tries to get inside, or rather tries to *be* the criminal. He sees himself as a kind of understudy who will know who has committed the crime once he has really learned the part. The reformed criminal Flambeau, for example, stopped stealing once Father Brown had explained to him why he stole. Far from seeing criminals as a race apart, Father Brown sees them as people like himself, that is, sinners. This is how he explains with unusual passion the source of his detective powers:

No man's really any good till he knows how bad he is, or might be; till he's realized exactly how much right he has to all this snobbery, and sneering, and talking about 'criminals,' as if they were apes in a forest ten thousand miles away; till he's got rid of all the dirty self-deception of talking about low types and deficient skulls; till he's squeezed out of his soul the last drop of the oil of the Pharisees; till his only hope is somehow or other to have captured one criminal, and kept him safe and sane under his own hat.

The other source of his knowledge of the human heart comes from his being a priest whose business, as it were, is sin, not least in the context of the confessional. In the first and most famous of the stories, 'The Blue Cross', Father Brown outwits Flambeau thanks to his knowledge of the tricks of the criminal trade which he has learned through hearing confessions. As a celibate living out of the world, like Father O'Connor, he knows about evil because he knows about real sins. And on one occasion he uncovers the villain because he can tell immediately that he has made a false confession. As a priest, too, he picks up vital information which the normal detective would never gather because he lacks that empathy which comes naturally to a good pastoral priest, used to mixing with all kinds of people.

Another critic has pointed out that it is impossible in a detective story to give any of the characters depth because every character has to be a suspect *except* the detective; but that in Father Brown's case, the detective is very much a character in his own right, and not only because of his knowledge of human nature, but because he *is* Chesterton in his views. As Knox observed, the sheer physical expansiveness of Chesterton was matched by the way in which he 'overflowed' every literary medium he tried, putting more of himself into it than it could contain. Even his great study of Dickens was 'really the Chestertonian philosophy as illustrated by the life of Dickens'. Similarly, the fact that Father Brown speaks with the voice of Chesterton makes him a larger personality than he would otherwise be. And so the Father Brown stories 'are something more' than detective stories: 'Like everything else Chesterton wrote, they are a Chestertonian manifesto.'[3]

Because Father Brown is a Catholic priest, it is no surpise to find that much of the Chestertonian manifesto in these stories is about Catholicism. A typically Chestertonian paradox is that Father Brown, in spite of being a Roman Catholic priest, never employs any specifically spiritual powers. The overwhelmingly Protestant readership that Chesterton was writing for would have naturally assumed that a detective priest would resort to all the tricks of 'priestcraft'. But Chesterton deliberately contrasts Father Brown, who categorically repudiates spiritual powers, with bogus characters who do (falsely) claim miraculous talents, as in 'The Red Moon of Meru'. Nor is there ever any suggestion that Father Brown ever employs any special supernatural insights.

The reason for this insistence is not just because Chesterton wants all the emphasis to fall upon Father Brown's experience of the human heart. At least as important is the theme that Catholicism and Catholic theology are entirely consonant with common sense and reason, while false religions dabble in the mysterious and occult. At the end of 'The Blue Cross', Father Brown completes his triumph over Flambeau by telling him that he knew the disguised Flambeau wasn't a real priest. How could he have known, the astonished Flambeau asks. 'You attacked reason. It's bad theology.' Flambeau had speculated that there might be other universes where reason was not rational, to which Father

Brown had responded: 'Alone on earth, the Church makes reason really supreme. Alone on earth, the Church affirms that God Himself is bound by reason.' In 'The Queer Feet', the author refers to the Catholic Church as 'wedded to common sense'. Elsewhere Father Brown is adamant that the first effect of not believing in God is that one loses one's common sense, which leads to superstitious gullibility. Mystery (in the non-Christian sense) is regularly denounced. In 'The Arrow of Heaven', Father Brown declares: 'Real mystics don't hide mysteries, they reveal them. They set up a thing in broad daylight, and when you've seen it it's still a mystery. But the mystagogues hide a thing in darkness and secrecy, and when you find it, it's a platitude.' In 'The Miracle of Moon Crescent', he goes further, saying that Satanism loves 'mysteries and initiations and secret societies and all the rest of it.' In 'The Doom of the Darnaways', the priest speaks of 'nonsense' as 'the most terrible thing' known to human beings. Whether it is 'scientific superstition' or 'other magical superstition', he believes in 'daylight' not 'subterranean superstition' that ends 'in the dark'. As he puts it in 'The Red Moon of Meru', 'Reason is from God, and when things are unreasonable there is something the matter.'

The voice of Father Brown is often audibly the voice of Chesterton. The Protestant doctrine of the Bible as the sole authority for Christians is answered by Father Brown with Chestertonian wit: 'When will people understand that it is useless for a man to read his Bible unless he also reads everybody else's Bible? A printer reads a Bible for misprints. A Mormon reads his Bible and finds polygamy; a Christian Scientist reads his and finds we have no arms and legs.' Naturally, too, Father Brown enjoys paradoxes: 'A thing can sometimes be too close to be seen, as, for instance, a man cannot see himself.' It may be the voice of Chesterton, but, far from being authorial intrusions, such observations can be very germane to the detective's investigation. It is important, for instance, to understand that:

The worldly man, who really lives only for this world and believes in no other, whose worldly success and pleasure are all he can ever snatch out of nothingness – *that* is the man who will really do anything, when he is in danger of losing the whole world and saving nothing. It is not the revolutionary man but the respectable man who would commit any crime – to save his respectability.

Whether strictly relevant or not, Father Brown, like Chesterton, has interesting, original, provocative things to say: such as that all genuine religions are materialistic; or that there is a difference (which the modern mind can't understand) between mystery 'in the sense of what is marvellous, and mystery in the sense of what is complicated', just as 'It really is more natural to believe a preternatural story that deals with things we don't understand, than a natural story that contradicts things we do understand'; or that 'People like frequent laughter, but I don't think they like a permanent smile. Cheerfulness without humour is a very trying thing'; or that so-called unbelievers are 'all balanced on the very edge of belief – of belief in almost anything'; that far from all religions being the same, 'some of them are so different that the best man of one creed will be callous, where the worst of another will be sensitive'; that there is indeed a limit to human charity 'and that is the real difference between human charity and Christian charity'. Father Brown's wisdom is Chesterton's wisdom, and that makes him a very unusual detective.

On the other hand, Chesterton's own extraordinary ingenuity – he is surely the most ingenious of all detective writers – in the plots he constructs may not exceed the bounds of possibility, but it certainly detracts from the realism of the stories. The detective genre was invented by Edgar Allen Poe, for whom crime was strictly an intellectual problem. But, while his detective Auguste Dupin purports to investigate solely by logical deduction, in fact what Poe achieves is 'not a triumph of reason, but a conjuring trick'. And it could be said that 'many of the Father Brown stories can be regarded as ingenious variations on the theme of "The Purloined Letter" ', the best known of the Dupin stories. What makes the difference between the two writers is that 'between Poe and Chesterton comes Conan Doyle'. For Sherlock Holmes is a character in a way that Dupin is not, just as Watson has a personality which Dupin's confidant totally lacks.[4]

There is a further debt that Chesterton owes to Conan Doyle and that is the way in which the Sherlock Holmes stories invest the most prosaic of London scenes with romance. But behind Conan Doyle is Dickens, 'the great master of the unfamiliarity in the familiar'.[5] In what is perhaps his finest work, *Charles Dickens* (1906), Chesterton gives a vivid example of 'that eerie realism with which Dickens could always vitalize some dark or dull corner of London', so that 'things seem more actual than things really are'. 'Indeed, that degree of realism does not exist in reality: it is the unbearable realism of a dream.' And Chesterton cites how Dickens

himself has given a perfect instance . . . He mentions among the coffee-shops into which he crept in those wretched days one in St Martin's Lane, 'of which I only recollect that it stood near the church, and that in the door there was an oval glass plate with 'COFFEE ROOM' painted on it, addressed towards the street. If I ever find myself in a very different kind of coffee room now, but where there is such an inscription on glass, and read it backwards on the wrong side, MOOR EEFFOC (as I often used to do then in a dismal reverie), a shock goes through my blood.' That wild word, 'Moor Eeffoc', is the motto of all effective realism; it is the masterpiece of the good realistic principle – the principle that the most fantastic thing of all is often the precise fact. And that elvish kind of realism Dickens adopted everywhere.[6]

Chesterton himself makes use of exactly the same visual effect in one of the Father Brown stories, but typically chooses a public house rather than a coffee shop:

Then his dubious eye roamed again to the white lettering on the glass front of the public-house. The young woman's eyes followed his, and rested there also, but in pure puzzledom.

'No,' said Father Brown, answering her thoughts. 'It doesn't say "Sela", like the thing in the Psalms; I read it like that myself when I was wool-gathering just now; it says "Ales".'

There is a further similarity with, or influence of, Dickens, the author of not only *Bleak House* but also the (unfinished) detective story, *The Mystery of Edwin Drood*. As W. W. Robson points out, 'The quality of Chesterton's work at its best, in the Father Brown stories, is comparable to that of *Edwin Drood* . . . full of suspense, sensation, genuine clues, red herrings, "atmosphere", real mystery and spurious mystery.'[7]

Like Dickens, moreover, especially in *Hard Times*, Chesterton does not hesitate to introduce social criticism into his stories. The fact that his protagonist, Father Brown, is himself on the fringe of society as a Roman Catholic priest rather than a clergyman of the Established Church, helps to encourage the reader to look critically at the English class system. As a nonconformist, Father Brown sees things which an insider would not notice, or pay any attention to. In 'The Blast of the Book', for instance, Professor Openshaw 'was rather surprised to find Father Brown talking to the waiter . . . apparently about the waiter's most private affairs', for, although he 'himself dined there about five times a week', he 'was conscious that he had never thought of talking to the man'. Here, too, the priestly dimension is also relevant in Father Brown's pastoral concern, which again gives him an intimate access to people which the ordinary detective would not have. At the end of the story, Father Brown explains the disappearance of Openshaw's clerk: '*because* you had never looked at him in your life . . . You never found out even what a stranger strolling into your office could find out, in five minutes' chat . . .'

Chesterton's views on the political as well as social scene are thus also aired in the stories. Capitalism is satirized in 'The Queer Feet', where the existence of the ridiculous select club of 'The Twelve True Fishermen' is accounted for by the fact that in 'a plutocracy tradesmen become cunning enough to be more fastidious than their customers. They positively create difficulties so that their wealthy and weary clients may spend money and diplomacy in overcoming them.' In this case the owner of the hotel where the club meets, 'made nearly a million out of it, by making it difficult to get into'. The waiter who comes to tell the club members that their silver fish service has disappeared, cannot bring himself to do so:

A genuine historic aristocrat would have thrown things at the waiter, beginning with empty bottles, and very probably ending with money. A genuine democrat would have asked him, with a comrade-like clearness of speech, what the devil he was doing. But these modern plutocrats could not bear a poor man near to them, either as a slave or as a friend.

But a socialist society is no more welcome, where, for example, chimney-sweeps may get properly paid, but, as Father Brown puts it, where you are not allowed 'to own your own soot'. Not that an aristocracy is any better: there, paradoxically, 'chivalric traditions' do not thrive, for 'Few except the poor preserve traditions. Aristocrats live not in traditions but in fashions.'

❋

Chesterton wrote a number of full-length novels, yet in his *Autobiography* he made no bones about the fact that he was primarily a journalist, not a novelist: '. . . I could not be a novelist; because I really like to see ideas or notions wrestling naked, as it were and not dressed up in a masquerade as men and women.'[8] Certainly, apart from *The Man Who Was Thursday* (1908), which is (as its subtitle 'a Nightmare' indicates) more of a nightmare than a novel, his most successful fictional work is the Father Brown stories. The tight form of the detective story meant that the problems of developing narrative and character which the novel demands did not present themselves. The only character that matters is Father Brown, who is part-Father O'Connor and part-Chesterton.

Chesterton's powers of description are also very apposite: he had, after all, begun life as an art student and his first work was as a painter rather than writer. The good mystery story requires the writer to evoke scene and atmosphere if the element of suspense is to be created. Chesterton is particularly good at describing light and sky, and in 'The Dagger with Wings', for example, the picture he paints gives just the right kind of thrill:

The rolling country round the little town was sealed and bound with frost, and the sky was as clear and cold as steel, except in the north-east, where clouds with lurid haloes were beginning to climb up the sky. It was against these darker and more sinister colours that the house on the hill gleamed with a row of pale pillars . . .

Chesterton is especially interested in the colours of dawn and dusk, as another instance from 'The Green Man' shows, where the briefest of pictures produces the appropriate shudder at the beginning of the story:

The last of the sunset lay in long bars of copper and gold above the last dark strip of sea that seemed rather black than blue. But blacker still against this gleam in the west, there passed in sharp outline, like figures in a shadow pantomime, two men with three-cornered cocked hats and swords . . .

In the Father Brown stories, then, Chesterton makes his own distinctive and original contribution to the genre of the detective story. Even though not the greatest of Chesterton's writings, as highly readable stories they will doubtless continue to be the most popular of his works. And because Chesterton was able to adapt the form to his own purposes, they also enable him both to demonstrate his own strengths as a writer and to express some of his most characteristic ideas. They thus form an admirable introduction to the writings and thought of G. K. Chesterton.

Ian Ker

Notes

1. G. K. Chesterton, *Autobiography* (Sevenoaks, Kent: Fisher Press, 1992), pp. 332–4, pp. 336–40.
2. Dorothy E. Collins, 'Recollections', *G. K. Chesterton: A Centenary Appraisal*, ed. John Sullivan (London: Paul Ellek, 1974), p. 158.
3. Ronald Knox, 'Chesterton's Father Brown', *A Half Century of Views*, ed. D. J. Conlon (Oxford: Oxford University Press, 1987), p. 133, p. 138.
4. W. W. Robson, 'Father Brown and Others', *G. K. Chesterton: A Centenary Appraisal*, p. 59.
5. Ibid., p. 61.
6. G. K. Chesterton, *Charles Dickens* (San Francisco: Ignatius Press, 1989), p. 65.
7. W. W. Robson, op. cit., p. 61.
8. *Autobiography*, p. 298.

The Innocence of Father Brown

To Waldo and Mildred d'Avigdor

1
The Blue Cross

Between the silver ribbon of morning and the green glittering ribbon of sea, the boat touched Harwich and let loose a swarm of folk like flies, among whom the man we must follow was by no means conspicuous – nor wished to be. There was nothing notable about him, except a slight contrast between the holiday gaiety of his clothes and the official gravity of his face. His clothes included a slight, pale grey jacket, a white waistcoat, and a silver straw hat with a grey-blue ribbon. His lean face was dark by contrast, and ended in a curt black beard that looked Spanish and suggested an Elizabethan ruff. He was smoking a cigarette with the seriousness of an idler. There was nothing about him to indicate the fact that the grey jacket covered a loaded revolver, that the white waistcoat covered a police card, or that the straw hat covered one of the most powerful intellects in Europe. For this was Valentin himself, the head of the Paris police and the most famous investigator of the world; and he was coming from Brussels to London to make the greatest arrest of the century.

Flambeau was in England. The police of three countries had tracked the great criminal at last from Ghent to Brussels, from Brussels to the Hook of Holland; and it was conjectured that he would take some advantage of the unfamiliarity and confusion of the Eucharistic Congress, then taking place in London. Probably he would travel as some minor clerk or secretary connected with it; but, of course, Valentin could not be certain; nobody could be certain about Flambeau.

It is many years now since this colossus of crime suddenly ceased keeping the world in a turmoil; and when he ceased, as they said after the death of Roland, there was a great quiet upon the earth. But in his best days (I mean, of course, his worst) Flambeau was a figure as statuesque and international as the Kaiser. Almost every morning the

3

daily paper announced that he had escaped the consequences of one extraordinary crime by committing another. He was a Gascon of gigantic stature and bodily daring; and the wildest tales were told of his outbursts of athletic humour; how he turned the *juge d'instruction* upside down and stood him on his head, 'to clear his mind'; how he ran down the Rue de Rivoli with a policeman under each arm. It is due to him to say that his fantastic physical strength was generally employed in such bloodless though undignified scenes; his real crimes were chiefly those of ingenious and wholesale robbery. But each of his thefts was almost a new sin, and would make a story by itself. It was he who ran the great Tyrolean Dairy Company in London, with no dairies, no cows, no carts, no milk, but with some thousand subscribers. These he served by the simple operation of moving the little milk-cans outside people's doors to the doors of his own customers. It was he who had kept up an unaccountable and close correspondence with a young lady whose whole letter-bag was intercepted, by the extraordinary trick of photographing his messages infinitesimally small upon the slides of a microscope. A sweeping simplicity, however, marked many of his experiments. It is said he once repainted all the numbers in a street in the dead of night merely to divert one traveller into a trap. It is quite certain that he invented a portable pillar-box, which he put up at corners in quiet suburbs on the chance of strangers dropping postal orders into it. Lastly he was known to be a startling acrobat; despite his huge figure, he could leap like a grasshopper and melt into the tree-tops like a monkey. Hence the great Valentin, when he set out to find Flambeau, was perfectly well aware that his adventures would not end when he had found him.

But how was he to find him? On this the great Valentin's ideas were still in process of settlement.

There was one thing which Flambeau, with all his dexterity of disguise, could not cover, and that was his singular height. If Valentin's quick eye had caught a tall apple-woman, a tall grenadier, or even a tolerably tall duchess, he might have arrested them on the spot. But all along his train there was nobody that could be a disguised Flambeau, any more than a cat could be a disguised giraffe. About the people on the boat he had already satisfied himself; and the people picked up at Harwich or on the journey limited themselves with certainty to six. There was a short railway official travelling up to the terminus, three fairly short market-gardeners picked up two stations afterwards, one very short widow lady going up from a small Essex town, and a very short Roman Catholic priest going up from a small Essex village. When it came to the last case, Valentin gave it up and almost laughed. The little priest was so much the essence of those Eastern flats: he had a face as round and dull as a Norfolk dumpling; he had eyes as empty as the North Sea; he had several brown-paper parcels which he was quite incapable of collecting. The Eucharistic Congress had doubtless sucked out of their local stagnation many such creatures, blind and helpless, like moles disinterred. Valentin was a sceptic in the severe style of France, and could have no love for priests. But he could have pity for them, and this one might have provoked pity in anybody. He had a large, shabby umbrella, which constantly fell on the floor. He did not seem to know which was the right end of his return ticket. He explained with a moon-calf simplicity to everybody in the carriage that he had to be careful, because he had something made of real silver 'with blue stones' in one of his brown-paper parcels. His quaint blending of Essex flatness with saintly simplicity continuously amused the Frenchman till the priest arrived (somehow) at Stratford with all his parcels, and came back for his umbrella. When he did the last, Valentin even had the good nature to warn him not to take care of the silver by telling everybody about it. But to whomever he talked, Valentin kept his eye open for some-one else; he looked out steadily for anyone, rich or poor, male or female, who was well up to six feet; for Flambeau was four inches above it.

He alighted at Liverpool Street, however, quite conscientiously secure that he had not missed the criminal so far. He then went to Scotland Yard to regularize his position and arrange for help in case of need; he then lit another cigarette and went for a long stroll in the streets of London. As he was walking in the streets and squares beyond Victoria, he paused suddenly and stood. It was a quaint, quiet square, very typical of London, full of an accidental stillness. The tall, flat houses round looked at once prosperous and uninhabited; the square of shrubbery in the centre looked as deserted as a green Pacific islet. One of the four sides was much higher than the rest, like a dais; and the line of this side was broken by one of London's admirable accidents – a restaurant that looked as if it had strayed from Soho. It was an unreasona-bly attractive object, with dwarf plants in pots and long, striped blinds

5

of lemon yellow and white. It stood specially high above the street, and in the usual patchwork way of London, a flight of steps from the street ran up to meet the front door almost as a fire-escape might run up to a first-floor window. Valentin stood and smoked in front of the yellow-white blinds and considered them long.

The most incredible thing about miracles is that they happen. A few clouds in heaven do come together into the staring shape of one human eye. A tree does stand up in the landscape of a doubtful journey in the exact and elaborate shape of a note of interrogation. I have seen both these things myself within the last few days. Nelson does die in the instant of victory; and a man named Williams does quite accidentally murder a man named Williamson; it sounds like a sort of infanticide. In short, there is in life an element of elfin coincidence which people reckoning on the prosaic may perpetually miss. As it has been well expressed in the paradox of Poe, wisdom should reckon on the unforeseen.

Aristide Valentin was unfathomably French; and the French intelligence is intelligence specially and solely. He was not 'a thinking machine'; for that is a brainless phrase of modern fatalism and materialism. A machine only *is* a machine because it cannot think. But he was a thinking man, and a plain man at the same time. All his wonderful successes, that looked like conjuring, had been gained by plodding logic, by clear and commonplace French thought. The French electrify the world not by starting any paradox, they electrify it by carrying out a truism. They carry a truism so far – as in the French Revolution. But exactly because Valentin understood reason, he understood the limits of reason. Only a man who knows nothing of motors talks of motoring without petrol; only a man who knows nothing of reason talks of reasoning without strong, undisputed first principles. Here he had no strong first principles. Flambeau had been missed at Harwich; and if he was in London at all, he might be anything from a tall tramp on Wimbledon Common to a tall toastmaster at the Hôtel Métropole. In such a naked state of nescience, Valentin had a view and a method of his own.

In such cases he reckoned on the unforeseen. In such cases, when he could not follow the train of the reasonable, he coldly and carefully followed the train of the unreasonable. Instead of going to the right places – banks, police-stations, rendezvous – he systematically went to the wrong places; knocked at every empty house, turned down every *cul de sac*, went up every lane blocked with rubbish, went round every crescent that led him uselessly out of the way. He defended this crazy course quite logically. He said that if one had a clue this was the worst way; but if one had no clue at all it was the best, because there was just the chance that any oddity that caught the eye of the pursuer might be the same that had caught the eye of the pursued. Somewhere a man must begin, and it had better be just where another man might stop. Something about that flight of steps up to the shop, something about the quietude and quaintness of the restaurant, roused all the detective's rare romantic fancy and made him resolve to strike at random. He went up the steps, and sitting down by the window, asked for a cup of black coffee.

It was half-way through the morning, and he had not breakfasted; the slight litter of other breakfasts stood about on the table to remind him of his hunger; and adding a poached egg to his order, he proceeded musingly to shake some white sugar into his coffee, thinking all the time about Flambeau. He remembered how Flambeau had escaped, once by a pair of nail scissors, and once by a house on fire; once by having to pay for an unstamped letter, and once by getting people to look through a telescope at a comet that might destroy the world. He thought his detective brain as good as the criminal's, which was true. But he fully realized the disadvantage. 'The criminal is the creative artist; the detective only the critic,' he said with a sour smile, and lifted his coffee cup to his lips slowly, and put it down very quickly. He had put salt in it.

He looked at the vessel from which the silvery powder had come; it was certainly a sugar-basin; as unmistakably meant for sugar as a champagne bottle for champagne. He wondered why they should keep salt in it. He looked to see if there were any more orthodox vessels. Yes, there were two salt-cellars quite full. Perhaps there was some speciality in the condiment in the salt-cellars. He tasted it; it was sugar. Then he looked round at the restaurant with a refreshed air of interest, to see if there were any other traces of that singular artistic taste which puts the sugar in the salt-cellars and the salt in the sugar-basin. Except for an odd splash of some dark fluid on one of the white-papered walls, the whole place appeared neat, cheerful and ordinary. He rang the bell for the waiter.

7

When that official hurried up, fuzzy-haired and somewhat blear-eyed at that early hour, the detective (who was not without an appreciation of the simpler forms of humour) asked him to taste the sugar and see if it was up to the high reputation of the hotel. The result was that the waiter yawned suddenly and woke up.

'Do you play this delicate joke on your customers every morning?' inquired Valentin. 'Does changing the salt and sugar never pall on you as a jest?'

The waiter, when this irony grew clearer, stammeringly assured him that the establishment had certainly no such intention; it must be a most curious mistake. He picked up the sugar-basin and looked at it; he picked up the salt-cellar and looked at that, his face growing more and more bewildered. At last he abruptly excused himself, and hurrying away, returned in a few seconds with the proprietor. The proprietor also examined the sugar-basin and then the salt-cellar; the proprietor also looked bewildered.

Suddenly the waiter seemed to grow inarticulate with a rush of words.

'I zink,' he stuttered eagerly, 'I zink it is those two clergymen.'

'What two clergymen?'

'The two clergymen,' said the waiter, 'that threw soup at the wall.'

'Threw soup at the wall?' repeated Valentin, feeling sure this must be some Italian metaphor.

'Yes, yes,' said the attendant excitedly, and pointing at the dark splash on the white paper; 'threw it over there on the wall.'

Valentin looked his query at the proprietor, who came to his rescue with fuller reports.

'Yes, sir,' he said, 'it's quite true, though I don't suppose it has anything to do with the sugar and salt. Two clergymen came in and drank soup here very early, as soon as the shutters were taken down. They were both very quiet, respectable people; one of them paid the bill and went out; the other, who seemed a slower coach altogether, was some minutes longer getting his things together. But he went at last. Only, the instant before he stepped into the street he deliberately picked up his cup, which he had only half emptied, and threw the soup slap on the wall. I was in the back room myself, and so was the waiter; so I could only rush out in time to find the wall splashed and the shop empty. It didn't do any particular damage, but it was confounded cheek; and I tried to catch the men in the street. They were too far off though; I only noticed they went round the corner into Carstairs Street.'

The detective was on his feet, hat settled and stick in hand. He had already decided that in the universal darkness of his mind he could only follow the first odd finger that pointed; and this finger was odd enough. Paying his bill and clashing the glass doors behind him, he was soon swinging round into the other street.

It was fortunate that even in such fevered moments his eye was cool and quick. Something in a shop-front went by him like a mere flash; yet he went back to look at it. The shop was a popular greengrocer and fruiterer's, an array of goods set out in the open air and plainly ticketed with their names and prices. In the two most prominent compartments were two heaps, of oranges and of nuts respectively. On the heap of nuts lay a scrap of cardboard, on which was written in bold, blue chalk, 'Best tangerine oranges, two a penny.' On the oranges was the equally clear and exact description, 'Finest Brazil nuts, 4d. a lb.' M. Valentin looked at these two placards and fancied he had met this highly subtle form of humour before, and that somewhat recently. He drew the attention of the red-faced fruiterer, who was looking rather sullenly up and down the street, to this inaccuracy in his advertisements. The fruiterer said nothing, but sharply put each card into its proper place. The detective, leaning elegantly on his walking-cane, continued to scrutinize the shop. At last he said: 'Pray excuse my apparent irrelevance, my good sir, but I should like to ask you a question in experimental psychology and the association of ideas.'

The red-faced shopman regarded him with an eye of menace; but he continued gaily, swinging his cane. 'Why,' he pursued, 'why are two tickets wrongly placed in a greengrocer's shop like a shovel hat that has come to London for a holiday? Or, in case I do not make myself clear, what is the mystical association which connects the idea of nuts marked as oranges with the idea of two clergymen, one tall and the other short?'

The eyes of the tradesman stood out of his head like a snail's; he really seemed for an instant likely to fling himself upon the stranger. At last he stammered angrily: 'I don't know what you 'ave to do with it, but if you're one of their friends, you can tell 'em from me that I'll knock their silly 'eads off, parsons or no parsons, if they upset my apples again.'

9

'Indeed?' asked the detective, with great sympathy. 'Did they upset your apples?'

'One of 'em did,' said the heated shopman; 'rolled 'em all over the street. I'd 'ave caught the fool but for havin' to pick 'em up.'

'Which way did these parsons go?' asked Valentin.

'Up that second road on the left-hand side, and then across the square,' said the other promptly.

'Thanks,' said Valentin, and vanished like a fairy. On the other side of the second square he found a policeman, and said: 'This is urgent, constable; have you seen two clergymen in shovel hats?'

The policeman began to chuckle heavily. 'I 'ave, sir; and if you arst me, one of 'em was drunk. He stood in the middle of the road that bewildered that –'

'Which way did they go?' snapped Valentin.

'They took one of them yellow buses over there,' answered the man; 'them that go to Hampstead.'

Valentin produced his official card and said very rapidly: 'Call up two of your men to come with me in pursuit,' and crossed the road with such contagious energy that the ponderous policeman was moved to almost agile obedience. In a minute and a half the French detective was joined on the opposite pavement by an inspector and a man in plain clothes.

'Well, sir,' began the former, with smiling importance, 'and what may – ?'

Valentin pointed suddenly with his cane. 'I'll tell you on the top of that omnibus,' he said, and was darting and dodging across the tangle of the traffic. When all three sank panting on the top seats of the yellow vehicle, the inspector said: 'We could go four times as quick in a taxi.'

'Quite true,' replied their leader placidly, 'if we only had an idea of where we were going.'

'Well, where *are* you going?' asked the other, staring.

Valentin smoked frowningly for a few seconds; then, removing his cigarette, he said: 'If you *know* what a man's doing, get in front of him; but if you want to guess what he's doing, keep behind him. Stray when he strays; stop when he stops; travel as slowly as he. Then you may see what he saw and may act as he acted. All we can do is to keep our eyes skinned for a queer thing.'

'What sort of a queer thing do you mean?' asked the inspector.

'Any sort of queer thing,' answered Valentin, and relapsed into obstinate silence.

The yellow omnibus crawled up the northern roads for what seemed like hours on end; the great detective would not explain further, and perhaps his assistants felt a silent and growing doubt of his errand. Perhaps, also, they felt a silent and growing desire for lunch, for the hours crept long past the normal luncheon hour, and the long roads of the North London suburbs seemed to shoot out into length after length like an infernal telescope. It was one of those journeys on which a man perpetually feels that now at last he must have come to the end of the universe, and then finds he has only come to the beginning of Tufnell Park. London died away in draggled taverns and dreary scrubs, and then was unaccountably born again in blazing high streets and blatant hotels. It was like passing through thirteen separate vulgar cities all just touching each other. But though the winter twilight was already threatening the road ahead of them, the Parisian detective still sat silent and watchful, eyeing the frontage of the streets that slid by on either side. By the time they had left Camden Town behind, the policemen were nearly asleep; at least, they gave something like a jump as Valentin leapt erect, struck a hand on each man's shoulder, and shouted to the driver to stop.

They tumbled down the steps into the road without realizing why they had been dislodged; when they looked round for enlightenment they found Valentin triumphantly pointing his finger towards a window on the left side of the road. It was a large window, forming part of the long façade of a gilt and palatial public house; it was the part reserved for respectable dining, and labelled 'Restaurant'. This window, like all the rest along the frontage of the hotel, was of frosted and figured glass, but in the middle of it was a big, black smash, like a star in the ice.

'Our cue at last,' cried Valentin, waving his stick; 'the place with the broken window.'

'What window? What cue?' asked his principal assistant. 'Why, what proof is there that this has anything to do with them?'

Valentin almost broke his bamboo stick with rage.

'Proof!' he cried. 'Good God! the man is looking for proof! Why, of course, the chances are twenty to one that it has *nothing* to do with

11

them. But what else can we do? Don't you see we must either follow one wild possibility or else go home to bed?' He banged his way into the restaurant, followed by his companions, and they were soon seated at a late luncheon at a little table, and looking at the star of smashed glass from the inside. Not that it was very informative to them even then.

'Got your window broken, I see,' said Valentin to the waiter, as he paid his bill.

'Yes, sir,' answered the attendant, bending busily over the change, to which Valentin silently added an enormous tip. The waiter straightened himself with mild but unmistakable animation.

'Ah, yes, sir,' he said. 'Very odd thing, that, sir.'

'Indeed? Tell us about it,' said the detective with careless curiosity.

'Well, two gents in black came in,' said the waiter; 'two of those foreign parsons that are running about. They had a cheap and quiet little lunch, and one of them paid for it and went out. The other was just going out to join him when I looked at my change again and found he'd paid me more than three times too much. "Here," I says to the chap who was nearly out of the door, "you've paid too much." "Oh," he says, very cool, "have we?" "Yes," I says, and picks up the bill to show him. Well, that was a knock-out.'

'What do you mean?' asked his interlocutor.

'Well, I'd have sworn on seven Bibles that I'd put 4s. on that bill. But now I saw I'd put 14s., as plain as paint.'

'Well?' cried Valentin, moving slowly, but with burning eyes, 'and then?'

'The parson at the door he says, all serene, "Sorry to confuse your accounts, but it'll pay for the window." "What window?" I says. "The one I'm going to break," he says, and smashed that blessed pane with his umbrella.'

All the inquirers made an exclamation; and the inspector said under his breath: 'Are we after escaped lunatics?' The waiter went on with some relish for the ridiculous story:

'I was so knocked silly for a second, I couldn't do anything. The man marched out of the place and joined his friend just round the corner. Then they went so quick up Bullock Street that I couldn't catch them, though I ran round the bars to do it.'

'Bullock Street,' said the detective, and shot up that thoroughfare as quickly as the strange couple he pursued.

Their journey now took them through bare brick ways like tunnels; streets with few lights and even with few windows; streets that seemed built out of the blank backs of everything and everywhere. Dusk was deepening, and it was not easy even for the London policemen to guess in what exact direction they were treading. The inspector, however, was pretty certain that they would eventually strike some part of Hampstead Heath. Abruptly one bulging and gas-lit window broke the blue twilight like a bull's-eye lantern; and Valentin stopped an instant before a little garish sweetstuff shop. After an instant's hesitation he went in; he stood amid the gaudy colours of the confectionery with entire gravity and bought thirteen chocolate cigars with a certain care. He was clearly preparing an opening; but he did not need one.

An angular, elderly young woman in the shop had regarded his elegant appearance with a merely automatic inquiry; but when she saw the door behind him blocked with the blue uniform of the inspector, her eyes seemed to wake up.

'Oh,' she said, 'if you've come about that parcel, I've sent it off already.'

'Parcel!' repeated Valentin; and it was his turn to look inquiring.

'I mean the parcel the gentleman left – the clergyman gentleman.'

'For goodness' sake,' said Valentin, leaning forward with his first real confession of eagerness, 'for Heaven's sake tell us what happened exactly.'

'Well,' said the woman, a little doubtfully, 'the clergymen came in about half an hour ago and bought some peppermints and talked a bit, and then went off towards the Heath. But a second after, one of them runs back into the shop and says, "Have I left a parcel?" Well, I looked everywhere and couldn't see one; so he says, "Never mind; but if it should turn up, please post it to this address," and he left me the address and a shilling for my trouble. And sure enough, though I thought I'd looked everywhere, I found he'd left a brown-paper parcel, so I posted it to the place he said. I can't remember the address now; it was somewhere in Westminster. But as the thing seemed so important, I thought perhaps the police had come about it.'

'So they have,' said Valentin shortly. 'Is Hampstead Heath near here?'

'Straight on for fifteen minutes,' said the woman, 'and you'll come right out on the open.' Valentin sprang out of the shop and began to run. The other detectives followed him at a reluctant trot.

The street they threaded was so narrow and shut in by shadows that when they came out unexpectedly into the void common and vast sky they were startled to find the evening still so light and clear. A perfect dome of peacock-green sank into gold amid the blackening trees and the dark violet distances. The glowing green tint was just deep enough to pick out in points of crystal one or two stars. All that was left of the daylight lay in a golden glitter across the edge of Hampstead and that popular hollow which is called the Vale of Health. The holiday makers who roam this region had not wholly dispersed: a few couples sat shapelessly on benches; and here and there a distant girl still shrieked on one of the swings. The glory of heaven deepened and darkened around the sublime vulgarity of man; and standing on the slope and looking across the valley, Valentin beheld the thing which he sought.

Among the black and breaking groups in that distance was one especially black which did not break – a group of two figures clerically clad. Though they seemed as small as insects, Valentin could see that one of them was much smaller than the other. Though the other had a student's stoop and an inconspicuous manner, he could see that the man was well over six feet high. He shut his teeth and went forward, whirling his stick impatiently. By the time he had substantially diminished the distance and magnified the two black figures as in a vast microscope, he had perceived something else; something which startled him, and yet which he had somehow expected. Whoever was the tall priest, there could be no doubt about the identity of the short one. It was his friend of the Harwich train, the stumpy little *curé* of Essex whom he had warned about his brown-paper parcels.

Now, so far as this went, everything fitted in finally and rationally enough. Valentin had learned by his inquiries that morning that a Father Brown from Essex was bringing up a silver cross with sapphires, a relic of considerable value, to show some of the foreign priests at the congress. This undoubtedly was the 'silver with blue stones'; and Father Brown undoubtedly was the little greenhorn in the train. Now there was nothing wonderful about the fact that what Valentin had found out

Flambeau had also found out; Flambeau found out everything. Also there was nothing wonderful in the fact that when Flambeau heard of a sapphire cross he should try to steal it; that was the most natural thing in all natural history. And most certainly there was nothing wonderful about the fact that Flambeau should have it all his own way with such a silly sheep as the man with the umbrella and the parcels. He was the sort of man whom anybody could lead on a string to the North Pole; it was not surprising that an actor like Flambeau, dressed as another priest, could lead him to Hampstead Heath. So far the crime seemed clear enough; and while the detective pitied the priest for his helplessness, he almost despised Flambeau for condescending to so gullible a victim. But when Valentin thought of all that had happened in between, of all that had led him to his triumph, he racked his brains for the smallest rhyme or reason in it. What had the stealing of a blue-and-silver cross from a priest from Essex to do with chucking soup at wallpaper? What had it to do with calling nuts oranges, or with paying for windows first and breaking them afterwards? He had come to the end of his chase; yet somehow he had missed the middle of it. When he failed (which was seldom), he had usually grasped the clue, but nevertheless missed the criminal. Here he had grasped the criminal, but still he could not grasp the clue.

The two figures that they followed were crawling like black flies across the huge green contour of a hill. They were evidently sunk in conversation, and perhaps did not notice where they were going; but they were certainly going to the wilder and more silent heights of the Heath. As their pursuers gained on them, the latter had to use the undignified attitudes of the deer-stalker, to crouch behind clumps of trees and even to crawl prostrate in deep grass. By these ungainly ingenuities the hunters even came close enough to the quarry to hear the murmur of the discussion, but no word could be distinguished except the word 'reason' recurring frequently in a high and almost childish voice. Once, over an abrupt dip of land and a dense tangle of thickets, the detectives actually lost the two figures they were following. They did not find the trail again for an agonizing ten minutes, and then it led round the brow of a great dome of hill overlooking an amphitheatre of rich and desolate sunset scenery. Under a tree in this commanding yet neglected spot was an old ramshackle wooden seat. On this seat sat the two priests still in serious speech together. The gorgeous green and gold still clung to the darkening horizon; but the dome above was turning slowly from peacock-green to peacock-blue, and the stars detached themselves more and more like solid jewels. Mutely motioning to his followers, Valentin contrived to creep up behind the big branching tree, and, standing there in deathly silence, heard the words of the strange priests for the first time.

After he had listened for a minute and a half, he was gripped by a devilish doubt. Perhaps he had dragged the two English policemen to the wastes of a nocturnal heath on an errand no saner than seeking figs on thistles. For the two priests were talking exactly like priests, piously, with learning and leisure, about the most aerial enigmas of theology. The little Essex priest spoke the more simply, with his round face turned to the strengthening stars; the other talked with his head bowed, as if he were even not worthy to look at them. But no more innocently clerical conversation could have been heard in any white Italian cloister or black Spanish cathedral.

The first he heard was the tail of one of Father Brown's sentences, which ended: '. . . what they really meant in the Middle Ages by the heavens being incorruptible.'

The taller priest nodded his bowed head and said:

'Ah, yes, these modern infidels appeal to their reason; but who can look at those millions of worlds and not feel that there may well be wonderful universes above us where reason is utterly unreasonable?'

'No,' said the other priest; 'reason is always reasonable, even in the last limbo, in the lost borderland of things. I know that people charge the Church with lowering reason, but it is just the other way. Alone on earth, the Church makes reason really supreme. Alone on earth, the Church affirms that God Himself is bound by reason.'

The other priest raised his austere face to the spangled sky and said:

'Yet who knows if in that infinite universe – ?'

'Only infinite physically,' said the little priest, turning sharply in his seat, 'not infinite in the sense of escaping from the laws of truth.'

Valentin behind his tree was tearing his finger-nails with silent fury. He seemed almost to hear the sniggers of the English detectives whom he had brought so far on a fantastic guess only to listen to the metaphysical gossip of two mild old parsons. In his impatience he lost the equally elaborate answer of the tall cleric, and when he listened again it was again Father Brown who was speaking:

'Reason and justice grip the remotest and the loneliest star. Look at those stars. Don't they look as if they were single diamonds and sapphires? Well, you can imagine any mad botany or geology you please. Think of forests of adamant with leaves of brilliants. Think the moon is a blue moon, a single elephantine sapphire. But don't fancy that all that frantic astronomy would make the smallest difference to the reason and justice of conduct. On plains of opal, under cliffs cut out of pearl, you would still find a notice-board, "Thou shalt not steal."'

Valentin was just in the act of rising from his rigid and crouching attitude and creeping away as softly as might be, felled by the one great folly of his life. But something in the very silence of the tall priest made him stop until the latter spoke. When at last he did speak, he said simply, his head bowed and his hands on his knees:

'Well, I still think that other worlds may perhaps rise higher than our reason. The mystery of heaven is unfathomable, and I for one can only bow my head.'

Then, with brow yet bent and without changing by the faintest shade his attitude or voice, he added:

'Just hand over that sapphire cross of yours, will you? We're all alone here, and I could pull you to pieces like a straw doll.'

The utterly unaltered voice and attitude added a strange violence to that shocking change of speech. But the guarder of the relic only seemed to turn his head by the smallest section of the compass. He seemed still to have a somewhat foolish face turned to the stars. Perhaps he had not understood. Or, perhaps, he had understood and sat rigid with terror.

'Yes,' said the tall priest, in the same low voice and in the same still posture, 'yes, I am Flambeau.'

Then, after a pause, he said:

'Come, will you give me that cross?'

'No,' said the other, and the monosyllable had an odd sound.

Flambeau suddenly flung off all his pontifical pretensions. The great robber leaned back in his seat and laughed low but long.

'No,' he cried; 'you won't give it me, you proud prelate. You won't give it me, you little celibate simpleton. Shall I tell you why you won't give it me? Because I've got it already in my own breast-pocket.'

The small man from Essex turned what seemed to be a dazed face in the dusk, and said, with the timid eagerness of 'The Private Secretary':

'Are – are you sure?'

Flambeau yelled with delight.

'Really, you're as good as a three-act farce,' he cried. 'Yes, you turnip, I am quite sure. I had the sense to make a duplicate of the right parcel, and now, my friend, you've got the duplicate, and I've got the jewels. An old dodge, Father Brown – a very old dodge.'

'Yes,' said Father Brown, and passed his hand through his hair with the same strange vagueness of manner. 'Yes, I've heard of it before.'

The colossus of crime leaned over to the little rustic priest with a sort of sudden interest.

'*You* have heard of it?' he asked. 'Where have *you* heard of it?'

'Well, I mustn't tell you his name, of course,' said the little man simply. 'He was a penitent, you know. He had lived prosperously for about twenty years entirely on duplicate brown-paper parcels. And so, you see, when I began to suspect you, I thought of this poor chap's way of doing it at once.'

'Began to suspect me?' repeated the outlaw with increased intensity. 'Did you really have the gumption to suspect me just because I brought you up to this bare part of the heath?'

'No, no,' said Brown with an air of apology. 'You see, I suspected you when we first met. It's that little bulge up the sleeve where you people have the spiked bracelet.'

'How in Tartarus,' cried Flambeau, 'did you ever hear of the spiked bracelet?'

'Oh, one's little flock, you know!' said Father Brown, arching his eyebrows rather blankly. 'When I was a curate in Hartlepool, there were three of them with spiked bracelets. So, as I suspected you from the first, don't you see, I made sure that the cross should go safe, anyhow. I'm afraid I watched you, you know. So at last I saw you change the parcels. Then, don't you see, I changed them back again. And then I left the right one behind.'

'Left it behind?' repeated Flambeau, and for the first time there was another note in his voice beside his triumph.

'Well, it was like this,' said the little priest, speaking in the same unaffected way. 'I went back to that sweet-shop and asked if I'd left a parcel, and gave them a particular address if it turned up. Well, I knew I hadn't; but when I went away again I did. So, instead of running after me with that valuable parcel, they have sent it flying to a friend of mine in Westminster.' Then he added rather sadly: 'I learnt that, too, from a poor fellow in Hartlepool. He used to do it with handbags he stole at railway stations, but he's in a monastery now. Oh, one gets to know, you know,' he added, rubbing his head again with the same sort of desperate apology. 'We can't help being priests. People come and tell us these things.'

Flambeau tore a brown-paper parcel out of his inner pocket and rent it in pieces. There was nothing but paper and sticks of lead inside it. He sprang to his feet with a gigantic gesture, and cried:

'I don't believe you. I don't believe a bumpkin like you could manage all that. I believe you've still got the stuff on you, and if you don't give it up – why, we're all alone, and I'll take it by force!'

'No,' said Father Brown simply, and stood up also; 'you won't take it by force. First, because I really haven't still got it. And, second, because we are not alone.'

Flambeau stopped in his stride forward.

'Behind that tree,' said Father Brown, pointing, 'are two strong policemen and the greatest detective alive. How did they come here, do you ask? Why, I brought them, of course! How did I do it? Why, I'll tell you if you like! Lord bless you, we have to know twenty such things when we work among the criminal classes! Well, I wasn't sure you were a thief, and it would never do to make a scandal against one of our own clergy. So I just tested you to see if anything would make you show yourself. A man generally makes a small scene if he finds salt in his coffee; if he doesn't, he has some reason for keeping quiet. I changed the salt and sugar, and *you* kept quiet. A man generally objects if his bill is three times too big. If he pays it, he has some motive for passing unnoticed. I altered your bill, and *you* paid it.'

The world seemed waiting for Flambeau to leap like a tiger. But he was held back as by a spell; he was stunned with the utmost curiosity.

'Well,' went on Father Brown, with lumbering lucidity, 'as you wouldn't leave any tracks for the police, of course somebody had to. At every place we went to, I took care to do something that would get us talked about for the rest of the day. I didn't do much harm – a splashed wall, spilt apples, a broken window; but I saved the cross, as the cross will always be saved. It is at Westminster by now. I rather wonder you didn't stop it with the Donkey's Whistle.'

'With the what?' asked Flambeau.

'I'm glad you've never heard of it,' said the priest, making a face. 'It's a foul thing. I'm sure you're too good a man for a Whistler. I couldn't have countered it even with the Spots myself; I'm not strong enough in the legs.'

'What on earth are you talking about?' asked the other.

'Well, I did think you'd know the Spots,' said Father Brown, agreeably surprised. 'Oh, you can't have gone so very wrong yet!'

'How in blazes do you know all these horrors?' cried Flambeau.

The shadow of a smile crossed the round, simple face of his clerical opponent.

'Oh, by being a celibate simpleton, I suppose,' he said. 'Has it never struck you that a man who does next to nothing but hear men's real sins is not likely to be wholly unaware of human evil? But, as a matter of fact, another part of my trade, too, made me sure you weren't a priest.'

'What?' asked the thief, almost gaping.

'You attacked reason,' said Father Brown. 'It's bad theology.'

And even as he turned away to collect his property, the three policemen came out from under the twilight trees. Flambeau was an artist and a sportsman. He stepped back and swept Valentin a great bow.

'Do not bow to me, *mon ami*,' said Valentin, with silver clearness. 'Let us both bow to our master.'

And they both stood an instant uncovered, while the little Essex priest blinked about for his umbrella.

2

The Secret Garden

Aristide Valentin, Chief of the Paris Police, was late for his dinner, and some of his guests began to arrive before him. These were, however, reassured by his confidential servant, Ivan, the old man with a scar and a face almost as grey as his moustaches, who always sat at a table in the entrance hall – a hall hung with weapons. Valentin's house was perhaps as peculiar and celebrated as its master. It was an old house, with high walls and tall poplars almost overhanging the Seine; but the oddity – and perhaps the police value – of its architecture was this: that there was no ultimate exit at all except through this front door, which was guarded by Ivan and the armoury. The garden was large and elaborate, and there were many exits from the house into the garden. But there was no exit from the garden into the world outside; all round it ran a tall, smooth unscalable wall with special spikes at the top; no bad garden, perhaps, for a man to reflect in whom some hundred criminals had sworn to kill.

As Ivan explained to the guests, their host had telephoned that he was detained for ten minutes. He was, in truth, making some last arrangements about executions and such ugly things; and though these duties were rootedly repulsive to him, he always performed them with precision. Ruthless in the pursuit of criminals, he was very mild about their punishment. Since he had been supreme over French – and largely over European – police methods, his great influence had been honourably used for the mitigation of sentences and the purification of prisons. He was one of the great humanitarian French freethinkers; and the only thing wrong with them is that they make mercy even colder than justice.

When Valentin arrived he was already dressed in black clothes and the red rosette – an elegant figure, his dark beard already streaked with grey. He went straight through his house to his study, which opened on the grounds behind. The garden door of it was open, and after he had carefully locked his box in its official place, he stood for a few seconds at the open door looking out upon the garden. A sharp moon was fighting with the flying rags and tatters of a storm, and Valentin regarded it with a wistfulness unusual in such scientific natures as his. Perhaps such scientific natures have some psychic prevision of the most tremendous problem of their lives. From any such occult mood, at least, he quickly recovered, for he knew he was late and that his guests had already begun to arrive. A glance at his drawing-room when he entered it was enough to make certain that his principal guest was not there, at any rate. He saw all the other pillars of the little party: he saw Lord Galloway, the English Ambassador – a choleric old man with a russet face like an apple, wearing the blue ribbon of the Garter. He saw Lady Galloway, slim and thread-like, with silver hair and a face sensitive and superior. He saw her daughter, Lady Margaret Graham, a pale and pretty girl with an elfish face and copper-coloured hair. He saw the Duchess of Mont St Michel, black-eyed and opulent, and with her her two daughters, black-eyed and opulent also. He saw Dr Simon, a typical French scientist, with glasses, a pointed brown beard, and a forehead barred with those parallel wrinkles which are the penalty of superciliousness, since they come through constantly elevating the eyebrows. He saw Father Brown of Cobhole, in Essex, whom he had recently met in England. He saw – perhaps with more interest than any of those – a tall man in uniform, who had bowed to the Galloways without receiving any very hearty acknowledgment, and who now advanced alone to pay his respects to his host. This was Commandant O'Brien, of the French Foreign Legion. He was a slim yet somewhat swaggering figure, clean-shaven, dark-haired, and blue-eyed, and as seemed natural in an officer of that famous regiment of victorious failures and successful suicides, he had an air at once dashing and melancholy. He was by birth an Irish gentleman, and in boyhood had known the Galloways – especially Margaret Graham. He had left his country after some crash of debts, and now expressed his complete freedom from British etiquette by swinging about in uniform, sabre and spurs. When he bowed to the Ambassador's family, Lord and Lady Galloway bent stiffly, and Lady Margaret looked away.

But for whatever old causes such people might be interested in each other, their distinguished host was not specially interested in them. No one of them at least was in his eyes the guest of the evening. Valentin was expecting, for special reasons, a man of world-wide fame, whose friendship he had secured during some of his great detective tours and triumphs in the United States. He was expecting Julius K. Brayne, that multi-millionaire whose colossal and even crushing endowments of small religions have occasioned so much easy sport and easier solemnity for the American and English papers. Nobody could quite make out whether Mr Brayne was an atheist or a Mormon, or a Christian Scientist; but he was ready to pour money into any intellectual vessel, so long as it was an untried vessel. One of his hobbies was to wait for the American Shakespeare – a hobby more patient than angling. He admired Walt Whitman, but thought that Luke P. Tanner, of Paris, Pa, was more 'progressive' than Whitman any day. He liked anything that he thought 'progressive'. He thought Valentin 'progressive', thereby doing him a grave injustice.

The solid appearance of Julius K. Brayne in the room was as decisive as a dinner bell. He had this great quality, which very few of us can claim, that his presence was as big as his absence. He was a huge fellow, as fat as he was tall, clad in complete evening black, without so much relief as a watch-chain or a ring. His hair was white and well brushed back like a German's; his face was red, fierce and cherubic, with one dark tuft under the lower lip that threw up that otherwise infantile visage with an effect theatrical and even Mephistophelean. Not long, however, did that *salon* merely stare at the celebrated American; his lateness had already become a domestic problem, and he was sent with all speed into the dining-room with Lady Galloway upon his arm.

Except on one point the Galloways were genial and casual enough. So long as Lady Margaret did not take the arm of that adventurer O'Brien her father was quite satisfied; and she had not done so; she had decorously gone in with Dr Simon. Nevertheless, old Lord Galloway was restless and almost rude. He was diplomatic enough during dinner, but when, over the cigars, three of the younger men – Simon the doctor, Brown the priest, and the detrimental O'Brien, the exile in a foreign uniform – all melted away to mix with the ladies or smoke in the conservatory, then the English diplomatist grew very undiplomatic indeed. He was stung every sixty seconds with the thought that the scamp O'Brien might be signalling to Margaret somehow; he did not attempt to imagine how. He was left over the coffee with Brayne, the hoary Yankee who believed in all religions, and Valentin, the grizzled Frenchman who believed in none. They could argue with each other, but neither could appeal to him. After a time this 'progressive' logomachy had reached a crisis of tedium; Lord Galloway got up also and sought the drawing-room. He lost his way in long passages for some six or eight minutes: till he heard the high-pitched, didactic voice of the doctor, and then the dull voice of the priest, followed by general laughter. They also, he thought with a curse, were probably arguing about 'science and religion'. But the instant he opened the *salon* door he saw only one thing – he saw what was not there. He saw that Commandant O'Brien was absent, and that Lady Margaret was absent, too.

Rising impatiently from the drawing-room, as he had from the dining-room, he stamped along the passage once more. His notion of protecting his daughter from the Irish-Algerian ne'er-do-weel had become something central and even mad in his mind. As he went towards the back of the house, where was Valentin's study, he was surprised to meet his daughter, who swept past with a white, scornful face, which was a second enigma. If she had been with O'Brien, where was O'Brien? If she had not been with O'Brien, where had she been? With a sort of senile and passionate suspicion he groped his way to the dark back parts of the mansion, and eventually found a servants' entrance that opened on to the garden. The moon with her scimitar had now ripped up and rolled away all the storm-wrack. The argent light lit up all four corners of the garden. A tall figure in blue was striding across the lawn towards the study door; a glint of moonlit silver on his facings picked him out as Commandant O'Brien.

He vanished through the french windows into the house, leaving Lord Galloway in an indescribable temper, at once virulent and vague. The blue-and-silver garden, like a scene in a theatre, seemed to taunt him with all that tyrannic tenderness against which his worldly authority was at war. The length and grace of the Irishman's stride enraged him as if he were a rival instead of a father; the moonlight maddened him. He was trapped as if by magic into a garden of troubadours, a Watteau fairyland; and, willing to shake off such amorous imbecilities by speech, he stepped briskly after his enemy. As he did so he tripped over some tree or stone in the grass; looked down at it first with irritation and then a second time with curiosity. The next instant the moon and the tall poplars looked at an unusual sight – an elderly English diplomatist running hard and crying or bellowing as he ran.

His hoarse shouts brought a pale face to the study door, the beaming glasses and worried brow of Dr Simon, who heard the nobleman's first clear words. Lord Galloway was crying: 'A corpse in the grass – a blood-stained corpse.' O'Brien at least had gone utterly from his mind.

'We must tell Valentin at once,' said the doctor, when the other had brokenly described all that he had dared to examine. 'It is fortunate that he is here'; and even as he spoke the great detective entered the study, attracted by the cry. It was almost amusing to note his typical transformation; he had come with the common concern of a host and a gentleman, fearing that some guest or servant was ill. When he was told the gory fact, he turned with all his gravity instantly bright and business-like; for this, however abrupt and awful, was his business.

'Strange, gentlemen,' he said, as they hurried out into the garden, 'that I should have hunted mysteries all over the earth, and now one comes and settles in my own backyard. But where is the place?' They crossed the lawn less easily, as a slight mist had begun to rise from the river; but under the guidance of the shaken Galloway they found the body sunken in deep grass – the body of a very tall and broad-shouldered man. He lay face downwards, so they could only see that his big shoulders were clad in black cloth, and that his big head was bald, except for a wisp or two of brown hair that clung to his skull like wet seaweed. A scarlet serpent of blood crawled from under his fallen face.

'At least,' said Simon, with a deep and singular intonation, 'he is none of our party.'

'Examine him, doctor,' cried Valentin rather sharply. 'He may not be dead.'

The doctor bent down. 'He is not quite cold, but I am afraid he is dead enough,' he answered. 'Just help me to lift him up.'

They lifted him carefully an inch from the ground, and all doubts as to his being really dead were settled at once and frightfully. The head fell away. It had been entirely sundered from the body; whoever had cut his throat had managed to sever the neck as well. Even Valentin was slightly shocked. 'He must have been as strong as a gorilla,' he muttered.

Not without a shiver, though he was used to anatomical abortions, Dr Simon lifted the head. It was slightly slashed about the neck and jaw, but the face was substantially unhurt. It was a ponderous, yellow face, at once sunken and swollen, with a hawk-like nose and heavy lids – the face of a wicked Roman emperor, with, perhaps, a distant touch of a Chinese emperor. All present seemed to look at it with the coldest eye of ignorance. Nothing else could be noted about the man except that, as they had lifted his body, they had seen underneath it the white gleam of a shirtfront defaced with a red gleam of blood. As Dr Simon said, the man had never been of their party. But he might very well have been trying to join it, for he had come dressed for such an occasion.

Valentin went down on his hands and knees and examined with his closest professional attention the grass and ground for some twenty yards round the body, in which he was assisted less skilfully by the doctor, and quite vaguely by the English lord. Nothing rewarded their grovellings except a few twigs, snapped or chopped into very small lengths, which Valentin lifted for an instant's examination, and then tossed away.

'Twigs,' he said gravely; 'twigs, and a total stranger with his head cut off; that is all there is on this lawn.'

There was an almost creepy stillness, and then the unnerved Galloway called out sharply:

'Who's that? Who's that over there by the garden wall?'

A small figure with a foolishly large head drew waveringly near them in the moonlit haze; looked for an instant like a goblin, but turned out to be the harmless little priest whom they had left in the drawing-room.

'I say,' he said meekly, 'there are no gates to this garden, do you know.'

Valentin's black brows had come together somewhat crossly, as they did on principle at the sight of the cassock. But he was far too just a man to deny the relevance of the remark. 'You are right,' he said. 'Before we find out how he came to be killed, we may have to find out how he came to be here. Now listen to me, gentlemen. If it can be done without prejudice to my position and duty, we shall all agree that certain distinguished names might well be kept out of this. There are ladies, gentlemen, and there is a foreign ambassador. If we must mark it down as a crime, then it must be followed up as a crime. But till then I can use my own discretion. I am the head of the police; I am so public that I can afford to be private. Please Heaven, I will clear every one of my own guests before I call in my men to look for anybody else. Gentlemen, upon your honour, you will none of you leave the house till to-morrow at noon; there are bedrooms, for all. Simon, I think you know where to find my man, Ivan, in the front hall; he is a confidential man. Tell him to leave another servant on guard and come to me at once. Lord Galloway, you are certainly the best person to tell the ladies what has happened, and prevent a panic. They also must stay. Father Brown and I will remain with the body.'

When this spirit of the captain spoke in Valentin he was obeyed like a bugle. Dr Simon went through to the armoury and routed out Ivan, the public detective's private detective. Galloway went to the drawing-room and told the terrible news tactfully enough, so that by the time the company assembled there the ladies were already startled and already soothed. Meanwhile the good priest and the good atheist stood at the head and foot of the dead man motionless in the moonlight, like symbolic statues of their two philosophies of death.

Ivan, the confidential man with the scar and the moustaches, came out of the house like a cannon ball, and came racing across the lawn to Valentin like a dog to his master. His livid face was quite lively with the glow of this domestic detective story, and it was with almost unpleasant eagerness that he asked his master's permission to examine the remains.

'Yes; look, if you like, Ivan,' said Valentin, 'but don't be long. We must go in and thrash this out in the house.'

Ivan lifted his head, and then almost let it drop.

'Why,' he gasped, 'it's – no, it isn't; it can't be. Do you know this man, sir?'

'No,' said Valentin indifferently; 'we had better go inside.'

Between them they carried the corpse to a sofa in the study, and then all made their way to the drawing-room.

The detective sat down at a desk quietly, and even with hesitation;

but his eye was the iron eye of a judge at assize. He made a few rapid notes upon paper in front of him, and then said shortly: 'Is everybody here?'

'Not Mr Brayne,' said the Duchess of Mont St Michel, looking round.

'No,' said Lord Galloway, in a hoarse, harsh voice. 'And not Mr Neil O'Brien, I fancy. I saw that gentleman walking in the garden when the corpse was still warm.'

'Ivan,' said the detective, 'go and fetch Commandant O'Brien and Mr Brayne. Mr Brayne, I know, is finishing a cigar in the dining-room; Commandant O'Brien, I think, is walking up and down the conservatory. I am not sure.'

The faithful attendant flashed from the room, and before anyone could stir or speak Valentin went on with the same soldierly swiftness of exposition.

'Everyone here knows that a dead man has been found in the garden, his head cut clean from his body. Dr Simon, you have examined it. Do you think that to cut a man's throat like that would need great force? Or, perhaps, only a very sharp knife?'

'I should say that it could not be done with a knife at all,' said the pale doctor.

'Have you any thought,' resumed Valentin, 'of a tool with which it could be done?'

'Speaking within modern probabilities, I really haven't,' said the doctor, arching his painful brows. 'It's not easy to hack a neck through even clumsily, and this was a very clean cut. It could be done with a battle-axe or an old headsman's axe, or an old two-handed sword.'

'But, good heavens!' cried the Duchess, almost in hysterics; 'there aren't any two-handed swords and battle-axes round here.'

Valentin was still busy with the paper in front of him. 'Tell me,' he said, still writing rapidly, 'could it have been done with a long French cavalry sabre?'

A low knocking came at the door, which for some unreasonable reason, curdled everyone's blood like the knocking in *Macbeth*. Amid that frozen silence Dr Simon managed to say: 'A sabre – yes, I suppose it could.'

'Thank you,' said Valentin. 'Come in, Ivan.'

The confidential Ivan opened the door and ushered in Commandant Neil O'Brien, whom he had found at last pacing the garden again.

The Irish officer stood disordered and defiant on the threshold. 'What do you want with me?' he cried.

'Please sit down,' said Valentin in pleasant, level tones. 'Why, you aren't wearing your sword! Where is it?'

'I left it on the library table,' said O'Brien, his brogue deepening in his disturbed mood. 'It was a nuisance, it was getting –'

'Ivan,' said Valentin: 'please go and get the Commandant's sword from the library.' Then, as the servant vanished: 'Lord Galloway says he saw you leaving the garden just before he found the corpse. What were you doing in the garden?'

The Commandant flung himself recklessly into a chair. 'Oh,' he cried in pure Irish; 'admirin' the moon. Communing with Nature, me boy.'

A heavy silence sank and endured, and at the end of it came again that trivial and terrible knocking. Ivan reappeared, carrying an empty steel scabbard. 'This is all I can find,' he said.

'Put it on the table,' said Valentin, without looking up.

There was an inhuman silence in the room, like that sea of inhuman silence round the dock of the condemned murderer. The Duchess's weak exclamations had long ago died away. Lord Galloway's swollen hatred was satisfied and even sobered. The voice that came was quite unexpected.

'I think I can tell you,' cried Lady Margaret, in that clear, quivering voice with which a courageous woman speaks publicly. 'I can tell you what Mr O'Brien was doing in the garden, since he is bound to silence. He was asking me to marry him. I refused; I said in my family circumstances I could give him nothing but my respect. He was a little angry at that; he did not seem to think much of my respect. I wonder,' she added, with rather a wan smile, 'if he will care at all for it now. For I offer it him now. I will swear anywhere that he never did a thing like this.'

Lord Galloway had edged up to his daughter, and was intimidating her in what he imagined to be an undertone. 'Hold your tongue, Maggie,' he said in a thunderous whisper. 'Why should you shield the fellow? Where's his sword? Where's his confounded cavalry –'

He stopped because of the singular stare with which his daughter was regarding him, a look that was indeed a lurid magnet for the whole group.

'You old fool!' she said, in a low voice without pretence of piety; 'what do you suppose you are trying to prove? I tell you this man was innocent while with me. But if he wasn't innocent, he was still with me. If he murdered a man in the garden, who was it who must have seen – who must at least have known? Do you hate Neil so much as to put your own daughter –'

Lady Galloway screamed. Everyone else sat tingling at the touch of those satanic tragedies that have been between lovers before now. They saw the proud, white face of the Scotch aristocrat and her lover, the Irish adventurer, like old portraits in a dark house. The long silence was full of formless historical memories of murdered husbands and poisonous paramours.

In the centre of this morbid silence an innocent voice said: 'Was it a very long cigar?'

The change of thought was so sharp that they had to look round to see who had spoken.

'I mean,' said little Father Brown, from the corner of the room. 'I mean that cigar Mr Brayne is finishing. It seems nearly as long as a walking-stick.'

Despite the irrelevance there was assent as well as irritation in Valentin's face as he lifted his head.

'Quite right,' he remarked sharply. 'Ivan, go and see about Mr Brayne again, and bring him here at once.'

The instant the factotum had closed the door, Valentin addressed the girl with an entirely new earnestness.

'Lady Margaret,' he said, 'we all feel, I am sure, both gratitude and admiration for your act in rising above your lower dignity and explaining the Commandant's conduct. But there is a hiatus still. Lord Galloway, I understand, met you passing from the study to the drawing-room, and it was only some minutes afterwards that he found the garden and the Commandant still walking there.'

'You have to remember,' replied Margaret, with a faint irony in her voice, 'that I had just refused him, so we should scarcely have come back arm in arm. He is a gentleman, anyhow; and he loitered behind – and so got charged with murder.'

'In those few moments,' said Valentin gravely, 'he might really –'

The knock came again, and Ivan put in his scarred face.

'Beg pardon, sir,' he said, 'but Mr Brayne has left the house.'

'Left!' cried Valentin, and rose for the first time to his feet.

'Gone. Scooted. Evaporated,' replied Ivan, in humorous French. 'His hat and coat are gone, too; and I'll tell you something to cap it all. I ran outside the house to find any traces of him, and I found one, and a big trace, too.'

'What do you mean?' asked Valentin.

'I'll show you,' said his servant, and reappeared with a flashing naked cavalry sabre, streaked with blood about the point and edge. Everyone in the room eyed it as if it were a thunderbolt; but the experienced Ivan went on quite quietly:

'I found this,' he said, 'flung among the bushes fifty yards up the road to Paris. In other words, I found it just where your respectable Mr Brayne threw it when he ran away.'

There was again a silence, but of a new sort. Valentin took the sabre, examined it, reflected with unaffected concentration of thought, and then turned a respectful face to O'Brien. 'Commandant,' he said, 'we trust you will always produce this weapon if it is wanted for police examination. Meanwhile,' he added, slapping the steel back in the ringing scabbard, 'let me return you your sword.'

At the military symbolism of the action the audience could hardly refrain from applause.

For Neil O'Brien, indeed, that gesture was the turning-point of existence. By the time he was wandering in the mysterious garden again in the colours of the morning the tragic futility of his ordinary mien had fallen from him; he was a man with many reasons for happiness. Lord Galloway was a gentleman, and had offered him an apology. Lady Margaret was something better than a lady, a woman at least, and had perhaps given him something better than an apology, as they drifted among the old flower-beds before breakfast. The whole company was more light-hearted and humane, for though the riddle of the death remained, the load of suspicion was lifted off them all, and sent flying off to Paris with the strange millionaire – a man they hardly knew. The devil was cast out of the house – he had cast himself out.

Still, the riddle remained; and when O'Brien threw himself on a garden seat beside Dr Simon, that keenly scientific person at once resumed it. He did not get much talk out of O'Brien, whose thoughts were on pleasanter things.

'I can't say it interests me much,' said the Irishman frankly, 'especially as it seems pretty plain now. Apparently Brayne hated this stranger for some reason; lured him into the garden, and killed him with my sword. Then he fled to the city, tossing the sword away as he went. By the way, Ivan tells me the dead man had a Yankee dollar in his pocket. So he was a countryman of Brayne's, and that seems to clinch it. I don't see any difficulties about the business.'

'There are five colossal difficulties,' said the doctor quietly; 'like high walls within walls. Don't mistake me. I don't doubt that Brayne did it; his flight, I fancy, proves that. But as to how he did it. First difficulty: Why should a man kill another man with a great hulking sabre, when he can almost kill him with a pocket knife and put it back in his pocket? Second difficulty: Why was there no noise or outcry? Does a man commonly see another come up waving a scimitar and offer no remarks? Third difficulty: A servant watched the front door all the evening; and a rat cannot get into Valentin's garden anywhere. How did the dead man get into the garden? Fourth difficulty: Given the same conditions, how did Brayne get out of the garden?'

'And the fifth,' said Neil, with eyes fixed on the English priest, who was coming slowly up the path.

'Is a trifle, I suppose,' said the doctor, 'but I think an odd one. When I first saw how the head had been slashed, I supposed the assassin had struck more than once. But on examination I found many cuts across the truncated section; in other words, they were struck *after* the head was off. Did Brayne hate his foe so fiendishly that he stood sabring his body in the moonlight?'

'Horrible!' said O'Brien, and shuddered.

The little priest, Brown, had arrived while they were talking, and had waited, with characteristic shyness, till they had finished. Then he said awkwardly:

'I say, I'm sorry to interrupt. But I was sent to tell you the news!'

'News?' repeated Simon, and stared at him rather painfully through his glasses.

'Yes, I'm sorry,' said Father Brown mildly. 'There's been another murder, you know.'

Both men on the seat sprang up, leaving it rocking.

'And, what's stranger still,' continued the priest, with his dull eyes on the rhododendrons, 'it's the same disgusting sort; it's another beheading. They found the second head actually bleeding in the river, a few yards along Brayne's road to Paris; so they suppose that he –'

'Great Heaven!' cried O'Brien. 'Is Brayne a monomaniac?'

'There are American vendettas,' said the priest impassively. Then he added: 'They want you to come to the library and see it.'

Commandant O'Brien followed the others towards the inquest, feeling decidedly sick. As a soldier, he loathed all this secretive carnage; where were these extravagant amputations going to stop? First one head was hacked off, and then another; in this case (he told himself bitterly) it was not true that two heads were better than one. As he crossed the study he almost staggered at a shocking coincidence. Upon Valentin's table lay the coloured picture of yet a third bleeding head; and it was the head of Valentin himself. A second glance showed him it was only a Nationalist paper, called *The Guillotine*, which every week showed one of its political opponents with rolling eyes and writhing features just after execution; for Valentin was an anti-clerical of some note. But O'Brien was an Irishman, with a kind of chastity even in his sins; and his gorge rose against that great brutality of the intellect which belongs only to France. He felt Paris as a whole, from the grotesques on the Gothic churches to the gross caricatures in the newspapers. He remembered the gigantic jests of the Revolution. He saw the whole city as one ugly energy, from the sanguinary sketch lying on Valentin's table up to where, above a mountain and forest of gargoyles, the great devil grins on Notre Dame.

The library was long, low, and dark; what light entered it shot from under low blinds and had still some of the ruddy tinge of morning. Valentin and his servant Ivan were waiting for them at the upper end of a long, slightly-sloping desk, on which lay the mortal remains, looking enormous in the twilight. The big black figure and yellow face of the man found in the garden confronted them essentially unchanged. The second head, which had been fished from among the river reeds that morning, lay streaming and dripping beside it; Valentin's men were still seeking to recover the rest of this second corpse, which was supposed to be afloat. Father Brown, who did not seem to share O'Brien's sensibilities in the least, went up to the second head and examined it with his blinking care. It was little more than a mop of wet, white hair, fringed with silver fire in the red and level morning light; the face, which seemed of an ugly, empurpled and perhaps criminal type, had been much battered against trees or stones as it tossed in the water.

'Good morning, Commandant O'Brien,' said Valentin, with quiet cordiality. 'You have heard of Brayne's last experiment in butchery, I suppose?'

Father Brown was still bending over the head with white hair, and he said, without looking up:

'I suppose it is quite certain that Brayne cut off this head, too.'

'Well, it seems common sense,' said Valentin, with his hands in his pockets. 'Killed in the same way as the other. Found within a few yards of the other. And sliced by the same weapon which we know he carried away.'

'Yes, yes; I know,' replied Father Brown, submissively. 'Yet, you know, I doubt whether Brayne could have cut off this head.'

'Why not?' inquired Dr Simon, with a rational stare.

'Well, doctor,' said the priest, looking up blinking, 'can a man cut off his own head? I don't know.'

O'Brien felt an insane universe crashing about his ears; but the doctor sprang forward with impetuous practicality and pushed back the wet, white hair.

'Oh, there's no doubt it's Brayne,' said the priest quietly. 'He had exactly that chip in the left ear.'

The detective, who had been regarding the priest with steady and glittering eyes, opened his clenched mouth and said sharply: 'You seem to know a lot about him, Father Brown.'

'I do,' said the little man simply. 'I've been about with him for some weeks. He was thinking of joining our church.'

The star of the fanatic sprang into Valentin's eyes; he strode towards the priest with clenched hands. 'And, perhaps,' he cried, with a blasting sneer: 'perhaps he was also thinking of leaving all his money to your church.'

'Perhaps he was,' said Brown stolidly; 'it is possible.'

'In that case,' cried Valentin, with a dreadful smile: 'you may indeed know a great deal about him. About his life and about his –'

Commandant O'Brien laid a hand on Valentin's arm. 'Drop that slanderous rubbish, Valentin,' he said: 'or there may be more swords yet.'

But Valentin (under the steady, humble gaze of the priest) had already recovered himself. 'Well,' he said shortly: 'people's private opinions can wait. You gentlemen are still bound by your promise to stay; you must enforce it on yourselves – and on each other. Ivan here will tell you anything more you want to know; I must get to business and write to the authorities. We can't keep this quiet any longer. I shall be writing in my study if there is any more news.'

'Is there any more news, Ivan?' asked Dr Simon, as the chief of police strode out of the room.

'Only one more thing, I think, sir,' said Ivan, wrinkling up his grey old face; 'but that's important, too, in its way. There's that old buffer you found on the lawn,' and he pointed without pretence of reverence at the big black body with the yellow head. 'We've found out who he is, anyhow.'

'Indeed!' cried the astonished doctor; 'and who is he?'

'His name was Arnold Becker,' said the under-detective, 'though he went by many aliases. He was a wandering sort of scamp, and is known to have been in America; so that was where Brayne got his knife into him. We didn't have much to do with him ourselves, for he worked mostly in Germany. We've communicated, of course, with the German police. But, oddly enough, there was a twin brother of his, named Louis Becker, whom we had a great deal to do with. In fact, we found it necessary to guillotine him only yesterday. Well, it's a rum thing, gentlemen, but when I saw that fellow flat on the lawn I had the greatest jump of my life. If I hadn't seen Louis Becker guillotined with my own eyes, I'd have sworn it was Louis Becker lying there in the grass. Then, of course, I remembered his twin brother in Germany, and following up the clue –'

The explanatory Ivan stopped, for the excellent reason that nobody was listening to him. The Commandant and the doctor were both staring at Father Brown, who had sprung stiffly to his feet, and was holding his temples tight like a man in sudden and violent pain.

'Stop, stop, stop!' he cried; 'stop talking a minute, for I see half. Will God give me strength? Will my brain make the one jump and see all? Heaven help me! I used to be fairly good at thinking. I could paraphrase any page in Aquinas once. Will my head split – or will it see? I see half – I only see half.'

He buried his head in his hands, and stood in a sort of rigid torture of thought or prayer, while the other three could only go on staring at this last prodigy of their wild twelve hours.

When Father Brown's hands fell they showed a face quite fresh and serious, like a child's. He heaved a huge sigh, and said: 'Let us get this said and done with as quickly as possible. Look here, this will be the quickest way to convince you all of the truth.' He turned to the doctor. 'Dr Simon,' he said, 'you have a strong head-piece, and I heard you this morning asking the five hardest questions about this business. Well, if you will now ask them again, I will answer them.'

Simon's pince-nez dropped from his nose in his doubt and wonder, but he answered at once. 'Well, the first question, you know, is why a man should kill another with a clumsy sabre at all when a man can kill with a bodkin?'

'A man cannot behead with a bodkin,' said Brown, calmly, 'and for *this* murder beheading was absolutely necessary.'

'Why?' asked O'Brien, with interest.

'And the next question?' asked Father Brown.

'Well, why didn't the man cry out or anything?' asked the doctor; 'sabres in gardens are certainly unusual.'

'Twigs,' said the priest gloomily, and turned to the window which looked on the scene of death. 'No one saw the point of the twigs. Why should they lie on that lawn (look at it) so far from any tree? They were not snapped off; they were chopped off. The murderer occupied his enemy with some tricks with the sabre, showing how he could cut a branch in mid-air, or what not. Then, while his enemy bent down to see the result, a silent slash, and the head fell.'

'Well,' said the doctor slowly, 'that seems plausible enough. But my next two questions will stump anyone.'

The priest still stood looking critically out of the window and waited.

'You know how all the garden was sealed up like an air-tight chamber,' went on the doctor. 'Well, how did the strange man get into the garden?'

Without turning round, the little priest answered: 'There never was any strange man in the garden.'

There was a silence, and then a sudden cackle of almost childish laughter relieved the strain. The absurdity of Brown's remark moved Ivan to open taunts.

'Oh!' he cried; 'then we didn't lug a great fat corpse on to a sofa last night? He hadn't got into the garden, I suppose?'

'Got into the garden?' repeated Brown reflectively. 'No, not entirely.'

'Hang it all,' cried Simon, 'a man gets into a garden, or he doesn't.'

'Not necessarily,' said the priest, with a faint smile. 'What is the next question, doctor?'

'I fancy you're ill,' exclaimed Dr Simon sharply; 'but I'll ask the next question if you like. How did Brayne get out of the garden?'

'He didn't get out of the garden,' said the priest, still looking out of the window.

'Didn't get out of the garden?' exploded Simon.

'Not completely,' said Father Brown.

Simon shook his fists in a frenzy of French logic. 'A man gets out of a garden, or he doesn't,' he cried.

'Not always,' said Father Brown.

Dr Simon sprang to his feet impatiently. 'I have no time to spare on such senseless talk,' he cried angrily. 'If you can't understand a man being on one side of the wall or the other, I won't trouble you further.'

'Doctor,' said the cleric very gently, 'we have always got on very pleasantly together. If only for the sake of old friendship, stop and tell me your fifth question.'

The impatient Simon sank into a chair by the door and said briefly: 'The head and shoulders were cut about in a queer way. It seemed to be done after death.'

'Yes,' said the motionless priest, 'it was done so as to make you assume exactly the one simple falsehood that you did assume. It was done to make you take for granted that the head belonged to the body.'

The borderland of the brain, where all the monsters are made, moved horribly in the Gaelic O'Brien. He felt the chaotic presence of all the horse-men and fish-women that man's unnatural fancy has begotten. A voice older than his first fathers seemed saying in his ear: 'Keep out of the monstrous garden where grows the tree with double fruit. Avoid the evil garden where died the man with two heads.' Yet, while these shameful symbolic shapes passed across the ancient mirror of his Irish soul, his Frenchified intellect was quite alert, and was watching the odd priest as closely and incredulously as all the rest.

Father Brown had turned round at last, and stood against the window with his face in dense shadow; but even in that shadow they could see it was pale as ashes. Nevertheless, he spoke quite sensibly, as if there were no Gaelic souls on earth.

'Gentlemen,' he said; 'you did not find the strange body of Becker in the garden. You did not find any strange body in the garden. In face of Dr Simon's rationalism, I still affirm that Becker was only partly present. Look here!' (pointing to the black bulk of the mysterious corpse); 'you never saw that man in your lives. Did you ever see this man?'

He rapidly rolled away the bald-yellow head of the unknown, and put in its place the white-maned head beside it. And there, complete, unified, unmistakable, lay Julius K. Brayne.

'The murderer,' went on Brown quietly, 'hacked off his enemy's head and flung the sword far over the wall. But he was too clever to fling the sword only. He flung the *head* over the wall also. Then he had only to clap on another head to the corpse, and (as he insisted on a private inquest) you all imagined a totally new man.'

'Clap on another head!' said O'Brien, staring. 'What other head? Heads don't grow on garden bushes, do they?'

'No,' said Father Brown huskily, and looking at his boots; 'there is only one place where they grow. They grow in the basket of the guillotine, beside which the Chief of Police, Aristide Valentin, was standing not an hour before the murder. Oh, my friends hear me a minute more before you tear me in pieces. Valentin is an honest man, if being mad for an arguable cause is honesty. But did you ever see in that cold, grey eye of his that he is mad? He would do anything, *anything*, to break what he calls the superstition of the Cross. He has fought for it and starved for it, and now he has murdered for it. Brayne's crazy millions had hitherto been scattered among so many sects that they did little to alter the balance of things. But Valentin heard a whisper that Brayne, like so many scatter-brained sceptics, was drifting to us; and that was quite a different thing. Brayne would pour supplies into the impoverished and pugnacious Church of France; he would support six Nationalist newspapers like *The Guillotine*. The battle was already balanced on a point, and the fanatic took flame at the risk. He resolved to destroy the millionaire, and he did it as one would expect the greatest of detectives to commit his only crime. He abstracted the severed head of Becker on some criminological excuse, and took it home in his official box. He had that last argument with Brayne, that Lord Galloway did not hear the end of; that failing, he led him out into the sealed garden, talked about swordsmanship, used twigs and a sabre for illustration, and –'

Ivan of the Scar sprang up. 'You lunatic,' he yelled; 'you'll go to my master now, if I take you by –'

'Why, I was going there,' said Brown heavily; 'I must ask him to confess, and all that.'

Driving the unhappy Brown before them like a hostage or sacrifice, they rushed together into the sudden stillness of Valentin's study.

The great detective sat at his desk apparently too occupied to hear their turbulent entrance. They paused a moment, and then something in the look of that upright and elegant back made the doctor run forward suddenly. A touch and a glance showed him that there was a small box of pills at Valentin's elbow, and that Valentin was dead in his chair; and on the blind face of the suicide was more than the pride of Cato.

3
The Queer Feet

If you meet a member of that select club, 'The Twelve True Fishermen,' entering the Vernon Hotel for the annual club dinner, you will observe, as he takes off his overcoat, that his evening coat is green and not black. If (supposing that you have the star-defying audacity to address such a being) you ask him why, he will probably answer that he does it to avoid being mistaken for a waiter. You will then retire crushed. But you will leave behind you a mystery as yet unsolved and a tale worth telling.

If (to pursue the same vein of improbable conjecture) you were to meet a mild, hard-working little priest, named Father Brown, and were to ask him what he thought was the most singular luck of his life, he would probably reply that upon the whole his best stroke was at the Vernon Hotel, where he had averted a crime and, perhaps, saved a soul, merely by listening to a few footsteps in a passage. He is perhaps a little proud of this wild and wonderful guess of his, and it is possible that he might refer to it. But since it is immeasurably unlikely that you will ever rise high enough in the social world to find 'The Twelve True Fishermen', or that you will ever sink low enough among slums and criminals to find Father Brown, I fear you will never hear the story at all unless you hear it from me.

The Vernon Hotel, at which The Twelve True Fishermen held their annual dinners, was an institution such as can only exist in an oligarchical society which has almost gone mad on good manners. It was that topsy-turvy product – an 'exclusive' commercial enterprise. That is, it was a thing which paid, not by attracting people, but actually by turning people away. In the heart of a plutocracy tradesmen become cunning enough to be more fastidious than their customers. They positively create difficulties so that their wealthy and weary clients may spend money and diplomacy in overcoming them. If there were a fashionable hotel in London which no man could enter who was under six foot, society would meekly make up parties of six-foot men to dine in it. If there were an expensive restaurant which by a mere caprice of its proprietor was only open on Thursday afternoon, it would be crowded on Thursday afternoon. The Vernon Hotel stood, as if by accident, in the corner of a square in Belgravia. It was a small hotel; and a very inconvenient one. But its very inconveniences were considered as walls protecting a particular class. One inconvenience, in particular, was held to be of vital importance: the fact that practically only twenty-four people could dine in the place at once. The only big dinner table was the celebrated terrace table, which stood open to the air on a sort of veranda overlooking one of the most exquisite old gardens in London. Thus it happened that even the twenty-four seats at this table could only be enjoyed in warm weather; and this making the enjoyment yet more difficult made it yet more desired. The existing owner of the hotel was a Jew named Lever; and he made nearly a million out of it, by making it difficult to get into. Of course he combined with this limitation in the scope of his enterprise the most careful polish in its performance. The wines and cooking were really as good as any in Europe, and the demeanour of the attendants exactly mirrored the fixed mood of the English upper class. The proprietor knew all his waiters like the fingers on his hand; there were only fifteen of them all told. It was much easier to become a Member of Parliament than to become a waiter in that hotel. Each waiter was trained in terrible silence and smoothness, as if he were a gentleman's servant. And, indeed, there was generally at least one waiter to every gentleman who dined.

The club of The Twelve True Fishermen would not have consented to dine anywhere but in such a place, for it insisted on a luxurious privacy; and would have been quite upset by the mere thought that any other club was even dining in the same building. On the occasion of their annual dinner the Fishermen were in the habit of exposing all their treasures, as if they were in a private house, especially the celebrated set of fish knives and forks which were, as it were, the insignia of the society, each being exquisitely wrought in silver in the form of a fish, and each loaded at the hilt with one large pearl. These were always laid out for the fish course, and the fish course was always the most magnificent in that magnificent repast. The society had a vast number of ceremonies and observances, but it had no history and no object; that was where it was so very aristocratic. You did not have to be anything in order to be one of the Twelve Fishers; unless you were already a certain sort of person, you never even heard of them. It had been in existence twelve years. Its president was Mr Audley. Its vice-president was the Duke of Chester.

If I have in any degree conveyed the atmosphere of this appalling hotel, the reader may feel a natural wonder as to how I came to know anything about it, and may even speculate as to how so ordinary a person as my friend Father Brown came to find himself in that golden gallery. As far as that is concerned, my story is simple, or even vulgar. There is in the world a very aged rioter and demagogue who breaks into the most refined retreats with the dreadful information that all men are brothers, and wherever this leveller went on his pale horse it was Father Brown's trade to follow. One of the waiters, an Italian, had been struck down with a paralytic stroke that afternoon; and his Jewish employer, marvelling mildly at such superstitions, had consented to send for the nearest Popish priest. With what the waiter confessed to Father Brown we are not concerned, for the excellent reason that the cleric kept it to himself; but apparently it involved him in writing out a note or statement for the conveying of some message or the righting of some wrong. Father Brown, therefore, with a meek impudence which he would have shown equally in Buckingham Palace, asked to be provided with a room and writing materials. Mr Lever was torn in two. He was a kind man, and had also that bad imitation of kindness, the dislike of any difficulty or scene. At the same time the presence of one unusual stranger in his hotel that evening was like a speck of dirt on something just cleaned. There was never any borderland or ante-room in the Vernon Hotel, no people waiting in the hall, no customers coming in on chance. There were fifteen waiters. There were twelve guests. It would be as startling to find a new guest in the hotel that night as to find a new brother taking breakfast or tea in one's own family. Moreover, the priest's appearance was second-rate and his clothes muddy; a mere glimpse of him afar off might precipitate a crisis in the club. Mr Lever at last hit on a plan to cover, since he might not obliterate, the disgrace. When you enter (as you never will) the Vernon Hotel, you pass down a short passage decorated with a few dingy but important pictures, and come to the main vestibule and lounge which opens on your right into passages leading to the public rooms, and on your left to a similar passage pointing to the kitchens and offices of the hotel. Immediately on your left hand is the corner of a glass office, which abuts upon the lounge – a house within a house, so to speak, like the old hotel bar which probably once occupied its place.

In this office sat the representative of the proprietor (nobody in this place ever appeared in person if he could help it), and just beyond the office, on the way to the servants' quarters, was the gentlemen's cloakroom, the last boundary of the gentlemen's domain. But between the office and the cloakroom was a small private room without other outlet, sometimes used by the proprietor for delicate and important matters, such as lending a duke a thousand pounds or declining to lend him sixpence. It is a mark of the magnificent tolerance of Mr Lever that he permitted this holy place to be for about half an hour profaned by a mere priest, scribbling away on a piece of paper. The story which Father Brown was writing down was very likely a much better story than this one, only it will never be known. I can merely state that it was very nearly as long, and that the last two or three paragraphs of it were the least exciting and absorbing.

For it was by the time he had reached these that the priest began a little to allow his thoughts to wander and his animal senses, which were commonly keen, to awaken. The time of darkness and dinner was drawing on; his own forgotten little room was without a light, and perhaps the gathering gloom, as occasionally happens, sharpened the sense of sound. As Father Brown wrote the last and least essential part of his document, he caught himself writing to the rhythm of a recurrent noise outside, just as one sometimes thinks to the tune of a railway train. When he became conscious of the thing he found what it was: only the ordinary patter of feet passing the door, which in an hotel was no very unlikely matter. Nevertheless, he stared at the darkened ceiling, and listened to the sound. After he had listened for a few seconds dreamily, he got to his feet and listened intently, with his head a little on one side. Then he sat down again and buried his brow in his hands, now not merely listening, but listening and thinking also.

The footsteps outside at any given moment were such as one might hear in any hotel; and yet, taken as a whole, there was something very strange about them. There were no other footsteps. It was always a very silent house, for the few familiar guests went at once to their own apartments, and the well-trained waiters were told to be almost invisible until they were wanted. One could not conceive any place where there was less reason to apprehend anything irregular. But these footsteps were so odd that one could not decide to call them regular or irregular. Father Brown followed them with his finger on the edge of the table, like a man trying to learn a tune on the piano.

First, there came a long rush of rapid little steps, such as a light man might make in winning a walking race. At a certain point they stopped and changed to a sort of slow-swinging stamp, numbering not a quarter of the steps, but occupying about the same time. The moment the last echoing stamp had died away would come again the run or ripple of light, hurrying feet, and then again the thud of the heavier walking. It was certainly the same pair of boots, partly because (as has been said) there were no other boots about, and partly because they had a small but unmistakable creak in them. Father Brown had the kind of head that cannot help asking questions; and on this apparently trivial question his head almost split. He had seen men run in order to jump. He had seen men run in order to slide. But why on earth should a man run in order to walk? Or, again, why should he walk in order to run? Yet no other description would cover the antics of this invisible pair of legs. The man was either walking very fast down one half of the corridor in order to walk very slow down the other half; or he was walking very slow at one end to have the rapture of walking fast at the other. Neither suggestion seemed to make much sense. His brain was growing darker and darker, like his room.

Yet, as he began to think steadily, the very blackness of his cell seemed to make his thoughts more vivid; he began to see as in a kind of vision the fantastic feet capering along the corridor in unnatural or symbolic attitudes. Was it a heathen religious dance? Or some entirely new kind of scientific exercise? Father Brown began to ask himself with more exactness what the steps suggested. Taking the slow step first; it certainly was not the step of the proprietor. Men of his type walk with a rapid waddle, or they sit still. It could not be any servant or messenger waiting for directions. It did not sound like it. The poorer orders (in an oligarchy) sometimes lurch about when they are slightly drunk, but generally, and especially in such gorgeous scenes, they stand or sit in constrained attitudes. No; that heavy yet springy step, with a kind of careless emphasis, not specially noisy, yet not caring what noise it made, belonged to only one of the animals of this earth. It was a gentleman of western Europe, and probably one who had never worked for his living.

Just as he came to this solid certainty, the step changed to the quicker one, and ran past the door as feverishly as a rat. The listener remarked that though this step was much swifter it was also much more noiseless, almost as if the man were walking on tiptoe. Yet it was not associated in his mind with secrecy, but with something else – something that he could not remember. He was maddened by one of those half-memories that make a man feel half-witted. Surely he had heard that strange, swift walking somewhere. Suddenly he sprang to his feet with a new idea in his head, and walked to the door. His room had no direct outlet on the passage, but led on one side into the glass office, and on the other into the cloak-room beyond. He tried the door into the office, and found it locked. Then he looked at the window, now a square pane full of purple cloud cleft by livid sunset, and for an instant he smelt evil as a dog smells rats.

The rational part of him (whether the wiser or not) regained its supremacy. He remembered that the proprietor had told him that he should lock the door, and would come later to release him. He told himself that twenty things he had not thought of might explain the eccentric sounds outside; he reminded himself that there was just enough light left to finish his own proper work. Bringing his paper to the window so as to catch the last stormy evening light, he resolutely plunged once more into the almost completed record. He had written for about twenty minutes, bending closer and closer to his paper in the lessening light; then suddenly he sat upright. He had heard the strange feet once more.

This time they had a third oddity. Previously the unknown man had walked, with levity indeed and lightning quickness, but he had walked. This time he ran. One could hear the swift, soft, bounding steps coming along the corridor, like the pads of a fleeing and leaping panther. Whoever was coming was a very strong, active man, in still yet tearing excitement. Yet, when the sound had swept up to the office like a sort of whispering whirlwind, it suddenly changed again to the old slow, swaggering stamp.

Father Brown flung down his paper, and, knowing the office door to be locked, went at once into the cloak-room on the other side. The attendant of this place was temporarily absent, probably because the only guests were at dinner, and his office was a sinecure. After groping through a grey forest of overcoats, he found that the dim cloak-room opened on the lighted corridor in the form of a sort of counter or half-door, like most of the counters across which we have all handed umbrellas and received tickets. There was a light immediately above the semi-circular arch of this opening. It threw little illumination on Father Brown himself, who seemed a mere dark outline against the dim sunset window behind him. But it threw an almost theatrical light on the man who stood outside the cloakroom in the corridor.

He was an elegant man in very plain evening dress; tall, but with an air of not taking up much room; one felt that he could have slid along like a shadow where many smaller men would have been obvious and obstructive. His face, now flung back in the lamplight, was swarthy and vivacious, the face of a foreigner. His figure was good, his manners good humoured and confident; a critic could only say that his black coat was a shade below his figure and manners, and even bulged and bagged in an odd way. The moment he caught sight of Brown's black silhouette against the sunset, he tossed down a scrap of paper with a number and called out with amiable authority: 'I want my hat and coat, please; I find I have to go away at once.'

Father Brown took the paper without a word, and obediently went to look for the coat; it was not the first menial work he had done in his life. He brought it and laid it on the counter; meanwhile, the strange gentleman who had been feeling in his waistcoat pocket, said, laughing: 'I haven't got any silver; you can keep this.' And he threw down half a sovereign, and caught up his coat.

Father Brown's figure remained quite dark and still; but in that instant he had lost his head. His head was always most valuable when he had lost it. In such moments he put two and two together and made four million. Often the Catholic Church (which is wedded to common sense) did not approve of it. Often he did not approve of it himself. But it was a real inspiration – important at rare crises – when whosoever shall lose his head the same shall save it.

'I think, sir,' he said civilly, 'that you have some silver in your pocket.'

The tall gentleman stared. 'Hang it,' he cried. 'If I give you gold, why should you complain?'

'Because silver is sometimes more valuable than gold,' said the priest mildly; 'that is, in large quantities.'

The stranger looked at him curiously. Then he looked still more curiously up the passage towards the main entrance. Then he looked back at Brown again, and then he looked very carefully at the window beyond Brown's head, still coloured with the after-glow of the storm. Then he seemed to make up his mind. He put one hand on the counter, vaulted over as easily as an acrobat and towered above the priest, putting one tremendous hand upon his collar.

'Stand still,' he said, in a hacking whisper. 'I don't want to threaten you, but –'

'I do want to threaten you,' said Father Brown, in a voice like a rolling drum. 'I want to threaten you with the worm that dieth not, and the fire that is not quenched.'

'You're a rum sort of cloak-room clerk,' said the other.

'I am a priest, Monsieur Flambeau,' said Brown, 'and I am ready to hear your confession.'

The other stood gasping for a few moments, and then staggered back into a chair.

The first two courses of the dinner of The Twelve True Fishermen had proceeded with placid success. I do not possess a copy of the menu; and if I did it would not convey anything to anybody. It was written in a sort of super-French employed by cooks, but quite unintelligible to Frenchmen. There was a tradition in the club that the *hors d'œuvres* should be various and manifold to the point of madness. They were taken seriously because they were avowedly useless extras, like the whole dinner and the whole club. There was also a tradition that the soup course should be light and unpretending – a sort of simple and austere vigil for the feast of fish that was to come. The talk was that strange, slight talk which governs the British Empire, which governs it in secret, and yet would scarcely enlighten an ordinary Englishman even if he could overhear it. Cabinet Ministers on both sides were alluded to by their Christian names with a sort of bored benignity. The Radical Chancellor of the Exchequer, whom the whole Tory party was supposed to be cursing for his extortions, was praised for his minor poetry, or his saddle in the hunting-field. The Tory leader, whom all Liberals were supposed to hate as a tyrant, was discussed and, on the whole, praised – as a Liberal. It seemed somehow that politicians were very important. And yet, anything seemed important about them except their politics. Mr Audley, the Chairman, was an amiable, elderly man who still wore Gladstone collars; he was a kind of symbol of all that phantasmal and yet fixed society. He had never done anything – not even anything wrong. He was not fast; he was not even particularly rich. He was simply in the thing; and there was an end of it. No party could ignore him, and if he had wished to be in the Cabinet he certainly would have been put there. The Duke of Chester, the vice-president, was a young and rising politician. That is to say, he was a pleasant youth, with flat, fair hair and a freckled face, with moderate intelligence and enormous estates. In public his appearances were always successful and his principle was simple enough. When he thought of a joke he made it, and was called brilliant. When he could not think of a joke he said that this was no time for trifling, and was called able. In private, in a club of his own class, he was simply quite pleasantly frank and silly, like a schoolboy. Mr Audley, never having been in politics, treated them a little more seriously. Sometimes he even embarrassed the company by phrases suggesting that there was some difference between a Liberal and a Conservative. He, himself, was a Conservative, even in private life. He had a roll of grey hair over the back of his collar like certain old-fashioned statesmen, and seen from behind he looked like the man the empire wants. Seen from the front he looked like a mild, self-indulgent bachelor, with rooms in the Albany – which he was.

As has been remarked, there were twenty-four seats at the terrace table, and only twelve members of the club. Thus they could occupy the terrace in the most luxurious style of all, being ranged along the inner side of the table, with no one opposite, commanding an uninterrupted view of the garden, the colours of which were still vivid, though evening was closing in somewhat luridly for the time of year. The Chairman sat in the centre of the line, and the vice-president at the right-hand end of it. When the twelve guests first trooped into their seats it was the custom (for some unknown reason) for all the fifteen waiters to stand lining the wall like troops presenting arms to the king, while the fat proprietor stood and bowed to the club with radiant surprise, as if he had never heard of them before. But before the first chink of knife and fork this army of retainers had vanished, only the one or two required to collect and distribute the plates darting about in deathly silence. Mr Lever, the proprietor, of course had disappeared in convulsions of courtesy long before. It would be exaggerative, indeed irreverent, to say that he ever positively appeared again. But when the important course, the fish course, was being brought on, there was – how shall I put it? – a vivid shadow, a projection of his personality, which told that he was hovering near. The sacred fish course consisted (to the eyes of the vulgar) in a sort of monstrous pudding, about the size and shape of a wedding cake, in which some considerable number of interesting fishes had finally lost the shapes which God had given to them. The Twelve True Fishermen took up their celebrated fish knives and fish forks, and approached it as gravely as if every inch of the pudding cost as much as the silver fork it was eaten with. So it did, for all I know. This course was dealt with in eager and devouring silence; and it was only when his plate was nearly empty that the young duke made the ritual remark: 'They can't do this anywhere but here.'

'Nowhere,' said Mr Audley, in a deep bass voice, turning to the speaker and nodding his venerable head a number of times. 'Nowhere, assuredly, except here. It was represented to me that at the Café Anglais –'

Here he was interrupted and even agitated for a moment by the removal of his plate, but he recaptured the valuable thread of his thoughts. 'It was represented to me that the same could be done at the Café Anglais. Nothing like it, sir,' he said, shaking his head ruthlessly, like a hanging judge. 'Nothing like it.'

'Overrated place,' said a certain Colonel Pound, speaking (by the look of him) for the first time for some months.

'Oh, I don't know,' said the Duke of Chester, who was an optimist, 'it's jolly good for some things. You can't beat it at –'

A waiter came swiftly along the room, and then stopped dead. His stoppage was as silent as his tread; but all those vague and kindly gentlemen were so used to the utter smoothness of the unseen machinery which surrounded and supported their lives, that a waiter doing anything unexpected was a start and a jar. They felt as you and I would feel if the inanimate world disobeyed – if a chair ran away from us.

The waiter stood staring a few seconds, while there deepened on every face at table a strange shame which is wholly the product of our time. It is the combination of modern humanitarianism with the horrible modern abyss between the souls of the rich and poor. A genuine historic aristocrat would have thrown things at the waiter, beginning with empty bottles, and very probably ending with money. A genuine democrat would have asked him, with a comrade-like clearness of speech, what the devil he was doing. But these modern plutocrats could not bear a poor man near to them, either as a slave or as a friend. That something had gone wrong with the servants was merely a dull, hot embarrassment. They did not want to be brutal, and they dreaded the need to be benevolent. They wanted the thing, whatever it was, to be over. It was over. The waiter, after standing for some seconds rigid, like a cataleptic, turned round and ran madly out of the room.

When he reappeared in the room, or rather in the doorway, it was in company with another waiter, with whom he whispered and gesticulated with southern fierceness. Then the first waiter went away, leaving the second waiter, and reappeared with a third waiter. By the time a fourth waiter had joined this hurried synod, Mr Audley felt it necessary to break the silence in the interests of Tact. He used a very loud cough, instead of the presidential hammer, and said: 'Splendid work young Moocher's doing in Burmah. Now, no other nation in the world could have –'

A fifth waiter had sped towards him like an arrow, and was whispering in his ear: 'So sorry. Important! Might the proprietor speak to you?'

The chairman turned in disorder, and with a dazed stare saw Mr Lever coming towards them with his lumbering quickness. The gait of the good proprietor was indeed his usual gait, but his face was by no means usual. Generally it was a genial copper-brown; now it was a sickly yellow.

'You will pardon me, Mr Audley,' he said, with asthmatic breathlessness. 'I have great apprehensions. Your fish-plates, they are cleared away with the knife and fork on them!'

'Well, I hope so,' said the chairman, with some warmth.

'You see him?' panted the excited hotel keeper; 'you see the waiter who took them away? You know him?'

'Know the waiter?' answered Mr Audley indignantly. 'Certainly not!'

Mr Lever opened his hands with a gesture of agony. 'I never send him,' he said. 'I know not when or why he come. I send my waiter to take away the plates, and he find them already away.'

Mr Audley still looked rather too bewildered to be really the man the empire wants; none of the company could say anything except the man of wood – Colonel Pound – who seemed galvanized into an unnatural life. He rose rigidly from his chair, leaving all the rest sitting, screwed his eyeglass into his eye, and spoke in a raucous undertone as if he had half-forgotten how to speak. 'Do you mean,' he said, 'that somebody has stolen our silver fish service?'

The proprietor repeated the open-handed gesture with even greater helplessness; and in a flash all the men at the table were on their feet.

'Are all your waiters here?' demanded the colonel, in his low, harsh accent.

'Yes; they're all here. I noticed it myself,' cried the young duke, pushing his boyish face into the inmost ring. 'Always count 'em as I come in; they look so queer standing up against the wall.'

'But surely one cannot exactly remember,' began Mr Audley, with heavy hesitation.

'I remember exactly, I tell you,' cried the duke excitedly. 'There never have been more than fifteen waiters at this place, and there were no more than fifteen to-night, I'll swear; no more and no less.'

The proprietor turned upon him, quaking in a kind of palsy of surprise. 'You say – you say,' he stammered, 'that you see all my fifteen waiters?'

'As usual,' assented the duke. 'What is the matter with that?'

'Nothing,' said Lever, with a deepening accent, 'only you did not. For one of zem is dead upstairs.'

There was a shocking stillness for an instant in that room. It may be (so supernatural is the word death) that each of those idle men looked for a second at his soul, and saw it as a small dried pea. One of them – the duke, I think – even said with the idiotic kindness of wealth: 'Is there anything we can do?'

'He has had a priest,' said the Jew, not untouched.

Then, as to the clang of doom, they awoke to their own position. For a few weird seconds they had really felt as if the fifteenth waiter might

51

be the ghost of the dead man upstairs. They had been dumb under that oppression, for ghosts were to them an embarrassment, like beggars. But the remembrance of the silver broke the spell of the miraculous; broke it abruptly and with a brutal reaction. The colonel flung over his chair and strode to the door. 'If there was a fifteenth man here, friends,' he said, 'that fifteenth fellow was a thief. Down at once to the front and back doors and secure everything; then we'll talk. The twenty-four pearls are worth recovering.'

Mr Audley seemed at first to hesitate about whether it was gentlemanly to be in such a hurry about anything; but, seeing the duke dash down the stairs with youthful energy, he followed with a more mature motion.

At the same instant a sixth waiter ran into the room, and declared that he had found the pile of fish-plates on a sideboard, with no trace of the silver.

The crowd of diners and attendants that tumbled helter-skelter down the passages divided into two groups. Most of the Fishermen followed the proprietor to the front room to demand news of any exit. Colonel Pound, with the Chairman, the vice-president, and one or two others, darted down the corridor leading to the servants' quarters, as the more likely line of escape. As they did so they passed the dim alcove or cavern of the cloak-room, and saw a short, black-coated figure, presumably an attendant, standing a little way back in the shadow of it.

'Hallo there!' called out the duke. 'Have you seen anyone pass?'

The short figure did not answer the question directly, but merely said: 'Perhaps I have got what you are looking for, gentlemen.'

They paused, wavering and wondering, while he quietly went to the back of the cloak-room, and came back with both hands full of shining silver, which he laid out on the counter as calmly as a salesman. It took the form of a dozen quaintly shaped forks and knives.

'You – you –' began the colonel, quite thrown off his balance at last. Then he peered into the dim little room and saw two things: first, that the short, black-clad man was dressed like a clergyman; and, second, that the window of the room behind him was burst, as if someone had passed violently through.

'Valuable things to deposit in a cloak-room, aren't they?' remarked the clergyman, with cheerful composure.

'Did – did you steal those things?' stammered Mr Audley, with staring eyes.

'If I did,' said the cleric pleasantly, 'at least I am bringing them back again.'

'But you didn't,' said Colonel Pound, still staring at the broken window.

'To make a clean breast of it, I didn't,' said the other, with some humour. And he seated himself quite gravely on a stool.

'But you know who did,' said the colonel.

'I don't know his real name,' said the priest placidly; 'but I know something of his fighting weight, and a great deal about his spiritual difficulties. I formed the physical estimate when he was trying to throttle me, and the moral estimate when he repented.'

'Oh, I say – repented!' cried young Chester, with a sort of crow of laughter.

Father Brown got to his feet, putting his hands behind him. 'Odd, isn't it,' he said, 'that a thief and a vagabond should repent, when so many who are rich and secure remain hard and frivolous, and without fruit for God or man? But there, if you will excuse me, you trespass a little upon my province. If you doubt the penitence as a practical fact, there are your knives and forks. You are The Twelve True Fishers, and there are all your silver fish. But He has made me a fisher of men.'

'Did you catch this man?' asked the colonel, frowning.

Father Brown looked him full in his frowning face. 'Yes,' he said, 'I caught him, with an unseen hook and an invisible line which is long enough to let him wander to the ends of the world, and still to bring him back with a twitch upon the thread.'

There was a long silence. All the other men present drifted away to carry the recovered silver to their comrades, or to consult the proprietor about the queer condition of affairs. But the grim-faced colonel still sat sideways on the counter, swinging his long, lank legs and biting his dark moustache.

At last he said quietly to the priest: 'He must have been a clever fellow, but I think I know a cleverer.'

'He was a clever fellow,' answered the other, 'but I am not quite sure of what other you mean.'

'I mean you,' said the colonel, with a short laugh. 'I don't want to get the fellow jailed; make yourself easy about that. But I'd give a good many silver forks to know exactly how you fell into this affair, and how you got the stuff out of him. I reckon you're the most up-to-date devil of the present company.'

Father Brown seemed rather to like the saturnine candour of the soldier. 'Well,' he said, smiling, 'I mustn't tell you anything of the man's identity, or his own story, of course; but there's no particular reason why I shouldn't tell you of the mere outside facts which I found out for myself.'

He hopped over the barrier with unexpected activity, and sat beside Colonel Pound, kicking his short legs like a little boy on a gate. He began to tell the story as easily as if he were telling it to an old friend by a Christmas fire.

'You see, colonel,' he said, 'I was shut up in that small room there doing some writing, when I heard a pair of feet in this passage doing a dance that was as queer as the dance of death. First came quick, funny little steps, like a man walking on tiptoe for a wager; then came slow, careless, creaking steps, as of a big man walking about with a cigar. But they were both made by the same feet, I swear, and they came in rotation; first the run and then the walk, and then the run again. I wondered at first idly, and then wildly why a man should act these two parts at once. One walk I knew; it was just like yours, colonel. It was the walk of a well-fed gentleman waiting for something, who strolls about rather because he is physically alert than because he is mentally impatient. I knew that I knew the other walk, too, but I could not remember what it was. What wild creature had I met on my travels that tore along on tiptoe in that extraordinary style? Then I heard a clink of plates somewhere; and the answer stood up as plain as St Peter's. It was the walk of a waiter — that walk with the body slanted forward, the eyes looking down, the ball of the toe spurning away the ground, the coat tails and napkin flying. Then I thought for a minute and a half more. And I believe I saw the manner of the crime, as clearly as if I were going to commit it.'

Colonel Pound looked at him keenly, but the speaker's mild grey eyes were fixed upon the ceiling with almost empty wistfulness.

'A crime,' he said slowly, 'is like any other work of art. Don't look surprised; crimes are by no means the only works of art that come from an infernal workshop. But every work of art, divine or diabolic, has one indispensable mark – I mean, that the centre of it is simple, however much the fulfilment may be complicated. Thus, in *Hamlet*, let us say, the grotesqueness of the grave-digger, the flowers of the mad girl, the fantastic finery of Osric, the pallor of the ghost and the grin of the skull are all oddities in a sort of tangled wreath round one plain tragic figure of a man in black. Well, this also,' he said, getting slowly down from his seat with a smile, 'this also is the plain tragedy of a man in black. Yes,' he went on, seeing the colonel look up in some wonder, 'the whole of this tale turns on a black coat. In this, as in *Hamlet*, there are the rococo excrescences – yourselves, let us say. There is the dead waiter, who was there when he could not be there. There is the invisible hand that swept your table clear of silver and melted into air. But every clever crime is founded ultimately on some one quite simple fact – some fact that is not itself mysterious. The mystification comes in covering it up, in leading men's thoughts away from it. This large and subtle and (in the ordinary course) most profitable crime, was built on the plain fact that a gentleman's evening dress is the same as a waiter's. All the rest was acting, and thundering good acting, too.'

'Still,' said the colonel, getting up and frowning at his boots. 'I am not sure that I understand.'

'Colonel,' said Father Brown, 'I tell you that this archangel of impudence who stole your forks walked up and down this passage twenty times in the blaze of all the lamps, in the glare of all the eyes. He did not go and hide in dim corners where suspicion might have searched for him. He kept constantly on the move in the lighted corridors, and everywhere that he went he seemed to be there by right. Don't ask me what he was like; you have seen him yourself six or seven times to-night. You were waiting with all the other grand people in the reception room at the end of the passage there, with the terrace just beyond. Whenever he came among you gentlemen, he came in the lightning style of a waiter, with bent head, flapping napkin and flying feet. He shot out on to the terrace, did something to the table-cloth, and shot back again towards the office and the waiters' quarters. By the time he had come under the eye of the office clerk and the waiters he had become another man in every inch of his body, in every instinctive gesture. He strolled among the servants with the absent-minded insolence which they have all seen in their patrons. It was no new thing to them that a swell from the dinner party should pace all parts of the house like an animal at the Zoo; they know that nothing marks the Smart Set more than a habit of walking where one chooses. When he was magnificently weary of walking down that particular passage he would wheel round and pace back past the office; in the shadow of the arch just beyond he was altered as by a blast of magic, and went hurrying forward again among the Twelve Fishermen, an obsequious attendant. Why should the gentlemen look at a chance waiter? Why should the waiters suspect a first-rate walking gentleman? Once or twice he played the coolest tricks. In the proprietor's private quarters he called out breezily for a syphon of soda water, saying he was thirsty. He said genially that he would carry it himself, and he did; he carried it quickly and correctly through the thick of you, a waiter with an obvious errand. Of course, it could not have been kept up long, but it only had to be kept up till the end of the fish course.

'His worst moment was when the waiters stood in a row; but even then he contrived to lean against the wall just around the corner in such a way that for that important instant the waiters thought him a gentleman, while the gentlemen thought him a waiter. The rest went like winking. If any waiter caught him away from the table, that waiter caught a languid aristocrat. He had only to time himself two minutes before the fish was cleared, become a swift servant, and clear it himself. He put the plates down on a sideboard, stuffed the silver in his breast pocket, giving it a bulgy look, and ran like a hare (I heard him coming) till he came to the cloak-room. There he had only to be a plutocrat again – a plutocrat called away suddenly on business. He had only to give his ticket to the cloak-room attendant, and go out again elegantly as he had come in. Only – only I happened to be the cloak-room attendant.'

'What did you do to him?' cried the colonel, with unusual intensity. 'What did he tell you?'

'I beg your pardon,' said the priest immovably, 'that is where the story ends.'

'And the interesting story begins,' muttered Pound. 'I think I understand his professional trick. But I don't seem to have got hold of yours.'

'I must be going,' said Father Brown.

They walked together along the passage to the entrance hall, where they saw the fresh, freckled face of the Duke of Chester, who was bounding buoyantly along towards them.

'Come along, Pound,' he cried breathlessly. 'I've been looking for you everywhere. The dinner's going again in spanking style, and old Audley has got to make a speech in honour of the forks being saved. We want to start some new ceremony, don't you know, to commemorate the occasion. I say, you really got the goods back, what do you suggest?'

'Why,' said the colonel, eyeing him with a certain sardonic approval. 'I should suggest that henceforward we wear green coats instead of black. One never knows what mistakes may arise when one looks so like a waiter.'

'Oh, hang it all!' said the young man, 'a gentleman never looks like a waiter.'

'Nor a waiter like a gentleman, I suppose,' said Colonel Pound, with the same lowering laughter on his face. 'Reverend sir, your friend must have been very smart to act the gentleman.'

Father Brown buttoned up his commonplace overcoat to the neck, for the night was stormy, and took his commonplace umbrella from the stand.

'Yes,' he said; 'it must be very hard work to be a gentleman; but, do you know, I have sometimes thought that it may be almost as laborious to be a waiter.'

And saying 'Good evening', he pushed open the heavy doors of that palace of pleasures. The golden gates closed behind him, and he went at a brisk walk through the damp, dark streets in search of a penny omnibus.

4
The Invisible Man

In the cool blue twilight of two steep streets in Camden Town, the shop at the corner, a confectioner's, glowed like the butt of a cigar. One should rather say, perhaps, like the butt of a firework, for the light was of many colours and some complexity, broken up by many mirrors and dancing on many gilt and gaily-coloured cakes and sweetmeats. Against this one fiery glass were glued the noses of many gutter-snipes, for the chocolates were all wrapped in those red and gold and green metallic colours which are almost better than chocolate itself; and the huge white wedding-cake in the window was somehow at once remote and satisfying, just as if the whole North Pole were good to eat. Such rainbow provocations could naturally collect the youth of the neighbourhood up to the ages of ten or twelve. But this corner was also attractive to youth at a later stage; and a young man, not less than twenty-four, was staring into the same shop-window. To him, also, the shop was of fiery charm, but this attraction was not wholly to be explained by chocolates; which, however, he was far from despising.

He was a tall, burly, red-haired young man, with a resolute face but a listless manner. He carried under his arm a flat, grey portfolio of black-and-white sketches which he had sold with more or less success to publishers ever since his uncle (who was an admiral) had disinherited him for Socialism, because of a lecture which he had delivered against that economic theory. His name was John Turnbull Angus.

Entering at last, he walked through the confectioner's shop into the back room, which was a sort of pastry-cook restaurant, merely raising his hat to the young lady who was serving there. She was a dark, elegant, alert girl in black, with a high colour and very quick, dark eyes; and after the ordinary interval she followed him into the inner room to take his order.

His order was evidently a usual one. 'I want, please,' he said with precision, 'one halfpenny bun and a small cup of black coffee.' An instant before the girl could turn away he added, 'Also, I want you to marry me.'

The young lady of the shop stiffened suddenly, and said: 'Those are jokes I don't allow.'

The red-haired young man lifted grey eyes of an unexpected gravity.

'Really and truly,' he said, 'it's as serious – as serious as the halfpenny bun. It is expensive, like the bun; one pays for it. It is indigestible, like the bun. It hurts.'

The dark young lady had never taken her dark eyes off him, but seemed to be studying him with almost tragic exactitude. At the end of her scrutiny she had something like the shadow of a smile, and she sat down in a chair.

'Don't you think,' observed Angus, absently, 'that it's rather cruel to eat these halfpenny buns? They might grow up into penny buns. I shall give up these brutal sports when we are married.'

The dark young lady rose from her chair and walked to the window, evidently in a state of strong but not unsympathetic cogitation. When at last she swung round again with an air of resolution, she was bewildered to observe that the young man was carefully laying out on the table various objects from the shop-window. They included a pyramid of highly coloured sweets, several plates of sandwiches, and the two decanters containing that mysterious port and sherry which are peculiar to pastry-cooks. In the middle of this neat arrangement he had carefully let down the enormous load of white sugared cake which had been the huge ornament of the window.

'What on earth are you doing?' she asked.

'Duty, my dear Laura,' he began.

'Oh, for the Lord's sake, stop a minute,' she cried, 'and don't talk to me in that way. I mean what is all that?'

'A ceremonial meal, Miss Hope.'

'And what is *that*?' she asked impatiently, pointing to the mountain of sugar.

'The wedding-cake, Mrs Angus,' he said.

The girl marched to that article, removed it with some clatter, and put it back in the shop-window; she then returned, and, putting her elegant elbows on the table, regarded the young man not unfavourably, but with considerable exasperation.

'You don't give me any time to think,' she said.

'I'm not such a fool,' he answered; 'that's my Christian humility.'

She was still looking at him; but she had grown considerably graver behind the smile.

'Mr Angus,' she said steadily, 'before there is a minute more of this nonsense I must tell you something about myself as shortly as I can.'

'Delighted,' replied Angus gravely. 'You might tell me something about myself, too, while you are about it.'

'Oh, do hold your tongue and listen,' she said. 'It's nothing that I'm ashamed of, and it isn't even anything that I'm specially sorry about. But what would you say if there were something that is no business of mine and yet is my nightmare?'

'In that case,' said the man seriously, 'I should suggest that you bring back the cake.'

'Well, you must listen to the story first,' said Laura, persistently. 'To begin with, I must tell you that my father owned the inn called the "Red Fish" at Ludbury, and I used to serve people in the bar.'

'I have often wondered,' he said, 'why there was a kind of a Christian air about this one confectioner's shop.'

'Ludbury is a sleepy, grassy little hole in the Eastern Counties, and the only kind of people who ever came to the "Red Fish" were occasional commercial travellers, and for the rest, the most awful people you can see, only you've never seen them. I mean little, loungy men, who had just enough to live on, and had nothing to do but lean about in bar-rooms and bet on horses, in bad clothes that were just too good for them. Even these wretched young rotters were not very common at our house; but there were two of them that were a lot too common – common in every sort of way. They both lived on money of their own, and were wearisomely idle and over-dressed. But yet I was a bit sorry for them, because I half believe they slunk into our little empty bar because each of them had a slight deformity; the sort of thing that some yokels laugh at. It wasn't exactly a deformity either; it was more an oddity. One of them was a surprisingly small man, something like a dwarf, or at least like a jockey. He was not at all jockeyish to look at, though, he had a round black head and a well-trimmed black beard, bright eyes like a bird's; he jingled money in his pockets; he jangled a great gold watch chain; and he never turned up except dressed just too much like a gentleman to be one. He was no fool, though a futile idler; he was curiously clever at all kinds of things that couldn't be the slightest use; a sort of impromptu conjuring; making fifteen matches set fire to each other like a regular firework; or cutting a banana or some such thing into a dancing doll. His name was Isidore Smythe; and I can see him still, with his little dark face, just coming up to the counter, making a jumping kangaroo out of five cigars.

'The other fellow was more silent and more ordinary; but somehow he alarmed me much more than poor little Smythe. He was very tall and slight, and light-haired; his nose had a high bridge, and he might almost have been handsome in a spectral sort of way; but he had one of the most appalling squints I have ever seen or heard of. When he looked straight at you, you didn't know where you were yourself, let alone what he was looking at. I fancy this sort of disfigurement embittered the poor chap a little; for while Smythe was ready to show off his monkey tricks anywhere, James Welkin (that was the squinting man's name) never did anything except soak in our bar parlour, and go for great walks by himself in the flat, grey country all round. All the same, I think Smythe too, was a little sensitive about being so small, though he carried it off more smartly. And so it was that I was really puzzled, as well as startled, and very sorry, when they both offered to marry me in the same week.

'Well, I did what I've since thought was perhaps a silly thing. But, after all, these freaks were my friends in a way; and I had a horror of their thinking I refused them for the real reason, which was that they were so impossibly ugly. So I made up some gas of another sort, about never meaning to marry anyone who hadn't carved his way in the world. I said it was a point of principle with me not to live on money that was just inherited like theirs. Two days after I had talked in this well-meaning sort of way, the whole trouble began. The first thing I heard was that both of them had gone off to seek their fortunes, as if they were in some silly fairy tale.

'Well, I've never seen either of them from that day to this. But I've had two letters from the little man called Smythe, and really they were rather exciting.'

'Ever heard of the other man?' asked Angus.

'No, he never wrote,' said the girl, after an instant's hesitation. 'Smythe's first letter was simply to say that he had started out walking with Welkin to London; but Welkin was such a good walker that the little man dropped out of it, and took a rest by the roadside. He happened to be picked up by some travelling show, and, partly because he was nearly a dwarf, and partly because he was really a clever little wretch, he got on quite well in the show business, and was soon sent up to the Aquarium, to do some tricks that I forgot. That was his first letter. His second was much more of a startler, and I only got it last week.'

The man called Angus emptied his coffee-cup and regarded her with mild and patient eyes. Her own mouth took a slight twist of laughter as she resumed: 'I suppose you've seen on the hoardings all about this "Smythe's Silent Service"? Or you must be the only person that hasn't. Oh, I don't know much about it, it's some clockwork invention for doing all the housework by machinery. You know the sort of thing: "Press a button – A Butler who Never Drinks." "Turn a handle – Ten House-maids who Never Flirt." You must have seen the advertisements. Well, whatever these machines are, they are making pots of money; and they are making it all for that little imp whom I knew down in Ludbury. I can't help feeling pleased the poor little chap has fallen on his feet; but the plain fact is, I'm in terror of his turning up any minute and telling me he's carved his way in the world – as he certainly has.'

'And the other man?' repeated Angus with a sort of obstinate quietude.

Laura Hope got to her feet suddenly. 'My friend,' she said: 'I think you are a witch. Yes, you are quite right. I have not seen a line of the other man's writing; and I have no more notion than the dead of what or where he is. But it is of him that I am frightened. It is he who is all about my path. It is he who has half driven me mad. Indeed, I think he has driven me mad; for I have felt him where he could not have been, and I have heard his voice when he could not have spoken.'

'Well, my dear,' said the young man, cheerfully, 'if he were Satan himself, he is done for now you have told somebody. One goes mad all alone, old girl. But when was it you fancied you felt and heard our squinting friend?'

'I heard James Welkin laugh as plainly as I hear you speak,' said the girl, steadily. 'There was nobody there, for I stood just outside the shop at the corner, and could see down both streets at once. I had forgotten how he laughed, though his laugh was as odd as his squint. I had not thought of him for nearly a year. But it's a solemn truth that a few seconds later the first letter came from his rival.'

'Did you ever make the spectre speak or squeak, or anything?' asked Angus, with some interest.

Laura suddenly shuddered, and then said with an unshaken voice: 'Yes. Just when I had finished reading the second letter from Isidore Smythe announcing his success, just then, I heard Welkin say: "He shan't have you, though." It was quite plain, as if he were in the room. It is awful; I think I must be mad.'

'If you really were mad,' said the young man, 'you would think you must be sane. But certainly there seems to me to be something a little rum about this unseen gentleman. Two heads are better than one – I spare you allusions to any other organs – and really, if you would allow me, as a sturdy, practical man, to bring back the wedding-cake out of the window –'

Even as he spoke, there was a sort of steely shriek in the street outside, and a small motor, driven at devilish speed, shot up to the door of the shop and stuck there. In the same flash of time a small man in a shiny top hat stood stamping in the outer room.

Angus, who had hitherto maintained hilarious ease from motives of mental hygiene, revealed the strain of his soul by striding abruptly out of the inner room and confronting the new-comer. A glance at him was quite sufficient to confirm the savage guesswork of a man in love. This very dapper but dwarfish figure, with the spike of black beard carried insolently forward, the clever unrestful eyes, the neat but very nervous fingers, could be none other than the man just described to him: Isidore Smythe, who made dolls out of banana skins and matchboxes: Isidore Smythe, who made millions out of undrinking butlers and unflirting housemaids of metal. For a moment the two men, instinctively under-standing each other's air of possession, looked at each other with that curious cold generosity which is the soul of rivalry.

Mr Smythe, however, made no allusion to the ultimate ground of their antagonism, but said simply and explosively: 'Has Miss Hope seen that thing on the window?'

'On the window?' repeated the staring Angus.

'There's no time to explain other things,' said the small millionaire shortly. 'There's some tomfoolery going on here that has to be investigated.'

He pointed his polished walking-stick at the window, recently depleted by the bridal preparations of Mr Angus; and that gentleman was astonished to see along the front of the glass a long strip of paper pasted, which had certainly not been on the window when he had looked through it some time before. Following the energetic Smythe outside into the street, he found that some yard and a half of stamp-paper had been carefully gummed along the glass outside, and on this was written in straggly characters: 'If you marry Smythe, he will die.'

'Laura,' said Angus, putting his big red head into the shop, 'you're not mad.'

'It's the writing of that fellow Welkin,' said Smythe gruffly. 'I haven't seen him for years, but he's always bothering me. Five times in the last fortnight he's had threatening letters left at my flat, and I can't even find out who leaves them, let alone if it is Welkin himself. The porter of the flats swears that no suspicious characters have been seen, and here he has pasted up a sort of dado on a public shop-window, while the people in the shop –'

'Quite so,' said Angus modestly, 'while the people in the shop were having tea. Well, sir, I can assure you I appreciate your common sense in dealing so directly with the matter. We can talk about other things afterwards. The fellow cannot be very far off yet, for I swear there was no paper there when I went last to the window, ten or fifteen minutes ago. On the other hand, he's too far off to be chased, as we don't even know the direction. If you'll take my advice, Mr Smythe, you'll put this at once in the hands of some energetic inquiry man, private rather than public. I know an extremely clever fellow, who has set up in business five minutes from here in your car. His name's Flambeau, and though his youth was a bit stormy, he's a strictly honest man now, and his brains are worth money. He lives in Lucknow Mansions, Hampstead.'

'That is odd,' said the little man, arching his black eyebrows. 'I live myself in Himalaya Mansions round the corner. Perhaps you might care to come with me; I can go to my rooms and sort out these queer Welkin documents, while you run round and get your friend the detective.'

'You are very good,' said Angus politely. 'Well, the sooner we act the better.'

Both men, with a queer kind of impromptu fairness, took the same sort of formal farewell of the lady, and both jumped into the brisk little car. As Smythe took the wheel and they turned the great corner of the street, Angus was amused to see a gigantesque poster of 'Smythe's Silent Service', with a picture of a huge headless iron doll, carrying a saucepan with the legend, 'A Cook Who is Never Cross'.

'I use them in my own flat,' said the little black-bearded man, laughing, 'partly for advertisement, and partly for real convenience. Honestly, and all above board, those big clockwork dolls of mine do bring you coals or claret or a time-table quicker than any live servants I've ever known, if you know which knob to press. But I'll never deny, between ourselves, that such servants have their disadvantages, too.'

'Indeed?' said Angus; 'is there something they can't do?'

'Yes,' replied Smythe coolly; 'they can't tell me who left those threatening letters at my flat.'

The man's motor was small and swift like himself; in fact, like his domestic service, it was of his own invention. If he was an advertising quack, he was one who believed in his own wares. The sense of something tiny and flying was accentuated as they swept up long white curves of road in the dead but open daylight of evening. Soon the white curves came sharper and dizzier; they were upon ascending spirals, as they say in the modern religions. For, indeed, they were cresting a corner of London which is almost as precipitous as Edinburgh, if not quite so picturesque. Terrace rose above terrace, and the special tower of flats they sought, rose above them all to almost Egyptian height, gilt by the level sunset. The change, as they turned the corner and entered the crescent known as Himalaya Mansions, was as abrupt as the opening of a window; for they found that pile of flats sitting above London as above a green sea of slate. Opposite to the mansions, on the other side of the gravel crescent, was a bushy enclosure more like a steep hedge or dyke than a garden, and some way below that ran a strip of artificial water, a sort of canal, like the moat of that embowered fortress. As the car swept round the crescent it passed, at one corner, the stray stall of a man selling chestnuts; and right away at the other end of the curve, Angus could see a dim blue policeman walking slowly. These were the only human shapes in that high suburban solitude; but he had an irrational sense that they expressed the speechless poetry of London. He felt as if they were figures in a story.

The little car shot up to the right house like a bullet, and shot out its owner like a bomb shell. He was immediately inquiring of a tall commissionaire in shining braid, and a short porter in shirt sleeves, whether anybody or anything had been seeking his apartments. He was assured that nobody and nothing had passed these officials since his last inquiries; whereupon he and the slightly bewildered Angus were shot up in the lift like a rocket, till they reached the top floor.

'Just come in for a minute,' said the breathless Smythe. 'I want to show you those Welkin letters. Then you might run round the corner and fetch your friend.' He pressed a button concealed in the wall, and the door opened of itself.

It opened on a long, commodious ante-room, of which the only arresting features, ordinarily speaking, were the rows of tall half-human mechanical figures that stood up on both sides like tailors' dummies. Like tailors' dummies they were headless; and like tailors' dummies they had a handsome unnecessary humpiness in the shoulders, and a pigeonbreasted protuberance of chest; but barring this, they were not much more like a human figure than any automatic machine at a station that is about the human height. They had two great hooks like arms, for carrying trays; and they were painted pea-green, or vermilion, or black for convenience of distinction; in every other way they were only automatic machines and nobody would have looked twice at them. On this occasion, at least, nobody did. For between the two rows of these domestic dummies lay something more interesting than most of the mechanics of the world. It was a white, tattered scrap of paper scrawled with red ink; and the agile inventor had snatched it up almost as soon as the door flew open. He handed it to Angus without a word. The red ink on it actually was not dry, and the message ran: 'If you have been to see her to-day, I shall kill you.'

There was a short silence, and then Isidore Smythe said quietly: 'Would you like a little whisky? I rather feel as if I should.'

'Thank you; I should like a little Flambeau,' said Angus, gloomily. 'This business seems to me to be getting rather grave. I'm going round at once to fetch him.'

'Right you are,' said the other, with admirable cheerfulness. 'Bring him round here as quick as you can.'

But as Angus closed the front door behind him he saw Smythe push back a button, and one of the clockwork images glided from its place and slid along a groove in the floor carrying a tray with syphon and decanter. There did seem something a trifle weird about leaving the little man alone among those dead servants, who were coming to life as the door closed.

Six steps down from Smythe's landing the man in shirt sleeves was doing something with a pail. Angus stopped to extract a promise, fortified with a prospective bribe, that he would remain in that place until the return with the detective, and would keep count of any kind of stranger coming up those stairs. Dashing down to the front hall he then laid similar charges of vigilance on the commissionaire at the front door, from whom he learned the simplifying circumstance that there was no back door. Not content with this, he captured the floating policeman and induced him to stand opposite the entrance and watch it; and finally paused an instant for a pennyworth of chestnuts, and an inquiry as to the probable length of the merchant's stay in the neighbourhood.

The chestnut seller, turning up the collar of his coat, told him he should probably be moving shortly, as he thought it was going to snow. Indeed, the evening was growing grey and bitter, but Angus, with all his eloquence, proceeded to nail the chestnut man to his post.

'Keep yourself warm on your own chestnuts,' he said earnestly. 'Eat up your whole stock; I'll make it worth your while. I'll give you a sovereign if you'll wait here till I come back, and then tell me whether any man, woman, or child has gone into that house where the commissionaire is standing.'

He then walked away smartly, with a last look at the besieged tower.

'I've made a ring round that room, anyhow,' he said. 'They can't all four of them be Mr Welkin's accomplices.'

Lucknow Mansions were, so to speak, on a lower platform of that hill of houses, of which Himalaya Mansions might be called the peak. Mr Flambeau's semi-official flat was on the ground floor, and presented in every way a marked contrast to the American machinery and cold hotel-like luxury of the flat of the Silent Service. Flambeau, who was a friend of Angus, received him in a rococo artistic den behind his office, of which the ornaments were sabres, harquebuses, Eastern curiosities, flasks of Italian wine, savage cooking-pots, a plumy Persian cat, and a small dusty-looking Roman Catholic priest, who looked particularly out of place.

'This is my friend, Father Brown,' said Flambeau. 'I've often wanted you to meet him. Splendid weather, this; a little cold for Southerners like me.'

'Yes, I think it will keep clear,' said Angus, sitting down on a violet-striped Eastern ottoman.

'No,' said the priest quietly; 'it has begun to snow.'

And indeed, as he spoke, the first few flakes, foreseen by the man of chestnuts, began to drift across the darkening window-pane.

'Well,' said Angus heavily. 'I'm afraid I've come on business, and rather jumpy business at that. The fact is, Flambeau, within a stone's throw of your house is a fellow who badly wants your help; he's perpetually being haunted and threatened by an invisible enemy – a scoundrel whom nobody has even seen.' As Angus proceeded to tell the whole tale of Smythe and Welkin beginning with Laura's story, and going on with his own, the supernatural laugh at the corner of two empty streets, the strange distinct words spoken in an empty room, Flambeau grew more and more vividly concerned, and the little priest seemed to be left out of it, like a piece of furniture. When it came to the scribbled stamp-paper pasted on the window, Flambeau rose, seeming to fill the room with his huge shoulders.

'If you don't mind,' he said, 'I think you had better tell me the rest on the nearest road to this man's house. It strikes me, somehow, that there is no time to be lost.'

'Delighted,' said Angus, rising also, 'though he's safe enough for the present, for I've set four men to watch the only hole to his burrow.'

They turned out into the street, the small priest trundling after them with the docility of a small dog. He merely said, in a cheerful way, like one making conversation: 'How quick the snow gets thick on the ground.'

As they threaded the steep side streets already powdered with silver, Angus finished his story; and by the time they reached the crescent with the towering flats, he had leisure to turn his attention to the four sentinels. The chestnut seller, both before and after receiving a sovereign, swore stubbornly that he had watched the door and seen no visitor enter. The policeman was even more emphatic. He said he had had experience of crooks of all kinds, in top hats and in rags; he wasn't so green as to expect suspicious characters to look suspicious; he looked out for anybody, and, so help him, there had been nobody. And when all three men gathered round the gilded commissionaire, who still stood smiling astride of the porch, the verdict was more final still.

'I've got a right to ask any man, duke or dustman, what he wants in these flats,' said the genial and gold-laced giant, 'and I'll swear there's been nobody to ask since this gentleman went away.'

The unimportant Father Brown, who stood back, looking modestly at the pavement, here ventured to say meekly: 'Has nobody been up and down stairs, then, since the snow began to fall? It began while we were all round at Flambeau's.'

'Nobody's been in here, sir, you can take it from me,' said the official, with beaming authority.

'Then I wonder what that is?' said the priest, and stared at the ground blankly like a fish.

The others all looked down also; and Flambeau used a fierce exclamation and a French gesture. For it was unquestionably true that down the middle of the entrance guarded by the man in gold lace, actually between the arrogant, stretched legs of that colossus, ran a stringy pattern of grey footprints stamped upon the white snow.

'God!' cried Angus involuntarily; 'the Invisible Man!'

Without another word he turned and dashed up the stairs, with Flambeau following; but Father Brown still stood looking about him in the snow-clad street as if he had lost interest in his query.

Flambeau was plainly in a mood to break down the door with his big shoulder; but the Scotsman, with more reason, if less intuition, fumbled about on the frame of the door till he found the invisible button; and the door swung slowly open.

It showed substantially the same serried interior; the hall had grown darker, though it was still struck here and there with the last crimson shafts of sunset, and one or two of the headless machines had been moved from their places for this or that purpose, and stood here and there about the twilit place. The green and red of their coats were all darkened in the dusk, and their likeness to human shapes slightly increased by their very shapelessness. But in the middle of them all, exactly where the paper with the red ink had lain, there lay something that looked very like red ink spilled out of its bottle. But it was not red ink.

With a French combination of reason and violence Flambeau simply said 'Murder!' and, plunging into the flat, had explored every corner and cupboard of it in five minutes. But if he expected to find a corpse he found none. Isidore Smythe simply was not in the place, either dead or alive. After the most tearing search the two men met each other in the outer hall with streaming faces and staring eyes. 'My friend,' said Flambeau, talking French in his excitement, 'not only is your murderer invisible, but he makes invisible also the murdered man.'

Angus looked round at the dim room full of dummies, and in some Celtic corner of his Scotch soul a shudder started. One of the life-size dolls stood immediately overshadowing the blood stain, summoned, perhaps, by the slain man an instant before he fell. One of the high-shouldered hooks that served the thing for arms, was a little lifted and Angus had suddenly the horrid fancy that poor Smythe's own iron child had struck him down. Matter had rebelled, and these machines had killed their master. But even so, what had they done with him?

'Eaten him?' said the nightmare at his ear; and he sickened for an instant at the idea of rent, human remains absorbed and crushed into all that acephalous clockwork.

He recovered his mental health by an emphatic effort, and said to Flambeau: 'Well, there it is. The poor fellow has evaporated like a cloud and left a red streak on the floor. The tale does not belong to this world.'

'There is only one thing to be done,' said Flambeau, 'whether it belongs to this world or the other, I must go down and talk to my friend.'

They descended, passing the man with the pail, who again asseverated that he had let no intruder pass, down to the commissionaire and the hovering chestnut man, who rightly reasserted their own watchfulness. But when Angus looked round for his fourth confirmation he could not see it, and called out with some nervousness: 'Where is the policeman?'

'I beg your pardon,' said Father Brown; 'that is my fault. I just sent him down the road to investigate something – that I just thought worth investigating.'

'Well, we want him back pretty soon,' said Angus abruptly, 'for the wretched man upstairs has not only been murdered, but wiped out.'

'How?' asked the priest.

'Father,' said Flambeau, after a pause, 'upon my soul I believe it is more in your department than mine. No friend or foe has entered the house, but Smythe is gone, as if stolen by the fairies. If that is not supernatural, I – '

As he spoke they were all checked by an unusual sight; the big blue policeman came round the corner of the crescent running. He came straight up to Brown.

'You're right, sir,' he panted, 'they've just found poor Mr Smythe's body in the canal down below.'

Angus put his hand wildly to his head. 'Did he run down and drown himself?' he asked.

'He never came down, I'll swear,' said the constable, 'and he wasn't drowned either, for he died of a great stab over the heart.'

'And yet you saw no one enter?' said Flambeau in a grave voice.

'Let us walk down the road a little,' said the priest.

As they reached the other end of the crescent he observed abruptly: 'Stupid of me! I forgot to ask the policeman something. I wonder if they found a light brown sack.'

'Why a light brown sack?' asked Angus, astonished.

'Because if it was any other coloured sack, the case must begin over again,' said Father Brown; 'but if it was a light brown sack, why, the case is finished.'

'I am pleased to hear it,' said Angus with hearty irony. 'It hasn't begun, so far as I am concerned.'

'You must tell us all about it,' said Flambeau, with a strange heavy simplicity, like a child.

Unconsciously they were walking with quickening steps down the long sweep of road on the other side of the high crescent, Father Brown leading briskly, though in silence. At last he said with an almost touching vagueness: 'Well, I'm afraid you'll think it so prosy. We always begin at the abstract end of things, and you can't begin this story anywhere else.

'Have you ever noticed this – that people never answer what you say? They answer what you mean – or what they think you mean. Suppose one lady says to another in a country house, "Is anybody staying with you?" the lady doesn't answer "Yes; the butler, the three footmen, the parlour-maid, and so on," though the parlour-maid may be in the room, or the butler behind her chair. She says: "There is *nobody* staying with us," meaning nobody of the sort you mean. But suppose a doctor inquiring into an epidemic asks, "Who is staying in the house?" then the lady will remember the butler, the parlour-maid, and the rest. All language is used like that; you never get a question answered literally, even when you get it answered truly. When those four quite honest men said that no man had gone into the Mansions, they did not really mean that *no man* had gone into them. They meant no man whom they could suspect of being your man. A man did go into the house, and did come out of it, but they never noticed him.'

'An invisible man?' inquired Angus, raising his red eyebrows.

'A mentally invisible man,' said Father Brown.

A minute or two after he resumed in the same unassuming voice, like a man thinking his way. 'Of course, you can't think of such a man, until you do think of him. That's where his cleverness comes in. But I came to think of him through two or three little things in the tale Mr Angus told us. First, there was the fact that this Welkin went for long walks. And then there was the vast lot of stamp-paper on the window. And then, most of all, there were the two things the young lady said – things that couldn't be true. Don't get annoyed,' he added hastily, noting a sudden movement of the Scotsman's head; 'she thought they were true all right, but they couldn't be true. A person *can't* be quite alone in a street a second before she receives a letter. She can't be quite alone in a street when she starts reading a letter just received. There must be somebody pretty near her; he must be mentally invisible.'

'Why must there be somebody near her?' asked Angus.

'Because,' said Father Brown: 'barring carrier-pigeons, somebody must have brought her the letter.'

'Do you really mean to say,' asked Flambeau, with energy, 'that Welkin carried his rival's letters to his lady?'

'Yes,' said the priest. 'Welkin carried his rival's letters to his lady. You see, he had to.'

'Oh, I can't stand much more of this,' exploded Flambeau. 'Who is this fellow? What does he look like. What is the usual get-up of a mentally invisible man?'

'He is dressed rather handsomely in red, blue and gold,' replied the priest promptly with decision, 'and in this striking, and even showy costume he entered Himalaya Mansions under eight human eyes; he killed Smythe in cold blood, and came down into the street again carrying the dead body in his arms – '

'Reverend sir,' cried Angus, standing still, 'are you raving mad, or am I?'

'You are not mad,' said Brown, 'only a little unobservant. You have not noticed such a man as this, for example.'

He took three quick strides forward, and put his hand on the shoulder of an ordinary passing postman who had bustled by them unnoticed under the shade of the trees.

'Nobody ever notices postmen, somehow,' he said thoughtfully; 'yet they have passions like other men, and even carry large bags where a small corpse can be stowed quite easily.'

The postman, instead of turning naturally, had ducked and tumbled against the garden fence. He was a lean fair-bearded man of very ordinary appearance, but as he turned an alarmed face over his shoulder, all three men were fixed with an almost fiendish squint.

Flambeau went back to his sabres, purple rugs and Persian cat, having many things to attend to. John Turnbull Angus went back to the lady at the shop, with whom that imprudent young man contrives to be extremely comfortable. But Father Brown walked those snow-covered hills under the stars for many hours with a murderer, and what they said to each other will never be known.

5
The Wrong Shape

Certain of the great roads going north out of London continue far into the country a sort of attenuated and interrupted spectre of a street, with great gaps in the building, but preserving the line. Here will be a group of shops, followed by a fenced field or paddock, and then a famous public house, and then perhaps a market garden or a nursery garden, and then one large private house, and then another field and another inn, and so on. If anyone walks along one of these roads he will pass a house which will probably catch his eye, though he may not be able to explain its attraction. It is a long, low house, running parallel with the road, painted mostly white and pale green, with a veranda and sun-blinds, and porches capped with those quaint sort of cupolas like wooden umbrellas that one sees in some old-fashioned houses. In fact, it is an old-fashioned house, very English and very suburban in the good old wealthy Clapham sense. And yet the house has a look of having been built chiefly for the hot weather. Looking at its white paint and sun-blinds one thinks vaguely of pugarees and even of palm trees. I cannot trace the feeling to its root; perhaps the place was built by an Anglo-Indian.

Anyone passing this house, I say, would be namelessly fascinated by it; would feel that it was a place about which some story was to be told. And he would have been right, as you shall shortly hear. For this is the story – the story of the strange things that did really happen in it in the Whitsuntide of the year 18 –:

Anyone passing the house on the Thursday before Whit-Sunday at about half-past four p.m. would have seen the front door open, and Father Brown, of the small church of St Mungo, come out smoking a large pipe in company with a very tall French friend of his called Flambeau, who was smoking a very small cigarette. These persons may or may not be of interest to the reader, but the truth is that they were not the only interesting things that were displayed when the front door of the white-and-green house was opened. There are further peculiarities about this house, which must be described to start with, not only that the reader may understand this tragic tale, but also that he may realize what it was that the opening of the door revealed.

The whole house was built upon the plan of a T, but a T with a very long cross piece and a very short tail piece. The long cross piece was the frontage that ran along in face of the street, with the front door in the middle; it was two storeys high, and contained nearly all the important rooms. The short tail piece, which ran out at the back immediately opposite the front door, was one storey high, and consisted only of two long rooms, the one leading into the other. The first of these two rooms was the study in which the celebrated Mr Quinton wrote his wild Oriental poems and romances. The farther room was a glass conservatory full of tropical blossoms of quite unique and almost monstrous beauty, and on such afternoons as these was glowing with gorgeous sunlight. Thus when the hall door was open, many a passerby literally stopped to stare and gasp; for he looked down a perspective of rich apartments to something really like a transformation scene in a fairy play: purple clouds and golden suns and crimson stars that were at once scorchingly vivid and yet transparent and far away.

Leonard Quinton, the poet, had himself most carefully arranged this effect; and it is doubtful whether he so perfectly expressed his personality in any of his poems. For he was a man who drank and bathed in colours, who indulged his lust for colour somewhat to the neglect of form – even of good form. This it was that had turned his genius so wholly to eastern art and imagery; to those bewildering carpets or blinding embroideries in which all the colours seem fallen into a fortunate chaos, having nothing to typify or to teach. He had attempted, not perhaps with complete artistic success, but with acknowledged imagination and invention, to compose epics and love stories reflecting the riot of violent and even cruel colour; tales of tropical heavens of burning gold or blood-red copper; of eastern heroes who rode with twelve-turbaned mitres upon elephants painted purple or peacock green; of gigantic jewels that a hundred negroes could not carry, but which burned with ancient and strange-hued fires.

In short (to put the matter from the more common point of view), he dealt much in eastern heavens, rather worse than most western hells; in eastern monarchs, whom we might possibly call maniacs; and in eastern jewels which a Bond Street jeweller (if the hundred staggering negroes brought them into his shop) might possibly not regard as genuine. Quinton was a genius, if a morbid one; and even his morbidity appeared more in his life than in his work. In temperament he was weak and waspish, and his health had suffered heavily from oriental experiments with opium. His wife – a handsome, hard-working, and, indeed, over-worked woman – objected to the opium, but objected much more to a live Indian hermit in white and yellow robes, whom her husband had insisted on entertaining for months together, a Virgil to guide his spirit through the heavens and the hells of the east.

It was out of this artistic household that Father Brown and his friend stepped on to the door-step; and to judge from their faces, they stepped out of it with much relief. Flambeau had known Quinton in wild student days in Paris, and they had renewed the acquaintance for a week-end; but apart from Flambeau's more responsible developments of late, he did not get on well with the poet now. Choking oneself with opium and writing little erotic verses on vellum was not his notion of how a gentleman should go to the devil. As the two paused on the door-step, before taking a turn in the garden, the front garden gate was thrown open with violence, and a young man with a billycock hat on the back of his head tumbled up the steps in his eagerness. He was a dissipated-looking youth with a gorgeous red necktie all awry, as if he had slept in it, and he kept fidgeting and lashing about with one of those little jointed canes.

'I say,' he said breathlessly, 'I want to see old Quinton. I must see him. Has he gone?'

'Mr Quinton is in, I believe,' said Father Brown, cleaning his pipe, 'but I do not know if you can see him. The doctor is with him at present.'

The young man, who seemed not to be perfectly sober, stumbled into the hall; and at the same moment the doctor came out of Quinton's study, shutting the door and beginning to put on his gloves.

'See Mr Quinton?' said the doctor coolly. 'No, I'm afraid you can't. In fact, you mustn't on any account. Nobody must see him; I've just given him his sleeping draught.'

'No, but look here, old chap,' said the youth in the red tie, trying affectionately to capture the doctor by the lapels of his coat. 'Look here. I'm simply sewn up, I tell you. I –'

'It's no good, Mr Atkinson,' said the doctor, forcing him to fall back; 'when you can alter the effects of a drug I'll alter my decision,' and, settling on his hat, he stepped out into the sunlight with the other two. He was a bull-necked, good-tempered little man with a small moustache, inexpressibly ordinary, yet giving an impression of capability.

The young man in the billycock, who did not seem to be gifted with any tact in dealing with people beyond the general idea of clutching hold of their coats, stood outside the door, as dazed as if he had been thrown out bodily, and silently watched the other three walk away together through the garden.

'That was a sound, spanking lie I told just now,' remarked the medical man, laughing. 'In point of fact, poor Quinton doesn't have his sleeping draught for nearly half an hour. But I'm not going to have him bothered with that little beast, who only wants to borrow money that he wouldn't pay back if he could. He's a dirty little scamp, though he is Mrs Quinton's brother, and she's as fine a woman as ever walked.'

'Yes,' said Father Brown. 'She's a good woman.'

'So I propose to hang about the garden till the creature has cleared off,' went on the doctor, 'and then I'll go in to Quinton with the medicine. Atkinson can't get in, because I locked the door.'

'In that case, Dr Harris,' said Flambeau, 'we might as well walk round at the back by the end of the conservatory. There's no entrance to it that way but it's worth seeing, even from the outside.'

'Yes, and I might get a squint at my patient,' laughed the doctor, 'for he prefers to lie on an ottoman right at the end of the conservatory amid all those blood-red poinsettias; it would give me the creeps. But what are you doing?'

Father Brown had stopped for a moment, and picked up out of the long grass, where it had almost been wholly hidden, a queer, crooked Oriental knife, inlaid exquisitely in coloured stones and metals.

'What is this?' asked Father Brown, regarding it with some disfavour.

'Oh, Quinton's, I suppose,' said Dr Harris carelessly; 'he has all sorts of Chinese knick-knacks about the place. Or perhaps it belongs to the mild Hindoo of his whom he keeps on a string.'

'What Hindoo?' asked Father Brown, still staring at the dagger in his hand.

'Oh, some Indian conjurer,' said the doctor lightly; 'a fraud, of course.'

'You don't believe in magic?' asked Father Brown without looking up.

'Oh crikey! magic!' said the doctor.

'It's very beautiful,' said the priest in a low, dreaming voice; 'the colours are very beautiful. But it's the wrong shape.'

'What for?' asked Flambeau, staring.

'For anything. It's the wrong shape in the abstract. Don't you ever feel that about Eastern art? The colours are intoxicatingly lovely; but the shapes are mean and bad – deliberately mean and bad. I have seen wicked things in a Turkey carpet.'

'*Mon Dieu!*' cried Flambeau, laughing.

'They are letters and symbols in a language I don't know; but I know they stand for evil words,' went on the priest, his voice growing lower and lower. 'The lines go wrong on purpose – like serpents doubling to escape.'

'What the devil are you talking about?' said the doctor with a loud laugh.

Flambeau spoke quietly to him in answer. 'The Father sometimes gets this mystic's cloud on him,' he said; 'but I give you fair warning that I have never known him have it except when there was some evil quite near.'

'Oh, rats!' said the scientist.

'Why, look at it,' cried Father Brown, holding out the crooked knife at arm's length, as if it were some glittering snake. 'Don't you see it is the wrong shape? Don't you see that it has no hearty and plain purpose? It does not point like a spear. It does not sweep like a scythe. It does not *look* like a weapon. It looks like an instrument of torture.'

'Well, as you don't seem to like it,' said the jolly Harris, 'it had better be taken back to its owner. Haven't we come to the end of this confounded conservatory yet? This house is the wrong shape, if you like.'

'You don't understand,' said Father Brown, shaking his head. 'The shape of this house is quaint – it is even laughable. But there is nothing *wrong* about it.'

As they spoke they came round the curve of glass that ended the conservatory, an uninterrupted curve, for there was neither door nor window by which to enter at that end. The glass, however, was clear, and the sun still bright, though beginning to set; and they could see not only the flamboyant blossoms inside, but the frail figure of the poet in a brown velvet coat lying languidly on the sofa, having, apparently, fallen half asleep over a book. He was a pale, slight man, with loose, chestnut hair and a fringe of beard that was the paradox of his face, for the beard made him look less manly. These traits were well known to all three of them; but even had it not been so, it may be doubted whether they would have looked at Quinton just then. Their eyes were riveted on another object.

Exactly in their path, immediately outside the round end of the glass building, was standing a tall man, whose drapery fell to his feet in faultless white, and whose bare, brown skull, face, and neck gleamed in the setting sun like splendid bronze. He was looking through the glass at the sleeper, and he was more motionless than a mountain.

'Who is that?' cried Father Brown, stepping back with a hissing intake of his breath.

'Oh, it is only that Hindoo humbug,' growled Harris; 'but I don't know what the deuce he's doing here.'

'It looks like hypnotism,' said Flambeau, biting his black moustache.

'Why are you unmedical fellows always talking bosh about hypnotism?' cried the doctor. 'It looks a deal more like burglary.'

'Well, we will speak to it, at any rate,' said Flambeau, who was always for action. One long stride took him to the place where the Indian stood. Bowing from his great height, which overtopped even the Oriental's, he said with placid impudence:

'Good evening, sir. Do you want anything?'

Quite slowly, like a great ship turning into a harbour, the great yellow face turned, and looked at last over its white shoulder. They were startled to see that its yellow eyelids were quite sealed, as in sleep. 'Thank you,' said the face in excellent English. 'I want nothing.' Then, half opening the lids, so as to show a slit of opalescent eyeball, he repeated, 'I want nothing.' Then he opened his eyes wide with a startling stare, said, 'I want nothing,' and went rustling away into the rapidly darkening garden.

'The Christian is more modest,' muttered Father Brown; 'he wants something.'

'What on earth was he doing?' asked Flambeau, knitting his black brows and lowering his voice.

'I should like to talk to you later,' said Father Brown.

The sunlight was still a reality, but it was the red light of evening, and the bulk of the garden trees and bushes grew blacker and blacker against it. They turned round the end of the conservatory, and walked in silence down the other side to get round to the front door. As they went they seemed to wake something, as one startles a bird, in the deeper corner between the study and the main building; and again they saw the white-robed fakir slide out of the shadow, and slip round towards the front door. To their surprise, however, he had not been alone. They found themselves abruptly pulled up and forced to banish their bewilderment by the appearance of Mrs Quinton, with her heavy golden hair and square pale face, advancing on them out of the twilight. She looked a little stern, but was entirely courteous.

'Good evening, Dr Harris.' was all she said.

'Good evening, Mrs Quinton,' said the little doctor heartily. 'I am just going to give your husband his sleeping draught.'

'Yes,' she said in a clear voice. 'I think it is quite time.' And she smiled at them, and went sweeping into the house.

'That woman's over-driven,' said Father Brown; 'that's the kind of woman that does her duty for twenty years, and then does something dreadful.'

The little doctor looked at him for the first time with an eye of interest. 'Did you ever study medicine?' he asked.

'You have to know something of the mind as well as the body,' answered the priest; 'we have to know something of the body as well as the mind.'

'Well,' said the doctor, 'I think I'll go and give Quinton his stuff.'

They had turned the corner of the front façade, and were approaching the front doorway. As they turned into it they saw the man in the white robe for the third time. He came so straight towards the front door that it seemed quite incredible that he had not just come out of the study opposite to it. Yet they knew that the study door was locked.

Father Brown and Flambeau, however, kept this weird contradiction to themselves, and Dr Harris was not a man to waste his thoughts on the impossible. He permitted the omnipresent Asiatic to make his exit, and then stepped briskly into the hall. There he found a figure which he had already forgotten. The inane Atkinson was still hanging about, humming and poking things with his knobby cane. The doctor's face had a spasm of disgust and decision, and he whispered rapidly to his companion: 'I must lock the door again, or this rat will get in. But I shall be out again in two minutes.'

He rapidly unlocked the door and locked it again behind him, just balking a blundering charge from the young man in the billycock. The young man threw himself impatiently on a hall chair. Flambeau looked at a Persian illumination on the wall; Father Brown, who seemed in a sort of daze, dully eyed the door. In about four minutes the door was opened again. Atkinson was quicker this time. He sprang forward, held the door open for an instant, and called out: 'Oh, I say, Quinton, I want –'

From the other end of the study came the clear voice of Quinton, in something between a yawn and a yell of weary laughter.

'Oh, I know what you want. Take it, and leave me in peace. I'm writing a song about peacocks.'

Before the door closed half a sovereign came flying through the aperture; and Atkinson, stumbling forward, caught it with singular dexterity.

'So that's settled,' said the doctor, and, locking the door savagely, he led the way out into the garden.

'Poor Leonard can get a little peace now,' he added to Father Brown; 'he's locked in all by himself for an hour or two.'

'Yes,' answered the priest; 'and his voice sounded jolly enough when we left him.' Then he looked gravely round the garden, and saw the loose figure of Atkinson standing and jingling the half-sovereign in his pocket, and beyond, in the purple twilight, the figure of the Indian sitting bolt upright upon a bank of grass with his face turned towards the setting sun. Then he said abruptly: 'Where is Mrs Quinton?'

'She has gone up to her room,' said the doctor. 'That is her shadow on the blind.'

Father Brown looked up, and frowningly scrutinized a dark outline at the gas-lit window.

'Yes,' he said, 'that is her shadow,' and he walked a yard or two and threw himself upon a garden seat.

Flambeau sat down beside him; but the doctor was one of those energetic people who live naturally on their legs. He walked away, smoking, into the twilight, and the two friends were left together.

'My father,' said Flambeau in French, 'what is the matter with you?'

Father Brown was silent and motionless for half a minute then he said: 'Superstition is irreligious, but there is something in the air of this place. I think it's that Indian – at least, partly.'

He sank into silence, and watched the distant outline of the Indian, who still sat rigid as if in prayer. At first sight he seemed motionless, but as Father Brown watched him he saw that the man swayed ever so slightly with a rhythmic movement, just as the dark tree-tops swayed ever so slightly in the little wind that was creeping up the dim garden paths and shuffling the fallen leaves a little.

The landscape was growing rapidly dark, as if for a storm, but they could still see all the figures in their various places. Atkinson was leaning against a tree, with a listless face; Quinton's wife was still at her window; the doctor had gone strolling round the end of the conservatory; they could see his cigar like a will-o'-the-wisp; and the fakir still sat rigid and yet rocking, while the trees above him began to rock and almost to roar. Storm was certainly coming.

'When that Indian spoke to us,' went on Brown in a conversational undertone, 'I had a sort of vision, a vision of him and all his universe. Yet he only said the same thing three times. When first he said, "I want nothing," it meant only that he was impenetrable, that Asia does not give itself away. Then he said again, "I want nothing," and I knew that he meant that he was sufficient to himself, like a cosmos, that he needed no God, neither admitted any sins. And when he said the third time, "I want nothing," he said it with blazing eyes. And I knew that he meant literally what he said; that nothing was his desire and his home; that he was weary for nothing as for wine; that annihilation, the mere destruction of everything or anything –'

Two drops of rain fell; and for some reason Flambeau started and looked up, as if they had stung him. And the same instant the doctor down by the end of the conservatory began running towards them, calling out something as he ran.

As he came among them like a bombshell the restless Atkinson happened to be taking a turn nearer to the house front; and the doctor clutched him by the collar in a convulsive grip. 'Foul play!' he cried; 'what have you been doing to him, you dog?'

The priest had sprung erect, and had the voice of steel of a soldier in command.

'No fighting,' he cried coolly; 'we are enough to hold anyone we want to. What is the matter, doctor?'

'Things are not right with Quinton,' said the doctor, quite white. 'I could just see him through the glass, and I don't like the way he's lying. It's not as I left him, anyhow.'

'Let us go in to him,' said Father Brown shortly. 'You can leave Mr Atkinson alone. I have had him in sight since we heard Quinton's voice.'

'I will stop here and watch him,' said Flambeau hurriedly. 'You go in and see.'

The doctor and the priest flew to the study door, unlocked it, and fell into the room. In doing so they nearly fell over the large mahogany table in the centre at which the poet usually wrote; for the place was lit only by a small fire kept for the invalid. In the middle of this table lay a single sheet of paper, evidently left there on purpose. The doctor snatched it up, glanced at it, handed it to Father Brown, and crying, 'Good God, look at that!' plunged towards the glass room beyond, where the terrible tropic flowers still seemed to keep a crimson memory of the sunset.

Father Brown read the words three times before he put down the paper. The words were: 'I die by my own hand; yet I die murdered!' They were in the quite inimitable, not to say illegible, handwriting of Leonard Quinton.

Then Father Brown, still keeping the paper in his hand, strode towards the conservatory, only to meet his medical friend coming back with a face of assurance and collapse. 'He's done it,' said Harris.

They went together through the gorgeous unnatural beauty of cactus and azalea and found Leonard Quinton, poet and romancer, with his head hanging downward off his ottoman and his red curls sweeping the ground. Inside his left side was thrust the queer dagger that they had picked up in the garden, and his limp hand still rested on the hilt.

Outside, the storm had come at one stride, like the night in Coleridge, and garden and glass roof were darkening with driving rain. Father

Brown seemed to be studying the paper more than the corpse; he held it close to his eyes; and seemed trying to read it in the twilight. Then he held it up against the faint light, and, as he did so, lightning stared at them for an instant so white that the paper looked black against it.

Darkness full of thunder followed, and after the thunder Father Brown's voice said out of the dark: 'Doctor, this paper is the wrong shape.'

'What do you mean?' asked Doctor Harris, with a frowning stare.

'It isn't square,' answered Brown. 'It has a sort of edge snipped off at the corner. What does it mean?'

'How the deuce should I know?' growled the doctor. 'Shall we move this poor chap, do you think? He's quite dead.'

'No,' answered the priest; 'we must leave him as he lies and send for the police.' But he was still scrutinizing the paper.

As they went back through the study he stopped by the table and picked up a small pair of nail scissors. 'Ah,' he said with a sort of relief; 'this is what he did it with. But yet –' And he knitted his brows.

'Oh, stop fooling with that scrap of paper,' said the doctor emphatically. 'It was a fad of his. He had hundreds of them. He cut all his paper like that,' as he pointed to a stack of sermon paper still unused on another and smaller table. Father Brown went up to it and held up a sheet. It was the same irregular shape.

'Quite so,' he said. 'And here I see the corners that were snipped off.' And to the indignation of his colleague he began to count them.

'That's all right,' he said, with an apologetic smile. 'Twenty-three sheets cut and twenty-two corners cut off them. And as I see you are impatient we will rejoin the others.'

'Who is to tell his wife?' asked Dr Harris. 'Will you go and tell her now, while I send a servant for the police?'

'As you will,' said Father Brown indifferently. And he went out to the hall door.

Here also he found a drama, though of a more grotesque sort. It showed nothing less than his big friend Flambeau in an attitude to which he had long been unaccustomed, while upon the pathway at the bottom of the steps was sprawling with his boots in the air the amiable Atkinson, his billycock hat and walking-cane sent flying in opposite directions along the path. Atkinson had at length wearied of Flambeau's almost paternal custody, and had endeavoured to knock him down, which was by no means a smooth game to play with the Roi des Apaches, even after that monarch's abdication.

Flambeau was about to leap upon his enemy and secure him once more, when the priest patted him easily on the shoulder.

'Make it up with Mr Atkinson, my friend,' he said. 'Beg a mutual pardon and say "Good night." We need not detain him any longer.' Then, as Atkinson rose somewhat doubtfully and gathered his hat and stick and went towards the garden gate, Father Brown said in a more serious voice: 'Where is that Indian?'

They all three (for the doctor had joined them) turned involuntarily towards the dim grassy bank amid the tossing trees, purple with twilight, where they had last seen the brown man swaying in his strange prayers. The Indian was gone.

'Confound him,' said the doctor, stamping furiously. 'Now I know that it was that nigger that did it.'

'I thought you didn't believe in magic,' said Father Brown quietly.

'No more I did,' said the doctor, rolling his eyes. 'I only know that I loathed that yellow devil when I thought he was a sham wizard. And I shall loathe him more if I come to think he was a real one.'

'Well, his having escaped is nothing,' said Flambeau. 'For we could have proved nothing and done nothing against him. One hardly goes to the parish constable with a story of suicide imposed by witchcraft or auto-suggestion.'

Meanwhile Father Brown had made his way into the house, and now went to break the news to the wife of the dead man.

When he came out again he looked a little pale and tragic; but what passed between them in that interview was never known, even when all was known.

Flambeau, who was talking quietly with the doctor, was surprised to see his friend reappear so soon at his elbow; but Brown took no notice, and merely drew the doctor apart. 'You have sent for the police, haven't you?' he asked.

'Yes,' answered Harris. 'They ought to be here in ten minutes.'

'Will you do me a favour?' said the priest quietly. 'The truth is, I make a collection of these curious stories, which often contain, as in the case of our Hindoo friend, elements which can hardly be put into a police report. Now, I want you to write out a report of this case for my private use. Yours is a clever trade,' he said, looking at the doctor gravely and steadily in the face. 'I sometimes think that you know some details of this matter which you have not thought fit to mention. Mine is a confidential trade like yours, and I will treat anything you write for me in strict confidence. But write the whole.'

The doctor, who had been listening thoughtfully with his head a little on one side, looked the priest in the face for an instant, and said: 'All right,' and went into the study, closing the door behind him.

'Flambeau,' said Father Brown, 'there is a long seat there under the veranda, where we can smoke, out of the rain. You are my only friend in the world, and I want to talk to you. Or, perhaps, be silent with you.'

They established themselves comfortably in the veranda seat; Father Brown, against his common habit, accepted a good cigar and smoked it steadily in silence, while the rain shrieked and rattled on the roof of the veranda.

'My friend,' he said at length, 'this is a very queer case. A very queer case.'

'I should think it was,' said Flambeau, with something like a shudder.

'You call it queer, and I call it queer,' said the other, 'and yet we mean quite opposite things. The modern mind always mixes up two different ideas: mystery in the sense of what is marvellous, and mystery in the sense of what is complicated. That is half its difficulty about miracles. A miracle is startling; but it is simple. It is simple because it *is* a miracle. It is power coming directly from God (or the devil) instead of indirectly through nature or human wills. Now you mean that this business is marvellous because it is miraculous, because it is witchcraft worked by a wicked Indian. Understand, I do not say that it was not spiritual or diabolic. Heaven and hell only know by what surrounding influences strange sins come into the lives of men. But for the present my point is this: if it was pure magic, as you think, then it is marvellous; but it is not mysterious – that is, it is not complicated. The quality of a miracle is mysterious, but its manner is simple. Now, the manner of this business has been the reverse of simple.'

The storm that had slackened for a little seemed to be swelling again, and there came heavy movements as of faint thunder. Father Brown let fall the ash of his cigar and went on:

'There has been in this incident,' he said, 'a twisted, ugly, complex quality that does not belong to the straight bolts either of heaven or hell. As one knows the crooked track of a snail, I know the crooked track of a man.'

The white lightning opened its enormous eye in one wink, the sky shut up again, and the priest went on:

'Of all these crooked things, the crookedest was the shape of that piece of paper. It was crookeder than the dagger that killed him.'

'You mean the paper on which Quinton confessed his suicide,' said Flambeau.

'I mean the paper on which Quinton wrote, "I die by my own hand,"' answered Father Brown. 'The shape of that paper, my friend, was the wrong shape; the wrong shape, if ever I have seen it in this wicked world.'

'It only had a corner snipped off,' said Flambeau, 'and I understand that all Quinton's paper was cut that way.'

'It was a very odd way,' said the other, 'and a very bad way, to my taste and fancy. Look here, Flambeau, this Quinton – God receive his soul! – was perhaps a bit of a cur in some ways, but he really was an artist, with the pencil as well as the pen. His handwriting, though hard to read, was bold and beautiful. I can't prove what I say; I can't prove anything. But I tell you with the full force of conviction that he could never have cut that mean little piece off a sheet of paper. If he had wanted to cut down paper for some purpose of fitting in, or binding up, or what not, he would have made quite a different slash with the scissors. Do you remember the shape? It was a mean shape. It was a wrong shape. Like this. Don't you remember?'

And he waved his burning cigar before him in the darkness, making irregular squares so rapidly that Flambeau really seemed to see them as fiery hieroglyphics upon the darkness – hieroglyphics such as his friend had spoken of, which are undecipherable, yet can have no good meaning.

'But,' said Flambeau, as the priest put his cigar in his mouth again and leaned back, staring at the roof. 'Suppose somebody else did use the scissors. Why should somebody else, cutting pieces off his sermon paper, make Quinton commit suicide?'

Father Brown was still leaning back and staring at the room, but he took his cigar out of his mouth and said: 'Quinton never did commit suicide.'

Flambeau stared at him. 'Why, confound it all,' he cried; 'then why did he confess to suicide?'

The priest leaned forward again, settled his elbows on his knees, looked at the ground, and said in a low distinct voice: 'He never did confess to suicide.'

Flambeau laid his cigar down. 'You mean,' he said, 'that the writing was forged?'

'No,' said Father Brown; 'Quinton wrote it all right.'

'Well, there you are,' said the aggravated Flambeau; 'Quinton wrote: "I die by my own hand," with his own hand on a plain piece of paper.'

'Of the wrong shape,' said the priest calmly.

'Oh, the shape be damned!' cried Flambeau. 'What has the shape to do with it?'

'There were twenty-three snipped papers,' resumed Brown unmoved, 'and only twenty-two pieces snipped off. Therefore one of the pieces had been destroyed, probably that from the written paper. Does that suggest anything to you?'

A light dawned on Flambeau's face, and he said: 'There was something else written by Quinton, some other words. "They will tell you I die by my own hand," or "Do not believe that –"'

'Hotter, as the children say,' said his friend. 'But the piece was hardly half an inch across; there was no room for one word, let alone five. Can you think of anything hardly bigger than a comma which the man with hell in his heart had to tear away as a testimony against him?'

'I can think of nothing,' said Flambeau at last.

'What about quotation marks?' said the priest, and flung his cigar far into the darkness like a shooting star.

All words had left the other man's mouth, and Father Brown, said, like one going back to fundamentals:

'Leonard Quinton was a romancer, and was writing an Oriental romance about wizardry and hypnotism. He –'

At this moment the door opened briskly behind them and the doctor came out with his hat on. He put a long envelope into the priest's hands.

'That's the document you wanted,' he said, 'and I must be getting home. Good night.'

'Good night,' said Father Brown, as the doctor walked briskly to the gate. He had left the front door open, so that a shaft of gaslight fell upon them. In the light of this Brown opened the envelope and read the following words:

DEAR FATHER BROWN, – *Vicisti, Galilœe!* Otherwise, damn your eyes, which are very penetrating ones. Can it be possible that there is something in all that stuff of yours after all?

'I am a man who has ever since boyhood believed in Nature and in all natural functions and instincts, whether men called them moral or immoral. Long before I became a doctor, when I was a schoolboy keeping mice and spiders, I believed that to be a good animal is the best thing in the world. But just now I am shaken; I have believed in Nature; but it seems as if Nature could betray a man. Can there be anything in your bosh? I am really getting morbid.

'I loved Quinton's wife. What was there wrong in that? Nature told me to, and it's love that makes the world go round. I also thought, quite sincerely, that she would be happier with a clean animal like me than with that tormenting little lunatic. What was there wrong in that? I was only facing facts, like a man of science. She would have been happier.

'According to my own creed I was quite free to kill Quinton, which was the best thing for everybody, even himself. But as a healthy animal I had no notion of killing myself. I resolved, therefore, that I would never do it until I saw a chance that would leave me scot free. I saw that chance this morning.

'I have been three times, all told, into Quinton's study to-day. The first time I went in he would talk about nothing but the weird tale, called "The Curse of a Saint", which he was writing, which was all about how some Indian hermit made an English colonel kill himself by thinking about him. He showed me the last sheets, and even read me the last paragraph, which was something like this: "The conqueror of the Punjab, a mere yellow skeleton, but still gigantic, managed to lift himself on his elbow and gasp in his nephew's ear: 'I die by my own hand, yet I die murdered!'" It so happened, by one chance out of a hundred, that those last words were written at the top of a new sheet of paper. I left the room, and went out into the garden intoxicated with a frightful opportunity.

'We walked round the house, and two more things happened in my favour. You suspected an Indian, and you found a dagger which the Indian might most probably use. Taking the opportunity to stuff it in my pocket I went back to Quinton's study, locked the door, and gave him his sleeping draught. He was against answering Atkinson at all, but I urged him to call out and quiet the fellow, because I wanted a clear proof that Quinton was alive when I left the room for the second time. Quinton lay down in the conservatory, and I came through the study. I am a quick man with my hands, and in a minute and a half I had done what I wanted to do. I had emptied all the first part of Quinton's romance into the fireplace, where it burnt to ashes. Then I saw that the quotation marks wouldn't do, so I snipped them off, and to make it seem likelier, snipped the whole quire to match. Then I came out with the knowledge that Quinton's confession of suicide lay on the front table, while Quinton lay alive, but asleep, in the conservatory beyond.

'The last act was a desperate one; you can guess it: I pretended to have seen Quinton dead and rushed to his room. I delayed you with the paper; and, being a quick man with my hands, killed Quinton while you were looking at his confession of suicide. He was half-asleep, being drugged, and I put his own hand on the knife and drove it into his body. The knife was of so queer a shape that no one but an operator could have calculated the angle that would reach his heart. I wonder if you noticed this.

'When I had done it the extraordinary thing happened. Nature deserted me. I felt ill. I felt just as if I had done something wrong. I think my brain is breaking up; I feel some sort of desperate pleasure in thinking I have told the thing to somebody; that I shall not have to be alone with it if I marry and have children. What is the matter with me? . . . Madness . . . or can one have remorse, just as if one were in Byron's poems! I cannot write any more. – JAMES ERSKINE HARRIS.

Father Brown carefully folded up the letter and put it in his breast pocket just as there came a loud peal at the gate bell, and the wet waterproofs of several policemen gleamed in the road outside.

The Incredulity of Father Brown

To Patricia Burke

NOTES: The archaeology and history in these stories are largely assumed for the sake of the plot. Problems of a very similar sort do exist; but no real ones have been reproduced.

1

The Resurrection of Father Brown

There was a brief period during which Father Brown enjoyed, or rather did not enjoy, something like fame. He was a nine days' wonder in the newspapers; he was even a common topic of controversy in the weekly reviews; his exploits were narrated eagerly and inaccurately in any number of clubs and drawing-rooms, especially in America. Incongruous and indeed incredible as it may seem to any one who knew him, his adventures as a detective were even made the subject of short stories appearing in magazines.

Strangely enough, this wandering limelight struck him in the most obscure, or at least the most remote, of his many places of residence. He had been sent out to officiate, as something between a missionary and a parish priest, in one of those sections of the northern coast of South America, where strips of country still cling insecurely to European powers, or are continually threatening to become independent republics, under the gigantic shadow of President Monroe. The population was red and brown with pink spots; that is, it was Spanish-American, and largely Spanish-American-Indian, but there was a considerable and increasing infiltration of Americans of the northern sort – Englishmen, Germans and the rest. And the trouble seems to have begun when one of these visitors, very recently landed and very much annoyed at having lost one of his bags, approached the first building of which he came in sight – which happened to be the mission-house and chapel attached to it, in front of which ran a long veranda and a long row of stakes, up which were trained the black twisted vines, their square leaves red with autumn. Behind them, also in a row, a number of human beings sat almost as rigid as the stakes, and coloured in some fashion like the vines. For while their broad-brimmed hats were as black as their unblinking eyes, the complexions of many of them might have been made out of the dark red timber of those transatlantic forests. Many of them were smoking very long, thin black cigars; and in all that group the smoke was almost the only moving thing. The visitor would probably have described them as natives, though some of them were very proud of Spanish blood. But he was not one to draw any fine distinction between Spaniards and Red Indians, being rather disposed to dismiss people from the scene when once he had convicted them of being native to it.

He was a newspaper man from Kansas City, a lean, light-haired man with what Meredith called an adventurous nose; one could almost fancy it found its way by feeling its way and moved like the proboscis of an ant-eater. His name was Snaith, and his parents, after some obscure meditation, had called him Saul, a fact which he had the good feeling to conceal as far as possible. Indeed, he had ultimately compromised by calling himself Paul, though by no means for the same reason that had affected the Apostle of the Gentiles. On the contrary, so far as he had any views on such things, the name of the persecutor would have been more appropriate; for he regarded organized religion with the conventional contempt which can be learnt more easily from Ingersoll than from Voltaire. And this was, as it happened, the not very important side of his character which he turned towards the mission-station and the groups in front of the veranda. Something in their shameless repose and indifference inflamed his own fury of efficiency; and, as he could get no particular answer to his first questions, he began to do all the talking himself.

Standing out there in the strong sunshine, a spick-and-span figure in his Panama hat and neat clothes, his grip-sack held in a steely grip, he began to shout at the people in the shadow. He began to explain to them very loudly why they were lazy and filthy, and bestially ignorant and lower than the beasts that perish, in case this problem should have previously exercised their minds. In his opinion it was the deleterious influence of priests that had made them so miserably poor and so hopelessly oppressed that they were able to sit in the shade and smoke and do nothing.

'And a mighty soft crowd you must be at that,' he said, 'to be bullied by these stuck-up josses because they walk about in their mitres and their tiaras and their gold copes and other glad rags, looking down on everybody else like dirt – being bamboozled by crowns and canopies and sacred umbrellas like a kid at a pantomime; just because a pompous old High Priest of Mumbo-Jumbo looks as if he was the lord of the earth. What about you? What do you look like, you poor simps? I tell you, that's why you're way-back in barbarism and can't read or write and –'

At this point the High Priest of Mumbo-Jumbo came in an undignified hurry out of the door of the mission-house, not looking very like a lord of the earth, but rather like a bundle of black second-hand clothes buttoned round a short bolster in the semblance of a guy. He was not wearing his tiara, supposing him to possess one, but a shabby broad hat not very dissimilar from those of the Spanish Indians, and it was thrust to the back of his head with a gesture of botheration. He seemed just about to speak to the motionless natives when he caught sight of the stranger and said quickly:

'Oh, can I be of any assistance? Would you like to come inside?'

Mr Paul Snaith came inside; and it was the beginning of a considerable increase of that journalist's information on many things. Presumably his journalistic instinct was stronger than his prejudices, as, indeed, it often is in clever journalists; and he asked a good many questions, the answers to which interested and surprised him. He discovered that the Indians could read and write, for the simple reason that the priest had taught them; but that they did not read or write any more than they could help, from a natural preference for more direct communications. He learned that these strange people, who sat about in heaps on the veranda without stirring a hair, could work quite hard on their own patches of land; especially those of them who were more than half Spanish; and he learned with still more astonishment that they all had patches of land that were really their own. That much was part of a stubborn tradition that seemed quite native to natives. But in that also the priest had played a certain part, and by doing so had taken perhaps what was his first and last part in politics, if it was only local politics. There had recently swept through that region one of those fevers of atheist and almost anarchist Radicalism which break out periodically in countries of the Latin culture, generally beginning in a secret society and generally ending in a civil war and in very little else. The local leader of the iconoclastic party was a certain Alvarez, a rather picturesque adventurer of Portuguese nationality but, as his enemies said, of partly negro origin, the head of any number of lodges and temples of initiation of the sort that in such places clothe even atheism with something mystical. The leader on the more conservative side was a much more common-place person, a very wealthy man named Mendoza, the owner of many factories and quite respectable, but not very exciting. It was the general opinion that the cause of law and order would have been entirely lost if it had not adopted a more popular policy of its own, in the form of securing land for the peasants; and this movement had mainly originated from the little mission-station of Father Brown.

While he was talking to the journalist, Mendoza, the Conservative leader, came in. He was a stout, dark man, with a bald head like a pear and a round body also like a pear; he was smoking a very fragrant cigar, but he threw it away, perhaps a little theatrically, when he came into the presence of the priest, as if he had been entering church; and bowed with a curve that in so corpulent a gentleman seemed quite improbable. He was always exceedingly serious in his social gestures, especially towards religious institutions. He was one of those laymen who are much more ecclesiastical than ecclesiastics. It embarrassed Father Brown a good deal, especially when carried thus into private life.

'I think I am an anti-clerical,' Father Brown would say with a faint smile; 'but there wouldn't be half so much clericalism if they would only leave things to the clerics.'

'Why, Mr Mendoza,' exclaimed the journalist with a new animation, 'I think we have met before. Weren't you at the Trade Congress in Mexico last year?' The heavy eyelids of Mr Mendoza showed a flutter of recognition, and he smiled in his slow way. 'I remember.'

'Pretty big business done there in an hour or two,' said Snaith with relish. 'Made a good deal of difference to you, too, I guess.'

'I have been very fortunate,' said Mendoza modestly.

'Don't you believe it!' cried the enthusiastic Snaith. 'Good fortune comes to the people who know when to catch hold; and you caught hold good and sure. But I hope I'm not interrupting your business?'

'Not at all,' said the other. 'I often have the honour of calling on the padre for a little talk. Merely for a little talk.'

It seemed as if this familiarity between Father Brown and a successful and even famous man of business completed the reconciliation between the priest and the practical Mr Snaith. He felt, it might be supposed, a new respectability clothe the station and the mission, and was ready to overlook such occasional reminders of the existence of religion as a chapel and a presbytery can seldom wholly avoid. He became quite enthusiastic about the priest's programme – at least on its secular and social side – and announced himself ready at any moment to act in the capacity of a live wire for its communication to the world at large. And it was at this point that Father Brown began to find the journalist rather more troublesome in his sympathy than in his hostility.

Mr Paul Snaith set out vigorously to feature Father Brown. He sent long and loud eulogies on him across the continent to his newspaper in the Middle West. He took snapshots of the unfortunate cleric in the most commonplace occupations, and exhibited them in gigantic photographs in the gigantic Sunday papers of the United States. He turned his sayings into slogans, and was continually presenting the world with 'A Message' from the reverend gentleman in South America. Any stock less strong and strenuously receptive than the American race would have become very much bored with Father Brown. As it was, he received handsome and eager offers to go on a lecturing tour in the States; and when he declined, the terms were raised with expressions of respectful wonder. A series of stories about him, like the stories of Sherlock Holmes, were, by the instrumentality of Mr Snaith, planned out and put before the hero with requests for his assistance and encouragement. As the priest found they had started, he could offer no suggestion except, that they should stop. And this in turn was taken by Mr Snaith as the text for a discussion on whether Father Brown should disappear temporarily over a cliff, in the manner of Dr Watson's hero. To all these demands the priest had patiently to reply in writing, saying that he would consent on such terms to the temporary cessation of the stories and begging that a considerable interval might occur before they began again. The notes he wrote grew shorter and shorter; and as he wrote the last of them, he sighed.

Needless to say, this strange boom in the North reacted on the little outpost in the South where he had expected to live in so lonely an exile. The considerable English and American population already on the spot began to be proud of possessing so widely advertised a person. American tourists, of the sort who land with a loud demand for Westminster Abbey, landed on that distant coast with a loud demand for Father

Brown. They were within measurable distance of running excursion trains named after him, and bringing crowds to see him as if he were a public monument. He was especially troubled by the active and ambitious new traders and shopkeepers of the place, who were perpetually pestering him to try their wares and to give them testimonials. Even if the testimonials were not forthcoming, they would prolong the correspondence for the purpose of collecting autographs. As he was a good-natured person they got a good deal of what they wanted out of him; and it was in answer to a particular request from a Frankfort wine-merchant named Eckstein that he wrote hastily a few words on a card, which were to prove a terrible turning-point in his life.

Eckstein was a fussy little man with fuzzy hair and pince-nez, who was wildly anxious that the priest should not only try some of his celebrated medicinal port, but should let him know where and when he would drink it, in acknowledging its receipt. The priest was not particularly surprised at the request, for he was long past surprise at the lunacies of advertisement. So he scribbled something down and turned to other business which seemed a little more sensible. He was again interrupted, by a note from no less a person than his political enemy Alvarez, asking him to come to a conference at which it was hoped that a compromise on an outstanding question might be reached; and suggesting an appointment that evening at a café just outside the walls of the little town. To this also he sent a message of acceptance by the rather florid and military messenger who was waiting for it; and then, having an hour or two before him, sat down to attempt to get through a little of his own legitimate business. At the end of the time he poured himself out a glass of Mr Eckstein's remarkable wine and, glancing at the clock with a humorous expression, drank it and went out into the night.

Strong moonlight lay on the little Spanish town, so that when he came to the picturesque gateway, with its rather rococo arch and the fantastic fringe of palms beyond it, it looked rather like a scene in a Spanish opera. One long leaf of palm with jagged edges, black against the moon, hung down on the other side of the arch, visible through the archway, and had something of the look of the jaw of a black crocodile. The fancy would not have lingered in his imagination but for something else that caught his naturally alert eye. The air was deathly still, and there was not a stir of wind; but he distinctly saw the pendent palm-leaf move.

He looked around him and realized that he was alone. He had left behind the last houses, which were mostly closed and shuttered, and was walking between two long blank walls built of large and shapeless but flattened stones, tufted here and there with the queer prickly weeds of that region – walls which ran parallel all the way to the gateway. He could not see the lights of the café outside the gate; probably it was too far away. Nothing could be seen under the arch but a wider expanse of large-flagged pavement, pale in the moon, with the straggling prickly pear here and there. He had a strong sense of the smell of evil; he felt queer physical oppression; but he did not think of stopping. His courage, which was considerable, was perhaps even less strong a part of him than his curiosity. All his life he had been led by an intellectual hunger for the truth, even of trifles. He often controlled it in the name of proportion; but it was always there. He walked straight through the gateway, and on the other side a man sprang like a monkey out of the tree-top and struck at him with a knife. At the same moment another man came crawling swiftly along the wall and, whirling a cudgel round his head, brought it down. Father Brown turned, staggered, and sank in a heap, but as he sank there dawned on his round face an expression of mild and immense surprise.

There was living in the same little town at this time another young American, particularly different from Mr Paul Snaith. His name was John Adams Race, and he was an electrical engineer, employed by Mendoza to fit out the old town with all the new conveniences. He was a figure far less familiar in satire and international gossip than that of the American journalist. Yet, as a matter of fact, America contains a million men of the moral type of Race to one of the moral type of Snaith. He was exceptional in being exceptionally good at his job, but in every other way he was very simple. He had begun life as a druggist's assistant in a Western village, and risen by sheer work and merit; but he still regarded his home town as the natural heart of the habitable world. He had been taught a very Puritan, or purely Evangelical, sort of Christianity from the Family Bible at his mother's knee; and in so far as he had time to have any religion, that was still his religion. Amid all the dazzling lights of the latest and even wildest discoveries, when he was at the very edge and extreme of experiment, working miracles of light and sound like a god creating new stars and solar systems, he never for a moment doubted that the things 'back home' were the best things in the world; his mother and the Family Bible and the quiet and quaint morality of his village. He had as serious and noble a sense of the sacredness of his mother as if he had been a frivolous Frenchman. He was quite sure the Bible religion was really the right thing; only he vaguely missed it wherever he went in the modern world. He could hardly be expected to sympathize with the religious externals of Catholic countries; and in a dislike of mitres and croziers he sympathized with Mr Snaith, though not in so cocksure a fashion. He had no liking for the public bowings and scrapings of Mendoza and certainly no temptation to the masonic mysticism of the atheist Alvarez. Perhaps all that semi-tropical life was too coloured for him, shot with Indian red and Spanish gold. Anyhow, when he said there was nothing to touch his home town, he was not boasting. He really meant that there was somewhere something plain and unpretentious and touching which he really respected more than anything else in the world. Such being the mental attitude of John Adams Race in a South American station, there had been growing on him for some time a curious feeling, which contradicted all his prejudices and for which he could not account. For the truth was this: that the only thing he had ever met in his travels that in the least reminded him of the old wood-pile and the provincial proprieties and the Bible on his mother's knee was (for some inscrutable reason) the round face and black clumsy umbrella of Father Brown.

He found himself insensibly watching that commonplace and even comic black figure as it went bustling about; watching it with an almost morbid fascination, as if it were a walking riddle or contradiction. He had found something he could not help liking in the heart of everything he hated; it was as if he had been horribly tormented by lesser demons and then found that the Devil was quite an ordinary person.

Thus it happened that, looking out of his window on that moonlit night, he saw the Devil go by, the demon of unaccountable blamelessness, in his broad black hat and long black coat, shuffling along the street towards the gateway, and saw it with an interest which he could not himself understand. He wondered where the priest was going, and what he was really up to; and remained gazing out into the moonlit street long after the little black figure had passed. And then he saw something else that intrigued him further. Two other men whom he recognized passed across his window as across a lighted stage. A sort of blue limelight of the moon ran in a spectral halo round the big bush of hair that stood erect on the head of little Eckstein, the wine-seller, and it outlined a taller and darker figure with an eagle profile and a queer old-fashioned and very top-heavy black hat, which seemed to make the whole outline still more bizarre, like a shape in a shadow pantomime. Race rebuked himself for allowing the moon to play such tricks with his fancy; for on a second glance he recognized the black Spanish side-whiskers and high-featured face of Dr Calderon, a worthy medical man of the town, whom he had once found attending professionally on Mendoza. Still, there was something in the way the men were whispering to each other and peering up the street that struck him as peculiar. On a sudden impulse he leapt over the low window-sill and himself went bareheaded up the road, following their trail. He saw them disappear under the dark archway, and a moment after there came a dreadful cry from beyond; curiously loud and piercing, and all the more blood-curdling to Race because it said something very distinctly in some tongue that he did not know.

The next moment there was a rushing of feet, more cries, and then a confused roar of rage or grief that shook the turrets and tall palm trees of the place; there was a movement in the mob that had gathered, as if they were sweeping backwards through the gateway. And then the dark archway resounded with a new voice, this time intelligible to him and falling with the note of doom, as someone shouted through the gateway:

'Father Brown is dead!'

He never knew what prop gave way in his mind, or why something on which he had been counting suddenly failed him; but he ran towards the gateway and was just in time to meet his countryman, the journalist Snaith, coming out of the dark entrance, deadly pale and snapping his fingers nervously.

'It's quite true,' said Snaith, with something which for him approached to reverence. 'He's a goner. The doctor's been looking at him, and there's no hope. Some of these damned Dagos clubbed him as he came through the gate – God knows why. It'll be a great loss to the place.'

Race did not or perhaps could not reply, but ran on under the arch to the scene beyond. The small black figure lay where it had fallen on the wilderness of wide stones starred here and there with green thorn; and the great crowd was being kept back, chiefly by the mere gestures of one gigantic figure in the foreground. For there were many there who swayed hither and thither at the mere movement of his hand, as if he had been a magician.

Alvarez, the dictator and demagogue, was a tall, swaggering figure always rather flamboyantly clad, and on this occasion he wore a green uniform with embroideries like silver snakes crawling all over it, with an order round his neck hung on a very vivid maroon ribbon. His close curling hair was already grey, and in contrast his complexion, which his friends called olive and his foes octoroon, looked almost literally golden, as if it were a mask moulded in gold. But his large-featured face, which was powerful and humorous, was at this moment properly grave and grim. He had been waiting, he explained, for Father Brown at the café, when he had heard a rustle and a fall and, coming out, had found the corpse lying on the flagstones.

'I know what some of you are thinking,' he said, looking round proudly, 'and if you are afraid of me – as you are – I will say it for you. I am an atheist; I have no god to call on for those who will not take my word. But I tell you in the name of every root of honour that may be left to a soldier and a man, that I had no part in this. If I had the men here that did it, I would rejoice to hang them on that tree.'

'Naturally we are glad to hear you say so,' said old Mendoza stiffly and solemnly, standing by the body of his fallen coadjutor. 'This blow has been too appalling for us to say what else we feel at present. I suggest that it will be more decent and proper if we remove my friend's body and break up this irregular meeting. I understand,' he added gravely to the doctor, 'that there is unfortunately no doubt.'

'There is no doubt,' said Dr Calderon.

John Race went back to his lodgings sad and with a singular sense of emptiness. It seemed impossible that he should miss a man whom he never knew. He learned that the funeral was to take place next day; for all felt that the crisis should be past as quickly as possible, for fear of riots that were hourly growing more probable. When Snaith had seen the row of Red Indians sitting on the veranda, they might have been a row of ancient Aztec images carved in red wood. But he had not seen them as they were when they heard that the priest was dead.

Indeed they would certainly have risen in revolution and lynched the republican leader, if they had not been immediately blocked by the direct necessity of behaving respectfully to the coffin of their own religious leader. The actual assassins, whom it would have been most natural to lynch, seemed to have vanished into thin air. Nobody knew their names; and nobody would ever know whether the dying man had even seen their faces. That strange look of surprise that was apparently his last look on earth might have been the recognition of their faces. Alvarez repeated violently that it was no work of his, and attended the funeral, walking behind the coffin in his splendid silver and green uniform with a sort of bravado of reverence.

Behind the veranda a flight of stone steps scaled a very steep green bank, fenced by a cactus-hedge, and up this the coffin was laboriously lifted to the ground above, and placed temporarily at the foot of the great gaunt crucifix that dominated the road and guarded the conse-crated ground. Below in the road were great seas of people lamenting and telling their beads – an orphan population that had lost a father. Despite all these symbols that were provocative enough to him, Alvarez behaved with restraint and respect; and all would have gone well – as Race told himself – had the others only let him alone.

Race told himself bitterly that old Mendoza had always looked like an old fool and had now very conspicuously and completely behaved like an old fool. By a custom common in simpler societies, the coffin was left open and the face uncovered, bringing the pathos to the point of agony for all those simple people. This, being consonant to tradition, need have done no harm; but some officious person had added to it the custom of the French free-thinkers, of having speeches by the graveside. Mendoza proceeded to make a speech – a rather long speech, and the longer it was, the longer and lower sank John Race's spirits and sympa-thies with the religious ritual involved. A list of saintly attributes, appa-rently of the most antiquated sort, was rolled out with the dilatory dullness of an after-dinner speaker who does not know how to sit down. That was bad enough; but Mendoza had also the ineffable stupidity to start reproaching and even taunting his political opponents. In three minutes he had succeeded in making a scene, and a very extraordinary scene it was.

'We may well ask,' he said, looking around him pompously; 'we may well ask where such virtues can be found among those who have madly abandoned the creed of their fathers. It is when we have atheists among us, atheist leaders, nay sometimes even atheist rulers, that we find their infamous philosophy bearing fruit in crimes like this. If we ask who murdered this holy man, we shall assuredly find –'

Africa of the forests looked out of the eyes of Alvarez the hybrid adventurer; and Race fancied he could see suddenly that the man was after all a barbarian, who could not control himself to the end; one might guess that all his 'illuminated' transcendentalism had a touch of Voodoo. Anyhow, Mendoza could not continue, for Alvarez had sprung up and was shouting back at him and shouting him down, with infinitely superior lungs.

'Who murdered him?' he roared. 'Your God murdered him! His own God murdered him! According to you, he murders all his faithful and foolish servants – as he murdered *that* one,' and he made a violent gesture, not towards the coffin but the crucifix. Seeming to control himself a little, he went on in a tone still angry but more argumentative: 'I don't believe it, but you do. Isn't it better to have no God than one that robs you in this fashion? I, at least, am not afraid to say that there is none. There is no power in all this blind and brainless universe that can hear your prayer or return your friend. Though you beg Heaven to raise him, he will not rise. Though I dare Heaven to raise him, he will not rise. Here and now I will put it to the test – I defy the God who is not there to waken the man who sleeps for ever.'

There was a shock of silence, and the demagogue had made his sensation.

'We might have known,' cried Mendoza in a thick gobbling voice, 'when we allowed such men as you –'

A new voice cut into his speech; a high and shrill voice with a Yankee accent.

'Stop! Stop!' cried Snaith the journalist; 'something's up! I swear I saw him move.'

He went racing up the steps and rushed to the coffin, while the mob below swayed with indescribable frenzies. The next moment he had turned a face of amazement over his shoulder and made a signal with his finger to Dr Calderon, who hastened forward to confer with him.

When the two men stepped away again from the coffin, all could see that the position of the head had altered. A roar of excitement rose from the crowd and seemed to stop suddenly, as if cut off in mid-air; for the priest in the coffin gave a groan and raised himself on one elbow, looking with bleared and blinking eyes at the crowd.

John Adams Race, who had hitherto known only miracles of science, never found himself able in after years to describe the topsy-turvydom of the next few days. He seemed to have burst out of the world of time and space, and to be living in the impossible. In half an hour the whole of that town and district had been transformed into something never known for a thousand years; a mediæval people turned to a mob of monks by a staggering miracle; a Greek city where the god had descended among men. Thousands prostrated themselves in the road; hundreds took vows on the spot; and even the outsiders, like the two Americans, were able to think and speak of nothing but the prodigy. Alvarez himself was shaken, as well he might be; and sat down, with his head upon his hands.

And in the midst of all this tornado of beatitude was a little man struggling to be heard. His voice was small and faint, and the noise was deafening. He made weak little gestures that seemed more those of irritation than anything else. He came to the edge of the parapet above the crowd, waving it to be quiet, with movements rather like the flap of the short wings of a penguin. There was something a little more like a lull in the noise; and then Father Brown for the first time reached the utmost stretch of the indignation that he could launch against his children.

'Oh, you *silly* people,' he said in a high and quavering voice; 'Oh, you silly, *silly* people.'

Then he suddenly seemed to pull himself together, made a bolt for the steps with his more normal gait, and began hurriedly to descend.

'Where are you going, Father?' said Mendoza, with more than his usual veneration.

'To the telegraph office,' said Father Brown hastily. 'What? No; of course it's not a miracle. Why should there be a miracle? Miracles are not so cheap as all that.'

And he came tumbling down the steps, the people flinging themselves before him to implore his blessing.

'Bless you, bless you,' said Father Brown hastily. 'God bless you all and give you more sense.'

And he scuttled away with extraordinary rapidity to the telegraph office, where he wired to his Bishop's secretary: 'There is some mad story about a miracle here; hope his lordship not give authority. Nothing in it.'

As he turned away from his effort, he tottered a little with the reaction, and John Race caught him by the arm.

'Let me see you home,' he said; 'you deserve more than these people are giving you.'

John Race and the priest were seated in the presbytery; the table was still piled up with the papers with which the latter had been wrestling the day before; the bottle of wine and the emptied wine-glass still stood where he had left them.

'And now,' said Father Brown almost grimly, 'I can begin to think.'

'I shouldn't think too hard just yet,' said the American. 'You must be wanting a rest. Besides, what are you going to think about?'

'I have pretty often had the task of investigating murders, as it happens,' said Father Brown. 'Now I have got to investigate my own murder.'

'If I were you,' said Race, 'I should take a little wine first.'

Father Brown stood up and filled himself another glass, lifted it, looked thoughtfully into vacancy and put it down again. Then he sat down once more and said:

'Do you know what I felt like when I died? You may not believe it, but my feeling was one of overwhelming astonishment.'

'Well,' answered Race, 'I suppose you were astonished at being knocked on the head.'

Father Brown leaned over to him and said in a low voice:

'I was astonished at not being knocked on the head.'

Race looked at him for a moment as if he thought the knock on the head had been only too effective; but he only said: 'What do you mean?'

'I mean that when that man brought his bludgeon down with a great swipe, it stopped at my head and did not even touch it. In the same way, the other fellow made as if to strike me with a knife, but he never gave me a scratch. It was just like play-acting. I think it was. But then followed the extraordinary thing.'

He looked thoughtfully at the papers on the table for a moment and then went on:

'Though I had not even been touched with knife or stick, I began to feel my legs doubling up under me and my very life failing. I knew I was being struck down by something, but it was not by those weapons. Do you know what I think it was?'

And he pointed to the wine on the table.

Race picked up the wine-glass and looked at it and smelt it.

'I think you are right,' he said. 'I began as a druggist and studied chemistry. I couldn't say for certain without an analysis, but I think there's something very unusual in this stuff. There are drugs by which the Asiatics produce a temporary sleep that looks like death.'

'Quite so,' said the priest calmly. 'The whole of this miracle was faked, for some reason or other. That funeral scene was staged – and timed. I think it is part of that raving madness of publicity that has got hold of Snaith; but I can hardly believe he would go quite so far, merely for that. After all, it's one thing to make copy out of me and run me as a sort of sham Sherlock Holmes, and –'

Even as the priest spoke his face altered. His blinking eyelids shut suddenly and he stood up as if he were choking. Then he put one wavering hand as if groping his way towards the door.

'Where are you going?' asked the other in some wonder.

'If you ask me,' said Father Brown, who was quite white, 'I was going to pray. Or rather, to praise.'

'I'm not sure I understand. What is the matter with you?'

'I was going to praise God for having so strangely and so incredibly saved me – saved me by an inch.'

'Of course,' said Race, 'I am not of your religion; but believe me, I have religion enough to understand that. Of course, you would thank God for saving you from death.'

'No,' said the priest. 'Not from death. From disgrace.'

The other sat staring; and the priest's next words broke out of him with a sort of cry.

'And if it had only been my disgrace! But it was the disgrace of all I stand for; the disgrace of the Faith that they went about to encompass.

What it might have been! The most huge and horrible scandal ever launched against us since the last lie was choked in the throat of Titus Oates.'

'What on earth are you talking about?' demanded his companion.

'Well, I had better tell you at once,' said the priest; and sitting down, he went on more composedly: 'It came to me in a flash when I happened to mention Snaith and Sherlock Holmes. Now I happen to remember what I wrote about his absurd scheme; it was the natural thing to write, and yet I think they had ingeniously manœuvred me into writing just those words. They were something like "I am ready to die and come to life again like Sherlock Holmes, if that is the best way." And the moment I thought of that, I realized that I had been made to write all sorts of things of that kind, all pointing to the same idea. I wrote, as if to an accomplice, saying that I would drink the drugged wine at a particular time. Now, don't you see?'

Race sprang to his feet still staring: 'Yes,' he said, 'I think I begin to see.'

'*They* would have boomed the miracle. Then *they* would have bust up the miracle. And what is the worst, they would have proved that *I* was in the conspiracy. It would have been *our* sham miracle. That's all there is to it; and about as near hell as you and I will ever be, I hope.'

Then he said, after a pause, in quite a mild voice:

'They certainly would have got quite a lot of good copy out of me.'

Race looked at the table and said darkly: 'How many of these brutes were in it?'

Father Brown shook his head. 'More than I like to think of,' he said; 'but I hope some of them were only tools. Alvarez might think that all's fair in war, perhaps; he has a queer mind. I'm very much afraid that Mendoza is an old hypocrite; I never trusted him, and he hated my action in an industrial matter. But all that will wait; I have only got to thank God for the escape. And especially that I wired at once to the Bishop.'

John Race appeared to be very thoughtful.

'You've told me a lot I didn't know,' he said at last, 'and I feel inclined to tell you the only thing you don't know. I can imagine how those fellows calculated well enough. They thought any man alive, waking up in a coffin to find himself canonized like a saint, and made into a walking miracle for everyone to admire, would be swept along with his worshippers and accept the crown of glory that fell on him out the sky. And I reckon their calculation was pretty practical psychology, as men go. I've seen all sorts of men in all sorts of places; and I tell you frankly I don't believe there's one man in a thousand who could wake up like that with all his wits about him; and while he was still almost talking in his sleep, would have the sanity and the simplicity and the humility to –' He was much surprised to find himself moved, and his level voice wavering.

Father Brown was gazing abstractedly, and in a rather cock-eyed fashion, at the bottle on the table. 'Look here,' he said, 'what about a bottle of real wine?'

2

The Arrow of Heaven

It is to be feared that about a hundred detective stories have begun with the discovery that an American millionaire has been murdered; an event which is, for some reason, treated as a sort of calamity. This story, I am happy to say, has to begin with a murdered millionaire; in one sense, indeed, it has to begin with three murdered millionaires, which some may regard as an *embarras de richesse*. But it was chiefly this coincidence or continuity of criminal policy that took the whole affair out of the ordinary run of criminal cases and made it the extraordinary problem that it was.

It was very generally said that they had all fallen victims to some vendetta or curse attaching to the possession of a relic of great value both intrinsically and historically: a sort of chalice inlaid with precious stones and commonly called the Coptic Cup. Its origin was obscure, but its use was conjectured to be religious; and some attributed the fate that followed its possessors to the fanaticism of some Oriental Christian horrified at its passing through such materialistic hands. But the mysterious slayer, whether or no he was such a fanatic, was already a figure of lurid and sensational interest in the world of journalism and gossip. The nameless being was provided with a name, or a nickname. But it is only with the story of the third victim that we are now concerned; for it was only in this case that a certain Father Brown, who is the subject of these sketches, had an opportunity of making his presence felt.

When Father Brown first stepped off an Atlantic liner on to American soil, he discovered, as many another Englishman has done, that he was a much more important person than he had ever supposed. His short figure, his short-sighted and undistinguished countenance, his rather rusty-black clerical clothes, could pass through any crowd in his own country without being noticed as anything unusual, except perhaps unusually insignificant. But America has a genius for the encouragement of fame; and his appearance in one or two curious criminal problems, together with his long association with Flambeau, the ex-criminal and detective, had consolidated a reputation in America out of what was little more than a rumour in England. His round face was blank with surprise when he found himself held up on the quay by a group of journalists, as by a gang of brigands, who asked him questions about all the subjects on which he was least likely to regard himself as an authority, such as the details of female dress and the criminal statistics of the country that he had only that moment clapped his eyes on. Perhaps it was the contrast with the black embattled solidarity of this group that made more vivid another figure that stood apart from it, equally black against the burning white daylight of that brilliant place and season, but entirely solitary; a tall, rather yellow-faced man in great goggles, who arrested him with a gesture when the journalists had finished and said: 'Excuse me, but maybe you are looking for Captain Wain.'

Some apology may be made for Father Brown; for he himself would have been sincerely apologetic. It must be remembered that he had never seen America before, and more especially that he had never seen that sort of tortoise-shell spectacles before; for the fashion at this time had not spread to England. His first sensation was that of gazing at some goggling sea-monster with a faint suggestion of a diver's helmet. Otherwise the man was exquisitely dressed; and to Brown, in his innocence, the spectacles seemed the queerest disfigurement for a dandy. It was as if a dandy had adorned himself with a wooden leg as an extra touch of elegance. The question also embarrassed him. An American aviator of the name of Wain, a friend of some friends of his own in France, was indeed one of a long list of people he had some hope of seeing during his American visit; but he had never expected to hear of him so soon.

'I beg your pardon,' he said doubtfully, 'are you Captain Wain? Do you – do you know him?'

'Well, I'm pretty confident I'm not Captain Wain,' said the man in goggles, with a face of wood. 'I was pretty clear about that when I saw him waiting for you over there in the car. But the other question's a bit more problematical. I reckon I know Wain and his uncle, and old man Merton, too. I know old man Merton, but old man Merton don't know me. And he thinks he has the advantage, and I think I have the advantage. See?'

Father Brown did not quite see. He blinked at the glittering seascape and the pinnacles of the city, and then at the man in goggles. It was not only the masking of the man's eyes that produced the impression of something impenetrable. Something in his yellow face was almost Asiatic, even Chinese; and his conversation seemed to consist of stratified layers of irony. He was a type to be found here and there in that hearty and sociable population; he was the inscrutable American.

'My name's Drage,' he said, 'Norman Drage, and I'm an American citizen, which explains everything. At least I imagine your friend Wain would like to explain the rest; so we'll postpone The Fourth of July till another date.'

Father Brown was dragged in a somewhat dazed condition towards a car at some little distance, in which a young man with tufts of untidy yellow hair and a rather harassed and haggard expression, hailed him from afar and presented himself as Peter Wain. Before he knew where he was he was stowed in the car and travelling with considerable speed through and beyond the city. He was unused to the impetuous practicality of such American action, and felt about as bewildered as if a chariot drawn by dragons had carried him away into fairyland. It was under these disconcerting conditions that he heard for the first time, in long monologues from Wain, and short sentences from Drage, the story of the Coptic Cup and the two crimes already connected with it.

It seemed that Wain had an uncle named Crake who had a partner named Merton, who was number three in the series of rich business men to whom the cup had belonged. The first of them, Titus P. Trant, the Copper King, had received threatening letters from somebody signing himself Daniel Doom. The name was presumably a pseudonym, but it had come to stand for a very public if not a very popular character; for somebody as well known as Robin Hood and Jack the Ripper combined. For it soon became clear that the writer of the threatening letter did not confine himself to threatening. Anyhow, the upshot was that old Trant was found one morning with his head in his own lilypond, and there was not the shadow of a clue. The cup was, fortunately, safe in the bank; and it passed with the rest of Trant's property to his cousin, Brian Horder, who was also a man of great wealth and who was also threatened by the nameless enemy. Brian Horder was picked up dead at the foot of a cliff outside his seaside residence, at which there was a burglary, this time on a large scale. For though the cup apparently again escaped, enough bonds and securities were stolen to leave Horder's financial affairs in confusion.

'Brian Horder's widow,' explained Wain, 'had to sell most of his valuables, I believe, and Brandon Merton must have purchased the cup at that time, for he had it when I first knew him. But you can guess for yourself that it's not a very comfortable thing to have.'

'Has Mr Merton ever had any of the threatening letters?' asked Father Brown, after a pause.

'I imagine he has,' said Mr Drage; and something in his voice made the priest look at him curiously, until he realized that the man in goggles was laughing silently, in a fashion that gave the new-comer something of a chill.

'I'm pretty sure he has,' said Peter Wain, frowning. 'I've not seen the letters, only his secretary sees any of his letters, for he is pretty reticent about business matters, as big business men have to be. But I've seen him real upset and annoyed with letters; and letters that he tore up, too, before even his secretary saw him. The secretary himself is getting nervous and says he is sure somebody is laying for the old man; and the long and the short of it is, that we'd be very grateful for a little advice in the matter. Everybody knows your great reputation, Father Brown, and the secretary asked me to see if you'd mind coming straight out to the Merton house at once.'

'Oh, I see,' said Father Brown, on whom the meaning of this apparent kidnapping began to dawn at last. 'But, really, I don't see that I can do any more than you can. You're on the spot, and must have a hundred times more data for a scientific conclusion than a chance visitor.'

'Yes,' said Mr Drage dryly; 'our conclusions are much too scientific to be true. I reckon if anything hit a man like Titus P. Trant, it just came out of the sky without waiting for any scientific explanation. What they call a bolt from the blue.'

'You can't possibly mean,' cried Wain, 'that it was supernatural!'

But it was by no means easy at any time to discover what Mr Drage could possibly mean; except that if he said somebody was a real smart man, he very probably meant he was a fool. Mr Drage maintained an oriental immobility until the car stopped, a little while after, at what was obviously their destination. It was rather a singular place. They had been driving through a thinly-wooded country that opened into a wide plain, and just in front of them was a building consisting of a single wall or very high fence, round, like a Roman camp and having rather the appearance of an aerodrome. The barrier did not look like wood or stone, and closer inspection proved it to be of metal.

They all alighted from the car, and one small door in the wall was slid open with considerable caution, after manipulations resembling the opening of a safe. But, much to Father Brown's surprise, the man called Norman Drage showed no disposition to enter, but took leave of them with sinister gaiety.

'I won't come in,' he said. 'It 'ud be too much pleasurable excitement for old man Merton, I reckon. He loves the sight of me so much that he'd die of joy.'

And he strode away, while Father Brown, with increasing wonder, was admitted through the steel door which instantly clicked behind him. Inside was a large and elaborate garden of gay and varied colours, but entirely without any trees or tall shrubs or flowers. In the centre of it rose a house of handsome and even striking architecture, but so high and narrow as rather to resemble a tower. The burning sunlight gleamed on glass roofing here and there at the top, but there seemed to be no windows at all in the lower part of it. Over everything was that spotless and sparkling cleanliness that seemed so native to the clear American air. When they came inside the portal, they stood amid resplendent marble and metals and enamels of brilliant colours, but there was no staircase. Nothing but a single shaft for a lift went up the centre between the solid walls, and the approach to it was guarded by heavy, powerful men like plain-clothes policemen.

'Pretty elaborate protection, I know,' said Wain. 'Maybe it makes you smile a little, Father Brown, to find Merton has to live in a fortress like this without even a tree in the garden for anyone to hide behind. But you don't know what sort of proposition we're up against in this country. And perhaps you don't know just what the name of Brander Merton means. He's a quiet-looking man enough, and anybody might pass him in the street; not that they get much chance nowadays, for he can only go out now and then in a closed car. But if anything happened to Brander Merton there'd be earthquakes from Alaska to the Cannibal Islands. I fancy there was never a king or emperor who had such power over the nations as he has. After all, I suppose if you'd been asked to visit the czar, or the king of England, you'd have had the curiosity to go. You mayn't care much for czars or millionaires; but it just means that power like that is always interesting. And I hope it's not against your principles to visit a modern sort of emperor like Merton.'

'Not at all,' said Father Brown, quietly. 'It is my duty to visit prisoners and all miserable men in captivity.'

There was a silence, and the young man frowned with a strange and almost shifty look on his lean face. Then he said, abruptly:

'Well, you've got to remember it isn't only common crooks or the Black Hand that's against him. This Daniel Doom is pretty much like the devil. Look how he dropped Trant in his own gardens and Horder outside his house, and got away with it.'

The top floor of the mansion, inside the enormously thick walls, consisted of two rooms; an outer room which they entered, and an inner room that was the great millionaire's sanctum. They entered the outer room just as two other visitors were coming out of the inner one. One was hailed by Peter Wain as his uncle – a small but very stalwart and active man with a shaven head that looked bald, and a brown face that looked almost too brown to have ever been white. This was old Crake, commonly called Hickory Crake in reminiscence of the more famous Old Hickory, because of his fame in the last Red Indian wars. His companion was a singular contrast – a very dapper gentleman with dark hair like a black varnish and a broad, black ribbon to his monocle: Barnard Blake, who was old Merton's lawyer and had been discussing with the partners the business of the firm. The four men met in the middle of the outer room and paused for a little polite conversation, in the act of respectively going and coming. And through all goings and comings another figure sat at the back of the room near the inner door, massive and motionless in the half-light from the inner window; a man with a negro face and enormous shoulders. This was what the humorous self-criticism of America playfully calls the Bad Man; whom his friends might call a bodyguard and his enemies a bravo.

This man never moved or stirred to greet anybody; but the sight of him in the outer room seemed to move Peter Wain to his first nervous query.

'Is anybody with the chief?' he asked.

'Don't get rattled, Peter,' chuckled his uncle. 'Wilton the secretary is with him, and I hope that's enough for anybody. I don't believe Wilton ever sleeps for watching Merton. He is better than twenty bodyguards. And he's quick and quiet as an Indian.'

'Well, you ought to know,' said his nephew, laughing. 'I remember the Red Indian tricks you used to teach me when I was a boy and liked to read Red Indian stories. But in my Red Indian stories Red Indians seemed always to have the worst of it.'

'They didn't in real life,' said the old frontiersman grimly.

'Indeed?' inquired the bland Mr Blake. 'I should have thought they could do very little against our firearms.'

'I've seen an Indian stand under a hundred guns with nothing but a little scalping-knife and kill a white man standing on the top of a fort,' said Crake.

'Why, what did he do with it?' asked the other.

'Threw it,' replied Crake, 'threw it in a flash before a shot could be fired. I don't know where he learnt the trick.'

'Well, I hope you didn't learn it,' said his nephew, laughing.

'It seems to me,' said Father Brown, thoughtfully, 'that the story might have a moral.'

While they were speaking Mr Wilton, the secretary, had come out of the inner room and stood waiting; a pale, fair-haired man with a square chin and steady eyes with a look like a dog's; it was not difficult to believe that he had the single-eye of a watchdog.

He only said, 'Mr Merton can see you in about ten minutes,' but it served for a signal to break up the gossiping group. Old Crake said he must be off, and his nephew went out with him and his legal companion, leaving Father Brown for the moment alone with his secretary; for the negroid giant at the other end of the room could hardly be felt as if he were human or alive; he sat so motionless with his broad back to them, staring towards the inner room.

'Arrangements rather elaborate here, I'm afraid,' said the secretary. 'You've probably heard all about this Daniel Doom, and why it isn't safe to leave the boss very much alone.'

'But he is alone just now, isn't he?' said Father Brown.

The secretary looked at him with grave, grey eyes.

'For fifteen minutes,' he said. 'For fifteen minutes out of the twenty-four hours. That is all the real solitude he has; and that he insists on, for a pretty remarkable reason.'

'And what is the reason?' inquired the visitor.

Wilton, the secretary, continued his steady gaze, but his mouth, that had been merely grave, became grim.

'The Coptic Cup,' he said. 'Perhaps you've forgotten the Coptic Cup; but he hasn't forgotten that or anything else. He doesn't trust any of us about the Coptic Cup. It's locked up somewhere and somehow in that room so that only he can find it; and he won't take it out till we're all out of the way. So we have to risk that quarter of an hour while he sits and worships it; I reckon it's the only worshipping he does. Not that there's any risk really; for I've turned all this place into a trap I don't believe the devil himself could get into – or at any rate, get out of. If this infernal Daniel Doom pays us a visit, he'll stay to dinner and a good bit later, by God! I'd sit here on hot bricks for the fifteen minutes, and the instant I heard a shot or a sound of struggle I'd press this button and an electrocuting current would run in a ring round that garden wall, so that it 'ud be death to cross or climb it. Of course, there couldn't be a shot, for this is the only way in; and the only window he sits at is away up on the top of a tower as smooth as a greasy pole. But, anyhow, we're all armed here, of course; and if Doom did get into that room he'd be dead before he got out.'

Father Brown was blinking at the carpet in a brown study. Then he said suddenly, with something like a jerk:

'I hope you won't mind my mentioning it, but a kind of a notion came into my head just this minute. It's about you.'

'Indeed,' remarked Wilton, 'and what about me?'

'I think you are a man of one idea,' said Father Brown, 'and you will forgive me for saying that it seems to be even more the idea of catching Daniel Doom than of defending Brander Merton.'

Wilton started a little and continued to stare at his companion; then very slowly his grim mouth took on a rather curious smile.

'How did you – what makes you think that?' he asked.

'You said that if you heard a shot you could instantly electrocute the

117

escaping enemy,' remarked the priest. 'I suppose it occurred to you that the shot might be fatal to your employer before the shock was fatal to his foe. I don't mean that you wouldn't protect Mr Merton if you could, but it seems to come rather second in your thoughts. The arrangements are very elaborate, as you say, and you seem to have elaborated them. But they seem even more designed to catch a murderer than to save a man.'

'Father Brown,' said the secretary, who had recovered his quiet tone, 'you're very smart, but there's something more to you than smartness. Somehow you're the sort of man to whom one wants to tell the truth; and besides, you'll probably hear it, anyhow, for in one way it's a joke against me already. They all say I'm a monomaniac about running down this big crook, and perhaps I am. But I'll tell you one thing that none of them know. My full name is John Wilton Horder.' Father Brown nodded as if he were completely enlightened, but the other went on.

'This fellow who calls himself Doom killed my father and uncle and ruined my mother. When Merton wanted a secretary I took the job, because I thought that where the cup was the criminal might sooner or later be. But I didn't know who the criminal was and could only wait for him; and I meant to serve Merton faithfully.'

'I understand,' said Father Brown gently; 'and, by the way, isn't it time that we attended on him?'

'Why, yes,' answered Wilton, again starting a little out of his brooding so that the priest concluded that his vindictive mania had again absorbed him for a moment. 'Go in now by all means.'

Father Brown walked straight into the inner room. No sound of greetings followed, but only a dead silence; and a moment after the priest reappeared in the doorway.

At the same moment the silent bodyguard sitting near the door moved suddenly; and it was as if a huge piece of furniture had come to life. It seemed as though something in the very attitude of the priest had been a signal; for his head was against the light from the inner window and his face was in shadow.

'I suppose you will press that button,' he said with a sort of sigh.

Wilton seemed to awake from his savage brooding with a bound and leapt up with a catch in his voice.

'There was no shot,' he cried.

'Well,' said Father Brown, 'it depends what you mean by a shot.'

Wilton rushed forward, and they plunged into the inner room together. It was a comparatively small room and simply though elegantly furnished. Opposite to them one wide window stood open, over-looking the garden and the wooded plain. Close up against the window stood a chair and a small table, as if the captive desired as much air and light as was allowed him during his brief luxury of loneliness.

On the little table under the window stood the Coptic Cup; its owner had evidently been looking at it in the best light. It was well worth looking at, for that white and brilliant daylight turned its precious stones to many-coloured flames so that it might have been a model of the Holy Grail. It was well worth looking at; but Brander Merton was not looking at it. For his head had fallen back over his chair, his mane of white hair hanging towards the floor, and his spike of grizzled beard thrust up towards the ceiling, and out of his throat stood a long, brown-painted arrow with red feathers at the other end.

'A silent shot,' said Father Brown, in a low voice; 'I was just wondering about those new inventions for silencing firearms. But this is a very old invention, and quite as silent.'

Then, after a moment, he added: 'I'm afraid he is dead. What are you going to do?'

The pale secretary roused himself with abrupt resolution. 'I'm going to press that button, of course,' he said, 'and if that doesn't do for Daniel Doom, I'm going to hunt him through the world till I find him.'

'Take care it doesn't do for any of our friends,' observed Father Brown; 'they can hardly be far off; we'd better call them.'

'That lot know all about the wall,' answered Wilton. 'None of them will try to climb it, unless one of them . . . is in a great hurry.'

Father Brown went to the window by which the arrow had evidently entered and looked out. The garden, with its flat flower-beds, lay far below like a delicately coloured map of the world. The whole vista seemed so vast and empty, the tower seemed set so far up in the sky that as he stared out a strange phrase came back to his memory.

'A bolt from the blue,' he said. 'What was that somebody said about a bolt from the blue and death coming out of the sky? Look how far away everything looks; it seems extraordinary that an arrow could come so far, unless it were an arrow from heaven.'

Wilton had returned, but did not reply, and the priest went on as in soliloquy.

'One thinks of aviation. We must ask young Wain . . . about aviation.'

'There's a lot of it round here,' said the secretary.

'Case of very old or very new weapons,' observed Father Brown. 'Some would be quite familiar to his old uncle, I suppose; we must ask him about arrows. This looks rather like a Red Indian arrow. I don't know where the Red Indian shot it from; but you remember the story the old man told. I said it had a moral.'

'If it had a moral,' said Wilton warmly, 'it was only that a real Red Indian might shoot a thing farther than you'd fancy. It's nonsense your suggesting a parallel.'

'I don't think you've got the moral quite right,' said Father Brown.

Although the little priest appeared to melt into the millions of New York next day, without any apparent attempt to be anything but a number in a numbered street, he was, in fact, unobtrusively busy for the next fortnight with the commission that had been given him, for he was filled with profound fear about a possible miscarriage of justice. Without having any particular air of singling them out from his other new acquaintances, he found it easy to fall into talk with the two or three men recently involved in the mystery; and with old Hickory Crake especially he had a curious and interesting conversation. It took place on a seat in Central Park, where the veteran sat with his bony hands and hatchet face resting on the oddly-shaped head of a walking-stick of dark red wood, possibly modelled on a tomahawk.

'Well, it may be a long shot,' he said, wagging his head, 'but I wouldn't advise you to be too positive about how far an Indian arrow could go. I've known some bow-shots that seemed to go straighter than any bullets, and hit the mark to amazement, considering how long they had been travelling. Of course, you practically never hear now of a Red Indian with a bow and arrows, still less of a Red Indian hanging about here. But if by any chance there were one of the old Indian marksmen, with one of the old Indian bows, hiding in those trees hundreds of yards beyond the Merton outer wall – why, then I wouldn't put it past the noble savage to be able to send an arrow over the wall and into the top window of Merton's house; no, nor into Merton, either. I've seen things quite as wonderful as that done in the old days.'

'No doubt,' said the priest, 'you have done things quite as wonderful, as well as seen them.'

Old Crake chuckled, and then said gruffly: 'Oh, that's all ancient history.'

'Some people have a way of studying ancient history,' the priest said. 'I suppose we may take it there is nothing in your old record to make people talk unpleasantly about this affair.'

'What do you mean?' demanded Crake, his eyes shifting sharply for the first time, in his red, wooden face, that was rather like the head of a tomahawk.

'Well, since you were so well acquainted with all the arts and crafts of the Redskin –' began Father Brown slowly.

Crake had had a hunched and almost shrunken appearance as he sat with his chin propped on its queer-shaped crutch. But the next instant he stood erect in the path like a fighting bravo with the crutch clutched like a cudgel.

'What?' he cried – in something like a raucous screech – 'what the hell! Are you standing up to me to tell me I might happen to have murdered my own brother-in-law?'

From a dozen seats dotted about the path people looked towards the disputants, as they stood facing each other in the middle of the path, the bald-headed energetic little man brandishing his outlandish stick like a club, and the black, dumpy figure of the little cleric looking at him without moving a muscle, save for his blinking eyelids. For a moment it looked as if the black, dumpy figure would be knocked on the head, and laid out with true Red Indian promptitude and dispatch; and the large form of an Irish policeman could be seen heaving up in the distance and bearing down on the group. But the priest only said, quite placidly, like one answering an ordinary query:

'I have formed certain conclusions about it, but I do not think I will mention them till I make my report.'

Whether under the influence of the footsteps of the policeman or of the eyes of the priest, old Hickory tucked his stick under his arm and put his hat on again, grunting. The priest bade him a placid good morning, and passed in an unhurried fashion out of the park, making his way to the lounge of the hotel where he knew that young Wain was to be found. The young man sprang up with a greeting; he looked even more haggard and harassed than before, as if some worry were eating him away; and the priest had a suspicion that his young friend had recently been engaged, with only too conspicuous success, in evading the last Amendment to the American Constitution. But at the first word about his hobby or favourite science he was vigilant and concentrated enough. For Father Brown had asked, in an idle and conversational fashion, whether much flying was done in that district, and had told how he had at first mistaken Mr Merton's circular wall for an aerodrome.

'It's a wonder you didn't see any while we were there,' answered Captain Wain. 'Sometimes they're as thick as flies; that open plain is a great place for them, and I shouldn't wonder if it were the chief breeding-ground, so to speak, for my sort of birds in the future. I've flown a good deal there myself, of course, and I know most of the fellows about here who flew in the war; but there are a whole lot of people taking to it out there now whom I never heard of in my life. I suppose it will be like motoring soon, and every man in the States will have one.'

'Being endowed by his Creator,' said Father Brown with a smile, 'with the right to life, liberty and the pursuit of motoring – not to mention aviation. So I suppose we may take it that one strange aeroplane passing over that house, at certain times, wouldn't be noticed much.'

'No,' replied the young man; 'I don't suppose it would.'

'Or even if the man were known,' went on the other, 'I suppose he might get hold of a machine that wouldn't be recognized as his. If you, for instance, flew in the ordinary way, Mr Merton and his friends might recognize the rig-out, perhaps; but you might pass pretty near that window on a different pattern of plane, or whatever you call it; near enough for practical purposes.'

'Well, yes,' began the young man, almost automatically, and then ceased, and remained staring at the cleric with an open mouth and eyes standing out of his head.

'My God!' he said, in a low voice; 'my God!'

Then he rose from the lounge seat, pale and shaking from head to foot and still staring at the priest.

'Are you mad?' he said; 'are you raving mad?'

There was a silence and then he spoke again in a swift hissing fashion. 'You positively come here to suggest –'

'No; only to collect suggestions,' said Father Brown, rising. 'I may have formed some conclusions provisionally, but I had better reserve them for the present.'

And then saluting the other with the same stiff civility, he passed out of the hotel to continue his curious peregrinations.

By the dusk of that day they had led him down the dingy streets and steps that straggled and tumbled towards the river in the oldest and most irregular part of the city. Immediately under the coloured lantern that marked the entrance to a rather low Chinese restaurant he encountered a figure he had seen before, though by no means presenting itself to the eye as he had seen it.

Mr Norman Drage still confronted the world grimly behind his great goggles, which seemed somehow to cover his face like a dark mask of glass. But except for the goggles, his appearance had undergone a strange transformation in the month that had elapsed since the murder. He had then, as Father Brown had noted, been dressed up to the nines – up to that point, indeed, where there begins to be too fine a distinction between the dandy and the dummy outside a tailor's shop. But now all those externals were mysteriously altered for the worse; as if the tailor's dummy had been turned into a scarecrow. His top hat still existed, but it was battered and shabby; his clothes were dilapidated; his watch-chain and minor ornaments were gone. Father Brown, however, addressed him as if they had met yesterday, and made no demur to sitting down with him on a bench in the cheap eating-house whither he was bound. It was not he, however, who began the conversation.

'Well?' growled Drage; 'and have you succeeded in avenging your holy and sainted millionaire? We know all millionaires are holy and sainted; you can find it all in the papers next day, about how they lived by the light of the Family Bible they read at their mother's knee. Gee! if they'd only read out some of the things there are in the Family Bible, the mother might have been startled some. And the millionaire, too, I reckon. The old Book's full of a lot of grand fierce old notions they don't grow nowadays; sort of wisdom of the Stone Age and buried under the Pyramids. Suppose somebody had flung old man Merton from the top of that tower of his, and let him be eaten by dogs at the bottom, it would be no worse than what happened to Jezebel. Wasn't Agag hacked into little pieces, for all he went walking delicately? Merton walked delicately all his life, damn him – until he got too delicate to walk at all. But the shaft of the Lord found him out, as it might have done in the old Book, and struck him dead on the top of his tower to be a spectacle to the people.'

'The shaft was material, at least,' said his companion.

'The Pyramids are mighty material, and they hold down the dead kings all right,' grinned the man in the goggles. 'I think there's a lot to be said for these old material religions. There's old carvings that have lasted for thousands of years, showing their gods and emperors with bended bows; with hands that look as if they could really bend bows of stone. Material, perhaps – but what materials! Don't you sometimes stand staring at those old Eastern patterns and things, till you have a hunch that that old Lord God is still driving like a dark Apollo, and shooting black rays of death?'

'If he is,' replied Father Brown, 'I might call him by another name. But I doubt whether Merton died by a dark ray or even a stone arrow.'

'I guess you think he's St Sebastian,' sneered Drage, 'killed with an arrow. A millionaire must be a martyr. How do you know he didn't deserve it? You don't know much about your millionaire, I fancy. Well, let me tell you he deserved it a hundred times over.'

'Well,' asked Father Brown gently, 'why didn't you murder him?'

'You want to know why I didn't?' said the other, staring. 'Well, you're a nice sort of clergyman.'

'Not at all,' said the other, as if waving away a compliment.

'I suppose it's your way of saying I did,' snarled Drage. 'Well, prove it, that's all. As for him, I reckon he was no loss.'

'Yes, he was,' said Father Brown, sharply. 'He was a loss to you. That's why you didn't kill him.'

And he walked out of the room, leaving the man in goggles gaping after him.

It was nearly a month later that Father Brown revisited the house where the third millionaire had suffered from the vendetta of Daniel Doom. A sort of council was held of the persons most interested. Old Crake sat at the head of the table with his nephew on his right hand, the lawyer on his left; the big man with the African features, whose name appeared to be Harris, was ponderously present, if only as a material witness; a red-haired, sharp-nosed individual addressed as Dixon seemed to be the representative of Pinkerton's or some such private agency; and Father Brown slipped unobtrusively into an empty seat beside him.

Every newspaper in the world was full of the catastrophe of the colossus of finance, of the great organizer of the Big Business that bestrides the modern world; but from the tiny group that had been nearest to him at the very instant of his death very little could be learned. The uncle, nephew, and attendant solicitor declared they were well outside the outer wall before the alarm was raised; and inquiries of the official guardians at both barriers brought answers that were rather confused, but on the whole confirmatory. Only one other complication seemed to call for consideration. It seemed that round about the time of the death, before or after, a stranger had been found hanging mysteriously round the entrance and asking to see Mr Merton. The servants had some difficulty in understanding what he meant, for his language was very obscure; but it was afterwards considered to be also very suspicious, since he had said something about a wicked man being destroyed by a word out of the sky.

Peter Wain leaned forward, the eyes bright in his haggard face, and said:

'I'll bet on that, anyhow, Norman Drage.'

'And who in the world is Norman Drage?' asked his uncle.

'That's what I want to know,' replied the young man. 'I practically asked him, but he has got a wonderful trick of twisting every straight question crooked; it's like lunging at a fencer. He hooked on to me with hints about the flying-ship of the future; but I never trusted him much.'

'But what sort of a man is he?' asked Crake.

'He's a mystagogue,' said Father Brown, with innocent promptitude. 'There are quite a lot of them about; the sort of men about town who hint to you in Paris cafés and cabarets that they've lifted the veil of Isis or know the secret of Stonehenge. In a case like this they're sure to have some sort of mystical explanations.'

The smooth, dark head of Mr Barnard Blake, the lawyer, was inclined politely towards the speaker, but his smile was faintly hostile.

'I should hardly have thought, sir,' he said, 'that you had any quarrel with mystical explanations.'

'On the contrary,' replied Father Brown, blinking amiably at him. 'That's just why I can quarrel with 'em. Any sham lawyer could bamboozle me, but he couldn't bamboozle you; because you're a lawyer yourself. Any fool could dress up as a Red Indian and I'd swallow him whole as the only original Hiawatha; but Mr Crake would see through him at once. A swindler could pretend to me that he knew all about aeroplanes, but not to Captain Wain. And it's just the same with the other, don't you see? It's just because I have picked up a little about mystics that I have no use for mystagogues. Real mystics don't hide mysteries, they reveal them. They set a thing up in broad daylight, and when you've seen it it's still a mystery. But the mystagogues hide a thing in darkness and secrecy, and when you find it, it's a platitude. But in the case of Drage, I admit he had also another and more practical notion in talking about fire from heaven or bolts from the blue.'

'And what was his notion?' asked Wain. 'I think it wants watching, whatever it is.'

'Well,' replied the priest, slowly, 'he wanted us to think the murders were miracles because . . . well, because he knew they weren't.'

'Ah,' said Wain, with a sort of hiss, 'I was waiting for that. In plain words, he is the criminal.'

'In plain words, he is the criminal who didn't commit the crime,' answered Father Brown calmly.

'Is that your conception of plain words?' inquired Blake politely.

'You'll be saying I'm the mystagogue now,' said Father Brown, somewhat abashed, but with a broad smile, 'but it was really quite accidental. Drage didn't commit the crime – I mean this crime. His only crime was blackmailing somebody, and he hung about here to do it; but he wasn't likely to want the secret to be public property or the whole business to be cut short by death. We can talk about him afterwards. Just at the moment, I only want him cleared out of the way.'

'Out of the way of what?' asked the other.

'Out of the way of the truth,' replied the priest, looking at him tranquilly, with level eyelids.

'Do you mean,' faltered the other, 'that you know the truth?'

'I rather think so,' said Father Brown modestly.

There was an abrupt silence, after which Crake cried out suddenly and irrelevantly in a rasping voice:

'Why, where is that secretary fellow? Wilton! He ought to be here.'

'I am in communication with Mr Wilton,' said Father Brown gravely;

'in fact, I asked him to ring me up here in a few minutes from now. I may say that we've worked the thing out together, in a manner of speaking.'

'If you're working together, I suppose it's all right,' grumbled Crake. 'I know he was always a sort of bloodhound on the trail of this vanishing crook, so perhaps it was well to hunt in couples with him. But if you know the truth about this, where the devil did you get it from?'

'I got it from you,' answered the priest, quietly, and continued to gaze mildly at the glaring veteran. 'I mean I made the first guess from a hint in a story of yours about an Indian who threw a knife and hit a man on the top of a fortress.'

'You've said that several times,' said Wain, with a puzzled air; 'but I can't see any inference, except that his murderer threw an arrow and hit a man on the top of a house very like a fortress. But of course the arrow wasn't thrown but shot, and would go much farther. Certainly it went uncommonly far; but I don't see how it brings us any farther.'

'I'm afraid you missed the point of the story,' said Father Brown. 'It isn't that if one thing can go far another can go farther. It is that the wrong use of a tool can cut both ways. The men on Crake's fort thought of a knife as a thing for a hand-to-hand fight and forgot that it could be a missile like a javelin. Some other people I know thought of a thing as a missile like a javelin and forgot that, after all, it could be used hand-to-hand as a spear. In short, the moral of the story is that since a dagger can be turned into an arrow, so can an arrow be turned into a dagger.'

They were all looking at him now; but he continued in the same casual and unconscious tone:

'Naturally we wondered and worried a good deal about who shot that arrow through the window and whether it came from far away, and so on. But the truth is that nobody shot the arrow at all. It never came in at the window at all.'

'Then how did it come there?' asked the swarthy lawyer, with a rather lowering face.

'Somebody brought it with him, I suppose,' said Father Brown; 'it wouldn't be hard to carry or conceal. Somebody had it in his hand as he stood with Merton in Merton's own room. Somebody thrust it into Merton's throat like a poignard, and then had the highly intelligent idea

FATHER BROWN

of placing the whole thing at such a place and angle that we all assumed in a flash that it had flown in at the window like a bird.'

'Somebody,' said old Crake, in a voice as heavy as stone.

The telephone bell rang with a strident and horrible clamour of insistence. It was in the adjoining room, and Father Brown had darted there before anybody else could move.

'What the devil is it all about?' cried Peter Wain, who seemed all shaken and distracted.

'He said he expected to be rung up by Wilton, the secretary,' replied his uncle in the same dead voice.

'I suppose it is Wilton?' observed the lawyer, like one speaking to fill up a silence. But nobody answered the question until Father Brown reappeared suddenly and silently in the room, bringing the answer.

'Gentlemen,' he said, when he had resumed his seat, 'it was you who asked me to look into the truth about this puzzle; and having found the truth, I must tell it, without any pretence of softening the shock. I'm afraid anybody who pokes his nose into things like this can't afford to be a respecter of persons.'

'I suppose,' said Crake, breaking the silence that followed, 'that means that some of us are accused, or suspected.'

'All of us are suspected,' answered Father Brown. 'I may be suspected myself, for I found the body.'

'Of course we're suspected,' snapped Wain. 'Father Brown kindly explained to me how I could have besieged the tower in a flying-machine.'

'No,' replied the priest, with a smile; 'you described to me how you could have done it. That was just the interesting part of it.'

'He seemed to think it likely,' growled Crake, 'that I killed him myself with a Red Indian arrow.'

'I thought it most unlikely,' said Father Brown, making rather a wry face. 'I'm sorry if I did wrong, but I couldn't think of any other way of testing the matter. I can hardly think of anything more improbable than the notion that Captain Wain went careering in a huge machine past the window, at the very moment of the murder, and nobody noticed it; unless, perhaps, it were the notion that a respectable old gentleman should play at Red Indians with a bow and arrow behind the bushes, to

128

kill somebody he could have killed in twenty much simpler ways. But I had to find out if they had had anything to do with it; and so I had to accuse them in order to prove their innocence.'

'And how have you proved their innocence?' asked Blake the lawyer, leaning forward eagerly.

'Only by the agitation they showed when they were accused,' answered the other.

'What do you mean, exactly?'

'If you will permit me to say so,' remarked Father Brown, composedly enough, 'I did undoubtedly think it my duty to suspect them and everybody else. I did suspect Mr Crake and I did suspect Captain Wain, in the sense that I considered the possibility or probability of their guilt. I told them I had formed conclusions about it; and I will now tell them what those conclusions were. I was sure they were innocent, because of the manner and the moment in which they passed from unconsciousness to indignation. So long as they never thought they were accused, they went on giving me materials to support the accusation. They practically explained to me how they might have committed the crime. Then they suddenly realized with a shock and a shout of rage that they were accused; they realized it long after they might well have expected to be accused, but long before I had accused them. Now no guilty person could possibly do that. He might be snappy and suspicious from the first; or he might simulate unconsciousness and innocence up to the end. But he wouldn't begin by making things worse for himself and then give a great jump and begin furiously denying the notion he had himself helped to suggest. That could only come by his having really failed to realize what he was suggesting. The self-consciousness of a murderer would always be at least morbidly vivid enough to prevent him first forgetting his relation with the thing and then remembering to deny it. So I ruled you both out and others for other reasons I needn't discuss now. For instance, there was the secretary –

'But I'm not talking about that just now. Look here, I've just heard from Wilton on the 'phone, and he's given me permission to tell you some rather serious news. Now I suppose you all know by this time who Wilton was, and what he was after.'

'I know he was after Daniel Doom and wouldn't be happy till he got him,' answered Peter Wain; 'and I've heard the story that he's the son of old Horder, and that's why he's the avenger of blood. Anyhow, he's certainly looking for the man called Doom.'

'Well,' said Father Brown, 'he has found him.'

Peter Wain sprang to his feet in excitement.

'The murderer!' he cried. 'Is the murderer in the lock-up already?'

'No,' said Father Brown, gravely; 'I said the news was serious, and it's more serious than that. I'm afraid poor Wilton has taken a terrible responsibility. I'm afraid he's going to put a terrible responsibility on us. He hunted the criminal down, and just when he had him cornered at last – well, he has taken the law into his own hands.'

'You mean that Daniel Doom –' began the lawyer.

'I mean that Daniel Doom is dead,' said the priest. 'There was some sort of wild struggle, and Wilton killed him.'

'Serve him right,' growled Mr Hickory Crake.

'Can't blame Wilton for downing a crook like that, especially considering the feud,' assented Wain; 'it was like stepping on a viper.'

'I don't agree with you,' said Father Brown. 'I suppose we all talk romantic stuff at random in defence of lynching and lawlessness; but I have a suspicion that if we lose our laws and liberties we shall regret it. Besides, it seems to me illogical to say there is something to be said for Wilton committing murder, without even inquiring whether there was anything to be said for Doom committing it. I rather doubt whether Doom was merely a vulgar assassin; he may have been a sort of outlaw with a mania about the cup, demanding it with threats and only killing after a struggle; both victims were thrown down just outside their houses. The objection to Wilton's way of doing it is that we shall never hear Doom's side of the case.'

'Oh, I've no patience with all this sentimental whitewashing of worthless, murderous blackguards,' cried Wain, heatedly. 'If Wilton croaked the criminal he did a jolly good day's work, and there's an end of it.'

'Quite so, quite so,' said his uncle, nodding vigorously.

Father Brown's face had a yet heavier gravity as he looked slowly round the semicircle of faces.

'Is that really what you all think?' he asked. Even as he did so he realized that he was an Englishman and an exile. He realized that he was among foreigners, even if he was among friends. Around that ring of foreigners ran a restless fire that was not native to his own breed; the fiercer spirit of the western nation that can rebel and lynch, and above all, combine. He knew that they had already combined.

'Well,' said Father Brown, with a sigh, 'I am to understand, then, that you do definitely condone this unfortunate man's crime, or act of private justice, or whatever you call it. In that case it will not hurt him if I tell you a little more about it.'

He rose suddenly to his feet; and though they saw no meaning in his movement, it seemed in some way to change or chill the very air in the room.

'Wilton killed Doom in a rather curious way,' he began.

'How did Wilton kill him?' asked Crake, abruptly.

'With an arrow,' said Father Brown.

Twilight was gathering in the long room, and daylight dwindling to a gleam from the great window in the inner room, where the great millionaire had died. Almost automatically the eyes of the group turned slowly towards it, but as yet there was no sound. Then the voice of Crake came cracked and high and senile in a sort of crowing gabble.

'What you mean? What you mean? Brander Merton killed by an arrow. This crook killed by an arrow –'

'By the same arrow,' said the priest, 'and at the same moment.'

Again there was a sort of strangled and yet swollen and bursting silence, and young Wain began: 'You mean –'

'I mean that your friend Merton was Daniel Doom,' said Father Brown firmly; 'and the only Daniel Doom you'll ever find. Your friend Merton was always crazy after that Coptic Cup that he used to worship like an idol every day; and in his wild youth he had really killed two men to get it, though I still think the deaths may have been in a sense accidents of the robbery. Anyhow, he had it; and that man Drage knew the story and was blackmailing him. But Wilton was after him for a very different purpose; I fancy he only discovered the truth when he'd got into this house. But anyhow, it was in this house, and in that room, that this hunt ended, and he slew the slayer of his father.'

For a long time nobody answered. Then old Crake could be heard drumming with his fingers on the table and muttering: 'Brander must have been mad. He must have been mad.'

'But, good Lord!' burst out Peter Wain; 'what are we to do? What are we to say? Oh, it's all quite different! What about the papers and the big business people? Brander Merton is a thing like the President or the Pope of Rome.'

'I certainly think it is rather different,' began Barnard Blake, the lawyer, in a low voice. 'The difference involves a whole –'

Father Brown struck the table so that the glasses on it rang; and they could almost fancy a ghostly echo from the mysterious chalice that still stood in the room beyond.

'No!' he cried, in a voice like a pistol-shot. 'There shall be no difference. I gave you your chance of pitying the poor devil when you thought he was a common criminal. You wouldn't listen then; you were all for private vengeance then. You were all for letting him be butchered like a wild beast without a hearing or a public trial, and said he had only got his deserts. Very well then, if Daniel Doom has got his deserts, Brander Merton has got his deserts. If that was good enough for Doom, by all that is holy it is good enough for Merton. Take your wild justice or our dull legality; but in the name of Almighty God, let there be an equal lawlessness or an equal law.'

Nobody answered except the lawyer, and he answered with something like a snarl:

'What will the police say if we tell them we mean to condone a crime?'

'What will they say if I tell them you did condone it?' replied Father Brown. 'Your respect for the law comes rather late, Mr Barnard Blake.'

After a pause he resumed in a milder tone: 'I, for one, am ready to tell the truth if the proper authorities ask me; and the rest of you can do as you like. But as a fact, it will make very little difference. Wilton only rang me up to tell me that I was now free to lay his confession before you; for when you heard it, he would be beyond pursuit.'

He walked slowly into the inner room and stood there by the little table beside which the millionaire had died. The Coptic Cup still stood in the same place, and he remained there for a space staring at its cluster of all the colours of the rainbow, and beyond it into a blue abyss of sky.

3
The Oracle of the Dog

'Yes,' said Father Brown, 'I always like a dog, so long as he isn't spelt backwards.'

Those who are quick in talking are not always quick in listening. Sometimes even their brilliancy produces a sort of stupidity. Father Brown's friend and companion was a young man with a stream of ideas and stories, an enthusiastic young man named Fiennes, with eager blue eyes and blond hair that seemed to be brushed back, not merely with a hair-brush but with the wind of the world as he rushed through it. But he stopped in the torrent of his talk in a momentary bewilderment before he saw the priest's very simple meaning.

'You mean that people make too much of them?' he said. 'Well, I don't know. They're marvellous creatures. Sometimes I think they know a lot more than we do.'

Father Brown said nothing, but continued to stroke the head of the big retriever in a half-abstracted but apparently soothing fashion.

'Why,' said Fiennes, warming again to his monologue, 'there was a dog in the case I've come to see you about: what they call the "Invisible Murder Case", you know. It's a strange story, but from my point of view the dog is about the strangest thing in it. Of course, there's the mystery of the crime itself, and how old Druce can have been killed by somebody else when he was all alone in the summer house –'

The hand stroking the dog stopped for a moment in its rhythmic movement, and Father Brown said calmly: 'Oh, it was a summer house, was it?'

'I thought you'd read all about it in the papers,' answered Fiennes. 'Stop a minute; I believe I've got a cutting that will give you all the particulars.' He produced a strip of newspaper from his pocket and handed it to the priest, who began to read it, holding it close to his blinking eyes with one hand while the other continued its half-conscious caresses of the dog. It looked like the parable of a man not letting his right hand know what his left hand did.

Many mystery stories, about men murdered behind locked doors and windows, and murderers escaping without means of entrance and exit, have come true in the course of the extraordinary events at Cranston on the coast of Yorkshire, where Colonel Druce was found stabbed from behind by a dagger that has entirely disappeared from the scene, and apparently even from the neighbourhood.

'The summer-house in which he died was indeed accessible at one entrance, the ordinary doorway which looked down the central walk of the garden towards the house. But, by a combination of events almost to be called a coincidence, it appears that both the path and the entrance were watched during the crucial time, and there is a chain of witnesses who confirm each other. The summer house stands at the extreme end of the garden, where there is no exit or entrance of any kind. The central garden path is a lane between two ranks of tall delphiniums, planted so close that any stray step off the path would leave its traces; and both path and plants run right up to the very mouth of the summer house, so that no one straying from that straight path could fail to be observed, and no other mode of entrance can be imagined.

'Patrick Floyd, secretary of the murdered man, testified that he had been in a position to overlook the whole garden from the time when Colonel Druce last appeared alive in the doorway to the time when he was found dead; as he, Floyd, had been on the top of a step-ladder clipping the garden hedge. Janet Druce, the dead man's daughter, confirmed this, saying that she had sat on the terrace of the house throughout that time and had seen Floyd at his work. Touching some part of the time, this is again supported by Donald Druce, her brother – who overlooked the garden – standing at his bedroom window in his dressing-gown, for he had risen late. Lastly, the account is consistent with that given by Dr Valentine, a neighbour, who called for a time to talk with Miss Druce on the terrace, and by the Colonel's solicitor, Mr Aubrey Traill, who was apparently the last to see the murdered man alive – presumably with the exception of the murderer.

'All are agreed that the course of events was as follows: About half-past three in the afternoon, Miss Druce went down the path to ask her father when he would like tea; but he said he did not want any and was waiting to see Traill, his lawyer, who was to be sent to him in the summer house. The girl then came away and met Traill coming down the path; she directed him to her father and he went in as directed. About half an hour afterwards he came out again, the Colonel coming with him to the door and showing himself to all appearance in health and even high spirits. He had been somewhat annoyed earlier in the day by his son's irregular hours, but seemed to recover his temper in a perfectly normal fashion, and had been rather markedly genial in receiving other visitors, including two of his nephews, who came over for the day. But as these were out walking during the whole period of the tragedy, they had no evidence to give. It is said, indeed, that the Colonel was not on very good terms with Dr Valentine, but that gentleman only had a brief interview with the daughter of the house, to whom he is supposed to be paying serious attentions.

'Traill, the solicitor, says he left the Colonel entirely alone in the summer house, and this is confirmed by Floyd's bird's-eye view of the garden, which showed nobody else passing the only entrance. Ten minutes later, Miss Druce again went down the garden and had not reached the end of the path when she saw her father, who was conspicuous by his white linen coat, lying in a heap on the floor. She uttered a scream which brought others to the spot, and on entering the place they found the Colonel lying dead beside his basket-chair, which was also upset. Dr Valentine, who was still in the immediate neighbourhood, testified that the wound was made by some sort of stiletto, entering under the shoulder blade and piercing the heart. The police have searched the neighbourhood for such a weapon, but no trace of it can be found.

'So Colonel Druce wore a white coat, did he?' said Father Brown as he put down the paper.

'Trick he learnt in the tropics,' replied Fiennes, with some wonder. 'He'd had some queer adventures there, by his own account; and I fancy his dislike of Valentine was connected with the doctor coming from the tropics, too. But it's all an infernal puzzle. The account there is pretty accurate; I didn't see the tragedy, in the sense of the discovery; I was out walking with the young nephews and the dog – the dog I wanted to tell you about. But I saw the stage set for it as described; the straight lane between the blue flowers right up to the dark entrance, and the lawyer going down it in his blacks and his silk hat, and the red head of the secretary showing high above the green hedge as he worked on it with his shears. Nobody could have mistaken that red head at any distance; and if people say they saw it there all the time, you may be sure they did. This red-haired secretary, Floyd, is quite a character; a breathless bounding sort of fellow, always doing everybody's work as he was doing the gardener's. I think he is an American; he's certainly got the American view of life – what they call the view-point, bless 'em.'

'What about the lawyer?' asked Father Brown.

There was a silence and then Fiennes spoke quite slowly for him. 'Traill struck me as a singular man. In his fine black clothes he was almost foppish, yet you can hardly call him fashionable. For he wore a pair of long, luxuriant black whiskers such as haven't been seen since Victorian times. He had rather a fine grave face and a fine grave manner, but every now and then he seemed to remember to smile. And when he showed his white teeth he seemed to lose a little of his dignity, and there was something faintly fawning about him. It may have been only embarrassment, for he would also fidget with his cravat and his tie-pin, which were at once handsome and unusual, like himself. If I could think of anybody – but what's the good, when the whole thing's impossible? Nobody knows who did it. Nobody knows how it could be done. At least there's only one exception I'd make, and that's why I really mentioned the whole thing. The dog knows.'

Father Brown sighed and then said absently: 'You were there as a friend of young Donald, weren't you? He didn't go on your walk with you?'

'No,' replied Fiennes smiling. 'The young scoundrel had gone to bed that morning and got up that afternoon. I went with his cousins, two young officers from India, and our conversation was trivial enough. I remember the elder, whose name I think is Herbert Druce and who is an authority on horse-breeding, talked about nothing but a mare he had bought and the moral character of the man who sold her; while his brother Harry seemed to be brooding on his bad luck at Monte Carlo. I only mention it to show you, in the light of what happened on our walk, that there was nothing psychic about us. The dog was the only mystic in our company.'

'What sort of a dog was he?' asked the priest.

'Same breed as that one,' answered Fiennes. 'That's what started me off on the story, your saying you didn't believe in believing in a dog. He's a big black retriever, named Nox, and a suggestive name, too; for

I think what he did a darker mystery than the murder. You know Druce's house and garden are by the sea; we walked about a mile from it along the sands and then turned back, going the other way. We passed a rather curious rock called the Rock of Fortune, famous in the neighbourhood because it's one of those examples of one stone barely balanced on another, so that a touch would knock it over. It is not really very high but the hanging outline of it makes it look a little wild and sinister; at least it made it look so to me, for I don't imagine my jolly young companions were afflicted with the picturesque. But it may be that I was beginning to feel an atmosphere; for just then the question arose of whether it was time to go back to tea, and even then I think I had a premonition that time counted for a good deal in the business. Neither Herbert Druce nor I had a watch, so we called out to his brother, who was some paces behind, having stopped to light his pipe under the hedge. Hence it happened that he shouted out the hour, which was twenty past four, in his big voice through the growing twilight; and somehow the loudness of it made it sound like the proclamation of something tremendous. His unconsciousness seemed to make it all the more so; but that was always the way with omens; and particular ticks of the clock were really very ominous things that afternoon. According to Dr Valentine's testimony, poor Druce had actually died just about half-past four.

'Well, they said we needn't go home for ten minutes, and we walked a little farther along the sands, doing nothing in particular – throwing stones for the dog and throwing sticks into the sea for him to swim after. But to me the twilight seemed to grow oddly oppressive, and the very shadow of the top-heavy Rock of Fortune lay on me like a load. And then the curious thing happened. Nox had just brought back Herbert's walking-stick out of the sea and his brother had thrown his in also. The dog swam out again, but just about what must have been the stroke of the half-hour, he stopped swimming. He came back again on to the shore and stood in front of us. Then he suddenly threw up his head and sent up a howl or wail of woe – if ever I heard one in the world.

'"What the devil's the matter with the dog?" asked Herbert; but none of us could answer. There was a long silence after the brute's wailing and whining died away on the desolate shore; and then the silence was broken. As I live, it was broken by a faint and far-off shriek, like the shriek of a woman from beyond the hedges inland. We didn't know what it was then; but we knew afterwards. It was the cry the girl gave when she first saw the body of her father.'

'You went back, I suppose,' said Father Brown patiently. 'What happened then?'

'I'll tell you what happened then,' said Fiennes with a grim emphasis. 'When we got back into that garden the first thing we saw was Traill, the lawyer; I can see him now with his black hat and black whiskers relieved against the perspective of the blue flowers stretching down to the summer-house, with the sunset and the strange outline of the Rock of Fortune in the distance. His face and figure were in shadow against the sunset; but I swear the white teeth were showing in his head and he was smiling.

'The moment Nox saw that man the dog dashed forward and stood in the middle of the path barking at him madly, murderously, volleying out curses that were almost verbal in their dreadful distinctness of hatred. And the man doubled up and fled along the path between the flowers.'

Father Brown sprang to his feet with a startling impatience.

'So the dog denounced him, did he?' he cried. 'The oracle of the dog condemned him. Did you see what birds were flying, and are you sure whether they were on the right hand or the left? Did you consult the augurs about the sacrifices? Surely you didn't omit to cut open the dog and examine his entrails. That is the sort of scientific test you heathen humanitarians seem to trust when you are thinking of taking away the life and honour of a man.'

Fiennes sat gaping for an instant before he found breath to say: 'Why, what's the matter with you? What have I done now?'

A sort of anxiety came back into the priest's eyes – the anxiety of a man who has run against a post in the dark and wonders for a moment whether he has hurt it.

'I'm most awfully sorry,' he said with sincere distress. 'I beg your pardon for being so rude; pray forgive me.'

Fiennes looked at him curiously. 'I sometimes think you are more of a mystery than any of the mysteries,' he said. 'But anyhow, if you don't believe in the mystery of the dog, at least you can't get over the mystery of the man. You can't deny that at the very moment when the beast came back from the sea and bellowed, his master's soul was driven out of his body by the blow of some unseen power that no mortal man can trace or even imagine. And as for the lawyer – I don't go only by the dog – there are other curious details, too. He struck me as a smooth smiling, equivocal sort of person; and one of his tricks seemed like a sort of hint. You know the doctor and the police were on the spot very quickly; Valentine was brought back when walking away from the house, and he telephoned instantly. That, with the secluded house, small numbers, and enclosed space, made it pretty possible to search everybody who could have been near; and everybody was thoroughly searched – for a weapon. The whole house, garden, and shore were combed for a weapon. The disappearance of the dagger is almost as crazy as the disappearance of the man.'

'The disappearance of the dagger,' said Father Brown, nodding. He seemed to have become suddenly attentive.

'Well,' continued Fiennes, 'I told you that man Traill had a trick of fidgeting with his tie and tie-pin – especially his tie-pin. His pin, like himself, was at once showy and old-fashioned. It had one of those stones with concentric coloured rings that look like an eye; and his own concentration on it got on my nerves, as if he had been a Cyclops with one eye in the middle of his body. But the pin was not only large but long; and it occurred to me that his anxiety about its adjustment was because it was even longer than it looked; as long as a stiletto in fact.'

Father Brown nodded thoughtfully. 'Was any other instrument ever suggested?' he asked.

'There was another suggestion,' answered Fiennes, 'from one of the young Druces – the cousins, I mean. Neither Herbert nor Harry Druce would have struck one at first as likely to be of assistance in scientific detection; but while Herbert was really the traditional type of heavy Dragoon, caring for nothing but horses and being an ornament to the Horse Guards, his younger brother Harry had been in the Indian Police and knew something about such things. Indeed, in his own way he was quite clever; and I rather fancy he had been too clever; I mean he had left the police through breaking some red-tape regulations and taking some sort of risk and responsibility of his own. Anyhow, he was in some sense a detective out of work, and threw himself into this business with more than the ardour of an amateur. And it was with him that I had an argument about the weapon – an argument that led to something new. It began by his countering my description of the dog barking at Traill; and he said that a dog at his worst didn't bark, but growled.'

'He was quite right there,' observed the priest.

'This young fellow went on to say that, if it came to that, he'd heard Nox growling at other people before then; and among others at Floyd, the secretary. I retorted that his own argument answered itself; for the crime couldn't be brought home to two or three people, and least of all to Floyd, who was as innocent as a harum-scarum schoolboy, and had been seen by everybody all the time perched above the garden hedge with his fan of red hair as conspicuous as a scarlet cockatoo. "I know there's difficulties anyhow," said my colleague; "but I wish you'd come with me down the garden a minute. I want to show you something I don't think any one else has seen." This was on the very day of the discovery, and the garden was just as it had been. The step-ladder was still standing by the hedge, and just under the hedge my guide stopped and disentangled something from the deep grass. It was the shears used for clipping the hedge, and on the point of one of them was a smear of blood.'

There was a short silence, and then Father Brown said suddenly. 'What was the lawyer there for?'

'He told us the Colonel sent for him to alter his will,' answered Fiennes. 'And, by the way, there was another thing about the business of the will that I ought to mention. You see, the will wasn't actually signed in the summer-house that afternoon.'

'I suppose not,' said Father Brown; 'there would have to be two witnesses.'

'The lawyer actually came down the day before and it was signed then; but he was sent for again next day because the old man had a doubt about one of the witnesses and had to be reassured.'

'Who were the witnesses?' asked Father Brown.

'That's just the point,' replied his informant eagerly, 'the witnesses were Floyd, the secretary, and this Dr Valentine, the foreign sort of surgeon or whatever he is; and the two have a quarrel. Now I'm bound to say that the secretary is something of a busybody. He's one of those hot and headlong people whose warmth of temperament has unfortunately turned mostly to pugnacity and bristling suspicion; to distrusting people instead of to trusting them. That sort of red-haired red-hot fellow is always either universally credulous or universally incredulous; and sometimes both. He was not only a Jack-of-all-trades, but he knew better than all tradesmen. He not only knew everything, but he warned everybody against everybody. All that must be taken into account in his suspicions about Valentine; but in that particular case there seems to have been something behind it. He said the name of Valentine was not really Valentine. He said he had seen him elsewhere known by the name of De Villon. He said it would invalidate the will; of course he was kind enough to explain to the lawyer what the law was on that point. They were both in a frightful wax.'

Father Brown laughed. 'People often are when they are to witness a will,' he said: 'for one thing, it means that they can't have any legacy under it. But what did Dr Valentine say? No doubt the universal secretary knew more about the doctor's name than the doctor did. But even the doctor might have some information about his own name.'

Fiennes paused a moment before he replied.

'Dr Valentine took it in a curious way. Dr Valentine is a curious man. His appearance is rather striking but very foreign. He is young but wears a beard cut square; and his face is very pale, dreadfully pale and dreadfully serious. His eyes have a sort of ache in them, as if he ought to wear glasses, or had given himself a headache with thinking; but he is quite handsome and always very formally dressed, with a top hat and a dark coat and a little red rosette. His manner is rather cold and haughty, and he has a way of staring at you which is very disconcerting. When thus charged with having changed his name, he merely stared like a sphinx and then said with a little laugh that he supposed Americans had no names to change. At that I think the Colonel also got into a fuss and said all sorts of angry things to the doctor; all the more angry because of the doctor's pretensions to a future place in his family. But I shouldn't have thought much of that but for a few words that I happened to hear later, early in the afternoon of the tragedy. I don't want to make a lot of them, for they weren't the sort of words on which one would like, in the ordinary way, to play the eavesdropper. As I was passing out towards the front gate with my two companions and the dog, I heard voices which told me that Dr Valentine and Miss Druce had withdrawn for a moment into the shadow of the house, in an angle behind a row of flowering plants, and were talking to each other in passionate whisperings – sometimes almost like hissings; for it was something of a lovers' quarrel as well as a lovers' tryst. Nobody repeats the sort of things they said for the most part; but in an unfortunate business like this I'm bound to say that there was repeated more than once a phrase about killing somebody. In fact, the girl seemed to be begging him not to kill somebody, or saying that no provocation could justify killing anybody; which seems an unusual sort of talk to address to a gentleman who has dropped in to tea.'

'Do you know,' asked the priest, 'whether Dr Valentine seemed to be very angry after the scene with the secretary and the Colonel – I mean about witnessing the will?'

'By all accounts,' replied the other, 'he wasn't half so angry as the secretary was. It was the secretary who went away raging after witnessing the will.'

'And now,' said Father Brown, 'what about the will itself?'

'The Colonel was a very wealthy man, and his will was important. Traill wouldn't tell us the alteration at that stage, but I have since heard only this morning in fact – that most of the money was transferred from the son to the daughter. I told you that Druce was wild with my friend Donald over his dissipated hours.'

'The question of motive has been rather over-shadowed by the question of method,' observed Father Brown thoughtfully. 'At that moment, apparently, Miss Druce was the immediate gainer by the death.'

'Good God! What a cold-blooded way of talking,' cried Fiennes, staring at him. 'You don't really mean to hint that she –'

'Is she going to marry that Dr Valentine?' asked the other.

'Some people are against it,' answered his friend. 'But he is liked and respected in the place and is a skilled and devoted surgeon.'

'So devoted a surgeon,' said Father Brown, 'that he had surgical instruments with him when he went to call on the young lady at teatime. For he must have used a lancet or something, and he never seems to have gone home.'

Fiennes sprang to his feet and looked at him in a heat of inquiry. 'You suggest he might have used the very same lancet –'

Father Brown shook his head. 'All these suggestions are fancies just now,' he said. 'The problem is not who did it or what did it, but how it was done. We might find many men and even many tools – pins and shears and lancets. But how did a man get into the room? How did even a pin get into it?'

He was staring reflectively at the ceiling as he spoke, but as he said the last words his eye cocked in an alert fashion as if he had suddenly seen a curious fly on the ceiling.

'Well, what would you do about it?' asked the young man. 'You have a lot of experience; what would you advise now?'

'I'm afraid I'm not much use,' said Father Brown with a sigh. 'I can't suggest very much without having ever been near the place or the people. For the moment you can only go on with local inquiries. I gather that your friend from the Indian Police is more or less in charge of your inquiry down there. I should run down and see how he is getting on. See what he's been doing in the way of amateur detection. There may be news already.'

As his guests, the biped and the quadruped, disappeared, Father Brown took up his pen and went back to his interrupted occupation of planning a course of lectures on the Encyclical *Rerum Novarum*. The subject was a large one and he had to re-cast it more than once, so that he was somewhat similarly employed some two days later when the big black dog again came bounding into the room and sprawled all over him with enthusiasm and excitement. The master who followed the dog shared the excitement if not the enthusiasm. He had been excited in a less pleasant fashion, for his blue eyes seemed to start from his head and his eager face was even a little pale.

'You told me,' he said abruptly and without preface, 'to find out what Harry Druce was doing. Do you know what he's done?'

The priest did not reply, and the young man went on in jerky tones:

'I'll tell you what he's done. He's killed himself.'

Father Brown's lips moved only faintly, and there was nothing practical about what he was saying – nothing that has anything to do with this story or this world.

'You give me the creeps sometimes,' said Fiennes. 'Did you – did you expect this?'

'I thought it possible,' said Father Brown; 'that was why I asked you to go and see what he was doing. I hoped you might not be too late.'

'It was I who found him,' said Fiennes rather huskily. 'It was the ugliest and most uncanny thing I ever knew. I went down that old garden again, and I knew there was something new and unnatural about it besides the murder. The flowers still tossed about in blue masses on each side of the black entrance into the old grey summer house; but to me the blue flowers looked like blue devils dancing before some dark cavern of the underworld. I looked all round, everything seemed to be in its ordinary place. But the queer notion grew on me that there was something wrong with the very shape of the sky. And then I saw what it was. The Rock of Fortune always rose in the background beyond the garden hedge and against the sea. And the Rock of Fortune was gone.'

Father Brown had lifted his head and was listening intently.

'It was as if a mountain had walked away out of a landscape or a moon fallen from the sky; though I knew, of course, that a touch at any time would have tipped the thing over. Something possessed me and I rushed down that garden path like the wind and went crashing through that hedge as if it were a spider's web. It was a thin hedge really, though its undisturbed trimness had made it serve all the purposes of a wall. On the shore I found the loose rock fallen from its pedestal; and poor Harry Druce lay like a wreck underneath it. One arm was thrown round it in a sort of embrace as if he had pulled it down on himself; and on the broad brown sands beside it, in large crazy lettering, he had scrawled the words: "The Rock of Fortune falls on the Fool."'

'It was the Colonel's will that did that,' observed Father Brown. 'The young man had staked everything on profiting himself by Donald's disgrace, especially when his uncle sent for him on the same day as the lawyer, and welcomed him with so much warmth. Otherwise he was done; he'd lost his police job; he was beggared at Monte Carlo. And he killed himself when he found he'd killed his kinsman for nothing.'

'Here, stop a minute!' cried the staring Fiennes. 'You're going too fast for me.'

'Talking about the will, by the way,' continued Father Brown calmly 'before I forget it, or we go on to bigger things, there was a simple explanation, I think, of all that business about the doctor's name. I rather fancy I have heard both names before somewhere. The doctor is really a French nobleman with the title of the Marquis de Villon. But he is also an ardent Republican and has abandoned his title and fallen back on the forgotten family surname. "With your Citizen Riquetti you have puzzled Europe for ten days."'

'What is that?' asked the young man blankly.

'Never mind,' said the priest. 'Nine times out of ten it is a rascally thing to change one's name; but this was a piece of fine fanaticism. That's the point of his sarcasm about Americans having no names – that is, no title. Now in England the Marquis of Hartington is never called Mr Hartington; but in France the Marquis de Villon is called M de Villon. So it might well look like a change of name. As for the talk about killing, I fancy that also was a point of French etiquette. The doctor was talking about challenging Floyd to a duel, and the girl was trying to dissuade him.'

'Oh, I *see*,' cried Fiennes slowly. 'Now I understand what she meant.'

'And what is that about?' asked his companion, smiling.

'Well,' said the young man, 'it was something that happened to me just before I found that poor fellow's body; only the catastrophe drove it out of my head. I suppose it's hard to remember a little romantic idyll when you've just come on top of a tragedy. But as I went down the lanes leading to the Colonel's old place I met his daughter walking with Dr Valentine. She was in mourning, of course, and he always wore black as if he were going to a funeral; but I can't say that their faces were very funereal. Never have I seen two people looking in their own way more respectably radiant and cheerful. They stopped and saluted me, and then she told me they were married and living in a little house on the outskirts of the town, where the doctor was continuing his practice. This rather surprised me, because I knew that her old father's will had left her his property; and I hinted at it delicately by saying I was going along to her father's old place and had half expected to meet her there. But she only laughed and said: "Oh, we've given up all that. My husband doesn't like heiresses." And I discovered with some astonishment they really had insisted on restoring the property to poor Donald; so I hope he's had a healthy shock and will treat it sensibly. There was never much really the matter with him; he was very young and his father was not very wise. But it was in connexion with that that she said something I didn't understand at the time; but now I'm sure it must be as you say. She said with a sort of sudden and splendid arrogance that was entirely altruistic:

145

'"I hope it'll stop that red-haired fool from fussing any more about the will. Does he think my husband, who has given up a crest and a coronet as old as the Crusades for his principles, would kill an old man in a summer house for a legacy like that?" Then she laughed again and said, "My husband isn't killing anybody except in the way of business. Why, he didn't even ask his friends to call on the secretary." Now, of course, I see what she meant.'

'I see part of what she meant, of course,' said Father Brown. 'What did she mean exactly by the secretary fussing about the will?'

Fiennes smiled as he answered. 'I wish you knew the secretary, Father Brown. It would be a joy to you to watch him make things hum, as he calls it. He made the house of mourning hum. He filled the funeral with all the snap and zip of the brightest sporting event. There was no holding him, after something had really happened. I've told you how he used to oversee the gardener as he did the garden, and how he instructed the lawyer in the law. Needless to say, he also instructed the surgeon in the practice of surgery; and as the surgeon was Dr Valentine, you may be sure it ended in accusing him of something worse than bad surgery. The secretary got it fixed in his red head that the doctor had committed the crime, and when the police arrived he was perfectly sublime. Need I say that he became, on the spot, the greatest of all amateur detectives? Sherlock Holmes never towered over Scotland Yard with more Titanic intellectual pride and scorn than Colonel Druce's private secretary over the police investigating Colonel Druce's death. I tell you it was a joy to see him. He strode about with an abstracted air, tossing his scarlet crest of hair and giving curt impatient replies. Of course it was his demeanour during these days that made Druce's daughter so wild with him. Of course he had a theory. It's just the sort of theory a man would have in a book; and Floyd is the sort of man who ought to be in a book. He'd be better fun and less bother in a book.'

'What was his theory?' asked the other.

'Oh, it was full of pep,' replied Fiennes gloomily. 'It would have been glorious copy if it could have held together for ten minutes longer. He said the Colonel was still alive when they found him in the summer house, and the doctor killed him with the surgical instrument on pretence of cutting the clothes.'

'I see,' said the priest. 'I suppose he was lying flat on his face on the mud floor as a form of siesta.'

'It's wonderful what hustle will do,' continued his informant. 'I believe Floyd would have got his great theory into the papers at any rate, and perhaps had the doctor arrested, when all these things were blown sky high as if by dynamite by the discovery of that dead body lying under the Rock of Fortune. And that's what we come back to after all. I suppose the suicide is almost a confession. But nobody will ever know the whole story.'

There was a silence, and then the priest said modestly: 'I rather think I know the whole story.'

Fiennes stared. 'But look here,' he cried; 'how do you come to know the whole story, or to be sure it's the true story? You've been sitting here a hundred miles away writing a sermon; do you mean to tell me you really know what happened already? If you've really come to the end, where in the world do you begin? What started you off with your own story?'

Father Brown jumped up with a very unusual excitement and his first exclamation was like an explosion.

'The dog!' he cried. 'The dog, of course! You had the whole story in your hands in the business of the dog on the beach, if you'd only noticed the dog properly.'

Fiennes stared still more. 'But you told me before that my feelings about the dog were all nonsense and the dog had nothing to do with it.'

'The dog had everything to do with it,' said Father Brown, 'as you'd have found out if you'd only treated the dog as a dog, and not as God Almighty judging the souls of men.'

He paused in an embarrassed way for a moment, and then said, with a rather pathetic air of apology: 'The truth is, I happen to be awfully fond of dogs. And it seemed to me that in all this lurid halo of dog superstitions nobody was really thinking about the poor dog at all. To begin with a small point, about his barking at the lawyer or growling at the secretary. You asked how I could guess things a hundred miles away; but honestly it's mostly to your credit, for you described people so well that I know the types. A man like Traill, who frowns usually and smiles suddenly, a man who fiddles with things, especially at his throat, is a nervous, easily embarrassed man. I shouldn't wonder if Floyd, the efficient secretary, is nervy and jumpy, too; those Yankee hustlers often are. Otherwise he wouldn't have cut his fingers on the shears and dropped them when he heard Janet Druce scream.

'Now dogs hate nervous people. I don't know whether they make the dog nervous, too; for whether, being after all a brute, he is a bit of a bully; or whether his canine vanity (which is colossal) is simply offended at not being liked. But anyhow there was nothing in poor Nox protesting against those people, except that he disliked them for being afraid of him. Now I know you're awfully clever, and nobody of sense sneers at cleverness. But I sometimes fancy, for instance, that you are too clever to understand animals. Sometimes you are too clever to understand men, especially when they act almost as simply as animals. Animals are very literal; they live in a world of truisms. Take this case: a dog barks at a man and a man runs away from a dog. Now you do not seem to be quite simple enough to see the fact: that the dog barked because he disliked the man and the man fled because he was frightened of the dog. They had no other motives and they needed none; but you must read psychological mysteries into it and suppose the dog had super-normal vision, and was a mysterious mouthpiece of doom. You must suppose the man was running away, not from the dog but from the hangman. And yet if you come to think of it, all this deeper psychology is exceedingly improbable. If the dog really could completely and consciously realize the murderer of his master he wouldn't stand yapping as he might at a curate at a tea-party; he's much more likely to fly at his throat. And on the other hand, do you really think a man who had hardened his heart to murder an old friend and then walk about smiling at the old friend's family, under the eyes of his old friend's daughter and post-mortem doctor – do you think a man like that would be doubled up by mere remorse because a dog barked? He might feel the tragic irony of it; it might shake his soul, like any other tragic trifle. But he wouldn't rush madly the length of a garden to escape from the only witness whom he knew to be unable to talk. People have a panic like that when they are frightened, not of tragic ironies, but of teeth. The whole thing is simpler than you can understand.

'But when we come to that business by the seashore, things are much more interesting. As you stated them, they were much more puzzling. I didn't understand that tale of the dog going in and out of the water; it didn't seem to me a doggy thing to do. If Nox had been very much upset about something else, he might possibly have refused to go after the stick at all. He'd probably go off nosing in whatever direction he suspected the mischief. But when once a dog is actually chasing a thing, a stone or a stick or a rabbit, my experience is that he won't stop for anything but the most peremptory command, and not always for that. That he should turn round because his mood changed seems to me unthinkable.'

'But he did turn round,' insisted Fiennes; 'and came back without the stick.'

'He came back without the stick for the best reason in the world,' replied the priest. 'He came back because he couldn't find it. He whined because he couldn't find it. That's the sort of thing a dog really does whine about. A dog is a devil of a ritualist. He is as particular about the precise routine of a game as a child about the precise repetition of a fairy-tale. In this case something had gone wrong with the game. He came back to complain seriously of the conduct of the stick. Never had such a thing happened before. Never had an eminent and distinguished dog been so treated by a rotten old walking-stick.'

'Why, what had the walking-stick done?' inquired the young man.

'It had sunk,' said Father Brown.

Fiennes said nothing, but continued to stare; and it was the priest who continued:

'It had sunk because it was not really a stick, but a rod of steel with a very thin shell of cane and a sharp point. In other words, it was a sword-stick. I suppose a murderer never gets rid of a bloody weapon so oddly and yet so naturally as by throwing it into the sea for a retriever.'

'I begin to see what you mean,' admitted Fiennes; 'but even if a sword-stick was used, I have no guess of how it was used.'

'I had a sort of guess,' said Father Brown, 'right at the beginning when you said the word summer house. And another when you said that Druce wore a white coat. As long as everybody was looking for a short dagger, nobody thought of it; but if we admit a rather long blade like a rapier, it's not so impossible.'

He was leaning back, looking at the ceiling, and began like one going back to his own first thoughts and fundamentals.

'All that discussion about detective stories like the Yellow Room, about a man found dead in sealed chambers which no one could enter, does not apply to the present case, because it is a summer house. When we talk of a Yellow Room, or any room, we imply walls that are really homogeneous and impenetrable. But a summer house is not made like that; it is often made, as it was in this case, of closely interlaced but separate boughs and strips of wood, in which there are chinks here and there. There was one of them just behind Druce's back as he sat in his chair up against the wall. But just as the room was a summer house, so the chair was a basket-chair. That also was a lattice of loopholes. Lastly, the summer-house was close up under the hedge; and you have just told me that it was really a thin hedge. A man standing outside it could easily see, amid a network of twigs and branches and canes, one white spot of the Colonel's coat as plain as the white of a target.

'Now, you left the geography a little vague; but it was possible to put two and two together. You said the Rock of Fortune was not really high; but you also said it could be seen dominating the garden like a mountain-peak. In other words, it was very near the end of the garden, though your walk had taken you a long way round to it. Also, it isn't likely the young lady really howled so as to be heard half a mile. She gave an ordinary involuntary cry, and yet you heard it on the shore. And among other interesting things that you told me, may I remind you that you said Harry Druce had fallen behind to light his pipe under a hedge.'

Fiennes shuddered slightly. 'You mean he drew his blade there and sent it through the hedge at the white spot. But surely it was a very odd chance and a very sudden choice. Besides, he couldn't be certain the old man's money had passed to him, and as a fact it hadn't.'

Father Brown's face became animated.

'You misunderstand the man's character,' he said, as if he himself had known the man all his life. 'A curious but not unknown type of character. If he had really *known* the money would come to him, I seriously believe he wouldn't have done it. He would have seen it as the dirty thing it was.'

'Isn't that rather paradoxical?' asked the other.

'This man was a gambler,' said the priest, 'and a man in disgrace for having taken risks and anticipated orders. It was probably for something pretty unscrupulous, for every imperial police is more like a Russian secret police than we like to think. But he had gone beyond the line and failed. Now, the temptation of that type of man is to do a mad thing precisely because the risk will be wonderful in retrospect. He wants to say, "Nobody but I could have seized that chance or seen that it was then or never. What a wild and wonderful guess it was, when I put all those things together; Donald in disgrace; and the lawyer being sent for; and Herbert and I sent for at the same time – and then nothing more but the way the old man grinned at me and shook hands. Anybody would say I was mad to risk it; but that is how fortunes are made, by the man mad enough to have a little foresight." In short, it is the vanity of guessing. It is the megalomania of the gambler. The more incongruous the coincidence, the more instantaneous the decision, the more likely he is to snatch the chance. The accident, the very triviality of the white speck and the hole in the hedge intoxicated him like a vision of the world's desire. Nobody clever enough to see such a combination of accidents could be cowardly enough not to use them! That is how the devil talks to the gambler. But the devil himself would hardly have induced that unhappy man to go down in a dull, deliberate way and kill an old uncle from whom he'd always had expectations. It would be too respectable.'

He paused a moment, and then went on with a certain quiet emphasis.

'And now try to call up the scene, even as you saw it yourself. As he stood there, dizzy with his diabolical opportunity, he looked up and saw that strange outline that might have been the image of his own tottering soul; the one great crag poised perilously on the other like a pyramid on its point, and remembered that it was called the Rock of Fortune. Can you guess how such a man at such a moment would read such a signal? I think it strung him up to action and even to vigilance. He who would be a tower must not fear to be a toppling tower. Anyhow, he acted; his next difficulty was to cover his tracks. To be found with a sword-stick, let alone a blood-stained sword-stick, would be fatal in the search that was certain to follow. If he left it anywhere, it would be found and probably traced. Even if he threw it into the sea the action might be noticed, and thought noticeable – unless indeed he could think of some more natural way of covering the action. As you know, he did think of one, and a very good one. Being the only one of you with a watch, he told you it was not yet time to return, strolled a little farther and started the game of throwing in sticks for the retriever. But how his eyes must have rolled darkly over all that desolate sea-shore before they alighted on the dog!'

Fiennes nodded, gazing thoughtfully into space. His mind seemed to have drifted back to a less practical part of the narrative.

'It's queer,' he said, 'that the dog really was in the story after all.'

'The dog could almost have told you the story, if he could talk,' said the priest. 'All I complain of is that because he couldn't talk, you made up his story for him, and made him talk with the tongues of men and angels. It's part of something I've noticed more and more in the modern world, appearing in all sorts of newspaper rumours and conversational catchwords; something that's arbitrary without being authoritative. People readily swallow the untested claims of this, that, or the other. It's drowning all your old rationalism and scepticism, it's coming in like a sea; and the name of it is superstition.' He stood up abruptly, his face heavy with a sort of frown, and went on talking almost as if he were alone. 'It's the first effect of not believing in God that you lose your common sense and can't see things as they are. Anything that anybody talks about, and says there's a good deal in it, extends itself indefinitely like a vista in a nightmare. And a dog is an omen, and a cat is a mystery, and a pig is a mascot and a beetle is a scarab, calling up all the menagerie of polytheism from Egypt and old India; Dog Anubis and great green-eyed Pasht and all the holy howling Bulls of Bashan; reeling back to the bestial gods of the beginning, escaping into elephants and snakes and crocodiles; and all because you are frightened of four words: "He was made Man".'

The young man got up with a little embarrassment, almost as if he had overheard a soliloquy. He called to the dog and left the room with vague but breezy farewells. But he had to call the dog twice, for the dog had remained behind quite motionless for a moment, looking up steadily at Father Brown as the wolf looked at St Francis.

4
The Miracle of Moon Crescent

Moon Crescent was meant in a sense to be as romantic as its name; and the things that happened there were romantic enough in their way. At least it had been an expression of that genuine element of sentiment – historic and almost heroic – which manages to remain side by side with commercialism in the elder cities on the eastern coast of America. It was originally a curve of classical architecture really recalling that eighteenth-century atmosphere in which men like Washington and Jefferson had seemed to be all the more republicans for being aristocrats. Travellers faced with the recurrent query of what they thought of our city were understood to be specially answerable for what they thought of our Moon Crescent. The very contrasts that confuse its original harmony were characteristic of its survival. At one extremity or horn of the crescent its last windows looked over an enclosure like a strip of a gentleman's park, with trees and hedges as formal as a Queen Anne garden. But immediately round the corner, the other windows, even of the same rooms, or rather 'apartments', looked out on the blank, unsightly wall of a huge warehouse attached to some ugly industry. The apartments of Moon Crescent itself were at that end remodelled on the monotonous pattern of an American hotel, and rose to a height, which, though lower than the colossal warehouse, would have been called a skyscraper in London. But the colonnade that ran round the whole frontage upon the street had a grey and weather-stained stateliness suggesting that the ghosts of the Fathers of the Republic might still be walking to and fro in it. The insides of the rooms, however, were as neat and new as the last New York fittings could make them, especially at the northern end between the neat garden and the blank warehouse wall. They were a system of very small flats, as we should say in England, each consisting of a sitting-room, bedroom, and bathroom, as identical as the hundred cells of a hive. In one of these the celebrated Warren Wynd sat at his desk sorting letters and scattering orders with wonderful rapidity and exactitude. He could only be compared to a tidy whirlwind.

Warren Wynd was a very little man with loose grey hair and a pointed beard, seemingly frail but fierily active. He had very wonderful eyes, brighter than stars and stronger than magnets, which nobody who had ever seen them could easily forget. And indeed in his work as a reformer and regulator of many good works he had shown at least that he had a pair of eyes in his head. All sorts of stories and even legends were told of the miraculous rapidity with which he could form a sound judgement, especially of human character. It was said that he selected the wife who worked with him so long in so charitable a fashion, by picking her out of a whole regiment of women in uniform marching past at some official celebration, some said of the Girl Guides and some of the Women Police. Another story was told of how three tramps, indistinguishable from each other in their community of filth and rags, had presented themselves before him asking for charity. Without a moment's hesitation he had sent one of them to a particular hospital devoted to a certain nervous disorder, had recommended the second to an inebriates' home, and had engaged the third at a handsome salary as his own private servant, a position which he filled successfully for years afterwards. There were, of course, the inevitable anecdotes of his prompt criticisms and curt repartees when brought in contact with Roosevelt, with Henry Ford, and with Mrs Asquith and all other persons with whom an American public man ought to have a historic interview, if only in the newspapers. Certainly he was not likely to be overawed by such personages; and at the moment here in question he continued very calmly his centrifugal whirl of papers, though the man confronting him was a personage of almost equal importance.

Silas T. Vandam, the millionaire and oil magnate, was a lean man with a long, yellow face and blue-black hair, colours which were the less conspicuous yet somehow the more sinister because his face and figure showed dark against the window and the white warehouse wall outside it; he was buttoned up tight in an elegant overcoat with strips of astrachan. The eager face and brilliant eyes of Wynd, on the other hand, were in the full light from the other window over-looking the little garden, for his chair and desk stood facing it; and though the face was preoccupied, it did not seem unduly preoccupied about the millionaire. Wynd's valet or personal servant, a big, powerful man with flat fair hair, was standing behind his master's desk holding a sheaf of letters; and Wynd's private secretary, a neat, red-haired youth with a sharp face, had his hand already on the door handle, as if guessing some purpose or obeying some gesture of his employer. The room was not only neat, but austere to the point of emptiness; for Wynd, with characteristic thoroughness, had rented the whole floor above, and turned it into a loft or storeroom, where all his other papers and possessions were stacked in boxes and corded bales.

'Give these to the floor-clerk, Wilson,' said Wynd to the servant holding the letters, 'and then get me the pamphlet on the Minneapolis Night Clubs; you'll find it in the bundle marked "G". I shall want it in half an hour, but don't disturb me till then. Well, Mr Vandam, I think your proposition sounds very promising; but I can't give a final answer till I've seen the report. It ought to reach me tomorrow afternoon, and I'll 'phone you at once. I'm sorry I can't say anything more definite just now.'

Mr Vandam seemed to feel that this was something like a polite dismissal; and his sallow, saturnine face suggested that he found a certain irony in the fact.

'Well, I suppose I must be going,' he said.

'Very good of you to call, Mr Vandam,' said Wynd, politely; 'you will excuse my not coming out, as I've something here I must fix at once. Fenner,' he added to the secretary, 'show Mr Vandam to his car, and don't come back again for half an hour. I've something here I want to work out by myself; after that I shall want you.'

The three men went out into the hallway together, closing the door behind them. The big servant, Wilson, was turning down the hallway in the direction of the floor-clerk, and the other two moving in the opposite direction towards the lift; for Wynd's apartment was high up on the fourteenth floor. They had hardly gone a yard from the closed door when they became conscious that the corridor was filled with a marching and even magnificent figure. The man was very tall and broad-shouldered, his bulk being the more conspicuous for being clad in white, or a light grey that looked like it, with a very wide white panama hat and an almost equally wide fringe or halo of almost equally white hair. Set in this aureole his face was strong and handsome, like that of a Roman emperor, save that there was something more than boyish, something a little childish, about the brightness of his eyes and the beatitude of his smile.

'Mr Warren Wynd in?' he asked, in hearty tones.

'Mr Warren Wynd is engaged,' said Fenner; 'he must not be disturbed on any account. I may say I am his secretary and can take any message.'

'Mr Warren Wynd is not at home to the Pope or the Crowned Heads,' said Vandam, the oil magnate, with sour satire. 'Mr Warren Wynd is mighty particular. I went in there to hand him over a trifle of twenty thousand dollars on certain conditions, and he told me to call again like as if I was a call-boy.'

'It's a fine thing to be a boy,' said the stranger, 'and a finer to have a call; and I've got a call he's just got to listen to. It's a call out of the great good country out West, where the real American is being made while you're all snoring. Just tell him that Art Alboin of Oklahoma City has come to convert him.'

'I tell you nobody can see him,' said the red-haired secretary sharply. 'He has given orders that he is not to be disturbed for half an hour.'

'You folks down East are all against being disturbed,' said the breezy Mr Alboin, 'but I calculate there's a big breeze getting up in the West that will have to disturb you. He's been figuring out how much money must go to this and that stuffy old religion; but I tell you any scheme that leaves out the new Great Spirit movement in Texas and Oklahoma, is leaving out the religion of the future.'

'Oh; I've sized up those religions of the future,' said the millionaire, contemptuously. 'I've been through them with a tooth-comb; and they're as mangy as yellow dog. There was that woman called herself Sophia: ought to have called herself Sapphira, I reckon. Just a plum fraud. Strings tied to all the tables and tambourines. Then there were the Invisible Life bunch; said they could vanish when they liked, and they did vanish, too, and a hundred thousand of my dollars vanished with them. I knew Jupiter Jesus out in Denver; saw him for weeks on end; and he was just a common crook. So was the Patagonian Prophet; you bet he's made a bolt for Patagonia. No, I'm through with all that; from now on I only believe what I see. I believe they call it being an atheist.'

'I guess you got me wrong,' said the man from Oklahoma, almost eagerly. 'I guess I'm as much of an atheist as you are. No supernatural or superstitious stuff in our movement; just plain science. The only real right science is just health, and the only real right health is just breathing. Fill your lungs with the wide air of the prairie and you could blow all your old eastern cities into the sea. You could just puff away their biggest men like thistledown. That's what we do in the new movement out home: we breathe. We don't pray; we breathe.'

'Well; I suppose you do,' said the secretary, wearily. He had a keen, intelligent face which could hardly conceal the weariness; but he had listened to the two monologues with the admirable patience and polite-ness (so much in contrast with the legends of impatience and insolence) with which such monologues are listened to in America.

'Nothing supernatural,' continued Alboin, 'just the great natural fact behind all the supernatural fancies. What did the Jews want with a God except to breathe into man's nostrils the breath of life? We do the breathing into our own nostrils out in Oklahoma. What's the meaning of the very word Spirit? It's just the Greek for breathing exercises. Life, progress, prophecy; it's all breath.'

'Some would allow it's all wind,' said Vandam; 'but I'm glad you've got rid of the divinity stunt, anyhow.'

The keen face of the secretary, rather pale against his red hair, showed a flicker of some odd feeling suggestive of a secret bitterness.

'I'm not glad,' he said, 'I'm just sure. You seem to like being atheists; so you may be just believing what you like to believe. But I wish to God there were a God; and there ain't. It's just my luck.'

Without a sound or stir they all became almost creepily conscious at this moment that the group, halted outside Wynd's door, had silently grown from three figures to four. How long the fourth figure had stood there none of the earnest disputants could tell, but he had every appearance of waiting respectfully and even timidly for the opportunity to say something urgent. But to their nervous sensibility he seemed to have sprung up suddenly and silently like a mushroom. And indeed, he looked rather like a big, black mushroom, for he was quite short and his small, stumpy figure was eclipsed by his big, black clerical hat; the resemblance might have been more complete if mushrooms were in the habit of carrying umbrellas, even of a shabby and shapeless sort.

Fenner, the secretary, was conscious of a curious additional surprise at recognizing the figure of a priest; but when the priest turned up a round face under the round hat and innocently asked for Mr Warren Wynd, he gave the regular negative answer rather more curtly than before. But the priest stood his ground.

'I do really want to see Mr Wynd,' he said. 'It seems odd, but that's exactly what I do want to do. I don't want to speak to him. I just want to see him. I just want to see if he's there to be seen.'

'Well, I tell you he's there and can't be seen,' said Fenner, with increasing annoyance. 'What do you mean by saying you want to see if he's there to be seen? Of course he's there. We all left him there five minutes ago, and we've stood outside this door ever since.'

'Well, I want to see if he's all right,' said the priest.

'Why?' demanded the secretary, in exasperation.

'Because I have a serious, I might say solemn, reason,' said the cleric, gravely, 'for doubting whether he is all right.'

'Oh, Lord!' cried Vandam, in a sort of fury; 'not more superstitions.'

'I see I shall have to give my reasons,' observed the little cleric, gravely. 'I suppose I can't expect you even to let me look through the crack of a door till I tell you the whole story.'

He was silent a moment as in reflection, and then went on without noticing the wondering faces around him. 'I was walking outside along the front of the colonnade when I saw a very ragged man running hard round the corner at the end of the crescent. He came pounding along the pavement towards me, revealing a great raw-boned figure and a face I knew. It was the face of a wild Irish fellow I once helped a little; I will not tell you his name. When he saw me he staggered, calling me by mine and saying, "Saints alive, it's Father Brown; you're the only man whose face could frighten me to-day." I knew he meant he'd been doing some wild thing or other, and I don't think my face frightened him much, for he was soon telling me about it. And a very strange thing it was. He asked me if I knew Warren Wynd, and I said no, though I knew he lived near the top of these flats. He said, "That's a man who thinks he's a saint of God; but if he knew what I was saying of him he should be ready to hang himself." And he repeated hysterically more than once, "Yes, ready to hang himself." I asked him if he'd done any harm to Wynd, and his answer was rather a queer one. He said: "I took

a pistol and I loaded it with neither shot nor slug, but only with a curse."
As far as I could make out, all he had done was to go down that little
alley between this building and the big warehouse, with an old pistol
loaded with a blank charge, and merely fire it against the wall, as if that
would bring down the building. "But as I did it," he said, "I cursed him
with the great curse, that the justice of God should take him by the hair
and the vengeance of hell by the heels, and he should be torn asunder
like Judas and the world know him no more. Well, it doesn't matter
now what else I said to the poor, crazy fellow; he went away quieted
down a little, and I went round to the back of the building to inspect.
And sure enough, in the little alley at the foot of this wall there lay a
rusty antiquated pistol; I know enough about pistols to know it had been
loaded only with a little powder; there were the black marks of powder
and smoke on the wall, and even the mark of the muzzle, but not even
a dent of any bullet. He had left no trace of destruction; he had left no
trace of anything, except those black marks and that black curse he had
hurled into heaven. So I came back here to ask for this Warren Wynd
and find out if he's all right.'

Fenner the secretary laughed. 'I can soon settle that difficulty for
you. I assure you he's quite all right; we left him writing at his desk only
a few minutes ago. He was alone in his flat; it's a hundred feet up from
the street, and so placed that no shot could have reached him, even if
your friend hadn't fired blank. There's no other entrance to this place
but this door, and we've been standing outside it ever since.'

'All the same,' said Father Brown, gravely, 'I should like to look in
and see.'

'Well, you can't,' retorted the other. 'Good Lord, you don't tell me
you think anything of the curse.'

'You forget,' said the millionaire, with a slight sneer, 'the reverend
gentleman's whole business is blessings and cursings. Come, sir, if he's
been cursed to hell, why don't you bless him back again? What's the
good of your blessings if they can't beat an Irish larrykin's curse.'

'Does anybody believe such things now?' protested the Westerner.

'Father Brown believes a good number of things, I take it,' said
Vandam, whose temper was suffering from the past snub and the
present bickering. 'Father Brown believes a hermit crossed a river on a
crocodile conjured out of nowhere, and then he told the crocodile to

159

die, and it sure did. Father Brown believes that some blessed saint or other died, and had his dead body turned into three dead bodies, to be served out to three parishes that were all bent on figuring as his home-town. Father Brown believes that a saint hung his cloak on a sunbeam, and another used his for a boat to cross the Atlantic. Father Brown believes the holy donkey had six legs and the house at Loretto flew through the air. He believes in hundreds of stone virgins winking and weeping all day long. It's nothing to him to believe that a man might escape through the keyhole or vanish out of a locked room. I reckon he doesn't take much stock of the laws of nature.'

'Anyhow, I have to take stock in the laws of Warren Wynd,' said the secretary, wearily, 'and it's his rule that he's to be left alone when he says so. Wilson will tell you just the same,' for the large servant who had been sent for the pamphlet, passed placidly down the corridor even as he spoke, carrying the pamphlet, but serenely passing the door. 'He'll go and sit on the bench by the floor-clerk and twiddle his thumbs till he's wanted; but he won't go in before then; and nor will I. I reckon we both know which side our bread is buttered, and it'd take a good many of Father Brown's saints and angels to make us forget it.'

'As for saints and angels –' began the priest.

'It's all nonsense,' repeated Fenner. 'I don't want to say anything offensive, but that sort of thing may be very well for crypts and cloisters and all sorts of moonshiny places. But ghosts can't get through a closed door in an American hotel.'

'But men can open a door, even in an American hotel,' replied Father Brown, patiently. 'And it seems to me the simplest thing would be to open it.'

'It would be simple enough to lose me my job,' answered the secretary, 'and Warren Wynd doesn't like his secretaries so simple as that. Not simple enough to believe in the sort of fairy tales you seem to believe in.'

'Well,' said the priest gravely, 'it is true enough that I believe in a good many things that you probably don't. But it would take a considerable time to explain all the things I believe in, and all the reasons I have for thinking I'm right. It would take about two seconds to open that door and prove I am wrong.'

Something in the phrase seemed to please the more wild and restless spirit of the man from the West.

'I'll allow I'd love to prove you wrong,' said Alboin, striding suddenly past them, 'and I will.'

He threw open the door of the flat and looked in. The first glimpse showed that Warren Wynd's chair was empty. The second glance showed that his room was empty also.

Fenner, electrified with energy in his turn, dashed past the other into the apartment.

'He's in his bedroom,' he said curtly, 'he must be.'

As he disappeared into the inner chamber the other men stood in the empty outer room staring about them. The severity and simplicity of its fittings, which had already been noted, returned on them with a rigid challenge. Certainly in this room there was no question of hiding a mouse, let alone a man. There were no curtains and, what is rare in American arrangements, no cupboards. Even the desk was no more than a plain table with a shallow drawer and a tilted lid. The chairs were hard and high-backed skeletons. A moment after the secretary reappeared at the inner door, having searched the two inner rooms. A staring negation stood in his eyes, and his mouth seemed to move in a mechanical detachment from it as he said sharply: 'He didn't come out through here?'

Somehow the others did not even think it necessary to answer that negation in the negative. Their minds had come up against something like the blank wall of the warehouse that stared in at the opposite window, gradually turning from white to grey as dusk slowly descended with the advancing afternoon. Vandam walked over to the window-sill against which he had leant half an hour before and looked out of the open window. There was no pipe or fire-escape, no shelf or foothold of any kind on the sheer fall to the little by-street below, there was nothing on the similar expanse of wall that rose many storeys above. There was even less variation on the other side of the street; there was nothing whatever but the wearisome expanse of whitewashed wall. He peered downwards, as if expecting to see the vanished philanthropist lying in a suicidal wreck on the path. He could see nothing but one small dark object which, though diminished by distance, might well be the pistol that the priest had found lying there. Meanwhile, Fenner had walked to the other window, which looked out from a wall equally blank and inaccessible, but looking out over a small ornamental park instead of a side street. Here a clump of trees interrupted the actual view of the ground; but they reached but a little way up the huge human cliff. Both turned back into the room and faced each other in the gathering twilight where the last silver gleams of daylight on the shiny tops of desks and tables were rapidly turning grey. As if the twilight itself irritated him, Fenner touched the switch and the scene sprang into the startling distinctness of electric light.

'As you said just now,' said Vandam grimly, 'there's no shot from down there could hit him, even if there was a shot in the gun. But even if he was hit with a bullet he wouldn't have just burst like a bubble.'

The secretary, who was paler than ever, glanced irritably at the bilious visage of the millionaire.

'What's got you started on those morbid notions? Who's talking about bullets and bubbles? Why shouldn't he be alive?'

'Why not indeed?' replied Vandam smoothly. 'If you'll tell me where he is, I'll tell you how he got there.'

After a pause the secretary muttered, rather sulkily: 'I suppose you're right. We're right up against the very thing we were talking about. It'd be a queer thing if you or I ever came to think there was anything in cursing. But who could have harmed Wynd shut up in here?'

Mr Alboin, of Oklahoma, had been standing rather astraddle in the middle of the room, his white, hairy halo as well as his round eyes, seeming to radiate astonishment. At this point he said, abstractedly, with something of the irrelevant impudence of an *enfant terrible*:

'You didn't cotton to him much, did you, Mr Vandam?'

Mr Vandam's long yellow face seemed to grow longer as it grew more sinister, while he smiled and answered quietly:

'If it comes to these coincidences, it was you, I think, who said that a wind from the West would blow away our big men like thistledown.'

'I know I said it would,' said the Westerner, with candour; 'but all the same, how the devil could it?'

The silence was broken by Fenner saying with an abruptness amounting to violence:

'There's only one thing to say about this affair. It simply hasn't happened. It can't have happened.'

'Oh, yes,' said Father Brown out of the corner; 'it has happened all right.'

They all jumped; for the truth was they had all forgotten the insignificant little man who had originally induced them to open the door. And the recovery of memory went with a sharp reversal of mood; it came back to them with a rush that they had all dismissed him as a superstitious dreamer for even hinting at the very thing that had since happened before their eyes.

'Snakes!' cried the impetuous Westerner, like one speaking before he could stop himself; 'suppose there were something in it, after all!'

'I must confess,' said Fenner, frowning at the table, 'that his reverence's anticipations were apparently well founded. I don't know whether he has anything else to tell us.'

'He might possibly tell us,' said Vandam, sardonically, 'what the devil we are to do now.'

The little priest seemed to accept the position in a modest, but matter-of-fact manner. 'The only thing I can think of,' he said, 'is first to tell the authorities of this place, and then to see if there were any more traces of my man who let off the pistol. He vanished round the other end of the Crescent where the little garden is. There are seats there, and it's a favourite place for tramps.'

Direct consultations with the headquarters of the hotel, leading to indirect consultations with the authorities of the police, occupied them for a considerable time; and it was already nightfall when they went out under the long, classical curve of the colonnade. The crescent looked as cold and hollow as the moon after which it was named, and the moon itself was rising luminous but spectral behind the black tree-tops when they turned the corner by the little public garden. Night veiled much of what was merely urban and artificial about the place; and as they melted into the shadows of the trees they had a strange feeling of having suddenly travelled many hundred miles from their homes. When they had walked in silence for a little, Alboin, who had something elemental about him, suddenly exploded.

'I give up,' he cried; 'I hand in my checks. I never thought I should come to such things; but what happens when the things come to you? I beg your pardon, Father Brown; I reckon I'll just come across, so far as you and your fairy-tales are concerned. After this, it's me for the fairy-tales. Why, you said yourself, Mr Vandam, that you're an atheist and only believe what you see. Well, what was it you did see? Or rather, what was it you didn't see?'

'I know,' said Vandam and nodded in a gloomy fashion.

'Oh, it's partly all this moon and trees that get on one's nerves,' said Fenner obstinately. 'Trees always look queer by moonlight, with their branches crawling about. Look at that – '

'Yes,' said Father Brown, standing still and peering at the moon through a tangle of trees. 'That's a very queer branch up there.'

When he spoke again he only said:

'I thought it was a broken branch.'

But this time there was a catch in his voice that unaccountably turned his hearers cold. Something that looked rather like a dead branch was certainly dependent in a limp fashion from the tree that showed dark against the moon; but it was not a dead branch. When they came close to it to see what it was, Fenner sprang away again with a ringing oath. Then he ran in again and loosened a rope from the neck of the dingy little body dangling with drooping plumes of grey hair. Somehow he knew that the body was a dead body before he managed to take it down from the tree. A very long coil of rope was wrapped round and round the branches, and a comparatively short length of it hung from the fork of the branch to the body. A long garden tub was rolled a yard or so from under the feet, like the stool kicked away from the feet of a suicide.

'Oh, my God!' said Alboin, so that it seemed as much a prayer as an oath. 'What was it that man said about him? – "If he knew, he would be ready to hang himself." Wasn't that what he said, Father Brown?'

'Yes,' said Father Brown.

'Well,' said Vandam in a hollow voice, 'I never thought to see or say such a thing. But what can one say except that the curse has worked?'

Fenner was standing with hands covering his face; and the priest laid a hand on his arm and said, gently, 'Were you very fond of him?'

The secretary dropped his hands and his white face was ghastly under the moon.

'I hated him like hell,' he said; 'and if he died by a curse it might have been mine.'

The pressure of the priest's hand on his arm tightened; and the priest said, with an earnestness he had hardly yet shown:

'It wasn't your curse; pray be comforted.'

The police of the district had considerable difficulty in dealing with the four witnesses who were involved in the case. All of them were reputable, and even reliable people in the ordinary sense; and one of them was a person of considerable power and importance: Silas Vandam of the Oil Trust. The first police-officer who tried to express scepticism about his story struck sparks from the steel of that magnate's mind very rapidly indeed.

'Don't you talk to me about sticking to the facts,' said the millionaire with asperity. 'I've stuck to a good many facts before you were born and a few of the facts have stuck to me. I'll give you the facts all right if you've got the sense to take 'em down correctly.'

The policeman in question was youthful and subordinate, and had a hazy idea that the millionaire was too political to be treated as an ordinary citizen; so he passed him and his companions on to a more stolid superior, one Inspector Collins, a grizzled man with a grimly comfortable way of talking; as one who was genial but would stand no nonsense.

'Well, well,' he said, looking at the three figures before him with twinkling eyes, 'this seems to be a funny sort of a tale.'

Father Brown had already gone about his daily business; but Silas Vandam had suspended even the gigantic business of the markets for an hour or so to testify to his remarkable experience. Fenner's business as secretary had ceased in a sense with his employer's life; and the great Art Alboin, having no business in New York or anywhere else except the spreading of the Breath of Life or religion of the Great Spirit, had nothing to draw him away at the moment from the immediate affair. So they stood in a row in the inspector's office, prepared to corroborate each other.

'Now I'd better tell you to start with,' said the inspector cheerfully, 'that it's no good for anybody to come to me with any miraculous stuff. I'm a practical man and a policeman, and that sort of thing is all very well for priests and parsons. This priest of yours seems to have got you all worked up about some story of a dreadful death and judgement; but I'm going to leave him and his religion out of it altogether. If Wynd came out of that room, somebody let him out. And if Wynd was found hanging on that tree, somebody hung him there.'

'Quite so,' said Fenner; 'but as our evidence is that nobody let him out, the question is how could anybody have hung him there?'

'How could anybody have a nose on his face?' asked the inspector. 'He had a nose on his face, and he had a noose round his neck. Those are facts; and, as I say, I'm a practical man and go by the facts. It can't have been done by a miracle, so it must have been done by a man.'

Alboin had been standing rather in the background; and indeed his broad figure seemed to form a natural background to the leaner and more vivacious men in front of him. His white head was bowed with a certain abstraction; but as the inspector said the last sentence, he lifted it, shaking his hoary mane in a leonine fashion, and looking dazed but awakened. He moved forward into the centre of the group, and they had a vague feeling that he was even vaster than before. They had been only too prone to take him for a fool or a mountebank; but he was not altogether wrong when he said that there was in him a certain depth of lungs and life, like a west wind stored up in its strength, which might some day puff lighter things away.

'So you're a practical man, Mr Collins,' he said, in a voice at once soft and heavy. 'It must be the second or third time you've mentioned in this little conversation that you are a practical man; so I can't be mistaken about that. And a very interesting little fact it is, for anybody engaged in writing your life, letters, and table-talk, with portrait at the age of five, daguerreotype of your grandmother and views of the old home-town; and I'm sure your biographer won't forget to mention it along with the fact that you had a pug nose with a pimple on it, and were nearly too fat to walk. And as you're a practical man, perhaps you would just go on practising till you've brought Warren Wynd to life again, and found out exactly how a practical man gets through a deal door. But I think you've got it wrong. You're not a practical man. You're a practical joke; that's what you are. The Almighty was having a bit of fun with us when he thought of you.'

With a characteristic sense of drama he went sailing towards the door before the astonished inspector could reply; and no after-recriminations could rob him of a certain appearance of triumph.

'I think you were perfectly right,' said Fenner. 'If those are practical men, give me priests.'

Another attempt was made to reach an official version of the event when the authorities fully realized who were the backers of the story, and what were the implications of it. Already it had broken out in the Press in its most sensationally and even shamelessly psychic form. Interviews with Vandam on his marvellous adventure, articles about Father Brown and his mystical intuitions, soon led those who feel responsible for guiding the public to wish to guide it into a wiser channel. Next time the inconvenient witnesses were approached in a more indirect and tactful manner. They were told, almost in an airy fashion, that Professor Vair was very much interested in such abnormal experiences; was especially interested in their own astonishing case. Professor Vair was a psychologist of great distinction; he had been known to take a detached interest in criminology; it was only some little time afterwards that they discovered that he was in any way connected with the police.

Professor Vair was a courteous gentleman, quietly dressed in pale grey clothes, with an artistic tie and a fair, pointed beard; he looked more like a landscape painter to anyone not acquainted with a certain special type of don. He had an air not only of courtesy, but of frankness.

'Yes, yes, I know,' he said smiling; 'I can guess what you must have gone through. The police do not shine in inquiries of a psychic sort, do they? Of course, dear old Collins said he only wanted the facts. What an absurd blunder! In a case of this kind we emphatically do *not* only want the facts. It is even more essential to have the fancies.'

'Do you mean,' asked Vandam gravely, 'that all that we call the facts were merely fancies?'

'Not at all,' said the professor, 'I only mean that the police are stupid in thinking they can leave out the psychological element in these things. Well, of course, the psychological element is everything in everything, though it is only just beginning to be understood. To begin with, take the element called personality. Now I have heard of this priest, Father Brown, before; and he is one of the most remarkable men of our time. Men of that sort carry a sort of atmosphere with them; and nobody knows how much his nerves and even his very senses are affected by it for the time being. People are hypnotized – yes, hypnotized; for hypnotism, like everything else, is a matter of degree; it enters slightly into all daily conversation: it is not necessarily conducted by a man in evening-dress on a platform in a public hall. Father Brown's religion has always understood the psychology of atmospheres, and knows how to appeal to everything simultaneously; even, for instance, to the sense of smell. It understands those curious effects produced by music on animals and human beings; it can –'

'Hang it,' protested Fenner, 'you don't think he walked down the corridor carrying a church organ?'

'He knows better than to do that,' said Professor Vair laughing. 'He knows how to concentrate the essence of all these spiritual sounds and sights, and even smells, in a few restrained gestures; in an art or school of manners. He could contrive so to concentrate your minds on the supernatural by his mere presence, that natural things slipped off your minds to left and right unnoticed. Now you know,' he proceeded with a return to cheerful good sense, 'that the more we study it the more queer the whole question of human evidence becomes. There is not one man in twenty who really observes things at all. There is not one man in a hundred who observes them with real precision; certainly not one in a hundred who can first observe, then remember, and finally describe. Scientific experiments have been made again and again showing that men under a strain have thought a door was shut when it was open, or open when it was shut. Men have differed about the number of doors or windows in a wall just in front of them. They have suffered optical illusions in broad daylight. They have done this even without the hypnotic effect of personality; but here we have a very powerful and persuasive personality bent upon fixing only one picture on your minds; the picture of the wild Irish rebel shaking his pistol at the sky and firing that vain volley, whose echoes were the thunders of heaven.'

'Professor,' cried Fenner, 'I'd swear on my deathbed that door never opened.'

'Recent experiments,' went on the professor, quietly, 'have suggested that our consciousness is not continuous, but is a succession of very rapid impressions like a cinema; it is possible that somebody or something may, so to speak, slip in or out between the scenes. It acts only in the instant while the curtain is down. Probably the patter of conjurers and all forms of sleight of hand depend on what we may call these black flashes of blindness between the flashes of sight. Now this priest and preacher of transcendental notions had filled you with a transcendental imagery; the image of the Celt like a Titan shaking the tower with his curse. Probably he accompanied it with some slight but compelling gesture, pointing your eyes and minds in the direction of the unknown destroyer below. Or perhaps something else happened, or somebody else passed by.'

'Wilson, the servant,' grunted Alboin, 'went down the hallway to wait on the bench, but I guess he didn't distract us much.'

'You never know how much,' replied Vair; 'it might have been that or more likely your eyes following some gesture of the priest as he told his tale of magic. It was in one of those black flashes that Mr Warren Wynd slipped out of his door and went to his death. That is the most probable explanation. It is an illustration of the new discovery. The mind is not a continuous line, but rather a dotted line.'

'Very dotted,' said Fenner feebly. 'Not to say dotty.'

'You don't really believe,' asked Vair, 'that your employer was shut up in a room like a box?'

'It's better than believing that I ought to be shut up in a room like a padded cell,' answered Fenner. 'That's what I complain of in your suggestions, professor. I'd as soon believe in a priest who believes in a miracle, as disbelieve in any man having any right to believe in a fact. The priest tells me that a man can appeal to a God I know nothing about to avenge him by the laws of some higher justice that I know nothing about. There's nothing for me to say except that I know nothing about it. But, at least, if the poor Paddy's prayer and pistol could be heard in a higher world, that higher world might act in some way that seems odd to us. But you ask me to disbelieve the facts of this world as they appear to my own five wits. According to you, a whole procession of Irishmen carrying blunderbusses may have walked through this room while we were talking, so long as they took care to tread on the blind spots in our minds. Miracles of the monkish sort, like materializing a crocodile or hanging a cloak on a sunbeam, seem quite sane compared to you.'

'Oh, well,' said Professor Vair, rather curtly, 'if you are resolved to believe in your priest and his miraculous Irishman I can say no more. I'm afraid you have not had an opportunity of studying psychology.'

'No,' said Fenner dryly; 'but I've had an opportunity of studying psychologists.'

And, bowing politely, he led his deputation out of the room and did not speak till he got into the street; then he addressed them rather explosively.

'Raving lunatics!' cried Fenner in a fume. 'What the devil do they think is to happen to the world if nobody knows whether he's seen anything or not? I wish I'd blown his silly head off with a blank charge, and then explained that I did it in a blind flash. Father Brown's miracle may be miraculous or no, but he said it would happen and it did happen. All these blasted cranks can do is to see a thing happen and then say it didn't. Look here, I think we owe it to the padre to testify to his little demonstration. We're all sane, solid men who never believed in anything. We weren't drunk. We weren't devout. It simply happened just as he said it would.'

'I quite agree,' said the millionaire. 'It may be the beginning of mighty big things in the spiritual line; but anyhow, the man who's in the spiritual line himself, Father Brown, has certainly scored over this business.'

A few days afterwards Father Brown received a very polite note signed Silas T. Vandam, and asking him if he could attend at a stated hour at the apartment which was the scene of the disappearance, in order to take steps for the establishment of that marvellous occurrence. The occurrence itself had already begun to break out in the newspapers, and was being taken up everywhere by the enthusiasts of occultism. Father Brown saw the flaring posters inscribed 'Suicide of Vanishing Man', and 'Man's Curse Hangs Philanthropist', as he passed towards Moon Crescent and mounted the steps on the way to the elevator. He found the little group much as he left it, Vandam, Alboin, and the secretary; but there was an entirely new respectfulness and even reverence in their tone towards himself. They were standing by Wynd's desk, on which lay a large paper and writing materials, as they turned to greet him.

'Father Brown,' said the spokesman, who was the white-haired Westerner, somewhat sobered with his responsibility, 'we asked you here in the first place to offer our apologies and our thanks. We recognize that it was you that spotted the spiritual manifestation from the first. We were hard-shell sceptics, all of us; but we realize now that a man must break that shell to get at the great things behind the world. You stand for those things; you stand for that super-normal explanation of things; and we have to hand it to you. And in the second place, we feel that this document would not be complete without your signature. We are notifying the exact facts to the Psychical Research Society, because the newspaper accounts are not what you might call exact. We've stated how the curse was spoken out in the street; how the man was sealed up here in a room like a box; how the curse dissolved him straight into thin air, and in some unthinkable way materialized him as a suicide hoisted on a gallows. That's all we can say about it; but all that we know, and have seen with our own eyes. And as you were the first to believe in the miracle, we all feel that you ought to be the first to sign.'

'No, really,' said Father Brown, in embarrassment. 'I don't think I should like to do that.'

'You mean you'd rather not sign first?'

'I mean I'd rather not sign at all,' said Father Brown, modestly. 'You see, it doesn't quite do for a man in my position to joke about miracles.'

'But it was you who said it was a miracle,' said Alboin, staring.

'I'm so sorry,' said Father Brown; 'I'm afraid there's some mistake. I don't think I ever said it was a miracle. All I said was that it might happen. What you said was that it couldn't happen because it would be a miracle if it did. And then it did. And so you said it was a miracle. But I never said a word about miracles or magic, or anything of the sort from beginning to end.'

'But I thought you believed in miracles,' broke out the secretary.

'Yes,' answered Father Brown, 'I believe in miracles. I believe in man-eating tigers, but I don't see them running about everywhere. If I want any miracles, I know where to get them.'

'I can't understand your taking this line, Father Brown,' said Vandam, earnestly. 'It seems so narrow; and you don't look narrow to me, though you are a parson. Don't you see, a miracle like this will knock all materialism endways? It will just tell the whole world in big print that spiritual powers can work and do work. You'll be serving religion as no parson ever served it yet.'

The priest had stiffened a little and seemed in some strange way clothed with unconscious and impersonal dignity, for all his stumpy figure. 'Well,' he said, 'you wouldn't suggest I should serve religion by what I know to be a lie? I don't know precisely what you mean by the phrase; and, to be quite candid, I'm not sure you do. Lying may be serving religion; I'm sure it's not serving God. And since you are harping so insistently on what I believe, wouldn't it be as well if you had some sort of notion of what it is?'

'I don't think I quite understand,' observed the millionaire, curiously.

'I don't think you do,' said Father Brown, with simplicity. 'You say this thing was done by spiritual powers. What spiritual powers? You don't think the holy angels took him and hung him on a garden tree, do you? And as for the unholy angels – no, no, no. The men who did this did a wicked thing, but they went no further than their own wickedness; they weren't wicked enough to be dealing with spiritual powers. I know something about Satanism, for my sins; I've been forced to know. I know what it is, what it practically always is. It's proud and it's sly. It likes to be superior; it loves to horrify the innocent with things half understood, to make children's flesh creep. That's why it's so fond of mysteries and initiations and secret societies and all the rest of it. Its eyes are turned inwards, and however grand and grave it may look, it's always hiding a small, mad smile.' He shuddered suddenly, as if caught in an icy draught of air. 'Never mind about them; they've got nothing to do with this, believe me. Do you think that poor, wild Irishman of mine, who ran raving down the street, who blurted out half of it when he first saw my face, and ran away for fear he should blurt out more, do you think Satan confides any secrets to him? I admit he joined in a plot, probably in a plot with two other men worse than himself; but for all that, he was just in an everlasting rage when he rushed down the lane and let off his pistol and his curse.'

'But what on earth does all this mean?' demanded Vandam. 'Letting off a toy pistol and a twopenny curse wouldn't do what was done, except by a miracle. It wouldn't make Wynd disappear like a fairy. It wouldn't make him reappear a quarter of a mile away with a rope round his neck.'

'No,' said Father Brown sharply; 'but what would it do?'

'And still I don't follow you,' said the millionaire gravely.

'I say, what would it do?' repeated the priest; showing, for the first time, a sort of animation verging on annoyance. 'You keep on repeating that a blank pistol-shot wouldn't do this and wouldn't do that; that if that was all, the murder wouldn't happen or the miracle wouldn't happen. It doesn't seem to occur to you to ask what would happen. What would happen to you if a lunatic let off a firearm without rhyme or reason right under your window? What's the very first thing that would happen?'

Vandam looked thoughtful. 'I guess I should look out of the window,' he said.

'Yes,' said Father Brown, 'you'd look out of the window. That's the whole story. It's a sad story, but it's finished now; and there were extenuating circumstances.'

'Why should looking out of the window hurt him?' asked Alboin. 'He didn't fall out, or he'd have been found in the lane.'

'No,' said Father Brown, in a low voice. 'He didn't fall. He rose.'

There was something in his voice like the groan of a gong, a note of doom, but otherwise he went on steadily:

'He rose, but not on wings; not on the wings of any holy or unholy angels. He rose at the end of a rope, exactly as you saw him in the garden: a noose dropped over the head the moment it was poked out of the window. Don't you remember Wilson, that big servant of his, a man of huge strength, while Wynd was the lightest of little shrimps? Didn't Wilson go to the floor above to get a pamphlet, to a room full of luggage corded in coils and coils of rope? Has Wilson been seen since that day? I fancy not.'

'Do you mean,' asked the secretary, 'that Wilson whisked him clean out of his own window like a trout on a line?'

'Yes,' said the other, 'and let him down again out of the other window into the park, where the third accomplice hooked him on to a tree. Remember the lane was always empty; remember the wall opposite was quite blank; remember it was all over in five minutes after the Irishman gave the signal with the pistol. There were three of them in it of course; and I wonder whether you can all guess who they were.'

They were all three staring at the plain, square window and the blank, white wall beyond; and nobody answered.

'By the way,' went on Father Brown, 'don't think I blame you for jumping to preternatural conclusions. The reason's very simple, really. You all swore you were hard-shelled materialists; and as a matter of fact you were all balanced on the very edge of belief – of belief in almost anything. There are thousands balanced on it to-day; but it's a sharp, uncomfortable edge to sit on. You won't rest till you believe something; that's why Mr Vandam went through new religions with a tooth-comb, and Mr Alboin quotes Scripture for his religion of breathing exercises, and Mr Fenner grumbles at the very God he denies. That's where you all split; it's natural to believe in the supernatural. It never feels natural to accept only natural things. But though it wanted only a touch to tip you into preternaturalism about these things, these things really were only natural things. They were not only natural, they were almost unnaturally simple. I suppose there never was quite so simple a story as this.'

Fenner laughed and then looked puzzled. 'I don't understand one thing,' he said. 'If it was Wilson, how did Wynd come to have a man like that on such intimate terms? How did he come to be killed by a man he'd seen every day for years? He was famous as being a judge of men.'

Father Brown thumped his umbrella on the ground with an emphasis he rarely showed.

'Yes,' he said, almost fiercely; 'that was how he came to be killed. He was killed for just that. He was killed for being a judge of men.'

They all stared at him, but he went on, almost as if they were not there.

'What is any man that he should be a judge of men?' he demanded. 'These three were the tramps that once stood before him and were dismissed rapidly right and left to one place or another; as if for them there were no cloak of courtesy, no stages of intimacy, no free-will in friendship. And twenty years has not exhausted the indignation born of that unfathomable insult in that moment when he dared to know them at a glance.'

'Yes,' said the secretary; 'I understand . . . and I understand how it is that you understand – all sorts of things.'

'Well, I'm blamed if I understand,' cried the breezy Western gentleman boisterously. 'Your Wilson and your Irishman seem to be just a couple of cut-throat murderers who killed their benefactor. I've no use for a black and bloody assassin of that sort in my morality, whether it's religion or not.'

'He was a black and bloody assassin, no doubt,' said Fenner, quietly. 'I'm not defending him; but I suppose it's Father Brown's business to pray for all men, even for a man like –'

'Yes,' assented Father Brown, 'it's my business to pray for all men, even for a man like Warren Wynd.'

5
The Dagger with Wings

Father Brown, at one period of his life, found it difficult to hang his hat on a hat-peg without repressing a slight shudder. The origin of this idiosyncrasy was indeed a mere detail in much more complicated events; but it was perhaps the only detail that remained to him in his busy life to remind him of the whole business. Its remote origin was to be found in the fact which led Dr Boyne, the medical officer attached to the police force, to send for the priest on a particular frosty morning in December.

Dr Boyne was a big dark Irishman, one of those rather baffling Irishmen to be found all over the world, who will talk scientific scepticism, materialism and cynicism at length and at large, but who never dream of referring anything touching the ritual of religion to anything except the traditional religion of their native land. It would be hard to say whether their creed is a very superficial varnish or a very fundamental substratum; but most probably it is both, with a mass of materialism in between. Anyhow, when he thought that matters of that sort might be involved, he asked Father Brown to call, though he made no pretence of preference for that aspect of them.

'I'm not sure I want you, you know,' was his greeting. 'I'm not sure about anything yet. I'm hanged if I can make out whether it's a case for a doctor, or a policeman, or a priest.'

'Well,' said Father Brown with a smile, 'as I suppose you're both a policeman and a doctor, I seem to be rather in a minority.'

'I admit you're what politicians call an instructed minority,' replied the doctor. 'I mean, I know you've had to do a little in our line as well as your own. But it's precious hard to say whether this business is in your line or ours, or merely in the line of the Commissioners in Lunacy. We've just had a message from a man living near here, in that white house on the hill, asking for protection against a murderous persecution. We've gone into the facts as far as we could, and perhaps I'd better tell you the story, as it is supposed to have happened, from the beginning.

'It seems that a man named Aylmer, who was a wealthy landowner in the West Country, married rather late in life and had three sons, Philip, Stephen and Arnold. But in his bachelor days, when he thought he would have no heir, he had adopted a boy whom he thought very brilliant and promising, who went by the name of John Strake. His origin seems to be vague; they say he was a foundling; some say he was a gipsy. I think the last notion is mixed up with the fact that Aylmer in his old age dabbled in all sorts of dingy occultism, including palmistry and astrology, and his three sons say that Strake encouraged him in it. But they said a great many other things besides that. They said Strake was an amazing scoundrel, and especially an amazing liar; a genius in inventing lies on the spur of the moment, and telling them so as to deceive a detective. But that might very well be a natural prejudice, in the light of what happened. Perhaps you can more or less imagine what happened. The old man left practically everything to the adopted son; and when he died the three real sons disputed the will. They said their father had been frightened into surrender and, not to put too fine a point on it, into gibbering idiocy. They said Strake had the strangest and most cunning ways of getting at him, in spite of the nurses and the family, and terrorizing him on his death-bed. Anyhow, they seemed to have proved something about the dead man's mental condition, for the courts set aside the will and the sons inherited. Strake is said to have broken out in the most dreadful fashion, and sworn he would kill all three of them, one after another, and that nothing could hide them from his vengeance. It is the third or last of the brothers, Arnold Aylmer, who is asking for police protection.'

'Third and last,' said the priest, looking at him gravely.

'Yes,' said Boyne. 'The other two are dead.'

There was a silence before he continued. 'That is where the doubt comes in. There is no proof they were murdered, but they might possibly have been. The eldest, who took up his position as squire, was supposed to have committed suicide in his garden. The second, who went into trade as a manufacturer, was knocked on the head by the machinery in his factory; he might very well have taken a false step and fallen. But if

Strake did kill them, he is certainly very cunning in his way of getting to work and getting away. On the other hand, it's more than likely that the whole thing is a mania of conspiracy founded on a coincidence. Look here, what I want is this. I want somebody of sense, who isn't an official, to go up and have a talk to this Mr Arnold Aylmer, and form an impression of him. You know what a man with a delusion is like, and how a man looks when he is telling the truth. I want you to be the advance guard, before we take the matter up.'

'It seems rather odd,' said Father Brown, 'that you haven't had to take it up before. If there is anything in this business, it seems to have been going on for a good time. Is there any particular reason why he should send for you just now, any more than any other time?'

'That had occurred to me, as you may imagine,' answered Dr Boyne. 'He does give a reason, but I confess it is one of the things that make me wonder whether the whole thing isn't only the whim of some half-witted crank. He declares that all his servants have suddenly gone on strike and left him, so that he is obliged to call on the police to look after his house. And on making inquiries, I certainly do find that there has been a general exodus of servants from that house on the hill; and of course the town is full of tales, very one-sided tales I dare say. Their account of it seems to be that their employer had become quite impossible in his fidgets and fears and exactions; that he wanted them to guard the house like sentries, or sit up like night nurses in a hospital; that they could never be left alone because he must never be left alone. So they all announced in a loud voice that he was a lunatic, and left. Of course that does not prove he is a lunatic; but it seems rather rum nowadays for a man to expect his valet or his parlour-maid to act as an armed guard.'

'And so,' said the priest with a smile, 'he wants a policeman to act as his parlour-maid because his parlour-maid won't act as a policeman.'

'I thought that rather thick, too,' agreed the doctor; 'but I can't take the responsibility of a flat refusal till I've tried a compromise. You are the compromise.'

'Very well,' said Father Brown simply. 'I'll go and call on him now if you like.'

The rolling country round the little town was sealed and bound with frost, and the sky was as clear and cold as steel, except in the north-east, where clouds with lurid haloes were beginning to climb up the sky. It was against these darker and more sinister colours that the house on the hill gleamed with a row of pale pillars, forming a short colonnade of the classical sort. A winding road led up to it across the curve of the down, and plunged into a mass of dark bushes. Just before it reached the bushes the air seemed to grow colder and colder, as if he were approaching an ice-house or the North Pole. But he was a highly practical person, never entertaining such fancies except as fancies. And he merely cocked his eye at the great livid cloud crawling up over the house, and remarked cheerfully:

'It's going to snow.'

Through a low ornamental iron gateway of the Italianate pattern he entered a garden having something of that desolation which only belongs to the disorder of orderly things. Deep-green growths were grey with the faint powder of the frost, large weeds had fringed the fading pattern of the flower-beds as if in a ragged frame; and the house stood as if waist-high in a stunted forest of shrubs and bushes. The vegetation consisted largely of evergreens or very hardy plants; and though it was thus thick and heavy, it was too northern to be called luxuriant. It might be described as an Arctic jungle. So it was in some sense with the house itself, which had a row of columns and a classical facade, which might have looked out on the Mediterranean; but which seemed now to be withering in the wind of the North Sea. Classical ornament here and there accentuated the contrast; caryatides and carved masks of comedy or tragedy looked down from corners of the building upon the grey confusion of the garden paths; but the faces seemed to be frost-bitten. The very volutes of the capitals might have curled up with the cold.

Father Brown went up the grassy steps to a square porch flanked by big pillars and knocked at the door. About four minutes afterwards he knocked again. Then he stood still patiently waiting with his back to the door and looked out on the slowly darkening landscape. It was darkening under the shadow of that one great continent of cloud that had come flying out of the north; and even as he looked out beyond the pillars of the porch, which seemed huge and black above him in the twilight, he saw the opalescent crawling rim of the great cloud as it sailed over the roof and bowed over the porch like a canopy. The grey canopy with its faintly coloured fringes seemed to sink lower and lower upon the garden beyond, until what had recently been a clear and pale-hued winter sky was left in a few silver ribbons and rags like a sickly sunset. Father Brown waited, and there was no sound within.

Then he betook himself briskly down the steps and round the house to look for another entrance. He eventually found one, a side door in the flat wall, and on this also he hammered and outside this also he waited. Then he tried the handle and found the door apparently bolted or fastened in some fashion; and then he moved along that side of the house, musing on the possibilities of the position, and wondering whether the eccentric Mr Aylmer had barricaded himself too deep in the house to hear any kind of summons; or whether perhaps he would barricade himself all the more, on the assumption that any summons must be the challenge of the avenging Strake. It might be that the decamping servants had only unlocked one door when they left in the morning, and that their master had locked that; but whatever he might have done it was unlikely that they, in the mood of that moment, had looked so carefully to the defences. He continued his prowl round the place; it was not really a large place, though perhaps a little pretentious; and in a few moments he found he had made the complete curcuit. A moment after he found what he suspected and sought. The french window of one room, curtained and shadowed with creeper, stood open by a crack, doubtless accidently left ajar, and he found himself in a central room, comfortably upholstered in a rather old-fashioned way, with a staircase leading up from it on one side and a door leading out of it on the other. Immediately opposite him was another door with red glass let into it, a little gaudily for later tastes; something that looked like a red-robed figure in cheap stained glass. On a round table to the right stood a sort of aquarium – a great bowl full of greenish water, in which fishes and similar things moved about as in a tank; and just opposite it a plant of the palm variety with very large green leaves. All this looked so very dusty and Early Victorian that the telephone, visible in the curtained alcove, was almost a surprise.

'Who is that?' a voice called out sharply and rather suspiciously from behind the stained-glass door.

'Could I see Mr Aylmer?' asked the priest apologetically.

The door opened and a gentleman in a peacock-green dressing-gown came out with an inquiring look. His hair was rather rough and untidy, as if he had been in bed or lived in a state of slowly getting up, but his eyes were not only awake but alert, and some would have said alarmed. Father Brown knew that the contradiction was likely enough in a man who had rather run to seed under the shadow either of a delusion or a danger. He had a fine aquiline face when seen in profile, but when seen full face the first impression was of the untidiness and even the wilderness of his loose brown beard.

'I am Mr Aylmer,' he said, 'but I have got out of the way of expecting visitors.'

Something about Mr Aylmer's unrestful eye prompted the priest to go straight to the point. If the man's persecution was only a monomania, he would be the less likely to resent it.

'I was wondering,' said Father Brown softly, 'whether it is quite true that you never expect visitors.'

'You are right,' replied his host steadily. 'I always expect one visitor. And he may be the last.'

'I hope not,' said Father Brown, 'but at least I am relieved to infer that I do not look very like him.'

Mr Aylmer shook himself with a sort of savage laugh. 'You certainly do not,' he said.

'Mr Aylmer,' said Father Brown frankly, 'I apologize for the liberty, but some friends of mine have told me about your trouble, and asked me to see if I could do anything for you. The truth is, I have some little experience in affairs like this.'

'There are no affairs like this,' said Aylmer.

'You mean,' observed Father Brown, 'that the tragedies in your unfortunate family were not normal deaths?'

'I mean they were not even normal murders,' answered the other. 'The man who is hounding us all to death is a hell-hound, and his power is from hell.'

'All evil has one origin,' said the priest gravely. 'But how do you know they were not normal murders?'

Aylmer answered with a gesture which offered his guest a chair; then he seated himself slowly in another, frowning, with his hands on his knees; but when he looked up his expression had grown milder and more thoughtful, and his voice was quite cordial and composed.

'Sir,' he said, 'I don't want you to imagine that I'm in the least an unreasonable person. I have come to these conclusions by reason, because unfortunately reason really leads there. I have read a great deal on these subjects; for I was the only one who inherited my father's scholarship in somewhat obscure matters, and I have since inherited his library. But what I tell you does not rest on what I have read but on what I have seen.'

Father Brown nodded, and the other proceeded, as if picking his words:

'In my elder brother's case I was not certain at first. There were no marks or footprints where he was found shot, and the pistol was left beside him. But he had just received a threatening letter, certainly from our enemy, for it was marked with a sign like a winged dagger, which was one of his infernal cabalistic tricks. And a servant said she had seen something moving along the garden wall in the twilight that was much too large to be a cat. I leave it there; all I can say is that if the murderer came, he managed to leave no traces of his coming. But when my brother Stephen died it was different; and since then I have known. A machine was working in an open scaffolding under the factory tower; I scaled the platform a moment after he had fallen under the iron hammer that struck him; I did not see anything else strike him, but I saw what I saw.

'A great drift of factory smoke was rolling between me and the factory tower; but through a rift of it I saw on the top of it a dark human figure wrapped in what looked like a black cloak. Then the sulphurous smoke drove between us again; and when it cleared I looked up at the distant chimney – there was nobody there. I am a rational man, and I will ask all rational men how he had reached that dizzy unapproachable turret, and how he left it.'

He stared across at the priest with a sphinx-like challenge; then after a silence he said abruptly:

'My brother's brains were knocked out, but his body was not much damaged. And in his pocket we found one of those warning messages dated the day before and stamped with the flying dagger.

'I am sure,' he went on gravely, 'that the symbol of the winged dagger is not merely arbitrary or accidental. Nothing about that abominable man is accidental. He is all design; though it is indeed a most dark and intricate design. His mind is woven not only out of elaborate schemes but out of all sorts of secret languages and signs, and dumb signals and wordless pictures which are the names of nameless things. He is the worst sort of man that the world knows: he is the wicked mystic. Now, I don't pretend to penetrate all that is conveyed by this symbol; but it seems surely that it must have a relation to all that was most remarkable, or even incredible, in his movements as he had hovered round my unfortunate family. Is there no connexion between the idea of a winged weapon and the mystery by which Philip was struck dead on his own lawn without the lightest touch of any footprint having disturbed the dust or grass? Is there no connexion between the plumed poignard flying like a feathered arrow and that figure which hung on the far top of the toppling chimney, clad in a cloak for pinions?'

'You mean,' said Father Brown thoughtfully, 'that he is in a perpetual state of levitation.'

'Simon Magus did it,' replied Aylmer, 'and it was one of the commonest predictions of the Dark Ages that Antichrist would be able to fly. Anyhow, there was the flying dagger on the document; and whether or no it could fly, it could certainly strike.'

'Did you notice what sort of paper it was on?' asked Father Brown 'Common paper?'

The sphinx-like face broke abruptly into a harsh laugh.

'You can see what they're like,' said Aylmer grimly, 'for I got one myself this morning.'

He was leaning back in his chair now, with his long legs thrust out from under the green dressing-gown, which was a little short for him, and his bearded chin pillowed on his chest. Without moving otherwise, he thrust his hand deep in the dressing-gown pocket and held out a fluttering scrap of paper at the end of a rigid arm. His whole attitude was suggestive of a sort of paralysis, that was both rigidity and collapse. But the next remark of the priest had a curious effect of rousing him.

Father Brown was blinking in his short-sighted way at the paper presented to him. It was a singular sort of paper, rough without being common, as from an artist's sketch-book; and on it was drawn boldly in red ink a dagger decorated with wings like the rod of Hermes, with the written words, 'Death comes the day after this, as it came to your brother.'

Father Brown tossed the paper on the floor and sat bolt upright in his chair.

'You mustn't let that sort of stuff stupefy you,' he said sharply. 'These devils always try to make us helpless by making us hopeless.'

Rather to his surprise, an awakening wave went over the prostrate figure, which sprang from its chair as if startled out of a dream.

'You're right, you're right!' cried Aylmer with a rather uncanny animation; 'and the devils shall find I'm not so hopeless after all, nor so helpless either. Perhaps I have more hope and better help than you fancy.'

He stood with his hands in his pockets, frowning down at the priest, who had a momentary doubt, during that strained silence, about whether the man's long peril had not touched his brain. But when he spoke it was quite soberly.

'I believe my unfortunate brothers failed because they used the wrong weapons. Philip carried a revolver, and that was how his death came to be called suicide. Stephen had police protection, but he also had a sense of what made him ridiculous; and he could not allow a policeman to climb up a ladder after him to a scaffolding where he stood only a moment. They were both scoffers, reacting into scepticism from the strange mysticism of my father's last days. But I always knew there was more in my father than they understood. It is true that by studying magic he fell at last under the blight of black magic; the black magic of this scoundrel Strake. But my brothers were wrong about the antidote. The antidote to black magic is not brute materialism or worldly wisdom. The antidote to black magic is white magic.'

'It rather depends,' said Father Brown, 'what you mean by white magic.'

'I mean silver magic,' said the other, in a low voice, like one speaking of a secret revelation. Then after a silence he said: 'Do you know what I mean by silver magic? Excuse me a moment.'

He turned and opened the central door with the red glass and went into a passage beyond it. The house had less depth than Brown had supposed; instead of the door opening into interior rooms, the corridor it revealed ended in another door on the garden. The door of one room was on one side of the passage; doubtless, the priest told himself, the proprietor's bedroom, whence he had rushed out in his dressing-gown.

There was nothing else on that side but an ordinary hat-stand with the ordinary dingy cluster of old hats and overcoats; but on the other side was something more interesting: a very dark old oak sideboard laid out with some old silver, and overhung by a trophy or ornament of old weapons. It was by that that Arnold Aylmer halted, looking up at a long, antiquated pistol with a bell-shaped mouth.

The door at the end of the passage was barely open, and through the crack came a streak of white daylight. The priest had very quick instincts about natural things, and something in the unusual brilliancy of that white line told him what had happened outside. It was indeed what he had prophesied when he was approaching the house. He ran past his rather startled host and opened the door, to face something that was at once a blank and a blaze. What he had seen shining through the crack was not only the most negative whiteness of daylight but the positive whiteness of snow. All round, the sweeping fall of the country was covered with that shining pallor that seems at once hoary and innocent.

'Here is white magic anyhow,' said Father Brown in his cheerful voice. Then, as he turned back into the hall, he murmured, 'And silver magic too, I suppose,' for the white lustre touched the silver with splendour and lit up the old steel here and there in the darkling armoury. The shaggy head of the brooding Aylmer seemed to have a halo of silver fire, as he turned with his face in shadow and the outlandish pistol in his hand.

'Do you know why I choose this sort of old blunderbuss?' he asked. 'Because I can load it with this sort of bullet.'

He had picked up a small apostle spoon from the sideboard, and by sheer violence broke off the small figure at the top. 'Let us go back into the other room,' he added.

'Did you ever read about the death of Dundee?' he asked when they had reseated themselves. He had recovered from his momentary annoyance at the priest's restlessness. 'Graham of Claverhouse, you know, who persecuted the Covenanters and had a black horse that could ride straight up a precipice. Don't you know he could only be shot with a silver bullet, because he had sold himself to the Devil? That's one comfort about you; at least you know enough to believe in the Devil.'

'Oh, yes,' replied Father Brown, 'I believe in the Devil. What I don't believe in is the Dundee. I mean the Dundee of Covenanting legends, with his nightmare of a horse. John Graham was simply a seventeenth-century professional soldier, rather better than most. If he dragooned them it was because he was a dragoon, but not a dragon. Now my experience is that it's not that sort of swaggering blade who sells himself to the Devil. The devil-worshippers I've known were quite different. Not to mention names, which might cause a social flutter, I'll take a man in Dundee's own day. Have you ever heard of Dalrymple of Stair?'

'No,' replied the other gruffly.

'You've heard of what he did,' said Father Brown, 'and it was worse than anything Dundee ever did; yet he escapes the infamy by oblivion. He was the man who made the Massacre of Glencoe. He was a very learned man and lucid lawyer, a statesman with very serious and enlarged ideas of statesmanship, a quiet man with a very refined and intellectual face. That's the sort of man who sells himself to the Devil.'

Aylmer half started from his chair with an enthusiasm of eager assent.

'By God! you are right,' he cried. 'A refined intellectual face! That is the face of John Strake.'

Then he raised himself and stood looking at the priest with a curious concentration. 'If you will wait here a little while,' he said, 'I will show you something.'

He went back through the central door, closing it after him; going, the priest presumed, to the old sideboard or possibly to his bedroom. Father Brown remained seated, gazing abstractedly at the carpet, where a faint red glimmer shone from the glass in the doorway. Once it seemed to brighten like a ruby and then darkened again, as if the sun of that stormy day had passed from cloud to cloud. Nothing moved except the aquatic creatures which floated to and fro in the dim green bowl. Father Brown was thinking hard.

A minute or two afterwards he got up and slipped quietly to the alcove of the telephone, where he rang up his friend Dr Boyne, at the official headquarters. 'I wanted to tell you about Aylmer and his affairs,' he said quietly. 'It's a queer story, but I rather think there's something in it. If I were you I'd send some men up here straight away; four or five men, I think, and surround the house. If anything does happen there'll probably be something startling in the way of an escape.'

Then he went back and sat down again, staring at the dark carpet, which again glowed blood-red with the light from the glass door. Something in that filtered light set his mind drifting on certain borderlands of thought, with the first white daybreak before the coming of colour, and all that mystery which is alternately veiled and revealed in the symbol of windows and of doors.

An inhuman howl in a human voice came from beyond the closed doors, almost simultaneously with the noise of firing. Before the echoes of the shot had died away the door was violently flung open and his host staggered into the room, the dressing-gown half torn from his shoulder and the long pistol smoking in his hand. He seemed to be shaking in every limb, yet he was shaken in part with an unnatural laughter.

'Glory be to the White Magic!' he cried; 'Glory be to the silver bullet! The hell-hound has hunted once too often, and my brothers are avenged at last.'

He sank into a chair and the pistol slid from his hand and fell on the floor. Father Brown darted past him, slipped through the glass door and went down the passage. As he did so he put his hand on the handle of the bedroom door, as if half intending to enter; then he stooped a moment, as if examining something – and then he ran to the outer door and opened it.

On the field of snow, which had been so blank a little while before, lay one black object. At the first glance it looked a little like an enormous bat. A second glance showed that it was, after all, a human figure; fallen on its face, the whole head covered by a broad black hat having something of a Latin-American look; while the appearance of batwings came from the two flaps or loose sleeves of a very vast black cloak spread out, perhaps by accident, to their utmost length on either side. Both the hands were hidden, though Father Brown thought he could detect the position of one of them, and saw close to it, under the edge of the cloak, the glimmer of some metallic weapon. The main effect, however, was curiously like that of the simple extravagances of heraldry; like a black eagle displayed on a white ground. But by walking round it and peering under the hat the priest got a glimpse of the face, which was indeed what his host had called refined and intellectual; even sceptical and austere: the face of John Strake.

'Well, I'm jiggered,' muttered Father Brown. 'It really does look like some vast vampire that has swooped down like a bird.'

'How else could he have come?' came a voice from the doorway, and Father Brown looked up to see Aylmer once more standing there.

'Couldn't he have walked?' replied Father Brown evasively.

Aylmer stretched out his arm and swept the white landscape with a gesture.

'Look at the snow,' he said in a deep voice that had a sort of roll and thrill in it. 'Is not the snow unspotted – pure as the white magic you yourself called it? Is there a speck on it for miles, save that one foul black blot that has fallen there? There are no footprints, but a few of yours and mine; there are none approaching the house from anywhere.'

Then he looked at the little priest for a moment with a concentrated and curious expression, and said:

'I will tell you something else. That cloak he flies with is too long to walk with. He was not a very tall man, and it would trail behind him like a royal train. Stretch it out over his body, if you like, and see.'

'What happened to you both?' asked Father Brown abruptly.

'It was too swift to describe,' answered Aylmer. 'I had looked out of the door and was turning back when there came a kind of rushing of wind all around me, as if I were being buffeted by a wheel revolving in mid-air. I spun round somehow and fired blindly; and then I saw nothing but what you see now. But I am morally certain you wouldn't see it if I had not had a silver shot in my gun. It would have been a different body lying there in the snow.'

'By the way,' remarked Father Brown, 'shall we leave it lying there in the snow? Or would you like it taken into your room – I suppose that's your bedroom in the passage?'

'No, no,' replied Aylmer hastily; 'we must leave it there till the police have seen it. Besides, I've had as much of such things as I can stand for the moment. Whatever else happens, I'm going to have a drink. After that, they can hang me if they like.'

Inside the central apartment, between the palm plant and the bowl of fishes, Aylmer tumbled into a chair. He had nearly knocked the bowl over as he lurched into the room, but he had managed to find the decanter of brandy after plunging his hand rather blindly into several cupboards and corners. He did not at any time look like a methodical person, but at this moment his distraction must have been extreme. He drank with a long gulp and began to talk rather feverishly, as if to fill up a silence.

'I see you are still doubtful,' he said, 'though you have seen the thing with your own eyes. Believe me, there was something more behind the quarrel between the spirit of Strake and the spirit of the house of Aylmer. Besides, you have no business to be an unbeliever. You ought to stand for all the things these stupid people call superstitions. Come now, don't you think there's a lot in those old wives' tales about luck and charms and so on, silver bullets included? What do you say about them as a Catholic?'

'I say I'm an agnostic,' replied Father Brown, smiling.

'Nonsense,' said Aylmer impatiently. 'It's your business to believe things.'

'Well, I do believe some things, of course,' conceded Father Brown; 'and therefore, of course, I don't believe other things.'

Aylmer was leaning forward, and looking at him with a strange intensity that was almost like that of a mesmerist.

'You do believe it,' he said. 'You do believe everything. We all believe everything, even when we deny everything. The deniers believe. The unbelievers believe. Don't you feel in your heart that these contradictions do not really contradict: that there is a cosmos that contains them all? The soul goes round upon a wheel of stars and all things return; perhaps Strake and I have striven in many shapes, beast against beast and bird against bird, and perhaps we shall strive for ever. But since we seek and need each other, even that eternal hatred is an eternal love. Good and evil go round in a wheel that is one thing and not many. Do you not realize in your heart, do you not believe behind all your beliefs, that there is but one reality and we are its shadows; and that all things are but aspects of one thing: a centre where men melt into Man and Man into God?'

'No,' said Father Brown.

Outside, twilight had begun to fall, in that phase of such a snow-laden evening when the land looks brighter than the sky. In the porch of the main entrance, visible through a half-curtained window, Father Brown could dimly see a bulky figure standing. He glanced casually at the french windows through which he had originally entered, and saw they were darkened with two equally motionless figures. The inner door with the coloured glass stood slightly ajar; and he could see in the short corridor beyond, the ends of two long shadows, exaggerated and distorted by the level light of evening, but still like grey caricatures of the figures of men. Dr Boyne had already obeyed his telephone message. The house was surrounded.

'What is the good of saying no?' insisted his host, still with the same hypnotic stare. 'You have seen part of that eternal drama with your own eyes. You have seen the threat of John Strake to slay Arnold Aylmer by black magic. You have seen Arnold Aylmer slay John Strake by white magic. You see Arnold Aylmer alive and talking to you now. And yet you do not believe it.'

'No, I do not believe it,' said Father Brown, and rose from his chair like one terminating a visit.

'Why not?' asked the other.

The priest only lifted his voice a little, but it sounded in every corner of the room like a bell.

'Because you are not Arnold Aylmer,' he said. 'I know who you are. Your name is John Strake; and you have murdered the last of the brothers, who is lying outside in the snow.'

A ring of white showed round the iris of the other man's eyes; he seemed to be making, with bursting eyeballs, a last effort to mesmerize and master his companion. Then he made a sudden movement sideways; and even as he did so the door behind him opened and a big detective in plain clothes put one hand quietly on his shoulder. The other hand hung down, but it held a revolver. The man looked wildly round, and saw plain-clothes men in all corners of the quiet room.

That evening Father Brown had another and longer conversation with Dr Boyne about the tragedy of the Aylmer family. By that time there was no longer any doubt of the central fact of the case, for John Strake had confessed his identity and even confessed his crimes; only it would be truer to say that he boasted of his victories. Compared to the fact that he had rounded off his life's work with the last Aylmer lying dead, everything else, including existence itself, seemed to be indifferent to him.

'The man is a sort of monomaniac,' said Father Brown. 'He is not interested in any other matter; not even in any other murder. I owe him something for that; for I had to comfort myself with the reflection a good many times this afternoon. As has doubtless occurred to you, instead of weaving all that wild but ingenious romance about winged vampires and silver bullets, he might have put an ordinary leaden bullet into me, and walked out of the house. I assure you it occurred quite frequently to me.'

'I wonder why he didn't,' observed Boyne. 'I don't understand it; but I don't understand anything yet. How on earth did you discover it, and what in the world did you discover?'

'Oh, you provided me with very valuable information,' replied Father Brown modestly, 'especially the one piece of information that really counted. I mean the statement that Strake was a very inventive and imaginative liar, with great presence of mind in producing his lies. This afternoon he needed it; but he rose to the occasion. Perhaps his only mistake was in choosing a preternatural story; he had the notion that because I am a clergyman I should believe anything. Many people have little notions of that kind.'

'But I can't make head or tail of it,' said the doctor. 'You must really begin at the beginning.'

'The beginning of it was a dressing-gown,' said Father Brown simply. 'It was the one really good disguise I've ever known. When you meet a man in a house with a dressing-gown on, you assume quite automatically that he's in his own house. I assumed it myself; but afterwards queer little things began to happen. When he took the pistol down he clicked it at arm's length, as a man does to make sure a strange weapon isn't loaded; of course he would know whether the pistols in his own hall were loaded or not. I didn't like the way he looked for the brandy, or the way he nearly barged into the bowl of fishes. For a man who has a fragile thing of that sort as a fixture in his rooms gets a quite mechanical habit of avoiding it. But these things might possibly have been fancies; the first real point was this. He came out from the little passage between the two doors; and in that passage there's only one other door leading to a room; so I assumed it was the bedroom he had just come from. I tried the handle; but it was locked. I thought this odd; and looked through the keyhole. It was an utterly bare room, obviously deserted; no bed, no anything. Therefore he had not come from inside any room, but from outside the house. And when I saw that, I think I saw the whole picture.

'Poor Arnold Aylmer doubtless slept and perhaps lived upstairs, and came down in his dressing-gown and passed through the red glass door. At the end of the passage, black against the winter daylight, he saw the enemy of his house. He saw a tall bearded man in a broad-brimmed black hat and a large flapping black cloak. He did not see much more in this world. Strake sprang on him, throttling or stabbing him; we cannot be sure till the inquest. Then Strake, standing in the narrow passage between the hat-stand and the old sideboard, and looking down in triumph on the last of his foes, heard something he had not expected. He heard footsteps in the parlour beyond. It was myself entering by the french windows.

'His masquerade was a miracle of promptitude. It involved not only a disguise but a romance – an impromptu romance. He took off his big black hat and cloak and put on the dead man's dressing-gown. Then he did a rather grisly thing; at least a thing that affects my fancy as more grisly than the rest. He hung the corpse like a coat on one of the hatpegs. He draped it in his own long cloak, and found it hung well below the heels; he covered the head entirely with his own wide hat. It was the only possible way of hiding it in that little passage with the locked door; but it was really a very clever one. I myself walked past the hat-stand once without knowing it was anything but a hat-stand. I think that unconsciousness of mine will always give me a shiver.

'He might perhaps have left it at that; but I might have discovered the corpse at any minute; and, hung where it was, it was a corpse calling for what you might call an explanation. He adopted the bolder stroke of discovering it himself and explaining it himself.

'Then there dawned on this strange and frightfully fertile mind the conception of a story of substitution; the reversal of the parts. He had already assumed the part of Arnold Aylmer. Why should not his dead enemy assume the part of John Strake? There must have been something in that topsy-turvydom to take the fancy of that darkly fanciful man. It was like some frightful fancy-dress ball to which the two mortal enemies were to go dressed up as each other. Only, the fancy-dress ball was to be a dance of death: and one of the dancers would be dead. That is why I can imagine that man putting it in his own mind, and I can imagine him smiling.'

Father Brown was gazing into vacancy with his large grey eyes, which, when not blurred by his trick of blinking, were the one notable thing in his face. He went on speaking simply and seriously:

'All things are from God; and above all, reason and imagination and the great gifts of the mind. They are good in themselves; and we must not altogether forget their origin even in their perversion. Now this man had in him a very noble power to be perverted; the power of telling stories. He was a great novelist; only he had twisted his fictive power to practical and to evil ends; to deceiving men with false fact instead of with true fiction. It began with his deceiving old Aylmer with elaborate excuses and ingeniously detailed lies; but even that may have been, at the beginning, little more than the tall stories and tarradiddles of the child who may say equally he has seen the King of England or the King of the Fairies. It grew strong in him through the vice that perpetuates all vices, pride; he grew more and more vain of his promptitude in producing stories of his originality, and subtlety in developing them. That is what the young Aylmers meant by saying that he could always cast a spell over their father; and it was true. It was the sort of spell that the story-teller cast over the tyrant in the Arabian Nights. And to the last he walked the world with the pride of a poet, and with the false yet unfathomable courage of a great liar. He could always produce more Arabian Nights if ever his neck was in danger. And to-day his neck was in danger.

'But I am sure, as I say, that he enjoyed it as a fantasy as well as a conspiracy. He set about the task of telling the true story the wrong way round: of treating the dead man as living and the live man as dead. He had already got into Aylmer's dressing-gown; he proceeded to get into Aylmer's body and soul. He looked at the corpse as if it were his own corpse lying cold in the snow. Then he spread-eagled it in that strange fashion to suggest the sweeping descent of a bird of prey, and decked it out not only in his own dark and flying garments but in a whole dark fairy-tale about the black bird that could only fall by the silver bullet. I do not know whether it was the silver glittering on the sideboard or the snow shining beyond the door that suggested to his intensely artistic temperament the theme of white magic and the white metal used against magicians. But whatever its origin, he made it his own like a poet; and did it very promptly, like a practical man. He completed the exchange and reversal of parts by flinging the corpse out on to the snow as the corpse of Strake. He did his best to work up a creepy conception of Strake as something hovering in the air everywhere, a harpy with wings of speed and claws of death; to explain the absence of footprints and other things. For one piece of artistic impudence I hugely admire him. He actually turned one of the contradictions in his case into an argument for it; and said that the man's cloak being too long for him proved that he never walked on the ground like an ordinary mortal. But he looked at me very hard while he said that; and something told me that he was at that moment trying a very big bluff.'

Dr Boyne looked thoughtful. 'Had you discovered the truth by then?' he asked. 'There is something very queer and close to the nerves, I think, about notions affecting identity. I don't know whether it would be more weird to get a guess like that swiftly or slowly. I wonder when you suspected and when you were sure.'

'I think I really suspected when I telephoned to you,' replied his friend. 'And it was nothing more than the red light from the closed door brightening and darkening on the carpet. It looked like a splash of blood that grew vivid as it cried for vengeance. Why should it change like that? I knew the sun had not come out; it could only be because the second door behind it had been opened and shut on the garden. But if he had gone out and seen his enemy then, he would have raised the alarm then; and it was some time afterwards that the fracas occurred. I began to feel he had gone out to do something . . . to prepare something . . . but as to when I was certain, that is a different matter. I knew that right at the end he was trying to hypnotize me, to master me by the black art of eyes like talismans and a voice like an incantation. That's what he used to do with old Aylmer, no doubt. But it wasn't only the way he said it, it was what he said. It was the religion and philosophy of it.'

'I'm afraid I'm a practical man,' said the doctor with gruff humour, 'and I don't bother much about religion and philosophy.'

'You'll never be a practical man till you do,' said Father Brown. 'Look here, doctor; you know me pretty well; I think you know I'm not a bigot. You know I know there are all sorts in all religions; good men in bad ones and bad men in good ones. But there's just one little fact I've learned simply as a practical man, an entirely practical point, that I've picked up by experience, like the tricks of an animal or the trade-mark of a good wine. I've scarcely ever met a criminal who philosophized at all, who didn't philosophize along those lines of orientalism and recurrence and reincarnation, and the wheel of destiny and the serpent biting its own tail. I have found merely in practice that there is a curse on the servants of that serpent; on their belly shall they go and the dust shall they eat; and there was never a blackguard or a profligate born who could not talk that sort of spirituality. It may not be like that in its real religious origins; but here in our working world it is the religion of rascals; and I knew it was a rascal who was speaking.'

'Why,' said Boyne, 'I should have thought that a rascal could pretty well profess any religion he chose.'

'Yes,' assented the other; 'he could profess any religion; that is he could pretend to any religion, if it was all a pretence. If it was mere mechanical hypocrisy and nothing else, no doubt it could be done by a mere mechanical hypocrite. Any sort of mask can be put on any sort of face. Anybody can learn certain phrases or state verbally that he holds certain views. I can go out into the street and state that I am a Wesleyan Methodist or a Sandemanian, though I fear in no very convincing accent. But we are talking about an artist; and for the enjoyment of the artist the mask must be to some extent moulded on the face. What he makes outside him must correspond to something inside him; he can only make his effects out of some of the materials of his soul. I suppose he could have said he was a Wesleyan Methodist; but he could never be an eloquent Methodist as he can be an eloquent mystic and fatalist. I am talking of the sort of ideal such a man thinks of if he really tries to be idealistic. It was his whole game with me to be as idealistic as possible; and whenever that is attempted by that sort of man, you will generally find it is that sort of ideal. That sort of man may be dripping with gore; but he will always be able to tell you quite sincerely that Buddhism is better than Christianity. Nay, he will tell you quite sincerely that Buddhism is more Christian than Christianity. That alone is enough to throw a hideous and ghastly ray of light on his notion of Christianity.'

'Upon my soul,' said the doctor, laughing, 'I can't make out whether you're denouncing or defending him.'

'It isn't defending a man to say he is a genius,' said Father Brown. 'Far from it. And it is simply a psychological fact that an artist will betray himself by some sort of sincerity. Leonardo da Vinci cannot draw as if he couldn't draw. Even if he tried, it will always be a strong parody of a weak thing. This man would have made something much too fearful and wonderful out of the Wesleyan Methodist.'

When the priest went forth again and set his face homeward, the cold had grown more intense and yet was somehow intoxicating. The trees stood up like silver candelabra of some incredible cold Candlemas of purification. It was a piercing cold, like that silver sword of pure pain that once pierced the very heart of purity. But it was not a killing cold, save in the sense of seeming to kill all the mortal obstructions to our immortal and immeasurable vitality. The pale green sky of twilight, with one star like the star of Bethlehem, seemed by some strange contradiction to be a cavern of clarity. It was as if there could be a green furnace of cold which wakened all things to life like warmth, and that the deeper they went into those cold crystalline colours the more were they light like winged creatures and clear like coloured glass. It tingled with truth and it divided truth from error with a blade like ice; but all that was left had never felt so much alive. It was as if all joy were a jewel in the heart of an iceberg. The priest hardly understood his own mood as he advanced deeper and deeper into the green gloaming, drinking deeper and deeper draughts of that virginal vivacity of the air. Some forgotten muddle and morbidity seemed to be left behind, or wiped out as the snow had painted out the footprints of the man of blood. As he shuffled homewards through the snow, he muttered to himself: 'And yet he is right enough about there being a white magic, if he only knows where to look for it.'

6

The Doom of the Darnaways

Two landscape-painters stood looking at one landscape, which was also a seascape, and both were curiously impressed by it, though their impressions were not exactly the same. To one of them, who was a rising artist from London, it was new as well as strange. To the other, who was a local artist but with something more than a local celebrity, it was better known; but perhaps all the more strange for what he knew of it.

In terms of tone and form, as these men saw it, it was a stretch of sands against a stretch of sunset, the whole scene lying in strips of sombre colour, dead green and bronze and brown and a drab that was not merely dull but in that gloaming in some way more mysterious than gold. All that broke these level lines was a long building which ran out from the fields into the sands of the sea, so that its fringe of dreary weeds and rushes seemed almost to meet the seaweed. But its most singular feature was that the upper part of it had the ragged outlines of a ruin, pierced by so many wide windows and large rents as to be a mere dark skeleton against the dying light; while the lower bulk of the building had hardly any windows at all, most of them being blind and bricked up and their outlines only faintly traceable in the twilight. But one window at least was still a window; and it seemed strangest of all that it showed a light.

'Who on earth can live in that old shell?' exclaimed the Londoner, who was a big, bohemian-looking man, young but with a shaggy red beard that made him look older; Chelsea knew him familiarly as Harry Payne.

'Ghosts, you might suppose,' replied his friend Martin Wood. 'Well, the people who live there really are rather like ghosts.'

It was perhaps rather a paradox that the London artist seemed almost bucolic in his boisterous freshness and wonder, while the local artist seemed a more shrewd and experienced person, regarding him with mature and amiable amusement; indeed, the latter was altogether a quieter and more conventional figure, wearing darker clothes and with his square and stolid face clean-shaven.

'It is only a sign of the times, of course,' he went on, 'or of the passing of old times and old families with them. The last of the great Darnaways live in that house, and not many of the new poor are as poor as they are. They can't even afford to make their own top storey habitable; but have to live in the lower rooms of a ruin, like bats and owls. Yet they have family portraits that go back to the Wars of the Roses and the first portrait-painting in England, and very fine some of them are; I happen to know, because they asked for my professional advice in overhauling them. There's one of them especially, and one of the earliest, but it's so good that it gives you the creeps.'

'The whole place gives you the creeps, I should think by the look of it,' replied Payne.

'Well,' said his friend, 'to tell you the truth, it does.'

The silence that followed was stirred by a faint rustle among the rushes by the moat; and it gave them, rationally enough, a slight nervous start when a dark figure brushed along the bank, moving rapidly and almost like a startled bird. But it was only a man walking briskly with a black bag in his hand; a man with a long sallow face and sharp eyes that glanced at the London stranger in a slightly darkling and suspicious manner.

'It's only Dr Barnet,' said Wood with a sort of relief. 'Good evening, Doctor. Are you going up to the house? I hope nobody's ill.'

'Everybody's always ill in a place like that,' growled the doctor; 'only sometimes they're too ill to know it. The very air of the place is a blight and a pestilence. I don't envy the young man from Australia.'

'And who,' asked Payne abruptly and rather absently, 'may the young man from Australia be?'

'Ah!' snorted the doctor; 'hasn't your friend told you about him? As a matter of fact I believe he is arriving to-day. Quite a romance in the old style of melodrama: the heir back from the colonies to his ruined castle, all complete even down to an old family compact for his marrying the lady watching in the ivied tower. Queer old stuff, isn't it? but it really happens sometimes. He's even got a little money, which is the only bright spot there ever was in this business.'

'What does Miss Darnaway herself, in her ivied tower, think of the business?' asked Martin Wood dryly.

'What she thinks of everything else by this time,' replied the doctor. 'They don't think in this weedy old den of superstitions, they only dream and drift. I think she accepts the family contract and the colonial husband as part of the Doom of the Darnaways, don't you know. I really think that if he turned out to be a hump-backed negro with one eye and a homicidal mania, she would only think it added a finishing touch and fitted in with the twilight scenery.'

'You're not giving my friend from London a very lively picture of my friends in the country,' said Wood, laughing. 'I had intended taking him there to call; no artist ought to miss those Darnaway portraits if he gets the chance. But perhaps I'd better postpone it if they're in the middle of the Australian invasion.'

'Oh, do go in and see them, for the Lord's sake,' said Dr Barnet warmly. 'Anything that will brighten their blighted lives will make my task easier. It will need a good many colonial cousins to cheer things up, I should think; and the more the merrier. Come, I'll take you in myself.'

As they drew nearer to the house it was seen to be isolated like an island in a moat of brackish water which they crossed by a bridge. On the other side spread a fairly wide stony floor or embankment with great cracks across it, in which little tufts of weed and thorn sprouted here and there. This rock platform looked large and bare in the grey twilight, and Payne could hardly have believed that such a corner of space could have contained so much of the soul of a wilderness. This platform only jutted out on one side, like a giant door-step and beyond it was the door; a very low-browed Tudor archway standing open, but dark like a cave.

When the brisk doctor led them inside without ceremony, Payne had, as it were, another shock of depression. He could have expected to find himself mounting to a very ruinous tower, by very narrow winding staircases; but in this case the first steps into the house were actually steps downwards. They went down several short and broken stairways into large twilit rooms which, but for their lines of dark pictures and dusty book-shelves, might have been the traditional dungeons beneath the castle moat. Here and there a candle in an old candlestick lit up some dusty accidental detail of a dead elegance; but the visitor was not so much impressed or depressed by this artificial light as by the one pale gleam of natural light. As he passed down the long room he saw the only window in that wall – a curious low oval window of a late-seventeenth-century fashion. But the strange thing about it was that it did not look out directly on any space of sky but only on a reflection of sky; a pale strip of daylight merely mirrored in the moat, under the hanging shadow of the bank. Payne had a memory of the Lady of Shallot who never saw the world outside except in a mirror. The lady of this Shallot not only in some sense saw the world in a mirror, but even saw the world upside-down.

'It's as if the house of Darnaway were falling literally as well as metaphorically,' said Wood in a low voice; 'as if it were sinking slowly into a swamp or a quicksand, until the sea goes over it like a green roof.'

Even the sturdy Dr Barnet started a little at the silent approach of the figure that came to receive them. Indeed, the room was so silent that they were all startled to realize that it was not empty. There were three people in it when they entered: three dim figures motionless in the dim room; all three dressed in black and looking like dark shadows. As the foremost figure drew nearer the grey light from the window, he showed a face that looked almost as grey as its frame of hair. This was old Vine, the steward, long left *in loco parentis* since the death of that eccentric parent, the last Lord Darnaway. He would have been a handsome old man if he had had no teeth. As it was, he had one which showed every now and then and gave him a rather sinister appearance. He received the doctor and his friends with a fine courtesy and escorted them to where the other two figures in black were seated. One of them seemed to Payne to give another appropriate touch of gloomy antiquity to the castle by the mere fact of being a Roman Catholic priest, who might have come out of a priest's hole in the dark old days. Payne could imagine him muttering prayers or telling beads, or tolling bells or doing a number of indistinct and melancholy things in that melancholy place. Just then he might be supposed to have been giving religious consolation to the lady; but it could hardly be supposed that the consolation was very consoling, or at any rate that it was very cheering. For the rest, the priest was personally insignificant enough, with plain and rather expressionless features; but the lady was a very different matter. Her face was very far from being plain or insignificant; it stood out from the darkness of her dress and hair and background with a pallor that was almost awful, but a beauty that was almost awfully alive. Payne looked at it as long as he dared; and he was to look at it a good deal longer before he died.

Wood merely exchanged with his friends such pleasant and polite phrases as would lead up to his purpose of revisiting the portraits. He apologized for calling on the day which he heard was to be one of family welcome; but he was soon convinced that the family was rather mildly relieved to have visitors to distract them or break the shock. He did not hesitate, therefore, to lead Payne through the central reception-room into the library beyond, where hung the portrait, for there was one which he was especially bent on showing, not only as a picture but almost as a puzzle. The little priest trudged along with them; he seemed to know something about old pictures as well as about old prayers.

'I'm rather proud of having spotted this,' said Wood. 'I believe it's a Holbein. If it isn't, there was somebody living in Holbein's time who was as great as Holbein.'

It was a portrait in the hard but sincere and living fashion of the period, representing a man clad in black trimmed with gold and fur, with a heavy, full, rather pale face but watchful eyes.

'What a pity art couldn't have stopped for ever at just that transition stage,' cried Wood, 'and never transitioned any more. Don't you see it's just realistic enough to be real? Don't you see the face speaks all the more because it stands out from a rather stiffer framework of less essential things? And the eyes are even more real than the face. On my soul, I think the eyes are too real for the face! It's just as if those sly, quick eyeballs were protruding out of a great pale mask.'

'The stiffness extends to the figure a little, I think,' said Payne. 'They hadn't quite mastered anatomy when mediævalism ended, at least in the north. That left leg looks to me a good deal out of drawing.'

'I'm not so sure,' replied Wood quietly. 'Those fellows who painted just when realism began to be done, and before it began to be overdone, were often more realistic than we think. They put real details of portraiture into things that are thought merely conventional. You might say this fellow's eyebrows or eye-sockets are a little lop-sided; but I bet if you knew him you'd find that one of his eyebrows did really stick up more than the other. And I shouldn't wonder if he was lame or something, and that black leg was meant to be crooked.'

'What an old devil he looks!' burst out Payne suddenly. 'I trust his reverence will excuse my language.'

'I believe in the devil, thank you,' said the priest with an inscrutable face. 'Curiously enough there was a legend that the devil was lame.'

'I say,' protested Payne, 'you can't really mean that he was the devil; but who the devil was he?'

'He was the Lord Darnaway under Henry VII and Henry VIII,' replied his companion. 'But there are curious legends about him, too; one of them is referred to in that inscription round the frame, and further developed in some notes left by somebody in a book I found here. They are both rather curious reading.'

Payne leaned forward, craning his head so as to follow the archaic inscription round the frame. Leaving out the antiquated lettering and spelling, it seemed to be a sort of rhyme running somewhat thus:

> In the seventh heir I shall return:
> In the seventh hour I shall depart:
> None in that hour shall hold my hand:
> And woe to her that holds my heart.

'It sounds creepy somehow,' said Payne, 'but that may be partly because I don't understand a word of it.'

'It's pretty creepy even when you do,' said Wood in a low voice. 'The record made at a later date, in the old book I found, is all about how this beauty deliberately killed himself in such a way that his wife was executed for his murder. Another note commemorates a later tragedy, seven successions later – under the Georges – in which another Darnaway committed suicide, having first thoughtfully left poison in his wife's wine. It's said that both suicides took place at seven in the evening. I suppose the inference is that he does really return with every seventh inheritor and makes things pleasant, as the rhyme suggests, for any lady unwise enough to marry him.'

'On that argument,' replied Payne, 'it would be a trifle uncomfortable for the next seventh gentleman.'

Wood's voice was lower still as he said:

'The new heir will be the seventh.'

Harry Payne suddenly heaved up his great chest and shoulders like a man flinging off a burden.

'What crazy stuff are we all talking?' he cried. 'We're all educated men in an enlightened age, I suppose. Before I came into this damned dank atmosphere I'd never have believed I should be talking of such things, except to laugh at them.'

'You are right,' said Wood. 'If you lived long enough in this underground palace you'd begin to feel differently about things. I've begun to feel very curiously about that picture, having had so much to do with handling and hanging it. It sometimes seems to me that the painted face is more alive than the dead faces of the people living here; that it is a sort of talisman or magnet: that it commands the elements and draws out the destinies of men and things. I suppose you would call it very fanciful.'

'What is that noise?' cried Payne suddenly.

They all listened, and there seemed to be no noise except the dull boom of the distant sea; then they began to have the sense of something mingling with it; something like a voice calling through the sound of the surf, dulled by it at first, but coming nearer and nearer. The next moment they were certain: someone was shouting outside in the dusk.

Payne turned to the low window behind him and bent to look out. It was the window from which nothing could be seen except the moat with its reflection of bank and sky. But that inverted vision was not the same that he had seen before. From the hanging shadow of the bank in the water depended two dark shadows reflected from the feet and legs of a figure standing above upon the bank. Through that limited aperture they could see nothing but the two legs black against the reflection of a pale and livid sunset. But somehow that very fact of the head being invisible, as if in the clouds, gave something dreadful to the sound that followed; the voice of a man crying aloud what they could not properly hear or understand. Payne especially was peering out of the little window with an altered face, and he spoke with an altered voice:

'How queerly he's standing!'

'No, no,' said Wood, in a sort of soothing whisper. 'Things often look like that in reflection. It's the wavering of the water that makes you think that.'

'Think what?' asked the priest shortly.

'That his left leg is crooked,' said Wood.

Payne had thought of the oval window as a sort of mystical mirror; and it seemed to him that there were in it other inscrutable images of doom. There was something else beside the figure that he did not understand; three thinner legs showing in dark lines against the light, as if some monstrous three-legged spider or bird were standing beside the stranger. Then he had the less crazy thought of a tripod like that of the heathen oracles; and the next moment the thing had vanished and the legs of the human figure passed out of the picture.

He turned to meet the pale face of old Vine, the steward, with his mouth open, eager to speak, and his single tooth showing.

'He has come,' he said. 'The boat arrived from Australia this morning.'

Even as they went back out of the library into the central salon they heard the footsteps of the newcomer clattering down the entrance steps, with various items of light luggage trailed behind him. When Payne saw one of them, he laughed with a reaction of relief. His tripod was nothing but the telescopic legs of a portable camera, easily packed and unpacked; and the man who was carrying it seemed so far to take on equally solid and normal qualities. He was dressed in dark clothes, but of a careless and holiday sort; his shirt was of grey flannel, and his boots echoed uncompromisingly enough in those still chambers. As he strode forward to greet his new circle his stride had scarcely more than the suggestion of a limp. But Payne and his companions were looking at his face, and could scarcely take their eyes from it.

He evidently felt there was something curious and uncomfortable about his reception; but they could have sworn that he did not himself know the cause of it. The lady, supposed to be in some sense already betrothed to him, was certainly beautiful enough to attract him; but she evidently also frightened him. The old steward brought him a sort of feudal homage, yet treated him as if he were the family ghost. The priest still looked at him with a face which was quite indecipherable, and therefore perhaps all the more unnerving. A new sort of irony, more like the Greek irony, began to pass over Payne's mind. He had dreamed of the stranger as a devil, but it seemed almost worse that he was an unconscious destiny. He seemed to march towards crime with the monstrous innocence of Œdipus. He had approached the family mansion in so blindly buoyant a spirit as to have set up his camera to photograph his first sight of it; and even the camera had taken on the semblance of the tripod of a tragic pythoness.

Payne was surprised, when taking his leave a little while after, at something which showed that the Australian was already less unconscious of his surroundings. He said in a low voice:

'Don't go . . . or come again soon. You look like a human being. This place fairly gives me the jumps.'

When Payne emerged out of those almost subterranean halls and came into the night air and the smell of the sea, he felt as if he had come out of that underworld of dreams in which events tumble on top of each other in a way at once unrestful and unreal. The arrival of the strange relative had been somehow unsatisfying and, as it were, unconvincing. The doubling of the same face in the old portrait and the new arrival troubled him like a two-headed monster. And yet it was not altogether a nightmare; nor was it that face, perhaps, that he saw most vividly.

'Did you say?' he asked of the doctor, as they strode together across the striped dark sands by the darkening sea; 'did you say that young man was betrothed to Miss Darnaway by a family compact or something? Sounds rather like a novel.'

'But an historical novel,' answered Dr Barnet. 'The Darnaways all went to sleep a few centuries ago, when things were really done that we only read of in romances. Yes; I believe there's some family tradition by which second or third cousins always marry when they stand in a certain relation of age, in order to unite the property. A damned silly tradition, I should say; and if they often married in and in, in that fashion, it may account on principles of heredity for their having gone so rotten.'

'I should hardly say,' answered Payne a little stiffly, 'that they had all gone rotten.'

'Well,' replied the doctor, 'the young man doesn't *look* rotten, of course, though he's certainly lame.'

'The young man!' cried Payne, who was suddenly and unreasonably angry. 'Well, if you think the young lady looks rotten, I think it's you who have rotten taste.'

The doctor's face grew dark and bitter. 'I fancy I know more about it than you do,' he snapped.

They completed the walk in silence, each feeling that he had been irrationally rude and had suffered equally irrational rudeness; and Payne was left to brood alone on the matter, for his friend Wood had remained behind to attend to some of his business in connexion with the pictures.

Payne took very full advantage of the invitation extended by the colonial cousin, who wanted somebody to cheer him up. During the next few weeks he saw a good deal of the dark interior of the Darnaway home; though it might be said that he did not confine himself entirely to cheering up the colonial cousin. The lady's melancholy was of longer standing and perhaps needed more lifting; anyhow, he showed a laborious readiness to lift it. He was not without a conscience, however, and the situation made him doubtful and uncomfortable. Weeks went by and nobody could discover from the demeanour of the new Darnaway whether he considered himself engaged according to the old compact or no. He went mooning about the dark galleries and stood staring vacantly at the dark and sinister picture. The shades of that prison-house were certainly beginning to close on him, and there was little of his Australian assurance left. But Payne could discover nothing upon the point that concerned him most. Once he attempted to confide in his friend Martin Wood, as he was pottering about in his capacity of picture-hanger; but even out of him he got very little satisfaction.

'It seems to me you can't butt in,' said Wood shortly, 'because of the engagement.'

'Of course I shan't butt in if there is an engagement,' retorted his friend; 'but is there? I haven't said a word to her of course; but I've seen enough of her to be pretty certain she doesn't think there is, even if she thinks there may be. He doesn't say there is, or even hint that there ought to be. It seems to me this shilly-shallying is rather unfair on everybody.'

'Especially on you, I suppose,' said Wood a little harshly. 'But if you ask me, I'll tell you what I think – I think he's afraid.'

'Afraid of being refused?' asked Payne.

'No; afraid of being accepted,' answered the other. 'Don't bite my head off – I don't mean afraid of the lady. I mean afraid of the picture.'

'Afraid of the picture!' repeated Payne.

'I mean afraid of the curse,' said Wood. 'Don't you remember the rhyme about the Darnaway doom falling on him and her?'

'Yes, but look here,' cried Payne; 'even the Darnaway doom can't have it both ways. You tell me first that I mustn't have my own way because of the compact, and then that the compact mustn't have its own way because of the curse. But if the curse can destroy the compact, why should she be tied to the compact? If they're frightened of marrying each other, they're free to marry anybody else, and there's an end of it. Why should I suffer for the observance of something they don't propose to observe? It seems to me your position is very unreasonable.'

'Of course it's all a tangle,' said Wood rather crossly, and went on hammering at the frame of a canvas.

Suddenly, one morning, the new heir broke his long and baffling silence. He did it in a curious fashion, a little crude, as was his way, but with an obvious anxiety to do the right thing. He asked frankly for advice, not of this or that individual as Payne had done, but collectively as of a crowd. When he did speak he threw himself on the whole company like a statesman going to the country. He called it 'a show-down'. Fortunately the lady was not included in this large gesture; and Payne shuddered when he thought of her feelings. But the Australian was quite honest; he thought the natural thing was to ask for help and for information, calling a sort of family council at which he put his cards on the table. It might be said that he flung down his cards on the table, for he did it with a rather desperate air, like one who had been harassed for days and nights by the increasing pressure of a problem. In that short time the shadows of that place of low windows and sinking pavements had curiously changed him, and increased a certain resemblance that crept through all their memories.

The five men, including the doctor, were sitting round a table; and Payne was idly reflecting that his own light tweeds and red hair must be the only colours in the room, for the priest and the steward were in black, and Wood and Darnaway habitually wore dark grey suits that looked almost like black. Perhaps this incongruity had been what the young man had meant by calling him a human being. At that moment the young man himself turned abruptly in his chair and began to talk. A moment after the dazed artist knew that he was talking about the most tremendous thing in the world.

'Is there anything it it?' he was saying. 'That is what I've come to asking myself till I'm nearly crazy. I'd never have believed I should come to thinking of such things; but I think of the portrait and the rhyme and the coincidences or whatever you call them, and I go cold. Is there anything in it? Is there any Doom of the Darnaways or only a damned queer accident? Have I got a right to marry, or shall I bring something big and black out of the sky, that I know nothing about, on myself and somebody else?'

His rolling eye had roamed round the table and rested on the plain face of the priest, to whom he now seemed to be speaking. Payne's submerged practicality rose in protest against the problem of super-stition being brought before that supremely superstitious tribunal. He was sitting next to Darnaway and struck in before the priest could answer.

'Well, the coincidences are curious, I admit,' he said, rather forcing a note of cheerfulness; 'but surely we –' and then he stopped as if he had been struck by lightning. For Darnaway had turned his head sharply over his shoulder at the interruption, and with the movement, his left eyebrow jerked up far above its fellow and for an instant the face of the portrait glared at him with a ghastly exaggeration of exactitude. The rest saw it; and all had the air of having been dazzled by an instant of light. The old steward gave a hollow groan.

'It is no good,' he said hoarsely; 'we are dealing with something too terrible.'

'Yes,' assented the priest in a low voice, 'we are dealing with something terrible; with the most terrible thing I know, and the name of it is nonsense.'

'What did you say?' said Darnaway, still looking towards him.

'I said nonsense,' repeated the priest. 'I have not said anything in particular up to now, for it was none of my business; I was only taking temporary duty in the neighbourhood and Miss Darnaway wanted to see me. But since you're asking me personally and point-blank, why, it's easy enough to answer. Of course there's no Doom of the Darnaways to prevent your marrying anybody you have any decent reason for marrying. A man isn't fated to fall into the smallest venial sin, let alone into crimes like suicide and murder. You can't be made to do wicked things against your will because your name is Darnaway, any more than I can because my name is Brown. The Doom of the Browns,' he added with relish – 'the Weird of the Browns would sound even better.'

'And you of all people,' repeated the Australian, staring, 'tell me to think like that about it.'

'I tell you to think about something else,' replied the priest cheerfully. 'What has become of the rising art of photography? How is the camera getting on? I know it's rather dark downstairs, but those hollow arches on the floor above could easily be turned into a first-rate photographic studio. A few workmen could fit it out with a glass roof in no time.'

'Really,' protested Martin Wood, 'I do think you should be the last man in the world to tinker about with those beautiful Gothic arches, which are about the best work your own religion has ever done in the world. I should have thought you'd have had some feeling for that sort of art; but I can't see why you should be so uncommonly keen on photography.'

'I'm uncommonly keen on daylight,' answered Father Brown, 'especially in this dingy business; and photography has the virtue of depending on daylight. And if you don't know that I would grind all the Gothic arches in the world to powder to save the sanity of a single human soul, you don't know so much about my religion as you think you do.'

The young Australian had sprung to his feet like a man rejuvenated. 'By George! that's the talk,' he cried; 'though I never thought to hear it from that quarter. I'll tell you what, reverend sir, I'll do something that will show I haven't lost my courage after all.'

The old steward was still looking at him with quaking watchfulness, as if he felt something fey about the young man's defiance. 'Oh,' he cried, 'what are you going to do now?'

'I am going to photograph the portrait,' replied Darnaway.

Yet it was barely a week afterwards that the storm of the catastrophe seemed to stoop out of the sky, darkening that sun of sanity to which the priest had appealed in vain, and plunging the mansion once more in the darkness of the Darnaway doom. It had been easy enough to fit up the new studio; and seen from inside it looked very like any other such studio, empty except for the fullness of the white light. A man coming from the gloomy rooms below had more than normally the sense of stepping into a more than modern brilliancy, as blank as the future. At the suggestion of Wood, who knew the castle well and had got over his first aesthetic grumblings, a small room remaining intact in the upper ruins was easily turned into a dark room, into which Darnaway went out of the white daylight to grope by the crimson gleams of a red lamp. Wood said, laughing, that the red lamp had reconciled him to the vandalism; as that bloodshot darkness was as romantic as an alchemist's cave.

Darnaway had risen at daybreak on the day that he meant to photograph the mysterious portrait, and had it carried up from the library by the single corkscrew staircase that connected the two floors. There he had set it up in the wide white daylight on a sort of easel and planted his photographic tripod in front of it. He said he was anxious to send a reproduction of it to a great antiquary who had written on the antiquities of the house; but the others knew that this was an excuse covering much deeper things. It was, if not exactly a spiritual duel between Darnaway and the demoniac picture, at least a duel between Darnaway and his own doubts. He wanted to bring the daylight of photography face to face with that dark masterpiece of painting; and to see whether the sunshine of the new art would not drive out the shadows of the old.

Perhaps this was why he preferred to do it by himself, even if some of the details seemed to take longer and involve more than normal delay. Anyhow, he rather discouraged the few who visited his studio during the day of the experiment, and who found him focusing and fussing about in a very isolated and impenetrable fashion. The steward had left a meal for him, as he refused to come down; the old gentleman also returned some hours afterwards and found the meal more or less normally disposed of; but when he brought it he got no more gratitude than a grunt. Payne went up once to see how he was getting on, but finding the photographer disinclined for conversation came down again. Father Brown had wandered that way in an unobtrusive style to take Darnaway a letter from the expert to whom the photograph was to be sent. But he left the letter on a tray, and whatever he thought of that great glasshouse full of daylight and devotion to a hobby, a world he had himself in some sense created, he kept it to himself and came down. He had reason to remember very soon that he was the last to come down the solitary staircase connecting the floors, leaving a lonely man and an empty room behind him. The others were standing in the salon that led into the library, just under the great black ebony clock that looked like a titanic coffin.

'How was Darnaway getting on,' asked Payne, a little later, 'when you last went up?'

The priest passed a hand over his forehead. 'Don't tell me I'm getting psychic,' he said with a sad smile. 'I believe I'm quite dazzled with daylight up in that room and couldn't see things straight. Honestly, I felt for a flash as if there were something uncanny about Darnaway's figure standing before that portrait.'

'Oh, that's the lame leg,' said Barnet promptly. 'We know all about that.'

'Do you know,' said Payne abruptly, but lowering his voice, 'I don't think we do know all about it or anything about it. What's the matter with his leg? What was the matter with his ancestor's leg?'

'Oh, there's something about that in the book I was reading in there, in the family archives,' said Wood; 'I'll fetch it for you.' And he stepped into the library just beyond.

'I think,' said Father Brown quietly, 'Mr Payne must have some particular reason for asking that.'

'I may as well blurt it out once and for all,' said Payne, but in a yet lower voice. 'After all, there is a rational explanation. A man from anywhere might have made up to look like the portrait. What do we know about Darnaway? He is behaving rather oddly –'

The others were staring at him in a rather startled fashion; but the priest seemed to take it very calmly.

'I don't think the old portrait's ever been photographed,' he said. 'That's why he wants to do it. I don't think there's anything odd about that.'

'Quite an ordinary state of things, in fact,' said Wood with a smile; he had just returned with the book in his hand. And even as he spoke there was a stir in the clockwork of the great dark clock behind him and successive strokes thrilled through the room up to the number of seven. With the last stroke there came a crash from the floor above that shook the house like a thunderbolt; and Father Brown was already two steps up the winding staircase before the sound had ceased.

'My God!' cried Payne involuntarily; 'he is alone up there.'

'Yes,' said Father Brown without turning, as he vanished up the stairway. 'We shall find him alone.'

When the rest recovered from their first paralysis and ran helter-skelter up the stone steps and found their way to the new studio, it was true in that sense that they found him alone. They found him lying in a wreck of his tall camera, with its long splintered legs standing out grotesquely at three different angles; and Darnaway had fallen on top of it with one black crooked leg lying at a fourth angle along the floor. For the moment the dark heap looked as if he were entangled with some huge and horrible spider. Little more than a glance and a touch were needed to tell them that he was dead. Only the portrait stood untouched upon the easel, and one could fancy the smiling eyes shone.

An hour afterwards Father Brown, in helping to calm the confusion of the stricken household, came upon the old steward muttering almost as mechanically as the clock had ticked and struck the terrible hour. Almost without hearing them, he knew what the muttered words must be.

> *In the seventh heir I shall return:*
> *In the seventh hour I shall depart:*

As he was about to say something soothing, the old man seemed suddenly to start awake and stiffen into anger; his mutterings changed to a fierce cry.

'You!' he cried; 'you and your daylight! Even you won't say now there is no Doom for the Darnaways.'

'My opinion about that is unchanged,' said Father Brown mildly.

Then after a pause he added: 'I hope you will observe poor Darnaway's last wish, and see the photograph is sent off.'

'The photograph!' cried the doctor sharply. 'What's the good of that? As a matter of fact, it's rather curious; but there isn't any photograph. It seems he never took it after all, after pottering about all day.'

Father Brown swung round sharply. 'Then take it yourselves,' he said. 'Poor Darnaway was perfectly right. It's most important that the photograph should be taken.'

As all the visitors, the doctor, the priest and the two artists trailed away in a black and dismal procession across the brown and yellow sands, they were at first more or less silent, rather as if they had been stunned. And certainly there had been something like a crack of thunder in a clear sky about the fulfilment of that forgotten superstition at the very time when they had most forgotten it; when the doctor and the priest had both filled their minds with rationalism as the photographer had filled his rooms with daylight. They might be as rationalistic as they liked; but in broad daylight the seventh heir had returned, and in broad daylight at the seventh hour he had perished.

'I'm afraid everybody will always believe in the Darnaway superstition now,' said Martin Wood.

'I know one who won't,' said the doctor sharply. 'Why should I indulge in superstition because somebody else indulges in suicide?'

'You think poor Mr Darnaway committed suicide?' asked the priest.

'I'm sure he committed suicide,' replied the doctor.

'It is possible,' agreed the other.

'He was quite alone up there, and he had a whole drug-store of poisons in the dark room. Besides, it's just the sort of thing that Darnaways do.'

'You don't think there's anything in the fulfilment of the family curse?'

'Yes,' said the doctor; 'I believe in one family curse, and that is the family constitution. I told you it was heredity, and they are all half mad. If you stagnate and breed in and brood in your own swamp like that, you're bound to degenerate whether you like it or not. The laws of heredity can't be dodged; the truths of science can't be denied. The minds of the Darnaways are falling to pieces, as their blighted old sticks and stones are falling to pieces, eaten away by the sea and the salt air. Suicide – of course he committed suicide; I dare say all the rest will commit suicide. Perhaps the best thing they could do.'

As the man of science spoke there sprang suddenly and with startling clearness into Payne's memory the face of the daughter of the Darnaways, a tragic mask pale against an unfathomable blackness, but itself of a blinding and more than mortal beauty. He opened his mouth to speak and found himself speechless.

'I see,' said Father Brown to the doctor; 'so you do believe in the superstition after all?'

'What do you mean – believe in the superstition? I believe in the suicide as a matter of scientific necessity.'

'Well,' replied the priest, 'I don't see a pin to choose between your scientific superstition and the other magical superstition. They both seem to end in turning people into paralytics, who can't move their own legs or arms or save their own lives or souls. The rhyme said it was the Doom of the Darnaways to be killed, and the scientific textbook says it is the Doom of the Darnaways to kill themselves. Both ways they seem to be slaves.'

'But I thought you said you believed in rational views of these things.' said Dr Barnet. 'Don't you believe in heredity?'

'I said I believed in daylight,' replied the priest in a loud and clear voice, 'and I won't choose between two tunnels of subterranean superstition that both end in the dark. And the proof of it is this: that you are all entirely in the dark about what really happened in that house.'

'Do you mean about the suicide?' asked Payne.

'I mean about the murder,' said Father Brown; and his voice, though only slightly lifted to a louder note, seemed somehow to resound over the whole shore. 'It was murder: but murder is of the will, which God made free.'

What the others said at the moment in answer to it Payne never knew. For the word had a rather curious effect on him; stirring him like the blast of a trumpet and yet bringing him to a halt. He stood still in the middle of the sandy waste and let the others go on in front of him; he felt the blood crawling through all his veins and the sensation that is called the hair standing on end; and yet he felt a new and unnatural happiness. A psychological process too quick and too complicated for himself to follow had already reached a conclusion that he could not analyse; but the conclusion was one of relief. After standing still for a moment he turned and went back slowly across the sands to the house of the Darnaways.

He crossed the moat with a stride that shook the bridge, descended the stairs and traversed the long rooms with a resounding tread, till he came to the place where Adelaide Darnaway sat haloed with the low light of the oval window, almost like some forgotten saint left behind in the land of death. She looked up, and an expression of wonder made her face yet more wonderful.

'What is it?' she said. 'Why have you come back?'

'I have come for the Sleeping Beauty,' he said in a tone that had the resonance of a laugh. 'This old house went to sleep long ago, as the doctor said; but it is silly for you to pretend to be old. Come up into the daylight and hear the truth. I have brought you a word; it is a terrible word, but it breaks the spell of your captivity.'

She did not understand a word he said, but something made her rise and let him lead her down the long hall and up the stairs and out under the evening sky. The ruins of a dead garden stretched towards the sea, and an old fountain with the figure of a triton, green with rust, remained poised there, pouring nothing out of a dried horn into an empty basin. He had often seen that desolate outline against the evening sky as he passed, and it had seemed to him a type of fallen fortunes in more ways than one. Before long, doubtless, those hollow fonts would be filled, but it would be with the pale green bitter waters of the sea and the flowers would be drowned and strangled in seaweed. So, he had told himself, the daughter of the Darnaways might indeed be wedded; but she would be wedded to death and a doom as deaf and ruthless as the sea. But now he laid a hand on the bronze triton that was like the hand of a giant, and shook it as if he meant to hurl it over like an idol or an evil god of the garden.

'What do you mean?' she asked steadily. 'What is this word that will set us free?'

'The word is murder,' he said, 'and the freedom it brings is as fresh as the flowers of spring. No; I do not mean I have murdered anybody. But the fact that anybody can be murdered is itself good news, after the evil dreams you have been living in. Don't you understand? In that dream of yours everything that happened to you came from inside you; the Doom of the Darnaways was stored up in the Darnaways; it unfolded itself like a horrible flower. There was no escape even by happy accident; it was all inevitable; whether it was Vine and his old-wives' tales, or Barnet and his new-fangled heredity. But this man who died was not the victim of a magic curse or an inherited madness. He was murdered; and for us that murder is simply an accident; yes, *requiescat in pace*: but a happy accident. It is a ray of daylight, because it comes from outside.'

She suddenly smiled. 'Yes, I believe I understand. I suppose you are talking like a lunatic, but I understand. But who murdered him?'

'I do not know,' he answered calmly, 'but Father Brown knows. And as Father Brown says, murder is at least done by the will, free as that wind from the sea.'

'Father Brown is a wonderful person,' she said after a pause; 'he was the only person who ever brightened my existence in any way at all until –'

'Until what?' asked Payne, and made a movement almost impetuous, leaning towards her and thrusting away the bronze monster so that it seemed to rock on its pedestal.

'Well, until you did,' she said and smiled again.

So was the sleeping palace awakened, and it is no part of this story to describe the stages of its awakening, though much of it had come to pass before the dark of that evening had fallen upon the shore. As Harry Payne strode homewards once more, across those dark sands that he had crossed in so many moods, he was at the highest turn of happiness that is given in this mortal life, and the whole red sea within him was at the top of its tide. He would have had no difficulty in picturing all that place again in flower, and the bronze triton bright as a golden god and the fountain flowing with water or wine. But all this brightness and blossoming had been unfolded for him by the one word 'murder', and it was still a word that he did not understand. He had taken it on trust, and he was not unwise; for he was one of those who have a sense of the sound of truth.

It was more than a month later that Payne returned to his London house to keep an appointment with Father Brown, taking the required photograph with him. His personal romance had prospered as well as was fitting under the shadow of such a tragedy, and the shadow itself therefore lay rather more lightly on him; but it was hard to view it as anything but the shadow of a family fatality. In many ways he had been much occupied; and it was not until the Darnaway household had resumed its somewhat stern routine, and the portrait had long been restored to its place in the library, that he had managed to photograph it with a magnesium flare. Before sending it to the antiquary, as originally arranged, he brought it to the priest who had so pressingly demanded it.

'I can't understand your attitude about all this, Father Brown,' he said. 'You act as if you had already solved the problem in some way of your own.'

The priest shook his head mournfully. 'Not a bit of it,' he answered. 'I must be very stupid, but I'm quite stuck; stuck about the most practical point of all. It's a queer business; so simple up to a point and then – Let me have a look at that photograph, will you?'

He held it close to his screwed, short-sighted eyes for a moment, and then said: 'Have you got a magnifying glass?'

Payne produced one, and the priest looked through it intently for some time and then said: 'Look at the title of that book at the edge of the bookshelf beside the frame: it's "The History of Pope Joan". Now, I wonder . . . yes, by George; and the one above is something or other of Iceland. Lord! what a queer way to find it out! What a dolt and donkey I was not to notice it when I was there!'

'But what have you found out?' asked Payne impatiently.

'The last link,' said Father Brown, 'and I'm not stuck any longer. Yes; I think I know how that unhappy story went from first to last now.'

'But why?' insisted the other.

'Why, because,' said the priest with a smile, 'the Darnaway library contained books about Pope Joan and Iceland, not to mention another I see with the title beginning "The Religion of Frederick", which is not so very hard to fill up.' Then, seeing the other's annoyance, his smile faded and he said more earnestly.

'As a matter of fact, this last point, though it is the last link, is not the main business. There were much more curious things in the case than that. One of them is rather a curiosity of evidence. Let me begin by saying something that may surprise you. Darnaway did not die at seven o'clock that evening. He had been already dead for a whole day.'

'Surprise is rather a mild word,' said Payne grimly, 'since you and I both saw him walking about afterwards.'

'No, we did not,' replied Father Brown quietly. 'I think we both saw him, or thought we saw him, fussing about with the focussing of his camera. Wasn't his head under that black cloak when you passed through the room? It was when I did. And that's why I felt there was something queer about the room and the figure. It wasn't that the leg was crooked, but rather that it wasn't crooked. It was dressed in the same sort of dark clothes; but if you see what you believe to be one man standing in the way that another man stands, you will think he's in a strange and strained attitude.'

'Do you really mean,' cried Payne with something like a shudder, 'that it was some unknown man?'

'It was the murderer,' said Father Brown. 'He had already killed Darnaway at daybreak and hid the corpse and himself in the dark room – an excellent hiding-place, because nobody normally goes into it or can see much if he does. But he let it fall out on the floor at seven o'clock, of course, that the whole thing might be explained by the curse.'

'But I don't understand,' observed Payne. 'Why didn't he kill him at seven o'clock then, instead of loading himself with a corpse for fourteen hours?'

'Let me ask you another question,' said the priest. 'Why was there no photograph taken? Because the murderer made sure of killing him when he first got up, and before he could take it. It was essential to the murderer to prevent that photograph reaching the expert on the Darnaway antiquities.'

There was a sudden silence for a moment, and then the priest went on in a lower tone:

'Don't you see how simple it is? Why, you yourself saw one side of the possibility; but it's simpler even than you thought. You said a man might be faked to resemble an old picture. Surely it's simpler that a picture should be faked to resemble a man. In plain words, it's true in a rather special way that there was no Doom of the Darnaways. There was no old picture; there was no old rhyme; there was no legend of a man who caused his wife's death. But there was a very wicked and a very clever man who was willing to cause another man's death in order to rob him of his promised wife.'

The priest suddenly gave Payne a sad smile, as if in reassurance. 'For the moment I believe you thought I meant you,' he said, 'but you were not the only person who haunted that house for sentimental reasons. You know the man, or rather you think you do. But there were depths in the man called Martin Wood, artist and antiquary, which none of his mere artistic acquaintances were likely to guess. Remember that he was called in to criticize and catalogue the pictures; in an aristocratic dustbin of that sort that practically means simply to tell the Darnaways what art treasures they had got. They would not be surprised at things turning up they had never noticed before. It had to be done well, and it was; perhaps he was right when he said that if it wasn't Holbein it was somebody of the same genius.'

'I feel rather stunned,' said Payne; 'and there are twenty things I don't see yet. How did he know what Darnaway looked like? How did he actually kill him? The doctors seem rather puzzled at present.'

'I saw a photograph the lady had which the Australian sent on before him,' said the priest, 'and there are several ways in which he could have learned things when the new heir was once recognized. We may not know these details; but they are not difficulties. You remember he used to help in the dark-room; it seems to me an ideal place, say, to prick a man with a poisoned pin, with the poisons all handy. No; I say these were not difficulties. The difficulty that stumped me was how Wood could be in two places at once. How could he take the corpse from the dark-room and prop it against the camera so that it would fall in a few seconds, without coming downstairs, when he was in the library looking out a book? And I was such a fool that I never looked at the books in the library; and it was only in this photograph, by very undeserved good luck, that I saw the simple fact of a book about Pope Joan.'

'You've kept your best riddle for the end,' said Payne grimly. 'What on earth can Pope Joan have to do with it?'

'Don't forget the book about the Something of Iceland,' advised the priest, 'or the religion of somebody called Frederick. It only remains to ask what sort of man was the late Lord Darnaway.'

'Oh, does it?' observed Payne heavily.

'He was a cultivated, humorous sort of eccentric, I believe,' went on Father Brown. 'Being cultivated, he knew there was no such person as Pope Joan. Being humorous, he was very likely to have thought of the title of "The Snakes of Iceland" or something else that didn't exist. I venture to reconstruct the third title as "The Religion of Frederick the Great" – which also doesn't exist. Now, doesn't it strike you that those would be just the titles to put on the backs of books that didn't exist; or in other words on a bookcase that wasn't a bookcase?'

'Ah!' cried Payne; 'I see what you mean now. There was some hidden staircase –'

'Up to the room Wood himself selected as a dark room,' said the priest nodding. 'I'm sorry. It couldn't be helped. It's dreadfully banal and stupid, as stupid as I have been on this pretty banal case. But we were mixed up in a real musty old romance of decayed gentility and a fallen family mansion; and it was too much to hope that we could escape having a secret passage. It was a priest's hole; and I deserve to be put in it.'

The Secret of Father Brown

1
The Song of the Flying Fish

The soul of Mr Peregrine Smart hovered like a fly round one possession and one joke. It might be considered a mild joke, for it consisted merely of asking people if they had seen his goldfish. It might also be considered an expensive joke; but it is doubtful whether he was not secretly more attached to the joke than to the evidence of expenditure. In talking to his neighbours in the little group of new houses that had grown up round the old village green, he lost no time in turning the conversation in the direction of his hobby. To Dr Burdock, a rising biologist with a resolute chin and hair brushed back like a German's, Mr Smart made the easy transition. 'You are interested in natural history; have you seen my goldfish?' To so orthodox an evolutionist as Dr Burdock doubtless all nature was one; but at first sight the link was not close, as he was a specialist who had concentrated entirely upon the primitive ancestry of the giraffe. To Father Brown, from a church in the neighbouring provincial town, he traced a rapid train of thought which touched on the topics of 'Rome – St Peter – fisherman – fish – goldfish'. In talking to Mr Imlack Smith, the bank manager, a slim and sallow gentleman of dressy appearance but quiet demeanour, he violently wrenched the conversation to the subject of the gold standard, from which it was merely a step to goldfish. In talking to that brilliant Oriental traveller and scholar, Count Yvon de Lara (whose title was French and his face rather Russian, not to say Tartar), the versatile conversationalist showed an intense and intelligent interest in the Ganges and the Indian Ocean, leading naturally to the possible presence of goldfish in those waters. From Mr Harry Hartopp, the very rich but very shy and silent young gentleman who had recently come down from London, he had at last extorted the information that the embarrassed youth in question was *not* interested in fishing, and had then added: 'Talking about fishing, have you seen my goldfish?'

The peculiar thing about the goldfish was that they were made of gold. They were part of an eccentric but expensive toy, said to have been made by the freak of some rich Eastern prince, and Mr Smart had picked it up at some sale or in some curiosity shop, such as he frequented for the purpose of lumbering up his house with unique and useless things. From the other end of the room it looked like a rather unusually large bowl containing rather unusually large living fish; a closer inspection showed it to be a huge bubble of beautifully blown Venetian glass, very thin and delicately clouded with faintly iridescent colour, in the tinted twilight of which hung grotesque golden fishes with great rubies for eyes. The whole thing was undoubtedly worth a great deal in solid material; how much more would depend upon the waves of lunacy passing over the world of collectors. Mr Smart's new secretary, a young man named Francis Boyle, though an Irishman and not credited with caution, was mildly surprised at his talking so freely of the gems of his collection to the group of comparative strangers who happened to have alighted in a rather nomadic fashion in the neighbourhood; for collectors are commonly vigilant and sometimes secretive. In the course of settling down to his new duties, Mr Boyle found he was not alone in this sentiment, and that in others, it passed from a mild wonder to a grave disapproval.

'It's a wonder his throat isn't cut,' said Mr Smart's valet, Harris, not without a hypothetical relish, almost as if he had said, in a purely artistic sense: 'It's a pity.'

'It's extraordinary how he leaves things about,' said Mr Smart's head clerk, Jameson, who had come up from the office to assist the new secretary, 'and he won't even put up those ramshackle old bars across his ramshackle old door.'

'It's all very well with Father Brown and the doctor,' said Mr Smart's housekeeper, with a certain vigorous vagueness that marked her opinions, 'but when it comes to foreigners, I call it tempting providence. It isn't only the Count, either; that man at the bank looks to me much too yellow to be English.'

'Well, that young Hartopp is English enough,' said Boyle good-humouredly, 'to the extent of not having a word to say for himself.'

'He thinks the more,' said the housekeeper. 'He may not be exactly a foreigner, but he is not such a fool as he looks. Foreign is as foreign does, I say,' she added darkly.

Her disapproval would probably have deepened if she had heard the conversation, in her master's drawing-room that afternoon, a conversation of which the goldfish were the text, though the offensive foreigner tended more and more to be the central figure. It was not that he spoke so very much; but even his silences had something positive about them. He looked the more massive for sitting in a sort of heap on a heap of cushions, and in the deepening twilight his wide Mongolian face seemed faintly luminous, like a moon. Perhaps his background brought out something atmospherically Asiatic about his face and figure, for the room was a chaos of more or less costly curiosities, amid which could be seen the crooked curves and burning colours of countless Eastern weapons, Eastern pipes and vessels, Eastern musical instruments and illuminated manuscripts. Anyhow, as the conversation proceeded, Boyle felt more and more that the figure seated on the cushions and dark against the twilight had the exact outline of a huge image of Buddha.

The conversation was general enough, for all the little local group were present. They were, indeed, often in the habit of dropping in at each other's houses, and by this time constituted a sort of club, of people coming from the four or five houses standing round the green. Of these houses Peregrine Smart's was the oldest, largest, and most picturesque; it straggled down almost the whole of one side of the square, leaving only room for a small villa, inhabited by a retired colonel named Varney, who was reported to be an invalid, and certainly was never seen to go abroad. At right angles to these stood two or three shops that served the simpler needs of the hamlet, and at the corner the inn of the Blue Dragon, at which Mr Hartopp, the stranger from London, was staying. On the opposite side were three houses, one rented by the Count de Lara, one by Dr Burdock, and the third still standing empty. On the fourth side was the bank, with an adjoining house for the bank manager, and a line of fence enclosing some land that was let for building. It was thus a very self-contained group, and the comparative emptiness of the open ground for miles round it threw the members more and more on each other's society. That afternoon, one stranger had indeed broken into the magic circle: a hatchet-faced fellow with fierce tufts of eyebrows and moustache, and so shabbily dressed that he must have been a millionaire or a duke if he had really (as was alleged) come down to do business with the old collector. But he was known, at the Blue Dragon at least, as Mr Harmer.

To him had been recounted anew the glories of the gilded fish and the criticisms regarding their custody.

'People are always telling me I ought to lock them up more carefully,' observed Mr Smart, cocking an eyebrow over his shoulder at the dependant who stood there holding some papers from the office. Smart was a round-faced, round-bodied little old man rather like a bald parrot. 'Jameson and Harris and the rest are always at me to bar the doors as if it were a mediaeval fortress, though really these rotten old rusty bars are too mediaeval to keep anybody out, I should think. I prefer to trust to luck and the local police.'

'It is not always the best bars that keep people out,' said the Count. 'It all depends on who's trying to get in. There was an ancient Hindu hermit who lived naked in a cave and passed through the three armies that encircled the Mogul and took the great ruby out of the tyrant's turban, and went back unscathed like a shadow. For he wished to teach the great how small are the laws of space and time.'

'When we really study the small laws of space and time,' said Dr Burdock dryly, 'we generally find out how those tricks are done. Western science has let in daylight on a good deal of Eastern magic. Doubtless a great deal can be done with hypnotism and suggestion, to say nothing of sleight-of-hand.'

'The ruby was not in the royal tent,' observed the Count in his dream fashion; 'but he found it among a hundred tents.'

'Can't all that be explained by telepathy?' asked the doctor sharply.

The question sounded the sharper because it was followed by a heavy silence, almost as if the distinguished Oriental traveller had, with imperfect politeness, gone to sleep.

'I beg your pardon,' he said rousing himself with a sudden smile. 'I had forgotten we were talking with words. In the east we talk with thoughts, and so we never misunderstand each other. It is strange how you people worship words and are satisfied with words. What difference does it make to a thing that you now call it telepathy, as you once called it tomfoolery? If a man climbs into the sky on a mango-tree, how is it

THE SONG OF THE FLYING FISH

altered by saying it is only levitation, instead of saying it is only lies. If a mediaeval witch waved a wand and turned me into a blue baboon, you would say it was only atavism.'

The doctor looked for a moment as if he might say that it would not be so great a change after all. But before his irritation could find that or any other vent, the man called Harmer interrupted gruffly:

'It's true enough those Indian conjurers can do queer things, but I notice they generally do them in India. Confederates, perhaps, or merely mass psychology. I don't think those tricks have ever been played in an English village, and I should say our friend's goldfish were quite safe.'

'I will tell you a story,' said de Lara, in his motionless way, 'which happened not in India, but outside an English barrack in the most modernized part of Cairo. A sentinel was standing inside the grating of an iron gateway looking out between the bars on to the street. There appeared outside the gate a beggar, barefoot and in native rags, who asked him, in English that was startlingly distinct and refined, for a certain official document kept in the building for safety. The soldier told the man, of course, that he could not come inside; and the man answered, smiling: "What is inside and what is outside?" The soldier was still staring scornfully through the iron grating when he gradually realized that, though neither he nor the gate had moved, he was actually standing in the street and looking in at the barrack yard, where the beggar stood still and smiling and equally motionless. Then, when the beggar turned towards the building, the sentry awoke to such sense as he had left, and shouted a warning to all the soldiers within the gated enclosure to hold the prisoner fast. "You won't get out of there anyhow," he said vindictively. Then the beggar said in his silvery voice: "What is outside and what is inside?" And the soldier, still glaring through the same bars, saw that they were once more between him and the street, where the beggar stood free and smiling with a paper in his hand.'

Mr Imlack Smith, the bank manager, was looking at the carpet with his dark sleek head bowed, and he spoke for the first time.

'Did anything happen about the paper?' he asked.

'Your professional instincts are correct, sir,' said the Count, with grim affability. 'It was a paper of considerable financial importance. Its consequences were international.'

'I hope they don't occur often,' said young Hartopp gloomily.

'I do not touch the political side,' said the Count serenely, 'but only the philosophical. It illustrates how the wise man can get behind time and space and turn the levers of them, so to speak, so that the whole world turns round before our eyes. But is it so hard for you people to believe that spiritual powers are really more powerful than material ones?'

'Well,' said old Smart cheerfully, 'I don't profess to be an authority on spiritual powers. What do you say, Father Brown?'

'The only thing that strikes me,' answered the little priest, 'is that all the supernatural acts we have yet heard of seem to be thefts. And stealing by spiritual methods seem to me much the same as stealing by material ones.'

'Father Brown is a Philistine,' said the smiling Smith.

'I have a sympathy with the tribe,' said Father Brown. 'A Philistine is only a man who is right without knowing why.'

'All this is too clever for me,' said Hartopp heartily.

'Perhaps,' said Father Brown with a smile, 'you would like to speak without words, as the Count suggests. He would begin by saying nothing in a pointed fashion, and you would retort with a burst of taciturnity.'

'Something might be done with music,' murmured the Count dreamily. 'It would be better than all these words.'

'Yes, I might understand that better,' said the young man in a low voice.

Boyle had followed the conversation with curious attention, for there was something in the demeanour of more than one of the talkers that seemed to him significant or even odd. As the talk drifted to music, with an appeal to the dapper bank manager (who was an amateur musician of some merit), the young secretary awoke with a start to his secretarial duties, and reminded his employer that the head clerk was still standing patiently with the papers in his hand.

'Oh, never mind about those just now, Jameson,' said Smart rather hurriedly. 'Only something about my account; I'll see Mr Smith about it later. You were saying that the 'cello, Mr Smith –'

But the cold breath of business had sufficed to disperse the fumes of transcendental talk, and the guests began one after another to say farewell. Only Mr Imlack Smith, bank manager and musician, remained to the last; and when the rest were gone he and his host went into the inner room, where the goldfish were kept, and closed the door.

The house was long and narrow, with a covered balcony running along the first floor, which consisted mostly of a sort of suite of rooms used by the householder himself, his bedroom and dressing-room, and an inner room in which his very valuable treasures were sometimes stored for the night instead of being left in the rooms below. This balcony, like the insufficiently barred door below it, was a matter of concern to the house-keeper and the head clerk and the others who lamented the carelessness of the collector; but, in truth, that cunning old gentleman was more careful than he seemed. He professed no great belief in the antiquated fastenings of the old house, which the house-keeper lamented to see rusting in idleness, but he had an eye to the more important point of strategy. He always put his favourite goldfish in the room at the back of his bedroom for the night, and slept in front of it, as it were, with a pistol under his pillow. And when Boyle and Jameson, awaiting his return from the *tête-à-tête*, at length saw the door open and their employer reappear, he was carrying the great glass bowl as reverently as if it had been the relic of a saint.

Outside, the last edges of the sunset still clung to the corners of the green square; but inside, a lamp had already been kindled; and in the mingling of the two lights the coloured globe glowed like some monstrous jewel, and the fantastic outlines of the fiery fishes seemed to give it, indeed, something of the mystery of a talisman, like strange shapes seen by a seer in the crystal of doom. Over the old man's shoulder the olive face of Imlack Smith stared like a sphinx.

'I am going up to London tonight, Mr Boyle,' said old Smart, with more gravity than he commonly showed. 'Mr Smith and I are catching the six-forty-five. I should prefer you, Jameson, to sleep upstairs in my room tonight; if you put the bowl in the back room as usual, it will be quite safe then. Not that I suppose anything could possibly happen.'

'Anything may happen anywhere,' said the smiling Mr Smith. 'I think you generally take a gun to bed with you. Perhaps you had better leave it behind in this case.'

Peregrine Smart did not reply, and they passed out of the house on to the road round the village green.

The secretary and the head clerk slept that night as directed in their employer's bedroom. To speak more strictly, Jameson, the head clerk, slept in a bed in the dressing-room, but the door stood open between, and the two rooms running along the front were practically one. Only the bedroom had a long french window giving on to the balcony, and an entrance at the back into the inner apartment, where the goldfish bowl had been placed for safety. Boyle dragged his bed right across so as to bar this entrance, put the revolver under his pillow, and then undressed and went to bed, feeling that he had taken all possible precautions against an impossible or improbable event. He did not see why there should be any particular danger of normal burglary; and as for the spiritual burglary that figured in the traveller's tales of the Count de Lara, if his thoughts ran on them so near to sleep it was because they were such stuff as dreams are made of. They soon turned into dreams with intervals of dreamless slumber. The old clerk was a little more restless as usual; but after fussing about a little longer and repeating some of his favourite regrets and warnings, he also retired to his bed in the same manner and slept. The moon brightened and grew dim again above the green square and the grey blocks of houses in a solitude and silence that seemed to have no human witness; and it was when the white cracks of daybreak had already appeared in the corners of the grey sky that the thing happened.

Boyle, being young, was naturally both the healthier and the heavier sleeper of the two. Though active enough when he was once awake, he always had a load to lift in waking. Moreover, he had dreams of the sort that cling to the emerging minds like the dim tentacles of an octopus. They were a medley of many things, including his last look from the balcony across the four grey roads and the green square. But the pattern of them changed and shifted and turned dizzily, to the accompaniment of a low grinding noise, which sounded somehow like a subterranean river, and may have been no more than old Mr Jameson snoring in the dressing-room. But in the dreamer's mind all that murmur and motion was vaguely connected with the words of the Count de Lara, about a wisdom that could hold the levers of time and space and turn the world. In the dream it seemed as if a vast murmuring machinery under the world were really moving whole landscapes hither and thither, so that the ends of the earth might appear in a man's front-garden, or his own front-garden be exiled beyond the sea.

The first complete impressions he had were the words of a song, with a rather thin metallic accompaniment; they were sung in a foreign accent and a voice that was still strange and yet faintly familiar. And yet he could hardly feel sure that he was not making up poetry in his sleep.

> *Over the land and over the sea*
> *My flying fishes will come to me,*
> *For the note is not of the world that wakes them,*
> *But in –*

He struggled to his feet and saw that his fellow-guardian was already out of bed; Jameson was peering out of the long window on to the balcony and calling out sharply to someone in the street below.

'Who's that?' he called out sharply. 'What do you want?'

He turned to Boyle in agitation, saying: 'There's somebody prowling about just outside. I knew it wasn't safe. I'm going down to bar that front door, whatever they say.'

He ran downstairs in a flutter and Boyle could hear the clattering of the bars upon the front door; but Boyle himself stepped out upon the balcony and looked out on the long grey road that led up to the house, and he thought he was still dreaming.

Upon that grey road leading across that empty moor and through that little English hamlet, there had appeared a figure that might have stepped straight out of the jungle or the bazaar – a figure out of one of the Count's fantastic stories; a figure out of the 'Arabian Nights'. The rather ghostly grey twilight which begins to define and yet to discolour everything when the light in the east has ceased to be localized, lifted slowly like a veil of grey gauze and showed him a figure wrapped in outlandish raiment. A scarf of a strange sea-blue, vast and voluminous, went round the head like a turban, and then again round the chin, giving rather the general character of a hood; so far as the face was concerned it had the effects of a mask. For the raiment round the head was drawn close as a veil; and the head itself was bowed over a queer-looking musical instrument made of silver or steel, and shaped like a deformed or crooked violin. It was played with something like a silver comb, and the notes were curiously thin and keen. Before Boyle could open his mouth, the same haunting alien accent came from under the shadow of the burnous, singing words of the same sort:

As the golden birds go back to the tree
My golden fishes return to me.
Return –

'You've no right here,' called out Boyle in exasperation, hardly knowing what he said.

'I have a right to the goldfish,' said the stranger, speaking more like King Solomon than an unsandalled Bedouin in a ragged blue cloak. 'And they will come to me. Come!'

He struck his strange fiddle as his voice rose sharply on the word. There was a pang of sound that seemed to pierce the mind, and then there came a fainter sound, like an answer: a vibrant whisper. It came from the dark room behind where the bowl of goldfish was standing.

Boyle turned towards it; and even as he turned the echo in the inner room changed to a long tingling sound like an electric bell, and then to a faint crash. It was still a matter of seconds since he had challenged the man from the balcony; but the old clerk had already regained the top of the stairs, panting a little, for he was an elderly gentleman.

'I've locked up the door, anyhow,' he said.

'The stable door,' said Boyle out of the darkness of the inner room.

Jameson followed him into that apartment and found him staring down at the floor, which was covered with a litter of coloured glass like the curved bits of a broken rainbow.

'What do you mean by the stable door?' began Jameson.

'I mean that the steed is stolen,' answered Boyle. 'The flying steeds. The flying fishes our Arab friend outside has just whistled to like so many performing puppies.'

'But how could he?' exploded the old clerk, as if such events were hardly respectable.

'Well, they're gone,' said Boyle shortly. 'The broken bowl is here, which would have taken a long time to open properly, but only a second to smash. But the fish are gone, God knows how, though I think our friend ought to be asked.'

'We are wasting time,' said the distracted Jameson. 'We ought to be after him at once.'

'Much better be telephoning the police at once,' answered Boyle. 'They ought to outstrip him in a flash with motors and telephones that go a good deal farther than we should ever get, running through the village in our nightgowns. But it may be there are things even the police cars and wires won't outstrip.'

While Jameson was talking to the police-station through the telephone in an agitated voice, Boyle went out again on to the balcony and hastily scanned that grey landscape of daybreak. There was no trace of the man in the turban, and no other sign of life, except some faint stirrings an expert might have recognized in the hotel of the Blue Dragon. Only Boyle, for the first time, noted consciously something that he had all along been noting unconsciously. It was like a fact struggling in the submerged mind and demanding its own meaning. It was simply the fact that the grey landscape had never been entirely grey; there was one gold spot amid its stripes of colourless colour, a lamp lighted in one of the houses on the other side of the green. Something, perhaps irrational, told him that it had been burning through all the hours of the darkness and was only fading with the dawn. He counted the houses, and his calculation brought out a result which seemed to fit in with something, he knew not what. Anyhow, it was apparently the house of the Count Yvon de Lara.

Inspector Pinner had arrived with several policemen, and done several things of a rapid and resolute sort, being conscious that the very absurdity of the costly trinkets might give the case considerable prominence in the newspapers. He had examined everything, measured everything, taken down everybody's deposition, taken everybody's finger-prints, put everybody's back up, and found himself at the end left facing a fact which he could not believe. An Arab from the desert had walked up the public road and stopped in front of the house of Mr Peregrine Smart, where a bowl of artificial goldfish was kept in an inner room; he had then sung or recited a little poem, and the bowl had exploded like a bomb and the fishes vanished into thin air. Nor did it soothe the inspector to be told by a foreign Count – in a soft, purring voice – that the bounds of experience were being enlarged.

Indeed, the attitude of each member of the little group was characteristic enough. Peregrine Smart himself had come back from London the next morning to hear the news of his loss. Naturally he admitted a shock; but it was typical of something sporting and spirited in the little old gentleman, something that always made his small strutting figure look like a cock-sparrow's, that he showed more vivacity in the search than depression at the loss. The man named Harmer, who had come to the village on purpose to buy the goldfish, might be excused for being a little testy on learning they were not there to be bought. But, in truth, his rather aggressive moustache and eyebrows seemed to bristle with something more definite than disappointment, and the eyes that darted over the company were bright with a vigilance that might well be suspicion. The sallow face of the bank manager, who had also returned from London though by a later train, seemed again and again to attract those shining and shifting eyes like a magnet. Of the two remaining figures of the original circle, Father Brown was generally silent when he was not spoken to, and the dazed Hartopp was often silent even when he was.

But the Count was not a man to let anything pass that gave an apparent advantage to his views. He smiled at his rationalistic rival, the doctor, in the manner of one who knows how it is possible to be irritating by being ingratiating.

'You will admit, doctor,' he said, 'that at least some of the stories you thought so improbable look a little more realistic to-day than they did yesterday. When a man as ragged as those I described is able, by speaking a word, to dissolve a solid vessel inside the four walls of the house he stands outside, it might perhaps be called an example of what I said about spiritual powers and material barriers.'

'And it might be called an example of what I said,' said the doctor sharply, 'about a little scientific knowledge being enough to show how the tricks are done.'

'Do you really mean, doctor,' asked Smart in some excitement, 'that you can throw any scientific light on this mystery?'

'I can throw light on what the Count calls a mystery,' said the doctor, 'because it is not a mystery at all. That part of it is plain enough. A sound is only a wave of vibration, and certain vibrations can break glass, if the sound is of a certain kind and the glass of a certain kind. The man did not stand in the road and think, which the Count tells us is the ideal method when Orientals want a little chat. He sang out what he wanted, quite loud, and struck a shrill note on an instrument. It is similar to many experiments by which glass of special composition has been cracked.'

'Such as the experiment,' said the Count lightly, 'by which several lumps of solid gold have suddenly ceased to exist.'

'Here comes Inspector Pinner,' said Boyle. 'Between ourselves, I think he would regard the doctor's natural explanation as quite as much of a fairy tale as the Count's preternatural one. A very sceptical intellect, Mr Pinner's, especially about me. I rather think I am under suspicion.'

'I think we are all under suspicion,' said the Count.

It was the presence of this suspicion in his own case that led Boyle to seek the personal advice of Father Brown. They were walking round the village green together, some hours later in the day, when the priest, who was frowning thoughtfully at the ground as he listened, suddenly stopped.

'Do you see that?' he asked. 'Somebody's been washing the pavement here – just this little strip of pavement outside Colonel Varney's house. I wonder whether that was done yesterday.'

Father Brown looked rather earnestly at the house, which was high and narrow, and carried rows of striped sun-blinds of gay but already faded colours. The chinks or crannies that gave glimpses of the interior looked all the darker; indeed, they looked almost black in contrast with the façade thus golden in the morning light.

'That is Colonel Varney's house, isn't it?' he asked. 'He comes from the East, too, I fancy. What sort of man is he?'

'I've never even seen him,' answered Boyle. 'I don't think anybody's seen him, except Dr Burdock, and I rather fancy the doctor doesn't see him more than he need.'

'Well, I'm going to see him for a minute,' said Father Brown.

The big front door opened and swallowed the small priest, and his friend stood staring at it in a dazed and irrational manner, as if wondering whether it would ever open again. It opened in a few minutes, and Father Brown emerged, still smiling, and continued his slow and pottering progress round the square of roads. Sometimes he seemed to have forgotten the matter in hand altogether, for he would make passing remarks on historical and social questions, or on the prospects of development in the district. He remarked on the soil used for the beginning of a new road by the bank; he looked across the old village green with a vague expression.

'Common land. I suppose people ought to feed their pigs and geese on it, if they had any pigs or geese; as it is, it seems to feed nothing but nettles and thistles. What a pity that what was supposed to be a sort of large meadow has been turned into a small and petty wilderness. That's Dr Burdock's house opposite, isn't it?'

'Yes,' answered Boyle, almost jumping at this abrupt postscript.

'Very well,' answered Father Brown, 'then I think we'll go indoors again.'

As they opened the front door of Smart's house and mounted the stairs, Boyle repeated to his companion many details of the drama enacted there at daybreak.

'I suppose you didn't doze off again?' asked Father Brown, 'giving time for somebody to scale the balcony while Jameson ran down to secure the door.'

'No,' answered Boyle; 'I am sure of that. I woke up to hear Jameson challenging the stranger from the balcony; then I heard him running downstairs and putting up the bars, and then in two strides I was on the balcony myself.'

'Or could he have slipped in between you from another angle? Are there any other entrances besides the front entrance?'

'Apparently there are not,' said Boyle gravely

'I had better make sure, don't you think?' asked Father Brown apologetically, and scuttled softly downstairs again. Boyle remained in the front bedroom gazing rather doubtfully after him. After a comparatively brief interval the round and rather rustic visage appeared again at the head of the stairs, looking rather like a turnip ghost with a broad grin.

'No; I think that settles the matter of entrances,' said the turnip ghost, cheerfully. 'And now, I think, having got everything in a tight box, so to speak, we can take stock of what we've got. It's rather a curious business.'

'Do you think,' asked Boyle, 'that the Count or the colonel, or any of these Eastern travellers have anything to do with it? Do you think it is – preternatural?'

'I will grant you this,' said the priest gravely, 'if the Count, or the colonel, or any of your neighbours did dress up in Arab masquerade and creep up to this house in the dark – then it *was* preternatural.'

'What do you mean? Why?'

'Because the Arab left no footprints,' answered Father Brown. 'The

234

colonel on the one side and the banker on the other are the nearest of your neighbours. That loose red soil is between you and the bank, it would print off bare feet like a plaster cast and probably leave red marks everywhere. I braved the colonel's curry-seasoned temper to verify the fact that the front pavement was washed yesterday and not to-day; it was wet enough to make wet footprints all along the road. Now, if the visitor were the Count or the doctor in the houses opposite, he might possibly, of course, have come across the common. But he must have found it exceedingly uncomfortable with bare feet, for it is, as I remarked, one mass of thorns and thistles and stinging nettles. He would surely have pricked himself and probably left traces of it. Unless, as you say, he was a preternatural being.'

Boyle looked steadily at the grave and indecipherable face of his clerical friend.

'Do you mean that he was?' he asked, at length.

'There is one general truth to remember,' said Father Brown, after a pause. 'A thing can sometimes be too close to be seen, as, for instance, a man cannot see himself. There was a man who had a fly in his eye when he looked through the telescope, and he discovered that there was a most incredible dragon in the moon. And I am told that if a man hears the exact reproduction of his own voice it sounds like the voice of a stranger. In the same way, if anything is right in the foreground of our life we hardly see it, and if we did we might think it quite odd. If the thing in the foreground got into the middle-distance, we should probably think it had come from the remote distance. Just come outside the house again for a moment. I want to show you how it looks from another standpoint.'

He had already risen, and as they descended the stairs he continued his remarks in a rather groping fashion as if he were thinking aloud.

'The Count and the Asiatic atmosphere all come in, because, in a case like this, everything depends on the preparation of the mind. A man can reach a condition in which a brick, falling on his head, will seem to be a Babylonian brick carved with cuneiform, and dropped from the Hanging Gardens of Babylon, so that he will never even look at the brick and see it is of one pattern with the bricks of his own house. So in your case –'

'What does this mean?' interrupted Boyle, staring and pointing at the entrance. 'What in the name of wonder does it mean? The door is barred again.'

He was staring at the front door by which they had entered but a little while before, and across which stood, once more, the great dark bands of rusty iron which had once, as he had said, locked the stable door too late. There was something darkly and dumbly ironic in those old fastenings closing behind them and imprisoning them as if of their own motion.

'Oh those!' said Father Brown casually. 'I put up those bars myself, just now. Didn't you hear me?'

'No,' answered Boyle, staring. 'I heard nothing.'

'Well, I rather thought you wouldn't,' said the other equably. 'There's really no reason why anybody upstairs should hear those bars being put up. A sort of hook fits easily into a sort of hole. When you're quite close you hear a dull click; but that's all. The only thing that makes any noise a man could hear upstairs, is this.'

And he lifted the bar out of its socket and let it fall with a clang at the side of the door.

'It does make a noise if you *unbar* the door,' said Father Brown gravely, 'even if you do it pretty carefully.'

'You mean –'

'I mean,' said Father Brown, 'that what you heard upstairs was Jameson opening the door and not shutting it. And now let's open the door ourselves and go outside.'

When they stood outside in the street, under the balcony, the little priest resumed his previous explanation as coolly as if it had been a chemical lecture.

'I was saying that a man may be in the mood to look for something very distant, and not realize that it is something very close, something very close to himself, perhaps something very like himself. It was a strange and outlandish thing that you saw when you looked down at this road. I suppose it never occurred to you to consider what he saw when he looked up at that balcony?'

Boyle was staring at the balcony and did not answer, and the other added:

'You thought it very wild and wonderful that an Arab should come through civilized England with bare feet. You did not remember that at the same moment you had bare feet yourself.'

Boyle at last found words, and it was to repeat words already spoken. 'Jameson opened the door,' he said mechanically.

'Yes,' assented his friend. 'Jameson opened the door and came out into the road in his nightclothes, just as you came out on the balcony. He caught up two things that you had seen a hundred times: the length of old blue curtain that he wrapped round his head, and the Oriental musical instrument you must have often seen in that heap of Oriental curiosities. The rest was atmosphere and acting, very fine acting, for he is a very fine artist in crime.'

'Jameson!' exclaimed Boyle incredulously. 'He was such a dull old stick that I never even noticed him.'

'Precisely,' said the priest, 'he was an artist. If he could act a wizard or a troubadour for six minutes, do you think he could not act a clerk for six weeks?'

'I am still not quite sure of his object,' said Boyle.

'His object has been achieved,' replied Father Brown, 'or very nearly achieved. He had taken the goldfish already, of course, as he had twenty chances of doing. But if he had simply taken them, everybody would have realized that he had twenty chances of doing it. By creating a mysterious magician from the end of the earth, he set everybody's thoughts wandering far afield to Arabia and India, so that you yourself can hardly believe that the whole thing was so near home. It was too close to you to be seen.'

'If this is true,' said Boyle, 'it was an extraordinary risk to run, and he had to cut it very fine. It's true I never heard the man in the street say anything while Jameson was talking from the balcony, so I suppose that was all a fake. And I suppose it's true that there was time for him to get outside before I had fully woken up and got out on to the balcony.'

'Every crime depends on somebody not waking up too soon,' replied Father Brown; 'and in every sense most of us wake up too late. I, for one, have woken up much too late. For I imagine he's bolted long ago, just before or just after they took his finger-prints.'

'You woke up before anybody else, anyhow,' said Boyle, 'and I should never have woken up in that sense. Jameson was so correct and colourless that I forgot all about him.'

'Beware of the man you forget,' replied his friend; 'he is the one man who has you entirely at a disadvantage. But I did not suspect him, either, until you told me how you had heard him barring the door.'

'Anyhow, we owe it all to you,' said Boyle warmly.

'You owe it all to Mrs Robinson,' said Father Brown with a smile.

'Mrs Robinson?' questioned the wondering secretary. 'You don't mean the housekeeper?'

'Beware of the woman you forget, and even more,' answered the other. 'This man was a very high-class criminal; he had been an excellent actor, and therefore he was a good psychologist. A man like the Count never hears any voice but his own; but this man could listen, when you had all forgotten he was there, and gather exactly the right materials for his romance and know exactly the right note to strike to lead you all astray. But he made one bad mistake in the psychology of Mrs Robinson, the housekeeper.'

'I don't understand,' answered Boyle, 'what she can have to do with it.'

'Jameson did not expect the doors to be barred,' said Father Brown. 'He knew that a lot of men, especially careless men like you and your employer, could go on saying for days that something ought to be done, or might as well be done. But if you convey to a woman that something ought to be done, there is always a dreadful danger that she will suddenly do it.'

2
The Worst Crime in the World

Father Brown was wandering through a picture gallery with an expression that suggested that he had not come there to look at the pictures. Indeed, he did not want to look at the pictures, though he liked pictures well enough. Not that there was anything immoral or improper about those highly modern pictorial designs. He would indeed be of an inflammable temperament who was stirred to any of the more pagan passions by the display of interrupted spirals, inverted cones and broken cylinders with which the art of the future inspired or menaced mankind. The truth is that Father Brown was looking for a young friend who had appointed that somewhat incongruous meeting-place, being herself of a more futuristic turn. The young friend was also a young relative; one of the few relatives that he had. Her name was Elizabeth Fane, simplified into Betty, and she was the child of a sister who had married into a race of refined but impoverished squires. As the squire was dead as well as impoverished, Father Brown stood in the relation of a protector as well as a priest, and in some sense a guardian as well as an uncle. At the moment, however, he was blinking about at the groups in the gallery without catching sight of the familiar brown hair and bright face of his niece. Nevertheless, he saw some people he knew and a number of people he did not know, including some that, as a mere matter of taste, he did not much want to know.

Among the people the priest did not know and who yet aroused his interest was a lithe and alert young man, very beautifully dressed and looking rather like a foreigner, because, while his beard was cut in a spade shape like an old Spaniard's, his dark hair was cropped so close as to look like a tight black skull-cap. Among the people the priest did not particularly want to know was a very dominant-looking lady, sensationally clad in scarlet, with a mane of yellow hair too long to be called bobbed, but too loose to be called anything else. She had a powerful and rather heavy face of a pale and rather unwholesome complexion, and when she looked at anybody she cultivated the fascinations of a basilisk. She towed in attendance behind her a short man with a big beard and a very broad face, with long sleepy slits of eyes. The expression of his face was beaming and benevolent, if only partially awake; but his bull neck, when seen from behind, looked a little brutal.

Father Brown gazed at the lady, feeling that the appearance and approach of his niece would be an agreeable contrast. Yet he continued to gaze, for some reason, until he reached the point of feeling that the appearance of anybody would be an agreeable contrast. It was therefore with a certain relief, though with a slight start as of awakening, that he turned at the sound of his name and saw another face that he knew.

It was the sharp but not unfriendly face of a lawyer named Granby, whose patches of grey hair might almost have been the powder from a wig, so incongruous were they with his youthful energy of movement. He was one of those men in the City who run about like schoolboys in and out of their offices. He could not run round the fashionable picture gallery quite in that fashion; but he looked as if he wanted to, and fretted as he glanced to left and right, seeking somebody he knew.

'I didn't know,' said Father Brown, smiling, 'that you were a patron of the New Art.'

'I didn't know that you were,' retorted the other. 'I came here to catch a man.'

'I hope you will have good sport,' answered the priest. 'I'm doing much the same.'

'Said he was passing through to the Continent,' snorted the solicitor, 'and could I meet him in this cranky place.' He ruminated a moment, and said abruptly: 'Look here, I know you can keep a secret. Do you know Sir John Musgrave?'

'No,' answered the priest; 'but I should hardly have thought he was a secret, though they say he does hide himself in a castle. Isn't he the old man they tell all those tales about – how he lives in a tower with a real portcullis and drawbridge, and generally refuses to emerge from the Dark Ages? Is he one of your clients?'

'No,' replied Granby shortly: 'it's his son, Captain Musgrave, who has come to us. But the old man counts for a good deal in the affair, and I don't know him; that's the point. Look here, this is confidential, as I say, but I can confide in you.' He dropped his voice and drew his friend apart into a side gallery containing representations of various real objects, which was comparatively empty.

'This young Musgrave,' he said, 'wants to raise a big sum from us on a *post obit* on his old father in Northumberland. The old man's long past seventy and presumably will *obit* some time or other; but what about the *post*, so to speak? What will happen afterwards to his cash and castles and portcullises and all the rest? It's a very fine old estate, and still worth a lot, but strangely enough it isn't entailed. So you see how we stand. The question is, as the man said in Dickens, is the old man friendly?'

'If he's friendly to his son you'll feel all the friendlier,' observed Father Brown. 'No, I'm afraid I can't help you. I never met Sir John Musgrave, and I understand very few people do meet him nowadays. But it seems obvious you have a right to an answer on that point before you lend the young gentleman your firm's money. Is he the sort that people cut off with a shilling?'

'Well, I'm doubtful,' answered the other. 'He's very popular and brilliant and a great figure in society; but he's a great deal abroad, and he's been a journalist.'

'Well,' said Father Brown, 'that's not a crime. At least not always.'

'Nonsense!' said Granby curtly. 'You know what I mean – he's rather a rolling stone, who's been a journalist and a lecturer and an actor, and all sorts of things. I've got to know where I stand . . . Why, there he is.'

And the solicitor, who had been stamping impatiently about the emptier gallery, turned suddenly and darted into the more crowded room at a run. He was running towards the tall and well-dressed young man with the short hair and the foreign-looking beard.

The two walked away together talking, and for some moments afterwards Father Brown followed them with his screwed, short-sighted eyes. His gaze was shifted and recalled, however, by the breathless and even boisterous arrival of his niece, Betty. Rather to the surprise of her uncle, she led him back into the emptier room and planted him on a seat that was like an island in that sea of floor.

'I've got something I must tell you,' she said. 'It's so silly that nobody else will understand it.'

'You overwhelm me,' said Father Brown. 'Is it about this business your mother started telling me about? Engagements and all that; not what the military historians call a general engagement.'

'You know,' she said, 'that she wants me to be engaged to Captain Musgrave.'

'I didn't,' said Father Brown with resignation; 'but Captain Musgrave seems to be quite a fashionable topic.'

'Of course we're very poor,' she said, 'and it's no good saying it makes no difference.'

'Do you want to marry him?' asked Father Brown, looking at her through his half-closed eyes.

She frowned at the floor, and answered in a lower tone:

'I thought I did. At least I think I thought I did. But I've just had rather a shock.'

'Then tell us all about it.'

'I heard him laugh,' she said.

'It is an excellent social accomplishment,' he replied.

'You don't understand,' said the girl. 'It wasn't social at all. That was just the point of it – that it wasn't social.'

She paused a moment, and then went on firmly:

'I came here quite early, and saw him sitting quite alone in the middle of that gallery with the new pictures, that was quite empty then. He had no idea I or anybody was near; he was sitting quite alone, and he laughed.'

'Well, no wonder,' said Father Brown. 'I'm not an art critic myself, but as a general view of the pictures taken as a whole –'

'Oh, you *won't* understand,' she said almost angrily. 'It wasn't a bit like that. He wasn't looking at the pictures. He was staring right up at the ceiling; but his eyes seemed to be turned inwards, and he laughed so that my blood ran cold.'

The priest had risen and was pacing the room with his hands behind him. 'You mustn't be hasty in a case of this sort,' he began. 'There are two kinds of men – but we can hardly discuss him just now, for here he is.'

Captain Musgrave entered the room swiftly and swept it with a smile. Granby, the lawyer, was just behind him, and his legal face bore a new expression of relief and satisfaction.

'I must apologize for everything I said about the Captain,' he said to the priest as they drifted together towards the door. 'He's a thoroughly sensible fellow and quite sees my point. He asked me himself why I didn't go north and see his old father; I could hear from the old man's own lips how it stood about the inheritance. Well, he couldn't say fairer than that, could he? But he's so anxious to get the thing settled that he offered to take me up in his own car to Musgrave Moss. That's the name of the estate. I suggested that, if he was so kind, we might go together; and we're starting to-morrow morning.'

As they spoke Betty and the Captain came through the doorway together, making in that framework at least a sort of picture that some would be sentimental enough to prefer to cones and cylinders. Whatever their other affinities, they were both very good-looking; and the lawyer was moved to a remark on the fact, when the picture abruptly altered.

Captain James Musgrave looked out into the main gallery, and his laughing and triumphant eyes were riveted on something that seemed to change him from head to foot. Father Brown looked round as under an advancing shadow of premonition; and he saw the lowering, almost livid face of the large woman in scarlet under its leonine yellow hair. She always stood with a slight stoop, like a bull lowering its horns, and the expression of her pale pasty face was so oppressive and hypnotic that they hardly saw the little man with the large beard standing beside her.

Musgrave advanced into the centre of the room towards her, almost like a beautifully dressed wax-work wound up to walk. He said a few words to her that could not be heard. She did not answer; but they turned away together, walking down the long gallery as if in debate, the short, bull-necked man with the beard bringing up the rear like some grotesque goblin page.

'Heaven help us!' muttered Father Brown, frowning after them. 'Who in the world is that woman?'

'No pal of mine, I'm happy to say,' replied Granby with grim flippancy. 'Looks as if a little flirtation with her might end fatally, doesn't it?'

'I don't think he's flirting with her,' said Father Brown.

Even as he spoke the group in question turned at the end of the gallery and broke up, and Captain Musgrave came back to them in hasty strides.

243

'Look here,' he cried, speaking naturally enough, though they fancied his colour was changed. 'I'm awfully sorry, Mr Granby, but I find I can't come north with you to-morrow. Of course, you will take the car all the same. Please do; I shan't want it. I – I have to be in London for some days. Take a friend with you if you like.'

'My friend, Father Brown –' began the lawyer.

'If Captain Musgrave is really so kind,' said Father Brown gravely. 'I may explain that I have some status in Mr Granby's inquiry, and it would be a great relief to my mind if I could go.'

Which was how it came about that a very elegant car, with an equally elegant chauffeur, shot north the next day over the Yorkshire moors, bearing the incongruous burden of a priest who looked rather like a black bundle, and a lawyer who had the habit of running about on his feet instead of racing on somebody else's wheels.

They broke their journey very agreeably in one of the great dales of the West Riding, dining and sleeping at a comfortable inn, and starting early next day, began to run along the Northumbrian coast till they reached a country that was a maze of sand dunes and rank sea meadows, somewhere in the heart of which lay the old Border castle which had remained so unique and yet so secretive a monument of the old Border wars. They found it at last, by following a path running beside a long arm of the sea that ran inland, and turned eventually into a sort of rude canal ending in the moat of the castle. The castle really was a castle, of the square, embattled plan that the Normans built everywhere from Galilee to the Grampians. It did really and truly have a portcullis and a drawbridge, and they were very realistically reminded of the fact by an accident that delayed their entrance.

They waded amid long coarse grass and thistle to the bank of the moat which ran in a ribbon of black with dead leaves and scum upon it, like ebony inlaid with a pattern of gold. Barely a yard or two beyond the black ribbon was the other green bank and the big stone pillars of the gateway. But so little, it would seem, had this lonely fastness been approached from outside that when the impatient Granby halloed across to the dim figures behind the portcullis, they seemed to have considerable difficulty even in lowering the great rusty drawbridge. It started on its way, turning over like a great falling tower above them, and then stuck, sticking out in mid-air at a threatening angle.

The impatient Granby, dancing upon the bank, called out to his companion:

'Oh, I can't stand these stick-in-the-mud ways! Why, it'd be less trouble to jump.'

And with characteristic impetuosity he did jump, landing with a slight stagger in safety on the inner shore. Father Brown's short legs were not adapted to jumping. But his temper was more adapted than most people's to falling with a splash into very muddy water. By the promptitude of his companion he escaped falling in very far. But as he was being hauled up the green, slimy bank, he stopped with bent head, peering at a particular point upon the grassy slope.

'Are you botanizing?' asked Granby irritably. 'We've got no time for you to collect rare plants after your last attempt as a diver among the wonders of the deep. Come on, muddy or no, we've got to present ourselves before the baronet.'

When they had penetrated into the castle, they were received courteously enough by an old servant, the only one in sight, and after indicating their business were shown into a long oak-panelled room with latticed windows of antiquated pattern. Weapons of many different centuries hung in balanced patterns on the dark walls, and a complete suit of fourteenth-century armour stood like a sentinel beside the large fireplace. In another long room beyond could be seen, through the half-open door, the dark colours of the rows of family portraits.

'I feel as if I'd got into a novel instead of a house,' said the lawyer. 'I'd no idea anybody did really keep up the "Mysteries of Udolpho" in this fashion.'

'Yes; the old gentleman certainly carries out his historical craze consistently,' answered the priest; 'and these things are not fakes, either. It's not done by somebody who thinks all mediaeval people lived at the same time. Sometimes they make up suits of armour out of different bits; but that suit all covered one man, and covered him very completely. You see it's the late sort of tilting-armour.'

'I think he's a late sort of host, if it comes to that,' grumbled Granby. 'He's keeping us waiting the devil of a time.'

'You must expect everything to go slowly in a place like this,' said Father Brown. 'I think it's very decent of him to see us at all: two total strangers come to ask him highly personal questions.'

And, indeed, when the master of the house appeared they had no reason to complain of their reception, but rather became conscious of something genuine in the traditions of breeding and behaviour that could retain their native dignity without difficulty in that barbarous solitude, and after those long years of rustication and moping. The baronet did not seem either surprised or embarrassed at the rare visitation; though they suspected that he had not had a stranger in his house for a quarter of a life-time, he behaved as if he had been bowing out duchesses a moment before. He showed neither shyness nor impatience when they touched on the very private matter of their errand; after a little leisurely reflection he seemed to recognize their curiosity as justified under the circumstances. He was a thin, keen-looking old gentleman, with black eyebrows and a long chin, and though the carefully-curled hair he wore was undoubtedly a wig, he had the wisdom to wear the grey wig of an elderly man.

'As regards the question that immediately concerns you,' he said, 'the answer is very simple indeed. I do most certainly propose to hand on the whole of my property to my son, as my father handed it on to me; and nothing – I say advisedly, nothing – would induce me to take any other course.'

'I am most profoundly grateful for the information,' answered the lawyer. 'But your kindness encourages me to say that you are putting it very strongly. I would not suggest that it is in the least likely that your son would do anything to make you doubt his fitness for the charge. Still he might –'

'Exactly,' said Sir John Musgrave dryly, 'he might. It is rather an under-statement to say that he might. Will you be good enough to step into the next room with me for a moment.'

He led them into the further gallery, of which they had already caught a glimpse, and gravely paused before a row of the blackened and lowering portraits.

'This is Sir Roger Musgrave,' he said, pointing to a long-faced person in a black periwig. 'He was one of the lowest liars and rascals in the rascally time of William of Orange, a traitor to two kings and something like the murderer of two wives. That is his father, Sir Robert, a perfectly honest old cavalier. That is his son, Sir James, one of the noblest of the Jacobite martyrs and one of the first men to attempt some reparation

246

to the Church and the poor. Does it matter that the House of Musgrave, the power, the honour, the authority, descended from one good man to another good man through the interval of a bad one? Edward I governed England well. Edward III covered England with glory. And yet the second glory came from the first glory through the infamy and imbecility of Edward II, who fawned upon Gaveston and ran away from Bruce. Believe me, Mr Granby, the greatness of a great house and history is something more than these accidental individuals who carry it on, even though they do not grace it. From father to son our heritage has come down, and from father to son it shall continue. You may assure yourselves, gentlemen, and you may assure my son, that I shall not leave my money to a home for lost cats. Musgrave shall leave it to Musgrave till the heavens fall.'

'Yes,' said Father Brown thoughtfully; 'I see what you mean.'

'And we shall be only too glad,' said the solicitor, 'to convey such a happy assurance to your son.'

'You may convey the assurance,' said their host gravely. 'He is secure in any event of having the castle, the title, the land and the money. There is only a small and merely private addition to that arrangement. Under no circumstances whatever will I ever speak to him as long as I live.'

The lawyer remained in the same respectful attitude, but he was now respectfully staring.

'Why, what on earth has he –'

'I am a private gentleman,' said Musgrave, 'as well as the custodian of a great inheritance. And my son did something so horrible that he has ceased to be – I will not say a gentleman – but even a human being. It is the worst crime in the world. Do you remember what Douglas said when Marmion, his guest, offered to shake hands with him?'

'Yes,' said Father Brown.

' "My castles are my king's alone, from turret to foundation stone," ' said Musgrave. ' "The hand of Douglas is his own." '

He turned towards the other room and showed his rather dazed visitors back into it.

'I hope you will take some refreshment,' he said, in the same equable fashion. 'If you have any doubt about your movements, I should be delighted to offer you the hospitality of the castle for the night.'

'Thank you, Sir John,' said the priest in a dull voice, 'but I think we had better go.'

'I will have the bridge lowered at once,' said their host; and in a few moments the creaking of that huge and absurdly antiquated apparatus filled the castle like the grinding of a mill. Rusty as it was, however, it worked successfully this time, and they found themselves standing once more on the grassy bank beyond the moat.

Granby was suddenly shaken by a shudder.

'What in hell was it that his son did?' he cried.

Father Brown made no answer. But when they had driven off again in their car and pursued their journey to a village not far off, called Gray-stones, where they alighted at the inn of the Seven Stars, the lawyer learned with a little mild surprise that the priest did not propose to travel much farther; in other words, that he had apparently every intention of remaining in the neighbourhood.

'I cannot bring myself to leave it like this,' he said gravely. 'I will send back the car, and you, of course, may very naturally want to go with it. Your question is answered; it is simply whether your firm can afford to lend money on young Musgrave's prospects. But my question isn't answered; it is whether he is a fit husband for Betty. I must try to discover whether he's really done something dreadful, or whether it's the delusion of an old lunatic.'

'But,' objected the lawyer, 'if you want to find out about him, why don't you go after him? Why should you hang about in this desolate hole where he hardly ever comes?'

'What would be the use of my going after him?' asked the other. 'There's no sense in going up to a fashionable young man in Bond Street and saying: "Excuse me, but have you committed a crime too horrible for a human being?" If he's bad enough to do it, he's certainly bad enough to deny it. And we don't even know what it is. No, there's only one man that knows, and *may* tell, in some further outburst of dignified eccentricity. I'm going to keep near him for the present.'

And in truth Father Brown did keep near the eccentric baronet, and did actually meet him on more than one occasion, with the utmost politeness on both sides. For the baronet, in spite of his years, was very vigorous and a great walker, and could often be seen stumping through the village, and along the country lanes. Only the day after their arrival,

Father Brown, coming out of the inn, on to the cobbled market-place, saw the dark and distinguished figure stride past in the direction of the post office. He was very quietly dressed in black, but his strong face was even more arresting in the strong sunlight; with his silvery hair, swarthy eyebrows and long chin, he had something of a reminiscence of Henry Irving, or some other famous actor. In spite of his hoary hair, his figure as well as his face suggested strength, and he carried his stick more like a cudgel than a crutch. He saluted the priest, and spoke with the same air of coming fearlessly to the point which had marked his revelations of yesterday.

'If you are still interested in my son,' he said, using the term with an icy indifference, 'you will not see very much of him. He has just left the country. Between ourselves, I might say fled the country.'

'Indeed,' said Father Brown with a grave stare.

'Some people I never heard of, called Grunov, have been pestering me, of all people, about his whereabouts,' said Sir John; 'and I've just come in to send off a wire to tell them that, so far as I know, he's living in the Poste Restante, Riga. Even that has been a nuisance. I came in yesterday to do it, but was five minutes too late for the post office. Are you staying long? I hope you will pay me another visit.'

When the priest recounted to the lawyer his little interview with old Musgrave in the village, the lawyer was both puzzled and interested.

'Why has the Captain bolted?' he asked. 'Who are the other people who want him? Who on earth are the Grunovs?'

'For the first, I don't know,' replied Father Brown. 'Possibly his mysterious sin has come to light. I should rather guess that the other people are blackmailing him about it. For the third, I think I do know. That horrible fat woman with yellow hair is called Madame Grunov, and that little man passes as her husband.'

The next day Father Brown came in rather wearily, and threw down his black bundle of an umbrella with the air of a pilgrim laying down his staff. He had an air of some depression. But it was as it was so often in his criminal investigations. It was not the depression of failure, but the depression of success.

'It's rather a shock,' he said in a dull voice; 'but I ought to have guessed it. I ought to have guessed it when I first went in and saw the thing standing there.'

'When you saw what?' asked Granby impatiently.

'When I saw there was only one suit of armour,' answered Father Brown.

There was a silence during which the lawyer only stared at his friend, and then the friend resumed.

'Only the other day I was just going to tell my niece that there are two types of men who can laugh when they are alone. One might almost say the man who does it is either very good or very bad. You see, he is either confiding the joke to God or confiding it to the Devil. But anyhow he has an inner life. Well, there really is a kind of man who confides the joke to the Devil. He does not mind if nobody sees the joke; if nobody can safely be allowed even to know the joke. The joke is enough in itself, if it is sufficiently sinister and malignant.'

'But what are you talking about?' demanded Granby. '*Whom* are you talking about? Which of them, I mean? *Who* is this person who is having a sinister joke with his Satanic Majesty?'

Father Brown looked across at him with a ghastly smile.

'Ah,' he said, 'that's the joke.'

There was another silence, but this time the silence seemed to be rather full and oppressive than merely empty; it seemed to settle down on them like the twilight that was gradually turning from dusk to dark. Father Brown went on speaking in a level voice, sitting stolidly with his elbows on the table.

'I've been looking up the Musgrave family,' he said. 'They are vigorous and long-lived stock, and even in the ordinary way I should think you would wait a good time for your money.'

'We're quite prepared for that,' answered the solicitor; 'but anyhow it can't last indefinitely. The old man is nearly eighty, though he still walks about, and the people at the inn here laugh and say they don't believe he will ever die.'

Father Brown jumped up with one of his rare but rapid movements, but remained with his hands on the table, leaning forward and looking his friend in the face.

'That's it,' he cried in a low but excited voice. 'That's the only problem. That's the only real difficulty. How will he die? How on earth is he to die?'

'What on earth do you mean?' asked Granby.

'I mean,' came the voice of the priest out of the darkening room, 'that I know the crime that James Musgrave committed.'

His tones had such a chill in them that Granby could hardly repress a shiver; he murmured a further question.

'It was really the worst crime in the world,' said Father Brown. 'At least, many communities and civilizations have accounted it so. It was always from the earliest times marked out in tribe and village for tremendous punishment. But anyhow, I know now what young Musgrave really did and why he did it.'

'And what did he do?' asked the lawyer.

'He killed his father,' answered the priest.

The lawyer in his turn rose from his seat and gazed across the table with wrinkled brows.

'But his father is at the castle,' he cried in sharp tones.

'His father is in the moat,' said the priest, 'and I was a fool not to have known it from the first when something bothered me about that suit of armour. Don't you remember the look of that room? How very carefully it was arranged and decorated? There were two crossed battleaxes hung on one side of the fire-place, two crossed battle-axes on the other. There was a round Scottish shield on one wall, a round Scottish shield on the other. And there was a stand of armour guarding one side of the hearth, and an empty space on the other. Nothing will make me believe that a man who arranged all the rest of that room with that exaggerated symmetry left that one feature of it lopsided. There was almost certainly another man in armour. And what has become of him?'

He paused a moment, and then went on in a more matter-of-fact tone:

'When you come to think of it, it's a very good plan for a murder, and meets the permanent problem of the disposal of the body. The body could stand inside that complete tilting-armour for hours, or even days, while servants came and went, until the murderer could simply drag it out in the dead of night and lower it into the moat, without even crossing the bridge. And then what a good chance he ran! As soon as the body was at all decayed in the stagnant water there would sooner or later be nothing but a skeleton in fourteenth-century armour, a thing very likely to be found in the moat of an old Border castle. It was unlikely that anybody would look for anything there, but if they did, that would soon be all they would find. And I got some confirmation of that. That was when you said I was looking for a rare plant; it was a plant in a good many senses, if you'll excuse the jest. I saw the marks of two feet sunk so deep into the solid bank I was sure that the man was either very heavy or was carrying something very heavy. Also, by the way, there's another moral from that little incident when I made my celebrated graceful and cat-like leap.'

'My brain is rather reeling,' said Granby, 'but I begin to have some notion of what all this nightmare is about. What about you and your cat-like leap?'

'At the post office to-day,' said Father Brown, 'I casually confirmed the statement the baronet made to me yesterday, that he had been there just after closing-time on the day previous – that is, not only on the very day we arrived, but at the very time we arrived. Don't you see what that means? It means that he was actually out when we called, and came back while we were waiting; and that was why we had to wait so long. And when I saw that, I suddenly saw a picture that told the whole story.'

'Well,' asked the other impatiently, 'and what about it?'

'An old man of eighty can walk,' said Father Brown. 'An old man can even walk a good deal, pottering about in country lanes. But an old man can't *jump*. He would be an even less graceful jumper than I was. Yet, if the baronet came back while we were waiting, he must have come in as we came in – by jumping the moat – for the bridge wasn't lowered till later. I rather guess he had hampered it himself to delay inconvenient visitors, to judge by the rapidity with which it was repaired. But that doesn't matter. When I saw that fancy picture of the black figure with the grey hair taking a flying leap across the moat I knew instantly that it was a young man dressed up as an old man. And there you have the whole story.'

'You mean,' said Granby slowly, 'that this pleasing youth killed his father, hid the corpse first in the armour and then in the moat, disguised himself and so on?'

'They happened to be almost exactly alike,' said the priest. 'You could see from the family portraits how strong the likeness ran. And then you talk of his disguising himself. But in a sense everybody's dress is a disguise. The old man disguised himself in a wig, and the young man in a foreign beard. When he shaved and put the wig on his cropped head he was exactly like his father, with a little make-up. Of course, you understand now why he was so very polite about getting you to come up next day here by car. It was because he himself was coming up that night by train. He got in front of you, committed his crime, assumed his disguise, and was ready for the legal negotiations.'

'Ah,' said Granby thoughtfully, 'the legal negotiations! You mean, of course, that the real old baronet would have negotiated very differently.'

'He would have told you plainly that the Captain would never get a penny,' said Father Brown. 'The plot, queer as it sounds, was really the only way of preventing his telling you so. But I want you to appreciate the cunning of what the fellow did tell you. His plan answered several purposes at once. He was being blackmailed by these Russians for some villainy; I suspect for treason during the war. He escaped from them at a stroke, and probably sent them chasing off to Riga after him. But the most beautiful refinement of all was that theory he enunciated about recognizing his son as an heir, but not as a human being. Don't you see that while it secured the *post obit*, it also provided some sort of answer to what would soon be the greatest difficulty of all?'

'I see several difficulties,' said Granby; 'which one do you mean?'

'I mean that if the son was not even disinherited, it would look rather odd that the father and son never met. The theory of a private repudiation answered that. So there only remained one difficulty, as I say, which is probably perplexing the gentleman now. How on earth is the old man to die?'

'I know how he ought to die,' said Granby.

Father Brown seemed to be a little bemused, and went on in a more abstracted fashion.

'And yet there is something more in it than that,' he said. 'There was something about that theory that he liked in a way that is more – well, more theoretical. It gave him an insane intellectual pleasure to tell you in one character that he had committed a crime in another character – when he really had. That is what I mean by the infernal irony; by the joke shared with the Devil. Shall I tell you something that sounds like what they call a paradox? Sometimes it is a joy in the very heart of hell to tell the truth. And above all, to tell it so that everybody misunderstands it. That is why he liked that antic of pretending to be somebody else, and then painting himself as black – as he was. And that was why my niece heard him laughing to himself all alone in the picture gallery.'

Granby gave a slight start, like a person brought back to common things with a bump.

'Your niece,' he cried. 'Didn't her mother want her to marry Musgrave? A question of wealth and position, I suppose.'

'Yes,' said Father Brown dryly; 'her mother was all in favour of a prudent marriage.'

3
The Red Moon of Meru

Everyone agreed that the bazaar at Mallowood Abbey (by kind permission of Lady Mounteagle) was a great success; there were roundabouts and swings and side-shows, which the people greatly enjoyed; I would also mention the Charity, which was the excellent object of the proceedings, if any of them could tell me what it was.

However, it is only with a few of them that we are here concerned; and especially with three of them, a lady and two gentlemen, who passed between two of the principal tents or pavilions, their voices high in argument. On their right was the tent of the Master of the Mountain, that world-famous fortune-teller by crystals and chiromancy; a rich purple tent, all over which were traced, in black and gold, the sprawling outlines of Asiatic gods waving any number of arms like octopods. Perhaps they symbolized the readiness of divine help to be had within; perhaps they merely implied that the ideal being of a pious palmist would have as many hands as possible. On the other side stood the plainer tent of Phroso the Phrenologist; more austerely decorated with diagrams of the heads of Socrates and Shakespeare, which were apparently of a lumpy sort. But these were presented merely in black and white, with numbers and notes, as became the rigid dignity of a purely rationalistic science. The purple tent had an opening like a black cavern, and all was fittingly silent within. But Phroso the Phrenologist, a lean, shabby, sunburnt person, with an almost improbably fierce black moustache and whiskers, was standing outside his own temple, and talking, at the top of his voice, to nobody in particular, explaining that the head of any passer-by would doubtless prove, on examination, to be every bit as knobbly as Shakespeare's. Indeed, the moment the lady appeared between the tents, the vigilant Phroso leapt on her and offered, with a pantomime of old-world courtesy, to feel her bumps.

She refused with civility that was rather like rudeness; but she must be excused, because she was in the middle of an argument. She also had to be excused, or at any rate was excused, because she was Lady Mounteagle. She was not a nonentity, however, in any sense; she was at once handsome and haggard, with a hungry look in her deep, dark eyes and something eager and almost fierce about her smile. Her dress was bizarre for the period; for it was before the Great War had left us in our present mood of gravity and recollection. Indeed, the dress was rather like the purple tent; being of a semi-oriental sort, covered with exotic and esoteric emblems. But everyone knew that the Mounteagles were mad; which was the popular way of saying that she and her husband were interested in the creeds and culture of the East.

The eccentricity of the lady was a great contrast to the conventionality of the two gentlemen, who were braced and buttoned up in all the stiffer fashion of that far-off day, from the tips of their gloves to their bright top hats. Yet even here there was a difference; for James Hardcastle managed at once to look correct and distinguished, while Tommy Hunter only looked correct and commonplace. Hardcastle was a promising politician; who seemed in society to be interested in everything except politics. It may be answered gloomily that every politician is emphatically a promising politician. But to do him justice, he had often exhibited himself as a performing politician. No purple tent in the bazaar, however, had been provided for him to perform in.

'For my part,' he said, screwing in the monocle that was the only gleam in his hard, legal face, 'I think we must exhaust the possibilities of mesmerism before we talk about magic. Remarkable psychological powers undoubtedly exist, even in apparently backward peoples. Marvellous things have been done by fakirs.'

'Did you say done by fakers?' asked the other young man, with doubtful innocence.

'Tommy, you are simply silly,' said the lady. 'Why will you keep barging in on things you don't understand? You're like a schoolboy screaming out that he knows how a conjuring trick is done. It's all so Early Victorian – that schoolboy scepticism. As for mesmerism, I doubt whether you can stretch it to –'

At this point Lady Mounteagle seemed to catch sight of somebody she wanted; a black stumpy figure standing at a booth where children were throwing hoops at hideous table ornaments. She darted across and cried:

'Father Brown, I've been looking for you. I want to ask you something. Do you believe in fortune-telling?'

The person addressed looked rather helplessly at the little hoop in his hand and said at last:

'I wonder in which sense you're using the word "believe". Of course, if it's all a fraud –'

'Oh, but the Master of the Mountain isn't a bit of a fraud,' she cried. 'He isn't a common conjurer or a fortune-teller at all. It's really a great honour for him to condescend to tell fortunes at my parties; he's a great religious leader in his own country; a Prophet and a Seer. And even his fortune-telling isn't vulgar stuff about coming into a fortune. He tells you great spiritual truths about yourself, about your ideals.'

'Quite so,' said Father Brown. 'That's what I object to. I was just going to say that if it's all a fraud, I don't mind it so much. It can't be much more of a fraud than most things at fancy bazaars; and there, in a way, it's a sort of practical joke. But if it's a religion and reveals spiritual truths – then it's all as false as hell and I wouldn't touch it with a bargepole.'

'That is something of a paradox,' said Hardcastle, with a smile. 'I wonder what a paradox is,' remarked the priest in a ruminant manner. 'It seems to me obvious enough. I suppose it wouldn't do very much harm if somebody dressed up as a German spy and pretended to have told all sorts of lies to the Germans. But if a man is trading in the *truth* with the Germans – well! So I think if a fortune-teller is trading in *truth* like that –'

'You really think,' began Hardcastle grimly.

'Yes,' said the other; 'I think he is trading with the enemy.'

Tommy Hunter broke into a chuckle. 'Well,' he said, 'if Father Brown thinks they're good so long as they're frauds, I should think he'd consider this copper-coloured prophet a sort of saint.'

'My cousin Tom is incorrigible,' said Lady Mounteagle. 'He's always going about showing up adepts, as he calls it. He only came down here in a hurry when he heard the Master was to be here, I believe. He'd have tried to show up Buddha or Moses.'

'Thought you wanted looking after a bit,' said the young man, with a grin on his round face. 'So I toddled down. Don't like this brown monkey crawling about.'

'There you go again!' said Lady Mounteagle. 'Years ago, when I was in India, I suppose we all had that sort of prejudice against brown people. But now I know something about their wonderful spiritual powers, I'm glad to say I know better.'

'Our prejudices seem to cut opposite ways,' said Father Brown. 'You excuse his being brown because he is brahminical; and I excuse his being brahminical because he is brown. Frankly, I don't care for spiritual powers much myself. I've got much more sympathy with spiritual weaknesses. But I can't see why anybody should dislike him merely because he is the same beautiful colour as copper, or coffee, or nut-brown ale, or those jolly peat-streams in the North. But then,' he added, looking across at the lady and screwing up his eyes, 'I suppose I'm prejudiced in favour of anything that's called brown.'

'There now!' cried Lady Mounteagle with a sort of triumph. 'I knew you were only talking nonsense!'

'Well,' grumbled the aggrieved youth with the round face. 'When anybody talks sense you call it schoolboy scepticism. When's the crystal-gazing going to begin?'

'Any time you like, I believe,' replied the lady. 'It isn't crystal-gazing, as a matter of fact, but palmistry; I suppose you would say it was all the same sort of nonsense.'

'I think there is a *via media* between sense and nonsense,' said Hardcastle, smiling. 'There are explanations that are natural and not at all nonsensical; and yet the results are very amazing. Are you coming in to be operated on? I confess I am full of curiosity.'

'Oh, I've no patience with such nonsense,' spluttered the sceptic, whose round face had become rather a red face with the heat of his contempt and incredulity. 'I'll let you waste your time on your mahogany mountebank; I'd rather go and throw at coco-nuts.'

The Phrenologist, still hovering near, darted at the opening.

'Heads, my dear sir,' he said, 'human skulls are of a contour far more subtle than that of coco-nuts. No coco-nut can compare with your own most –'

Hardcastle had already dived into the dark entry of the purple tent; and they heard a low murmur of voices within. As Tom Hunter turned on the Phrenologist with an impatient answer, in which he showed a regrettable indifference to the line between natural and preternatural sciences, the lady was just about to continue her little argument with the little priest, when she stopped in some surprise.

James Hardcastle had come out of the tent again, and in his grim face and glaring monocle, surprise was even more vividly depicted.

'He's not there,' remarked the politician abruptly. 'He's gone. Some aged nigger, who seems to constitute his *suite*, jabbered something to me to the effect that the Master had gone forth rather than sell sacred secrets for gold.'

Lady Mounteagle turned radiantly to the rest. 'There now,' she cried. 'I told you he was a cut above anything you fancied! He hates being here in a crowd; he's gone back to his solitude.'

'I am sorry,' said Father Brown gravely. 'I may have done him an injustice. Do you know where he has gone?'

'I think so,' said his hostess equally gravely. 'When he wants to be alone, he always goes to the cloisters, just at the end of the left wing, beyond my husband's study and private museum, you know. Perhaps you know this house was once an abbey.'

'I have heard something about it,' answered the priest, with a faint smile.

'We'll go there, if you like,' said the lady, briskly. 'You really ought to see my husband's collection; or the Red Moon at any rate. Haven't you ever heard of the Red Moon of Meru? Yes, it's a ruby.'

'I should be delighted to see the collection,' said Hardcastle quietly, 'including the Master of the Mountain, if that prophet is one exhibit in the museum.' And they all turned towards the path leading to the house.

'All the same,' muttered the sceptical Thomas, as he brought up the rear, 'I should very much like to know what the brown beast *did* come here for, if he didn't come to tell fortunes.'

As he disappeared, the indomitable Phroso made one more dart after him, almost snatching at his coat-tails.

'The bump – ' he began.

'No bump,' said the youth, 'only a hump. Hump I always have when I come down to see Mounteagle.' And he took to his heels to escape the embrace of the man of science.

On their way to the cloisters the visitors had to pass through the long room that was devoted by Lord Mounteagle to his remarkable private museum of Asiatic charms and mascots. Through one open door, in the length of the wall opposite, they could see the Gothic arches and the glimmer of daylight between them, marking the square open space, round the roofed border of which the monks had walked in older days. But they had to pass something that seemed at first sight rather more extraordinary than the ghost of a monk.

It was an elderly gentleman, robed from head to foot in white, with a pale green turban, but a very pink and white English complexion and the smooth white moustaches of some amiable Anglo-Indian colonel. This was Lord Mounteagle, who had taken his Oriental pleasures more sadly, or at least more seriously than his wife. He could talk of nothing whatever, except Oriental religion and philosophy; and had thought it necessary even to dress in the manner of an Oriental hermit. While he was delighted to show his treasures, he seemed to treasure them much more for the truths supposed to be symbolized in them than for their value in collections, let alone cash. Even when he brought out the great ruby, perhaps the only thing of great value in the museum, in a merely monetary sense, he seemed to be much more interested in its name than in its size, let alone its price.

The others were all staring at what seemed a stupendously large red stone, burning like a bonfire seen through a rain of blood. But Lord Mounteagle rolled it loosely in his palm without looking at it; and staring at the ceiling, told them a long tale about the legendary character of Mount Meru, and how, in the Gnostic mythology, it had been the place of the wrestling of nameless primeval powers.

Towards the end of the lecture on the Demiurge of the Gnostics (not forgetting its connexion with the parallel concept of Manichæus), even the tactful Mr Hardcastle thought it time to create a diversion. He asked to be allowed to look at the stone; and as evening was closing in, and the long room with its single door was steadily darkening, he stepped out in the cloister beyond, to examine the jewel by a better light. It was then that they first became conscious, slowly and almost creepily conscious, of the living presence of the Master of the Mountain.

The cloister was on the usual plan, as regards its original structure;

but the line of Gothic pillars and pointed arches that formed the inner square was linked together all along by a low wall, about waist high, turning the Gothic doors into Gothic windows and giving each a sort of flat window-sill of stone. This alteration was probably of ancient date; but there were other alterations of a quainter sort, which witnessed to the rather unusual individual ideas of Lord and Lady Mounteagle. Between the pillars hung thin curtains, or rather veils, made of beads or light canes, in a continental or southern manner; and on these again could be traced the lines and colours of Asiatic dragons or idols, that contrasted with the grey Gothic framework in which they were suspended. But this, while it further troubled the dying light of the place, was the least of the incongruities of which the company, with very varying feelings, became aware.

In the open space surrounded by the cloisters, there ran, like a circle in a square, a circular path paved with pale stones and edged with some sort of green enamel like an imitation lawn. Inside that, in the very centre, rose the basin of a dark-green fountain, or raised pond, in which water lilies floated and goldfish flashed to and fro; and high above these, its outline dark against the dying light, was a great green image. Its back was turned to them and its face so completely invisible in the hunched posture that the statue might almost have been headless. But in that mere dark outline, in the dim twilight, some of them could see instantly that it was the shape of no Christian thing.

A few yards away, on the circular path, and looking towards the great green god, stood the man called the Master of the Mountain. His pointed and finely-finished features seemed moulded by some skilful craftsman as a mask of copper. In contrast with this, his dark-grey beard looked almost blue like indigo; it began in a narrow tuft on his chin, and then spread outwards like a great fan or the tail of a bird. He was robed in peacock green and wore on his bald head a high cap of uncommon outline: a head-dress none of them had ever seen before; but it looked rather Egyptian than Indian. The man was standing with staring eyes; wide open, fish-shaped eyes, so motionless that they looked like the eyes painted on a mummy-case. But though the figure of the Master of the Mountain was singular enough, some of the company, including Father Brown, did not look at him; they still looked at the dark-green idol at which he himself was looking.

'This seems a queer thing,' said Hardcastle, frowning a little, 'to set up in the middle of an old abbey cloister.'

'Now, don't tell me you're going to be silly,' said Lady Mounteagle. 'That's just what we meant; to link up the great religions of East and West; Buddha and Christ. Surely you must understand that all religions are really the same.'

'If they are,' said Father Brown mildly, 'it seems rather unnecessary to go into the middle of Asia to get one.'

'Lady Mounteagle means that they are different aspects or facets, as there are of this stone,' began Hardcastle; and becoming interested in the new topic, laid the great ruby down on the stone sill or ledge under the Gothic arch. 'But it does not follow that we can mix the aspects in one artistic style. You may mix Christianity and Islam, but you can't mix Gothic and Saracenic, let alone real Indian.'

As he spoke, the Master of the Mountain seemed to come to life like a cataleptic, and moved gravely round another quarter segment of the circle, and took up his position outside their own row of arches, standing with his back to them and looking now towards the idol's back. It was obvious that he was moving by stages round the whole circle, like a hand round a clock; but pausing for prayer or contemplation.

'What *is* his religion?' asked Hardcastle, with a faint touch of impatience.

'He says,' replied Lord Mounteagle, reverently, 'that it is older than Brahminism and purer than Buddhism.'

'Oh,' said Hardcastle, and continued to stare through his single eyeglass, standing with both his hands in his pockets.

'They say,' observed the nobleman in his gentle but didactic voice, 'that the deity called the God of Gods is carved in a colossal form in the cavern of Mount Meru –'

Even his lordship's lecturing serenity was broken abruptly by the voice that came over his shoulder. It came out of the darkness of the museum they had just left, when they stepped out into the cloister. At the sound of it the two younger men looked first incredulous, then furious, and then almost collapsed into laughter.

'I hope I do not intrude,' said the urbane and seductive voice of Professor Phroso, that unconquerable wrestler of the truth, 'but it occurred to me that some of you might spare a little time for that much despised science of Bumps, which –'

'Look here,' cried the impetuous Tommy Hunter, 'I haven't got any bumps; but you'll jolly well have some soon, you –'

Hardcastle mildly restrained him as he plunged back through the door; and for the moment all the group had turned again and were looking back into the inner room.

It was at that moment that the thing happened. It was the impetuous Tommy, once more, who was the first to move, and this time to better effect. Before anyone else had seen anything, when Hardcastle had barely remembered with a jump that he had left the gem on the stone sill, Tommy was across the cloister with the leap of a cat and, leaning with his head and shoulders out of the aperture between two columns, had cried out in a voice that rang down all the arches: 'I've got him!'

In that instant of time, just after they turned, and just before they heard his triumphant cry, they had all seen it happen. Round the corner of one of the two columns, there had darted in and out again a brown or rather bronze-coloured hand, the colour of dead gold; such as they had seen elsewhere. The hand had struck as straight as a striking snake; as instantaneous as the flick of the long tongue of an ant-eater. But it had licked up the jewel. The stone slab of the window-sill shone bare in the pale and fading light.

'I've got him,' gasped Tommy Hunter; 'but he's wriggling pretty hard. You fellows run round him in front – he can't have got rid of it, anyhow.'

The others obeyed, some racing down the corridor and some leaping over the low wall, with the result that a little crowd, consisting of Hardcastle, Lord Mounteagle, Father Brown, and even the undetachable Mr Phroso of the bumps, had soon surrounded the captive Master of the Mountain, whom Hunter was hanging on to desperately by the collar with one hand, and shaking every now and then in a manner highly insensible to the dignity of Prophets as a class.

'Now we've got him, anyhow,' said Hunter, letting go with a sigh. 'We've only got to search him. The thing must be here.'

Three-quarters of an hour later, Hunter and Hardcastle, their top-hats, ties, gloves, slips and spats somewhat the worse for their recent activities, came face to face in the cloister and gazed at each other.

'Well,' asked Hardcastle with restraint, 'have you any views on the mystery?'

'Hang it all,' replied Hunter; 'you can't call it a mystery. Why, we all saw him take it ourselves.'

'Yes,' replied the other, 'but we didn't all see him lose it ourselves. And the mystery is, where has he lost it so that we can't find it?'

'It must be somewhere,' said Hunter. 'Have you searched the fountain and all round that rotten old god there?'

'I haven't dissected the little fishes,' said Hardcastle, lifting his eye-glass and surveying the other. 'Are you thinking of the ring of Poly-crates?'

Apparently the survey, through the eye-glass, of the round face before him, convinced him that it covered no such meditation on Greek legend.

'It's not on him, I admit,' repeated Hunter, suddenly, 'unless he's swallowed it.'

'Are we to dissect the Prophet, too?' asked the other smiling. 'But here comes our host.'

'This is a most distressing matter,' said Lord Mounteagle, twisting his white moustache with a nervous and even tremulous hand. 'Horrible thing to have a theft in one's house, let alone connecting it with a man like the Master. But, I confess, I can't quite make head or tail of the way in which he is talking about it. I wish you'd come inside and see what you think.'

They went in together, Hunter falling behind and dropping into conversation with Father Brown, who was kicking his heels round the cloister.

'You must be very strong,' said the priest pleasantly. 'You held him with one hand; and he seemed pretty vigorous, even when we had eight hands to hold him, like one of those Indian gods.'

They took a turn or two round the cloister, talking; and then they also went into the inner room, where the Master of the Mountain was seated on a bench, in the capacity of a captive, but with more of the air of a king.

It was true, as Lord Mounteagle said, that his air and tone were not very easy to understand. He spoke with a serene, and yet secretive sense of power. He seemed rather amused at their suggestions about trivial hiding-places for the gem; and certainly he showed no resentment whatever. He seemed to be laughing, in a still unfathomable fashion at their efforts to trace what they had all seen him take.

'You are learning a little,' he said, with insolent benevolence, 'of the laws of time and space; about which your latest science is a thousand years behind our oldest religion. You do not even know what is really meant by hiding a thing. Nay, my poor little friends, you do not even know what is meant by *seeing* a thing; or perhaps you would see this as plainly as I do.'

'Do you mean it is here?' demanded Hardcastle harshly.

'Here is a word of many meanings, also,' replied the mystic. 'But I did not say it was here. I only said I could see it.'

There was an irritated silence, and he went on sleepily.

'If you were to be utterly, unfathomably, silent, do you think you might hear a cry from the other end of the world? The cry of a worshipper alone in those mountains, where the original image sits, itself like a mountain. Some say that even Jews and Moslems might worship that image; because it was never made by man. Hark! Do you hear the cry with which he lifts his head and sees in that socket of stone, that has been hollow for ages, the one red and angry moon that is the eye of the mountain?'

'Do you really mean,' cried Lord Mounteagle, a little shaken, 'that you could make it pass from here to Mount Meru? I used to believe you had great spiritual powers, but – '

'Perhaps,' said the Master, 'I have more than you will ever believe.'

Hardcastle rose impatiently and began to pace the room with his hands in his pockets.

'I never believed so much as you did; but I admit that powers of a certain type may . . . Good God!'

His high, hard voice had been cut off in mid-air, and he stopped staring; the eye-glass fell out of his eye. They all turned their faces in the same direction; and on every face there seemed to be the same suspended animation.

The Red Moon of Meru lay on the stone window-sill, exactly as they had last seen it. It might have been a red spark blown there from a bonfire, or a red rose-petal tossed from a broken rose; but it had fallen in precisely the same spot where Hardcastle had thoughtlessly laid it down.

This time Hardcastle did not attempt to pick it up again; but his demeanour was somewhat notable. He turned slowly and began to stride about the room again; but there was in his movements something masterful, where before it had been only restless. Finally, he brought himself to a standstill in front of the seated Master, and bowed with a somewhat sardonic smile.

'Master,' he said, 'we all owe you an apology and, what is more important, you have taught us all a lesson. Believe me, it will serve as a lesson as well as a joke. I shall always remember the very remarkable powers you really possess, and how harmlessly you use them. Lady Mounteagle,' he went on, turning towards her, 'you will forgive me for having addressed the Master first; but it was to you I had the honour of offering this explanation some time ago. I may say that I explained it before it had happened. I told you that most of these things could be interpreted by some kind of hypnotism. Many believe that this is the explanation of all those Indian stories about the mango plant and the boy who climbs a rope thrown into the air. It does not really happen; but the spectators are mesmerized into imagining that it happened. So we were all mesmerized into imagining this theft had happened. That brown hand coming in at the window, and whisking away the gem, was a momentary delusion; a hand in a dream. Only, having seen the stone vanish, we never looked for it where it was before. We plunged into the pond and turned every leaf of the water lilies; we were almost giving emetics to the goldfish. But the ruby has been here all the time.'

And he glanced across at the opalescent eyes and smiling bearded mouth of the Master, and saw that the smile was just a shade broader. There was something in it that made the others jump to their feet with an air of sudden relaxation and general, gasping relief.

'This is a very fortunate escape for us all,' said Lord Mounteagle, smiling rather nervously. 'There cannot be the least doubt it is as you say. It has been a most painful episode and I really don't know what apologies –'

'I have no complaints,' said the Master of the Mountain, still smiling. 'You have never touched Me at all.'

While the rest went off rejoicing, with Hardcastle for the hero of the hour, the little Phrenologist with the whiskers sauntered back towards his preposterous tent. Looking over his shoulder he was surprised to find Father Brown following him.

'Can I feel your bumps?' asked the expert, in his mildly sarcastic tone.

'I don't think you want to feel any more, do you?' said the priest good-humouredly. 'You're a detective, aren't you?'

'Yep,' replied the other. 'Lady Mounteagle asked me to keep an eye on the Master, being no fool, for all her mysticism; and when he left his tent, I could only follow by behaving like a nuisance and a monomaniac. If anybody had come into my tent, I'd have had to look up Bumps in an encyclopaedia.'

'Bumps, What Ho She; see Folk-Lore,' observed Father Brown, dreamily. 'Well, you were quite in the part in pestering people – at a bazaar.'

'Rum case, wasn't it?' remarked the fallacious Phrenologist. 'Queer to think the thing was there all the time.'

'Very queer,' said the priest.

Something in his voice made the other man stop and stare.

'Look here!' he cried; 'what's the matter with you? What are you looking like that for! Don't you *believe* that it was there all the time?'

Father Brown blinked rather as if he had received a buffet; then he said slowly and with hesitation: 'No . . . the fact is . . . I can't – I can't quite bring myself to believe it.'

'You're not the sort of chap,' said the other shrewdly, 'who'd say that without reason. Why don't you think the ruby had been there all the time?'

'Only because I put it back myself,' said Father Brown.

The other man stood rooted to the spot, like one whose hair was standing on end. He opened his mouth without speech.

'Or rather,' went on the priest, 'I persuaded the thief to let me put it back. I told him what I'd guessed and showed him there was still time for repentance. I don't mind telling you in professional confidence; besides, I don't think the Mounteagles would prosecute, now they've got the thing back, especially considering who stole it.'

'Do you mean the Master?' asked the late Phroso.

'No,' said Father Brown, 'the Master didn't steal it.'

'But I don't understand,' objected the other. 'Nobody was outside the window except the Master; and a hand certainly came from outside.'

'The hand came from outside, but the thief came from the inside,' said Father Brown.

'We seem to be back among the mystics again. Look here, I'm a practical man; I only wanted to know if it is all right with the ruby –'

'I knew it was all wrong,' said Father Brown, 'before I even knew there was a ruby.'

After a pause he went on thoughtfully. 'Right away back in that argument of theirs, by the tents, I knew things were going wrong. People will tell you that theories don't matter and that logic and philosophy aren't practical. Don't you believe them. Reason is from God, and when things are unreasonable there is something the matter. Now, that quite abstract argument ended with something funny. Consider what the theories were. Hardcastle was a trifle superior and said that all things were perfectly possible; but they were mostly done merely by mesmerism, or clairvoyance; scientific names for philosophical puzzles, in the usual style. But Hunter thought it all sheer fraud and wanted to show it up. By Lady Mounteagle's testimony, he not only went about showing up fortune-tellers and such like, but he had actually come down specially to confront this one. He didn't often come; he didn't get on with Mounteagle, from whom, being a spendthrift, he always tried to borrow; but when he heard the Master was coming, he came hurrying down. Very well. In spite of that, it was Hardcastle who went to consult the wizard and Hunter who refused. He said he'd waste no time on such nonsense; having apparently wasted a lot of his life on proving it to be nonsense. That seems inconsistent. He thought in this case it was crystal-gazing; but he found it was palmistry.'

'Do you mean he made that an excuse?' asked his companion, puzzled.

'I thought so at first,' replied the priest; 'but I know now it was not an excuse, but a reason. He really was put off by finding it was a palmist, because –'

'Well,' demanded the other impatiently.

'Because he didn't want to take his glove off,' said Father Brown.

'Take his glove off?' repeated the inquirer.

'If he had,' said Father Brown mildly, 'we should all have seen that his hand was painted pale brown already ... Oh, yes, he did come down specially because the Master was here. He came down very fully prepared.'

'You mean,' cried Phroso, 'that it was Hunter's hand, painted brown, that came in at the window? Why, he was with us all the time!'

'Go and try it on the spot and you'll find it's quite possible,' said the priest. 'Hunter leapt forward and leaned out of the window; in a flash he could tear off his glove, tuck up his sleeve, and thrust his hand back round the other side of the pillar, while he gripped the Indian with the other hand and hallooed out that he'd caught the thief. I remarked at the time that he held the thief with one hand, where any sane man would have used two. But the other hand was slipping the jewel into his trouser pocket.'

There was a long pause and then the ex-Phrenologist said slowly 'Well, that's a staggerer. But the thing stumps me still. For one thing, it doesn't explain the queer behaviour of the old magician himself. If he was entirely innocent, why the devil didn't he say so? Why wasn't he indignant at being accused and searched? Why did he only sit smiling and hinting in a sly way what wild and wonderful things he could do?'

'Ah!' cried Father Brown, with a sharp note in his voice: 'there you come up against it! Against everything these people don't and won't understand. All religions are the same, says Lady Mounteagle. Are they, by George! I tell you some of them are so different that the best man of one creed will be callous, where the worst man of another will be sensitive. I told you I didn't like spiritual power, because the accent is on the word power. I don't say the Master would steal a ruby, very likely he wouldn't; very likely he wouldn't think it worth stealing. It wouldn't be specially his temptation to take jewels; but it would be his temptation to take credit for miracles that didn't belong to him any more than the jewels. It was to *that* sort of temptation, to *that* sort of stealing that he yielded today. He liked us to think that he had marvellous mental powers that could make a material object fly through space; and even when he hadn't done it, he allowed us to think he had. The point about private property wouldn't occur primarily to him at all. The question wouldn't present itself in the form: "Shall I *steal* this pebble?" but only in the form: "Could I make a pebble vanish and re-appear on a distant mountain?" The question of *whose* pebble would strike him as irrelevant. That is what I mean by religions being different. He is very proud of having what he calls spiritual powers. But what he calls spiritual doesn't mean what we call moral. It means rather mental; the power of the mind over matter; the magician controlling the elements. Now we are not like that, even when we are no better; even when we are worse. We, whose fathers at least were Christians, who have grown up under those mediæval arches even if we bedizen them with all the demons in Asia – we have the very opposite ambition and the very opposite shame. We should all be anxious that nobody should think we had done it. He was actually anxious that everybody should think he had – even when he hadn't. He actually stole the credit of stealing. While we were all casting the crime from us like a snake, he was actually luring it to him like a snake charmer. But snakes are not pets in this country! Here the traditions of Christendom tell at once under a test like this. Look at old Mounteagle himself, for instance! Ah, you may be as Eastern and esoteric as you like, and wear a turban and a long robe and live on messages from Mahatmas; but if a bit of stone is stolen in your house, and your friends are suspected, you will jolly soon find out that you're an ordinary English gentleman in a fuss. The man who really did it would never want us to think he did it, for he also was an English gentleman. He was also something very much better; he was a Christian thief. I hope and believe he was a penitent thief.'

'By your account,' said his companion laughing, 'the Christian thief and the heathen fraud went by contraries. One was sorry he'd done it and the other was sorry he hadn't.'

'We mustn't be too hard on either of them,' said Father Brown. 'Other English gentlemen have stolen before now, and been covered by legal and political protection; and the West also has its own way of covering theft with sophistry. After all, the ruby is not the only kind of valuable stone in the world that has changed owners; it is true of other precious stones; often carved like cameos and coloured like flowers.'

The other looked at him inquiringly; and the priest's finger was pointed to the Gothic outline of the great Abbey.

'A great graven stone,' he said, 'and that was also stolen.'

4

The Chief Mourner of Marne

A blaze of lightning blanched the grey woods tracing all the wrinkled foliage down to the last curled leaf, as if every detail were drawn in silverpoint or graven in silver. The same strange trick of lightning by which it seems to record millions of minute things in an instant of time, picked out everything, from the elegant litter of the picnic spread under the spreading tree to the pale lengths of winding road, at the end of which a white car was waiting. In the distance a melancholy mansion with four towers like a castle, which in the grey evening had been but a dim and distant huddle of walls like a crumbling cloud, seemed to spring into the foreground, and stood up with all its embattled roofs and blank and staring windows. And in this, at least, the light had something in it of revelation. For to some of those grouped under the tree that castle was, indeed, a thing faded and almost forgotten, which was to prove its power to spring up again in the foreground of their lives.

The light also clothed for an instant, in the same silver splendour, at least one human figure that stood up as motionless as one of the towers. It was that of a tall man standing on a rise of ground above the rest, who were mostly sitting on the grass or stooping to gather up the hamper and crockery. He wore a picturesque short cloak or cape clasped with a silver clasp and chain, which blazed like a star when the flash touched it; and something metallic in his motionless figure was emphasized by the fact that his closely-curled hair was of the burnished yellow that can be really called gold; and had the look of being younger than his face, which was handsome in a hard aquiline fashion, but looked, under the strong light, a little wrinkled and withered. Possibly it had suffered from wearing a mask of make-up, for Hugo Romaine was the greatest actor of his day. For that instant of illumination the golden curls and ivory mask and silver ornament made his figure gleam like that of a man in armour; the next instant his figure was a dark and even black silhouette against the sickly grey of the rainy evening sky.

But there was something about its stillness, like that of a statue, that distinguished it from the group at his feet. All the other figures around him had made the ordinary involuntary movement at the unexpected shock of light; for though the skies were rainy it was the first flash of the storm. The only lady present, whose air of carrying grey hair gracefully, as if she were really proud of it, marked her a matron of the United States, unaffectedly shut her eyes and uttered a sharp cry. Her English husband, General Outram, a very stolid Anglo-Indian with a bald head and black moustache and whiskers of antiquated pattern, looked up with one stiff movement and then resumed his occupation of tidying up. A young man of the name of Mallow, very big and shy, with brown eyes like a dog's, dropped a cup and apologized awkwardly. A third man, much more dressy, with a resolute head, like an inquisitive terrier's, and grey hair brushed stiffly back, was no other than the great newspaper proprietor, Sir John Cockspur; he cursed freely, but not in an English idiom or accent, for he came from Toronto. But the tall man in the short cloak stood up literally like a statue in the twilight; his eagle face under the full glare had been like the bust of a Roman emperor, and the carved eyelids had not moved.

A moment after, the dark dome cracked across with thunder, and the statue seemed to come to life. He turned his head over his shoulder and said casually;

'About a minute and half between the flash and the bang, but I think the storm's coming nearer. A tree is not supposed to be a good umbrella for the lightning, but we shall want it soon for the rain. I think it will be a deluge.'

The young man glanced at the lady a little anxiously and said: 'Can't we get shelter anywhere? There seems to be a house over there.'

'There is a house over there,' remarked the general, rather grimly; 'but not quite what you'd call a hospitable hotel.'

'It's curious,' said his wife sadly, 'that we should be caught in a storm with no house near but that one, of all others.'

Something in her tone seemed to check the younger man, who was both sensitive and comprehending; but nothing of that sort daunted the man from Toronto.

'What's the matter with it?' he asked. 'Looks rather like a ruin.'

'That place,' said the general dryly, 'belongs to the Marquis of Marne.'

'Gee!' said Sir John Cockspur. 'I've heard all about that bird, anyhow; and a queer bird, too. Ran him as a front-page mystery in the *Comet* last year. "The Nobleman Nobody Knows."'

'Yes, I've heard of him, too,' said young Mallow in a low voice. 'There seem to be all sorts of weird stories about why he hides himself like that. I've heard that he wears a mask because he's a leper. But somebody else told me quite seriously that there's a curse on the family; a child born with some frightful deformity that's kept in a dark room.'

'The Marquis of Marne has three heads,' remarked Romaine quite gravely. 'Once in every three hundred years a three-headed nobleman adorns the family tree. No human being dares approach the accursed house except a silent procession of hatters, sent to provide an abnormal number of hats. But' – and his voice took one of those deep and terrible turns, that could cause such a thrill in the theatre – 'my friends, *those hats are of no human shape*.'

The American lady looked at him with a frown and a slight air of distrust, as if that trick of voice had moved her in spite of herself.

'I don't like your ghoulish jokes,' she said; 'and I'd rather you didn't joke about this, anyhow.'

'I hear and obey,' replied the actor; 'but am I, like the Light Brigade, forbidden even to reason why?'

'The reason,' she replied, 'is that he isn't the Nobleman Nobody Knows. I know him myself, or, at least, I knew him very well when he was an attaché at Washington thirty years ago, when we were all young. And he didn't wear a mask, at least, he didn't wear it with me. He wasn't a leper, though he may be almost as lonely. And he had only one head and only one heart, and that was broken.'

'Unfortunate love affair, of course,' said Cockspur. 'I should like that for the *Comet*.'

'I suppose it's a compliment to us,' she replied thoughtfully, 'that you always assume a man's heart is broken by a woman. But there are other kinds of love and bereavement. Have you never read "In Memoriam"? Have you never heard of David and Jonathan? What broke poor Marne up was the death of his brother; at least, he was really a first cousin, but had been brought up with him like a brother, and was much nearer

273

than most brothers. James Mair, as the marquis was called when I knew him, was the elder of the two, but he always played the part of worshipper, with Maurice Mair as a god. And, by his account, Maurice Mair was certainly a wonder. James was no fool, and very good at his own political job; but it seems that Maurice could do that and everything else; that he was a brilliant artist and amateur actor and musician, and all the rest of it. James was very good-looking himself, long and strong and strenuous, with a high-bridged nose; though I suppose the young people would think he looked very quaint with his beard divided into two bushy whiskers in the fashion of those Victorian times. But Maurice was clean-shaven, and, by the portraits shown to me, certainly quite beautiful; though he looked a little more like a tenor than a gentleman ought to look. James was always asking me again and again whether his friend was not a marvel, whether any woman wouldn't fall in love with him, and so on, until it became rather a bore, except that it turned so suddenly into a tragedy. His whole life seemed to be in that idolatry, and one day the idol tumbled down, and was broken like any china doll. A chill caught at the seaside, and it was all over.'

'And after that,' asked the young man, 'did he shut himself up like this?'

'He went abroad at first,' she answered; 'away to Asia and the Cannibal Islands and Lord knows where. These deadly strokes take different people in different ways. It took him in the way of an utter sundering or severance from everything, even from tradition and as far as possible from memory. He could not bear a reference to the old tie; a portrait or an anecdote or even an association. He couldn't bear the business of a great public funeral. He longed to get away. He stayed away for ten years. I heard some rumour that he had begun to revive a little at the end of the exile; but when he came back to his own home he relapsed completely. He settled down into religious melancholia, and that's practically madness.'

'The priests got hold of him, they say,' grumbled the old general. 'I know he gave thousands to found a monastery, and lives himself rather like a monk – or, at any rate, a hermit. Can't understand what good they think that will do.'

'Goddarned superstition,' snorted Cockspur; 'that sort of thing ought to be shown up. Here's a man that might have been useful to the Empire and the world, and these vampires get hold of him and suck him dry. I bet with their unnatural notions they haven't even let him marry.'

'No, he has never married,' said the lady. 'He was engaged when I knew him, as a matter of fact, but I don't think it ever came first with him, and I think it went with the rest when everything else went. Like Hamlet and Ophelia – he lost hold of love because he lost hold of life. But I knew the girl; indeed, I know her still. Between ourselves, it was Viola Grayson, daughter of the old admiral. She's never married either.'

'It's infamous! It's infernal!' cried Sir John, bounding up. 'It's not only a tragedy, but a crime. I've got a duty to the public, and I mean to see all this nonsensical nightmare . . . in the twentieth century –'

He was almost choked with his own protest, and then, after a silence, the old soldier said:

'Well, I don't profess to know much about those things, but I think these religious people need to study a text which says: "Let the dead bury their dead."'

'Only, unfortunately, that's just what it looks like,' said his wife with a sigh. 'It's just like some creepy story of a dead man burying another dead man, over and over again for ever.'

'The storm has passed over us,' said Romaine, with a rather inscrutable smile. 'You will not have to visit the inhospitable house after all.'

She suddenly shuddered.

'Oh, I'll never do that again!' she exclaimed.

Mallow was staring at her.

'Again! Have you tried it before?' he cried.

'Well, I did once,' she said, with a lightness not without a touch of pride; 'but we needn't go back on all that. It's not raining now, but I think we'd better be moving back to the car.'

As they moved off in procession, Mallow and the general brought up the rear; and the latter said abruptly, lowering his voice:

'I don't want that little cad Cockspur to hear but as you've asked you'd better know. It's the one thing I can't forgive Marne; but I suppose these monks have drilled him that way. My wife, who had been the best friend he ever had in America, actually came to that house when he was walking in the garden. He was looking at the ground like a monk, and hidden in a black hood that was really as ridiculous as any mask. She had sent her card in, and stood there in his very path. And he walked past her without a word or a glance, as if she had been a stone. He wasn't human; he was like some horrible automaton. She may well call him a dead man.'

'It's all very strange,' said the young man rather vaguely. 'It isn't like – like what I should have expected.'

Young Mr Mallow, when he left that rather dismal picnic, took himself thoughtfully in search of a friend. He did not know any monks, but he knew one priest, whom he was very much concerned to confront with the curious revelations he had heard that afternoon. He felt he would very much like to know the truth about the cruel superstition that hung over the house of Marne, like the black thundercloud he had seen hovering over it.

After being referred from one place to another, he finally ran his friend Father Brown to earth in the house of another friend, a Roman Catholic friend with a large family. He entered somewhat abruptly to find Father Brown sitting on the floor with a serious expression, and attempting to pin the somewhat florid hat belonging to a wax doll on to the head of a teddy bear.

Mallow felt a faint sense of incongruity; but he was far too full of his problem to put off the conversation if he could help it. He was staggering from a sort of set-back in a subconscious process that had been going on for some time. He poured out the whole tragedy of the house of Marne as he had heard it from the general's wife, along with most of the comments of the general and the newspaper proprietor. A new atmosphere of attention seemed to be created with the mention of the newspaper proprietor.

Father Brown neither knew nor cared that his attitudes were comic or commonplace. He continued to sit on the floor, where his large head and short legs made him look very like a baby playing with toys. But there came into his great grey eyes a certain expression that has been seen in the eyes of many men in many centuries through the story of nineteen hundred years; only the men were not generally sitting on floors, but at council tables, or on the seats of chapters, or the thrones of bishops and cardinals; a far-off, watchful look, heavy with the humility of a charge too great for men. Something of that anxious and far-reaching look is found in the eyes of sailors and of those who have steered through so many storms the ship of St Peter.

'It's very good of you to tell me this,' he said. 'I'm really awfully grateful, for we may have to do something about it. If it were only people
like you and the general, it might be only a private matter; but if Sir John
Cockspur is going to spread some sort of scare in his papers – well, he's
a Toronto Orangeman, and we can hardly keep out of it.'

'But what will you say about it?' asked Mallow anxiously.

'The first thing I should say about it,' said Father Brown, 'is that, as
you tell it, it doesn't sound like life. Suppose, for the sake of argument,
that we are all pessimistic vampires blighting all human happiness.
Suppose I'm a pessimistic vampire.' He scratched his nose with the
teddy bear, became faintly conscious of the incongruity, and put it
down. 'Suppose we do destroy all human and family ties. Why should
we entangle a man again in an old family tie just when he showed signs
of getting loose from it? Surely it's a little unfair to charge us both with
crushing such affection and encouraging such infatuation. I don't see
why even a religious maniac should be that particular sort of monomaniac, or how religion could increase that mania, except by brightening
it with a little hope.'

Then he said, after a pause: 'I should like to talk to that general of
yours.'

'It was his wife who told me,' said Mallow.

'Yes,' replied the other; 'but I'm more interested in what he didn't
tell you than in what she did.'

'You think he knows more than she does?'

'I think he knows more than she says,' answered Father Brown. 'You
tell me he used a phrase about forgiving everything except the rudeness
to his wife. After all, what else was there to forgive?'

Father Brown had risen and shaken his shapeless clothes, and stood
looking at the young man with screwed up eyes and slightly quizzical
expression. The next moment he had turned, and picking up his equally
shapeless umbrella and large shabby hat, went stumping down the
street.

He plodded through a variety of wide streets and squares till he came
to a handsome old-fashioned house in the West End, where he asked
the servant if he could see General Outram. After some little palaver
he was shown into a study, fitted out less with books than with maps
and globes, where the bald-headed, black-whiskered Anglo-Indian

sat smoking a long, thin, black cigar and playing with pins on a chart.

'I am sorry to intrude,' said the priest, 'and all the more because I can't help the intrusion looking like interference. I want to speak to you about a private matter, but only in the hope of keeping it private. Unfortunately, some people are likely to make it public. I think, general, that you know Sir John Cockspur.'

The mass of black moustache and whisker served as a sort of mask for the lower half of the old general's face; it was always hard to see whether he smiled, but his brown eyes often had a certain twinkle.

'Everybody knows him, I suppose,' he said. 'I don't know him very well.'

'Well, you know everybody knows whatever he knows,' said Father Brown, smiling, 'when he thinks it convenient to print it. And I understand from my friend Mr Mallow, whom, I think, you know, that Sir John is going to print some scorching anti-clerical articles founded on what he would call the Marne Mystery. "Monks Drive Marquis Mad," etc.'

'If he is,' replied the general, 'I don't see why you should come to me about it. I ought to tell you I'm a strong Protestant.'

'I'm very fond of strong Protestants,' said Father Brown. 'I came to you because I was sure you would tell the truth. I hope it is not uncharitable to feel less sure of Sir John Cockspur.'

The brown eyes twinkled again, but the general said nothing.

'General,' said Father Brown, 'suppose Cockspur or his sort were going to make the world ring with tales against your country and your flag. Suppose he said your regiment ran away in battle, or your staff were in the pay of the enemy. Would you let anything stand between you and the facts that would refute him? Wouldn't you get on the track of the truth at all costs to anybody? Well, I have a regiment, and I belong to an army. It is being discredited by what I am certain is a fictitious story; but I don't know the true story. Can you blame me for trying to find it out?'

The soldier was silent, and the priest continued:

'I have heard the story Mallow was told yesterday, about Marne retiring with a broken heart through the death of his more than brother. I am sure there was more in it than that. I came to ask you if you know any more.'

'No,' said the general shortly; 'I cannot tell you any more.'

'General,' said Father Brown with a broad grin, 'you would have called me a Jesuit if I had used that equivocation.'

The soldier laughed gruffly, and then growled with much greater hostility.

'Well, I won't tell you, then,' he said. 'What do you say to that?'

'I only say,' said the priest mildly, 'that in that case I shall have to tell you.'

The brown eyes stared at him; but there was no twinkle in them now. He went on:

'You compel me to state, less sympathetically perhaps than you could, why it is obvious that there is more behind. I am quite sure the marquis has better cause for his brooding and secretiveness than merely having lost an old friend. I doubt whether priests have anything to do with it; I don't even know if he's a convert or merely a man comforting his conscience with charities; but I'm sure he's something more than a chief mourner. Since you insist, I will tell you one or two of the things that made me think so.

'First, it was stated that James Mair was engaged to be married, but somehow became unattached again after the death of Maurice Mair. Why should an honourable man break off his engagement merely because he was depressed by the death of a third party? He's much more likely to have turned for consolation to it; but, anyhow, he was bound in decency to go through with it.'

The general was biting his black moustache, and his brown eyes had become very watchful and even anxious, but he did not answer.

'A second point,' said Father Brown, frowning at the table. 'James Mair was always asking his lady friend whether his cousin Maurice was not very fascinating, and whether women would not admire him. I don't know if it occurred to the lady that there might be another meaning to that inquiry.'

The general got to his feet and began to walk or stamp about the room.

'Oh, damn it all,' he said, but without any air of animosity.

'The third point,' went on Father Brown, 'is James Mair's curious manner of mourning – destroying all relics, veiling all portraits, and so on. It does sometimes happen, I admit; it might mean mere affectionate bereavement. But it might mean something else.'

'Confound you,' said the other. 'How long are you going on piling this up?'

'The fourth and fifth points are pretty conclusive,' said the priest calmly, 'especially if you take them together. The first is that Maurice Mair seems to have had no funeral in particular, considering he was a cadet of a great family. He must have been buried hurriedly; perhaps secretly. And the last point is, that James Mair instantly disappeared to foreign parts; fled, in fact, to the ends of the earth.

'And so,' he went on, still in the same soft voice, 'when you would blacken my religion to brighten the story of the pure and perfect affection of two brothers, it seems –'

'Stop!' cried Outram in a tone like a pistol shot. 'I must tell you more, or you will fancy worse. Let me tell you one thing to start with. It was a fair fight.'

'Ah,' said Father Brown, and seemed to exhale a huge breath.

'It was a duel,' said the other. 'It was probably the last duel fought in England, and it is long ago now.'

'That's better,' said Father Brown. 'Thank God; that's a great deal better.'

'Better than the ugly things you thought of, I suppose?' said the general gruffly. 'Well, it's all very well for you to sneer at the pure and perfect affection; but it was true for all that. James Mair really was devoted to his cousin, who'd grown up with him like a younger brother. Elder brothers and sisters do sometimes devote themselves to a child like that, especially when he's a sort of infant phenomenon. But James Mair was the sort of simple character in whom even hate is in a sense unselfish. I mean that even when his tenderness turns to rage it is still objective, directed outwards to its object; he isn't conscious of himself. Now poor Maurice Mair was just the opposite. He was far more friendly and popular; but his success had made him live in a house of mirrors. He was first in every sort of sport and art and accomplishment; he nearly always won and took his winning amiably. But if ever, by any chance, he lost, there was just a glimpse of something not so amiable; he was a little jealous. I needn't tell you the whole miserable story of how he was a little jealous of his cousin's engagement; how he couldn't keep his restless vanity from interfering. It's enough to say that one of the few things in which James Mair was admittedly ahead of him was marksmanship with a pistol; and with that the tragedy ended.'

'You mean the tragedy began,' replied the priest. 'The tragedy of the survivor. I thought he did not need any monkish vampires to make him miserable.'

'To my mind he's more miserable than he need be,' said the general. 'After all, as I say, it was a ghastly tragedy, but it was a fair fight. And Jim had great provocation.'

'How do you know all this?' asked the priest.

'I know it because I saw it,' answered Outram stolidly. 'I was James Mair's second, and I saw Maurice Mair shot dead on the sands before my very eyes.'

'I wish you would tell me more about it,' said Father Brown reflectively. 'Who was Maurice Mair's second?'

'He had a more distinguished backing,' replied the general grimly. 'Hugo Romaine was his second; the great actor, you know. Maurice was mad on acting and had taken up Romaine (who was then a rising but still a struggling man), and financed the fellow and his ventures in return for taking lessons from the professional in his own hobby of amateur acting. But Romaine was then, I suppose, practically dependent on his rich friend; though he's richer now than any aristocrat. So his serving as second proves very little about what he thought of the quarrel. They fought in the English fashion, with only one second apiece; I wanted at least to have a surgeon, but Maurice boisterously refused it, saying the fewer people who knew, the better; and at the worst we could immediately get help. "There's a doctor in the village not half a mile away," he said; "I know him and he's got the fastest horse in the country. He could be brought here in no time; but there's no need to bring him here till we know." Well, we all knew that Maurice ran most risk, as the pistol was not his weapon; so when he refused aid nobody liked to ask for it. The duel was fought on a flat stretch of sand on the east coast of Scotland; and both the sight and sound of it were masked from the hamlets inland by a long rampart of sandhills patched with rank grass; probably part of the links, though in those days no Englishman had heard of golf. There was one deep, crooked cranny in the sandhills through which we came out on the sands. I can see them now; first a wide strip of dead yellow, and beyond, a narrower strip of dark red; a dark red that seemed already like the long shadow of a deed of blood.

'The thing itself seemed to happen with horrible speed; as if a whirlwind had struck the sand. With the very crack of sound Maurice Mair seemed to spin like a teetotum and pitch upon his face like a ninepin. And queerly enough, while I'd been worrying about him up to that moment, the instant he was dead all my pity was for the man who killed him; as it is to this day and hour. I knew that with that, the whole huge terrible pendulum of my friend's life-long love would swing back; and that whatever cause others might find to pardon him, he would never pardon himself for ever and ever. And so, somehow, the really vivid thing, the picture that burns in my memory so that I can't forget it, is not that of the catastrophe, the smoke and the flash and the falling figure. That seemed to be all over, like the noise that wakes a man up. What I saw, what I shall always see, is poor Jim hurrying across towards his fallen friend and foe; his brown beard looking black against the ghastly pallor of his face, with its high features cut out against the sea; and the frantic gestures with which he waved me to run for the surgeon in the hamlet behind the sandhills. He had dropped his pistol as he ran; he had a glove in one hand and the loose and fluttering fingers of it seemed to elongate and emphasize his wild pantomime of pointing or hailing for help. That is the picture that really remains with me; and there is nothing else in that picture, except the striped background of sands and sea and the dark, dead body lying still as a stone, and the dark figure of the dead man's second standing grim and motionless against the horizon.'

'Did Romaine stand motionless?' asked the priest. 'I should have thought he would have run even quicker towards the corpse.'

'Perhaps he did when I had left,' replied the general. 'I took in that undying picture in an instant and the next instant I had dived among the sandhills, and was far out of sight of the others. Well, poor Maurice had made a good choice in the matter of doctors; though the doctor came too late, he came quicker than I should have thought possible. This village surgeon was a very remarkable man, red-haired, irascible, but extraordinarily strong in promptitude and presence of mind. I saw him but for a flash as he leapt on his horse and went thundering away to the scene of death, leaving me far behind. But in that flash I had so strong a sense of his personality that I wished to God he had really been called in before the duel began; for I believe on my soul he would have prevented it somehow. As it was, he cleaned up the mess with marvellous swiftness; long before I could trail back to the sea-shore on my two feet his impetuous practicality had managed everything; the corpse was temporarily buried in the sandhills and the unhappy homicide has been persuaded to do the only thing he could do – to flee for his life. He slipped along the coast till he came to a port and managed to get out of the country. You know the rest; poor Jim remained abroad for many years; later, when the whole thing had been hushed up or forgotten, he returned to his dismal castle and automatically inherited the title. I have never seen him from that day to this, and yet I know what is written in red letters in the inmost darkness of his brain.'

'I understand,' said Father Brown, 'that some of you have made efforts to see him?'

'My wife never relaxed her efforts,' said the general. 'She refuses to admit that such a crime ought to cut a man off for ever; and I confess I am inclined to agree with her. Eighty years before it would have been thought quite normal; and really it was manslaughter rather than murder. My wife is a great friend of the unfortunate lady who was the occasion of the quarrel and she has an idea that if Jim would consent to see Viola Grayson once again, and receive her assurance that old quarrels are buried, it might restore his sanity. My wife is calling a sort of council of old friends to-morrow, I believe. She is very energetic.'

Father Brown was playing with the pins that lay beside the general's map; he seemed to listen rather absent-mindedly. He had the sort of mind that sees things in pictures; and the picture which had coloured even the prosaic mind of the practical soldier took on tints, yet more significant and sinister in the more mystical mind of the priest. He saw the dark-red desolation of sand, the very hue of Aceldama, and the dead man lying in a dark heap, and the slayer, stooping as he ran, gesticulating with a glove in demented remorse, and always his imagination came back to the third thing that he could not yet fit into any human picture: the second of the slain man standing motionless and mysterious, like a dark statue on the edge of the sea. It might seem to some a detail: but for him it was that stiff figure that stood up like a standing note of interrogation.

Why had not Romaine moved instantly? It was the natural thing for a second to do, in common humanity, let alone friendship. Even if there were some double-dealing or darker motive not yet understood, one would think it would be done for the sake of appearances. Anyhow, when the thing was all over, it would be natural for the second to stir long before the other second had vanished beyond the sandhills.

'Does this man Romaine move very slowly?' he asked.

'It's queer you should ask that,' answered Outram, with a sharp glance. 'No, as a matter of fact he moves very quickly when he moves at all. But, curiously enough, I was just thinking that only this afternoon I saw him stand exactly like that, during the thunderstorm. He stood in that silver-clasped cape of his, and with one hand on his hip, exactly and in every line as he stood on those bloody sands long ago. The lightning blinded us all, but he did not blink. When it was dark again he was standing there still.'

'I suppose he isn't standing there now?' inquired Father Brown, 'I mean, I suppose he moved sometime?'

'No, he moved quite sharply when the thunder came,' replied the other. 'He seemed to have been waiting for it, for he told us the exact time of the interval . . . is anything the matter?'

'I've pricked myself with one of your pins,' said Father Brown. 'I hope I haven't damaged it.' But his eyes had snapped and his mouth abruptly shut.

'Are you ill?' inquired the general, staring at him.

'No,' answered the priest; 'I'm only not quite so stoical as your friend Romaine. I can't help blinking when I see light.'

He turned to gather up his hat and umbrella; but when he had got to the door he seemed to remember something and turned back. Coming up close to Outram, he gazed up into his face with a rather helpless expression, as of a dying fish, and made a motion as if to hold him by the waistcoat.

'General,' he almost whispered, 'for God's sake don't let your wife and that other woman insist on seeing Marne again. Let sleeping dogs lie, or you'll unleash all the hounds of hell.'

The general was left alone with a look of bewilderment in his brown eyes, as he sat down again to play with his pins.

Even greater, however, was the bewilderment which attended the successive stages of the benevolent conspiracy of the general's wife, who had assembled her little group of sympathizers to storm the castle of the misanthrope. The first surprise she encountered was the unexplained absence of one of the actors in the ancient tragedy. When they assembled by agreement at a quiet hotel quite near the castle, there was no sign of Hugo Romaine, until a belated telegram from a lawyer told them that the great actor had suddenly left the country. The second surprise, when they began the bombardment by sending up word to the castle with an urgent request for an interview, was the figure which came forth from those gloomy gates to receive the deputation in the name of the noble owner. It was no such figure as they would have conceived suitable to those sombre avenues or those almost feudal formalities. It was not some stately steward or major-domo, nor even a dignified butler or tall and ornamental footman. The only figure that came out of the cavernous castle doorway was the short and shabby figure of Father Brown.

'Look here,' he said, in his simple, bothered fashion, 'I told you you'd much better leave him alone. He knows what he's doing and it'll only make everybody unhappy.'

Lady Outram, who was accompanied by a tall and quietly-dressed lady, still very handsome, presumably the original Miss Grayson, looked at the little priest with cold contempt.

'Really, sir,' she said; 'this is a private occasion, and I don't understand what you have to do with it.'

'Trust a priest to have to do with a private occasion,' snarled Sir John Cockspur. Don't you know they live behind the scenes like rats behind a wainscot burrowing their way into everybody's private rooms? See how he's already in possession of poor Marne.' Sir John was slightly sulky, as his aristocratic friends had persuaded him to give up the great scoop of publicity in return for the privilege of being really inside a Society secret. It never occurred to him to ask himself whether *he* was at all like a rat in a wainscot.

'Oh, that's all right,' said Father Brown, with the impatience of anxiety. 'I've talked it over with the marquis and the only priest he's ever had anything to do with; his clerical tastes have been much exaggerated. I tell you he knows what he's about; and I do implore you all to leave him alone.'

'You mean to leave him to this living death of moping and going mad in a ruin!' cried Lady Outram, in a voice that shook a little. 'And all because he had the bad luck to shoot a man in a duel more than a quarter of a century ago. Is that what you call Christian charity?'

'Yes,' answered the priest stolidly; 'that is what I call Christian charity.'

'It's about all the Christian charity you'll ever get out of these priests,' cried Cockspur bitterly. 'That's their only idea of pardoning a poor fellow for a piece of folly; to wall him up alive and starve him to death with fasts and penances and pictures of hell-fire. And all because a bullet went wrong.'

'Really, Father Brown,' said General Outram, 'do you honestly think he deserves this? Is that your Christianity?'

'Surely the true Christianity,' pleaded his wife more gently, 'is that which knows all and pardons all; the love that can remember – and forget.'

'Father Brown,' said young Mallow, very earnestly, 'I generally agree with what you say; but I'm hanged if I can follow you here. A shot in a duel, followed instantly by remorse, is not such an awful offence.'

'I admit,' said Father Brown dully, 'that I take a more serious view of his offence.'

'God soften your hard heart,' said the strange lady speaking for the first time. 'I am going to speak to my old friend.'

Almost as if her voice had raised a ghost in that great grey house, something stirred within and a figure stood in the dark doorway at the top of the great stone flight of steps. It was clad in dead black, but there was something wild about the blanched hair and something in the pale features that was like the wreck of a marble statue.

Viola Grayson began calmly to move up the great flight of steps; and Outram muttered in his thick black moustache: 'He won't cut her dead as he did my wife, I fancy.'

Father Brown, who seemed in a collapse of resignation, looked up at him for a moment.

'Poor Marne has enough on his conscience,' he said. 'Let us acquit him of what we can. At least he never cut your wife.'

'What do you mean by that?'

'He never knew her,' said Father Brown.

As they spoke, the tall lady proudly mounted the last step and came face to face with the Marquis of Marne. His lips moved, but something happened before he could speak.

A scream rang across the open space and went wailing away in echoes along those hollow walls. By the abruptness and agony with which it broke from the woman's lips it might have been a mere inarticulate cry. But it was an articulated word; and they all heard it with a horrible distinctness.

'Maurice!'

'What is it, dear?' cried Lady Outram, and began to run up the steps; for the other woman was swaying as if she might fall down the whole stone flight. Then she faced about and began to descend, all bowed and shrunken and shuddering. 'Oh, my God,' she was saying. 'Oh, my God . . . it isn't Jim at all . . . it's Maurice!'

'I think, Lady Outram,' said the priest gravely, 'you had better go with your friend.'

As they turned, a voice fell on them like a stone from the top of the stone stair, a voice that might have come out of an open grave. It was hoarse and unnatural, like the voices of men who are left alone with wild birds on desert islands. It was the voice of the Marquis of Marne, and it said: 'Stop!'

'Father Brown,' he said, 'before your friends disperse I authorize you to tell them all I have told you. Whatever follows, I will hide from it no longer.'

'You are right,' said the priest, 'and it shall be counted to you.'

'Yes,' said Father Brown quietly to the questioning company afterwards. 'He has given me the right to speak; but I will not tell it as he told me, but as I found it out for myself. Well, I knew from the first that the blighting monkish influence was all nonsense out of novels. Our people might possibly, in certain cases, encourage a man to go regularly into a monastery, but certainly not to hang about in a mediæval castle. In the same way, they certainly wouldn't want him to dress up as a monk when he wasn't a monk. But it struck me that he might himself want to wear a monk's hood or even a mask. I had heard of him as a mourner, and then as a murderer; but already I had hazy suspicions that his reason for hiding might not only be concerned with what he was, but with who he was.

'Then came the general's vivid description of the duel; and the most vivid thing in it to me was the figure of Mr Romaine in the background; it was vivid because it was in the background. Why did the general leave behind him on the sand a dead man, whose friend stood yards away from him like a stock or a stone? Then I heard something, a mere trifle, about a trick habit that Romaine has of standing quite still when he is waiting for something to happen; as he waited for the thunder to follow the lightning. Well, that automatic trick in this case betrayed everything. Hugo Romaine on that old occasion, also, was waiting for something.'

'But it was all over,' said the general. 'What could he have been waiting for?'

'He was waiting for the duel,' said Father Brown.

'But I tell you I saw the duel!' cried the general.

'And I tell you you didn't see the duel,' said the priest.

'Are you mad?' demanded the other. 'Or why should you think I am blind?'

'Because you were blinded – that you might not see,' said the priest. 'Because you are a good man and God had mercy on your innocence, and he turned your face away from that unnatural strife. He set a wall of sand and silence between you and what really happened on that horrible red shore, abandoned to the raging spirits of Judas and of Cain.'

'Tell us what happened!' gasped the lady impatiently.

'I will tell it as I found it,' proceeded the priest. 'The next thing I found was that Romaine the actor had been training Maurice Mair in all the tricks of the trade of acting. I once had a friend who went in for acting. He gave me a very amusing account of how his first week's training consisted entirely of falling down; of learning how to fall flat without a stagger, as if he were stone dead.'

'God have mercy on us!' cried the general, and gripped the arms of his chair as if to rise.

'Amen,' said Father Brown. 'You told me how quickly it seemed to come; in fact, Maurice fell before the bullet flew, and lay perfectly still, waiting. And his wicked friend and teacher stood also in the background, waiting.'

'We are waiting,' said Cockspur, 'and I feel as if I couldn't wait.'

'James Mair, already broken with remorse, rushed across to the fallen man and bent over to lift him up. He had thrown away his pistol like an unclean thing; but Maurice's pistol still lay under his hand and it was undischarged. Then as the elder man bent over the younger, the younger lifted himself on his left arm and shot the elder through the body. He knew he was not so good a shot, but there was no question of missing the heart at that distance.'

The rest of the company had risen and stood staring down at the narrator with pale faces. 'Are you sure of this?' asked Sir John at last, in a thick voice.

'I am sure of it,' said Father Brown, 'and now I leave Maurice Mair, the present Marquis of Marne, to your Christian charity. You have told me something to-day about Christian charity. You seemed to me to give it almost too large a place; but how fortunate it is for poor sinners like this man that you err so much on the side of mercy, and are ready to be reconciled to all mankind.'

'Hang it all,' exploded the general; 'if you think I'm going to be reconciled to a filthy viper like that, I tell you I wouldn't say a word to save him from hell. I said I could pardon a regular decent duel, but of all the treacherous assassins –'

'He ought to be lynched,' cried Cockspur excitedly. 'He ought to burn alive like a nigger in the States. And if there is such a thing as burning for ever, he jolly well –'

'I wouldn't touch him with a bargepole myself,' said Mallow.

'There is a limit to human charity,' said Lady Outram, trembling all over.

'There is,' said Father Brown dryly; 'and that is the real difference between human charity and Christian charity. You must forgive me if I was not altogether crushed by your contempt for my uncharitableness to-day; or by the lectures you read me about pardon for every sinner. For it seems to me that you only pardon the sins that you don't really think sinful. You only forgive criminals when they commit what you don't regard as crimes, but rather as conventions. So you tolerate a conventional duel, just as you tolerate a conventional divorce. You forgive because there isn't anything to be forgiven.'

'But, hang it all,' cried Mallow, 'you don't expect us to be able to pardon a vile thing like this?'

'No,' said the priest; 'but *we* have to be able to pardon it.'

He stood up abruptly and looked round at them.

'We have to touch such men, not with a bargepole, but with a benediction,' he said. 'We have to say the word that will save them from hell. We alone are left to deliver them from despair when your human charity deserts them. Go on your own primrose path pardoning all your favourite vices and being generous to your fashionable crimes; and leave us in the darkness, vampires of the night, to console those who really need consolation; who do things really indefensible, things that neither the world nor they themselves can defend; and none but a priest will pardon. Leave us with the men who commit the mean and revolting and real crimes; mean as St Peter when the cock crew, and yet the dawn came.'

'The dawn,' repeated Mallow doubtfully. 'You mean hope – for *him*?'

'Yes,' replied the other. 'Let me ask you one question. You are great ladies and men of honour and secure of yourselves; you would never, you can tell yourselves, stoop to such squalid reason as that. But tell me this. If any of you had so stooped, which of you, years afterwards, when you were old and rich and safe, would have been driven by conscience or confessor to tell such a story of yourself? You say you could not commit so base a crime. Could you confess so base a crime?'

The others gathered their possessions together and drifted by twos and threes out of the room in silence. And Father Brown, also in silence, went back to the melancholy castle of Marne.

The Scandal of Father Brown

1

The Scandal of Father Brown

It would not be fair to record the adventures of Father Brown, without admitting that he was once involved in a grave scandal. There still are persons, perhaps even of his own community, who would say that there was a sort of blot upon his name. It happened in a picturesque Mexican road-house of rather loose repute, as appeared later; and to some it seemed that for once the priest had allowed a romantic streak in him, and his sympathy for human weakness, to lead him into loose and unorthodox action. The story in itself was a simple one; and perhaps the whole surprise of it consisted in its simplicity.

Burning Troy began with Helen; this disgraceful story began with the beauty of Hypatia Potter. Americans have a great power, which Europeans do not always appreciate, of creating institutions from below; that is by popular initiative. Like every other good thing, it has its lighter aspects; one of which, as has been remarked by Mr Wells and others, is that a person may become a public institution without becoming an official institution. A girl of great beauty or brilliancy will be a sort of uncrowned queen, even if she is not a Film Star or the original of a Gibson Girl. Among those who had the fortune, or misfortune, to exist beautifully in public in this manner, was a certain Hypatia Hard, who had passed through the preliminary stage of receiving florid compliments in society paragraphs of the local press, to the position of one who is actually interviewed by real pressmen. On War and Peace and Patriotism and Prohibition and Evolution and the Bible she had made her pronouncements with a charming smile; and if none of them seemed very near to the real grounds of her own reputation, it was almost equally hard to say what the grounds of her reputation really were. Beauty, and being the daughter of a rich man, are things not rare in her country; but to these she added whatever it is that attracts the wandering eye of journalism. Next to none of her admirers had even seen her, or even hoped to do so; and none of them could possibly derive any sordid benefit from her father's wealth. It was simply a sort of popular romance, the modern substitute for mythology; and it laid the first foundations of the more turgid and tempestuous sort of romance in which she was to figure later on; and in which many held that the reputation of Father Brown, as well as of others, had been blown to rags.

It was accepted, sometimes romantically, sometimes resignedly, by those whom American satire has named the Sob Sisters, that she had already married a very worthy and respectable business man of the name of Potter. It was even possible to regard her for a moment as Mrs Potter, on the universal understanding that her husband was only the husband of Mrs Potter.

Then came the Great Scandal, by which her friends and enemies were horrified beyond their wildest hopes. Her name was coupled (as the queer phrase goes) with a literary man living in Mexico; in status an American, but in spirit a very Spanish American. Unfortunately his vices resembled her virtues, in being good copy. He was no less a person than the famous or infamous Rudel Romanes; the poet whose works had been so universally popularized by being vetoed by libraries or prosecuted by the police. Anyhow, her pure and placid star was seen in conjunction with this comet. He was of the sort to be compared to a comet, being hairy and hot; the first in his portraits, the second in his poetry. He was also destructive; the comet's tail was a trail of divorces, which some called his success as a lover and some his prolonged failure as a husband. It was hard on Hypatia; there are disadvantages in conducting the perfect private life in public; like a domestic interior in a shop-window. Interviewers reported doubtful utterances about Love's Larger Law of Supreme Self-Realization. The Pagans applauded. The Sob Sisterhood permitted themselves a note of romantic regret; some having even the hardened audacity to quote from the poem of Maud Mueller, to the effect that of all the words of tongue or pen, the saddest are 'It might have been.' And Mr Agar P. Rock, who hated the Sob Sisterhood with a holy and righteous hatred, said that in this case he thoroughly agreed with Bret Harte's emendation of the poem: 'More sad are those we daily see; it is, but it hadn't ought to be.'

For Mr Rock was very firmly and rightly convinced that a very large number of things hadn't ought to be. He was a slashing and savage critic of national degeneration, on the *Minneapolis Meteor*, and a bold and honest man. He had perhaps come to specialize too much in the spirit of indignation, but it had had a healthy enough origin in his reaction against sloppy attempts to confuse right and wrong in modern journalism and gossip. He expressed it first in the form of a protest against an unholy halo of romance being thrown round the gunman and the gangster. Perhaps he was rather too much inclined to assume, in robust impatience, that all gangsters were Dagos and that all Dagos were gangsters. But his prejudices, even when they were a little provincial, were rather refreshing after a certain sort of maudlin and unmanly hero-worship, which was ready to regard a professional murderer as a leader of fashion, so long as the pressmen reported that his smile was irresistible or his tuxedo was all right. Anyhow, the prejudices did not boil the less in the bosom of Mr Rock, because he was actually in the land of the Dagos when this story opens; striding furiously up a hill beyond the Mexican border, to the white hotel, fringed with ornamental palms, in which it was supposed that the Potters were staying and that the mysterious Hypatia now held her court. Agar Rock was a good specimen of a Puritan, even to look at; he might even have been a virile Puritan of the seventeenth century, rather than the softer and more sophisticated Puritan of the twentieth. If you had told him that his antiquated black hat and habitual black frown, and fine flinty features, cast a gloom over the sunny land of palms and vines, he would have been very much gratified. He looked to right and left with eyes bright with universal suspicions. And, as he did so, he saw two figures on the ridge above him, outlined against the clear sub-tropical sunset; figures in a momentary posture which might have made even a less suspicious man suspect something.

One of the figures was rather remarkable in itself. It was poised at the exact angle of the turning road above the valley, as if by an instinct for the site as well as the attitude of statuary. It was wrapt in a great black cloak, in the Byronic manner, and the head that rose above it in swarthy beauty was remarkably like Byron's. This man had the same curling hair and curling nostrils; and he seemed to be snorting something of the same scorn and indignation against the world. He grasped in his hand a rather long cane or walking-stick, which having a spike of

the sort used for mountaineering, carried at the moment a fanciful
suggestion of a spear. It was rendered all the more fanciful by something
comically contradictory in the figure of the other man, who carried an
umbrella. It was indeed a new and neatly-rolled umbrella, very different,
for instance, from Father Brown's umbrella: and he was neatly clad like
a clerk in light holiday clothes; a stumpy stoutish bearded man; but the
prosaic umbrella was raised and even brandished at an acute angle of
attack. The taller man thrust back at him, but in a hasty defensive
manner; and then the scene rather collapsed into comedy; for the
umbrella opened of itself and its owner almost seemed to sink behind
it, while the other man had the air of pushing his spear through a great
grotesque shield. But the other man did not push it, or the quarrel, very
far; he plucked out the point, turned away impatiently and strode down
the road; while the other, rising and carefully refolding his umbrella,
turned in the opposite direction towards the hotel. Rock had not heard
any of the words of the quarrel, which must have immediately preceded
this brief and rather absurd bodily conflict; but as he went up the road
in the track of the short man with the beard, he revolved many things.
And the romantic cloak and rather operatic good looks of the one man,
combined with the sturdy self-assertion of the other, fitted in with
the whole story which he had come to seek; and he knew that he could
have fixed those two strange figures with their names: Romanes and
Potter.

His view was in every way confirmed when he entered the pillared
porch; and heard the voice of the bearded man raised high in altercation
or command. He was evidently speaking to the manager or staff of the
hotel, and Rock heard enough to know that he was warning them of a
wild and dangerous character in the neighbourhood.

'If he's really been to the hotel already,' the little man was saying, in
answer to some murmur, 'all I can say is that you'd better not let him
in again. Your police ought to be looking after a fellow of that sort, but
anyhow, I won't have the lady pestered with him.'

Rock listened in grim silence and growing conviction; then he
slid across the vestibule to an alcove where he saw the hotel register
and turning to the last page, saw 'the fellow' had indeed been to the
hotel already. There appeared the name of 'Rudel Romanes,' that
romantic public character in very large and florid foreign lettering;

and after a space under it, rather close together, the names of Hypatia Potter and Ellis T. Potter, in a correct and quite American hand-writing.

Agar Rock looked moodily about him, and saw in the surroundings and even the small decorations of the hotel everything that he hated most. It is perhaps unreasonable to complain of oranges growing on orange trees, even in small tubs; still more of their only growing on threadbare curtains or faded wallpapers as a formal scheme of ornament. But to him those red and golden moons, decoratively alternated with silver moons, were in a queer way the quintessence of all moonshine. He saw in them all that sentimental deterioration which his principles deplored in modern manners, and which his prejudices vaguely connec-ted with the warmth and softness of the South. It annoyed him even to catch sight of a patch of dark canvas, half-showing a Watteau shepherd with a guitar, or a blue tile with a commonplace design of a Cupid on a dolphin. His common sense would have told him that he might have seen these things in a shop-window on Fifth Avenue; but where they were, they seemed like a taunting siren voice of the Paganism of the Mediterranean. And then suddenly, the look of all these things seemed to alter, as a still mirror will flicker when a figure has flashed past it for a moment; and he knew the whole room was full of a challenging presence. He turned almost stiffly, and with a sort of resistance, and knew that he was facing the famous Hypatia, of whom he had read and heard for so many years.

Hypatia Potter, *née* Hard, was one of those people to whom the word 'radiant' really does apply definitely and derivatively. That is, she allowed what the papers called her Personality to go out from her in rays. She would have been equally beautiful, and to some tastes more attractive, if she had been self-contained; but she had always been taught to believe that self-containment was only selfishness. She would have said that she had lost Self in Service; it would perhaps be truer to say that she had asserted Self in Service; but she was quite in good faith about the service. Therefore her outstanding starry blue eyes really struck outwards, as in the old metaphor that made eyes like Cupid's darts, killing at a distance; but with an abstract conception of conquest beyond any mere coquetry. Her pale fair hair, though arranged in a saintly halo, had a look of almost electric radiation. And when she understood that the stranger before her was Mr Agar Rock, of the *Minneapolis Meteor*, her eyes took on themselves the range of long searchlights, sweeping the horizon of the States.

But in this the lady was mistaken; as she sometimes was. For Agar Rock was not Agar Rock of the *Minneapolis Meteor*. He was at that moment merely Agar Rock; there had surged up in him a great and sincere moral impulsion, beyond the coarse courage of the interviewer. A feeling profoundly mixed of a chivalrous and national sensibility to beauty, with an instant itch for moral action of some definite sort, which was also national, nerved him to face a great scene; and to deliver a noble insult. He remembered the original Hypatia, the beautiful Neo-Platonist, and how he had been thrilled as a boy by Kingsley's romance in which the young monk denounces her for harlotries and idolatries. He confronted her with an iron gravity and said:

'If you'll pardon me, Madam, I should like to have a word with you in private.'

'Well,' she said, sweeping the room with her splendid gaze, 'I don't know whether you consider this place private.'

Rock also gazed round the room and could see no sign of life less vegetable than the orange trees, except what looked like a large black mushroom, which he recognized as the hat of some native priest or other, stolidly smoking a black local cigar, and otherwise as stagnant as any vegetable. He looked for a moment at the heavy, expressionless features, noting the rudeness of that peasant type from which priests so often come, in Latin and especially Latin-American countries; and lowered his voice a little as he laughed.

'I don't imagine that Mexican padre knows our language,' he said. 'Catch those lumps of laziness learning any language but their own. Oh, I can't swear he's a Mexican; he might be anything; mongrel Indian or nigger, I suppose. But I'll answer for it he's not an American. Our ministries don't produce that debased type.'

'As a matter of fact,' said the debased type, removing his black cigar, 'I'm English and my name is Brown. But pray let me leave you if you wish to be private.'

'If you're English,' said Rock warmly, 'you ought to have some normal Nordic instinct for protesting against all this nonsense. Well, it's enough to say now that I'm in a position to testify that there's a pretty dangerous fellow hanging round this place; a tall fellow in a cloak, like those old pictures of crazy poets.'

'Well, you can't go much by that,' said the priest mildly; 'a lot of people round here use those cloaks, because the chill strikes very suddenly after sunset.'

Rock darted a dark and doubtful glance at him; as if suspecting some evasion in the interests of all that was symbolized to him by mushroom hats and moonshine. 'It wasn't only the cloak,' he growled, 'though it was partly the way he wore it. The whole look of the fellow was theatrical, down to his damned theatrical good looks. And if you'll forgive me, Madam, I strongly advise you to have nothing to do with him, if he comes bothering here. Your husband has already told the hotel people to keep him out –'

Hypatia sprang to her feet and, with a very unusual gesture, covered her face, thrusting her fingers into her hair. She seemed to be shaken, possibly with sobs, but by the time she had recovered they had turned into a sort of wild laughter.

'Oh, you are all too funny,' she said, and, in a way very unusual with her, ducked and darted to the door and disappeared.

'Bit hysterical when they laugh like that,' said Rock uncomfortably; then, rather at a loss, and turning to the little priest: 'as I say, if you're English, you ought really to be on my side against these Dagos, anyhow. Oh, I'm not one of those who talk tosh about Anglo-Saxons; but there is such a thing as history. You can always claim that America got her civilization from England.'

'Also, to temper our pride,' said Father Brown, 'we must always admit that England got her civilization from Dagos.'

Again there glowed in the other's mind the exasperated sense that his interlocutor was fencing with him, and fencing on the wrong side, in some secret and evasive way; and he curtly professed a failure to comprehend.

'Well, there was a Dago, or possibly a Wop, called Julius Caesar,' said Father Brown; 'he was afterwards killed in a stabbing match; you know these Dagos always use knives. And there was another one called Augustine, who brought Christianity to our little island; and really, I don't think we should have had much civilization without those two.'

'Anyhow, that's all ancient history,' said the somewhat irritated journalist, 'and I'm very much interested in modern history. What I see is that these scoundrels are bringing Paganism to our country, and destroying all the Christianity there is. Also destroying all the common sense there is. All settled habits, all solid social order, all the way in which the farmers who were our fathers and grandfathers did manage to live in the world, melted into a hot mush by sensations and sensualities about film stars who are divorced every month or so, and make every silly girl think that marriage is only a way of getting divorced.'

'You are quite right,' said Father Brown. 'Of course I quite agree with you there. But you must make some allowances. Perhaps these Southern people are a little prone to that sort of fault. You must remember that Northern people have other kinds of faults. Perhaps these surroundings do encourage people to give too rich an importance to mere romance . . .'

The whole integral indignation of Agar Rock's life rose up within him at the word.

'I hate Romance,' he said, hitting the little table before him. 'I've fought the papers I worked for for forty years about the infernal trash. Every blackguard bolting with a barmaid is called a romantic elopement or something; and now our own Hypatia Hard, a daughter of decent people, may get dragged into some rotten romantic divorce case, that will be trumpeted to the whole world as happily as a royal wedding. This mad poet Romanes is hanging round her; and you bet the spotlight will follow him, as if he were any rotten little Dago who is called the Great Lover on the films. I saw him outside; and he's got the regular spotlight face. Now my sympathies are with decency and common sense. My sympathies are with poor Potter, a plain straightforward broker from Pittsburg, who thinks he has a right to his own home. And he's making a fight for it, too. I heard him hollering at the management, telling them to keep that rascal out; and quite right too. The people here seem a sly and slinky lot; but I rather fancy he's put the fear of God into them already.'

'As a matter of fact,' said Father Brown, 'I rather agree with you about the manager and the men in this hotel; but you mustn't judge all Mexicans by them. Also I fancy the gentleman you speak of has not only hollered, but handed round dollars enough to get the whole staff on his side. I saw them locking doors and whispering most excitedly. By the way, your plain straightforward friend seems to have a lot of money.'

'I've no doubt his business does well,' said Rock. 'He's quite the best type of sound business man. What do you mean?'

'I fancied it might suggest another thought to you,' said Father Brown; and, rising with rather heavy civility, he left the room.

Rock watched the Potters very carefully that evening at dinner; and gained some new impressions, though none that disturbed his deep sense of the wrong that probably threatened the peace of the Potter home. Potter himself proved worthy of somewhat closer study; though the journalist had at first accepted him as prosaic and unpretentious, there was a pleasure in recognizing finer lines in what he considered the hero or victim of a tragedy. Potter had really rather a thoughtful and distinguished face, though worried and occasionally petulant. Rock got an impression that the man was recovering from an illness; his faded hair was thin but rather long, as if it had been lately neglected, and his rather unusual beard gave the onlooker the same notion. Certainly he spoke once or twice to his wife in a rather sharp and acid manner, fussing about tablets or some detail of digestive science; but his real worry was doubtless concerned with the danger from without. His wife played up to him in the splendid if somewhat condescending manner of a Patient Griselda; but her eyes also roamed continually to the doors and shutters, as if in half-hearted fear of an invasion. Rock had only too good reason to dread, after her curious outbreak, the fact that her fear might turn out to be only half-hearted.

It was in the middle of that night that the extraordinary event occurred. Rock, imagining himself to be the last to go up to bed, was surprised to find Father Brown still tucked obscurely under an orange-tree in the hall, and placidly reading a book. He returned the other's farewell without further words, and the journalist had his foot on the lowest step of the stair, when suddenly the outer door sprang on its hinges and shook and rattled under the shock of blows planted from without; and a great voice louder than the blows was heard violently demanding admission. Somehow the journalist was certain that the blows had been struck with a pointed stick like an alpenstock. He looked back at the darkened lower floor, and saw the servants of the hotel sliding here and there to see that the doors were locked; and not unlocking them. Then he slowly mounted to his room, and sat down furiously to write his report.

He described the siege of the hotel; the evil atmosphere; the shabby luxury of the place; the shifty evasions of the priest; above all, that terrible voice crying without, like a wolf prowling round the house. Then, as he wrote, he heard a new sound and sat up suddenly. It was a long repeated whistle, and in his mood he hated it doubly, because it was like the signal of a conspirator and like the love-call of a bird. There followed an utter silence, in which he sat rigid; then he rose abruptly; for he had heard yet another noise. It was a faint swish followed by a sharp rap or rattle; and he was almost certain that somebody was throwing something at a window. He walked stiffly downstairs, to the floor which was now dark and deserted; or nearly deserted. For the little priest was still sitting under the orange shrub, lit by a low lamp; and still reading his book.

'You seem to be sitting up late,' he said harshly.

'Quite a dissipated character,' said Father Brown, looking up with a broad smile, 'reading Economics of Usury at all wild hours of the night.'

'The place is locked up,' said Rock.

'Very thoroughly locked up,' replied the other. 'Your friend with the beard seems to have taken every precaution. By the way, your friend with the beard is a little rattled; I thought he was rather cross at dinner.'

'Natural enough,' growled the other, 'if he thinks savages in this savage place are out to wreck his home life.'

'Wouldn't it be better,' said Father Brown, 'if a man tried to make his home life nice inside, while he was protecting it from the things outside.'

'Oh, I know you will work up all the casuistical excuses,' said the other; 'perhaps he was rather snappy with his wife; but he's got the right on his side. Look here, you seem to me to be rather a deep dog. I believe you know more about this than you say. What the devil is going on in this infernal place? Why are you sitting up all night to see it through?'

'Well,' said Father Brown patiently, 'I rather thought my bedroom might be wanted.'

'Wanted by whom?'

'As a matter of fact, Mrs Potter wanted another room,' explained

Father Brown with limpid clearness. 'I gave her mine, because I could open the window. Go and see, if you like.'

'I'll see to something else first,' said Rock grinding his teeth. 'You can play your monkey tricks in this Spanish monkey-house, but I'm still in touch with civilization.' He strode into the telephone-booth and rang up his paper; pouring out the whole tale of the wicked priest who helped the wicked poet. Then he ran upstairs into the priest's room, in which the priest had just lit a short candle, showing the windows beyond wide open.

He was just in time to see a sort of rude rope-ladder unhooked from the window-sill and rolled up by a laughing gentleman on the lawn below. The laughing gentleman was a tall and swarthy gentleman, and was accompanied by a blonde but equally laughing lady. This time, Mr Rock could not even comfort himself by calling her laughter hysterical. It was too horribly genuine; and rang down the rambling garden-paths as she and her troubadour disappeared into the dark thickets.

Agar Rock turned on his companion a face of final and awful justice; like the Day of Judgement.

'Well, all America is going to hear of this,' he said. 'In plain words, you helped her to bolt with that curly-haired lover.'

'Yes,' said Father Brown, 'I helped her to bolt with that curly-haired lover.'

'You call yourself a minister of Jesus Christ,' cried Rock, 'and you boast of a crime.'

'I have been mixed up with several crimes,' said the priest gently. 'Happily for once this is a story without a crime. This is a simple fireside idyll; that ends with a glow of domesticity.'

'And ends with a rope-ladder instead of a rope,' said Rock. 'Isn't she a married woman?'

'Oh, yes,' said Father Brown.

'Well, oughtn't she to be with her husband?' demanded Rock.

'She is with her husband,' said Father Brown.

The other was startled into anger. 'You lie,' he said. 'The poor little man is still snoring in bed.'

'You seem to know a lot about his private affairs,' said Father Brown plaintively. 'You could almost write a life of the Man with a Beard. The only thing you don't seem ever to have found out about him is his name.'

'Nonsense,' said Rock. 'His name is in the hotel book.'

'I know it is,' answered the priest, nodding gravely, 'in very large letters; the name of Rudel Romanes. Hypatia Potter, who met him here, put her name boldly under his, when she meant to elope with him; and her husband put his name under that, when he pursued them to this place. He put it very close under hers, by way of protest. Then Romanes (who has pots of money, as a popular misanthrope despising men) bribed the brutes in this hotel to bar and bolt it and keep the lawful husband out. And I, as you truly say, helped him to get in.'

When a man is told something that turns things upside-down; that the tail wags the dog; that the fish has caught the fisherman; that the earth goes round the moon; he takes some little time before he even asks seriously if it is true. He is still content with the consciousness that it is the opposite of the obvious truth. Rock said at last: 'You don't mean that little fellow is the romantic Rudel we're always reading about; and that curly-haired fellow is Mr Potter of Pittsburgh.'

'Yes,' said Father Brown. 'I knew it the moment I clapped eyes on both of them. But I verified it afterwards.'

Rock ruminated for a time and said at last: 'I suppose it's barely possible you're right. But how did you come to have such a notion, in the face of the facts?'

Father Brown looked rather abashed; subsided into a chair, and stared into vacancy, until a faint smile began to dawn on his round and rather foolish face.

'Well,' he said, 'you see – the truth is, I'm not romantic.'

'I don't know what the devil you are,' said Rock roughly.

'Now *you* are romantic,' said Father Brown helpfully. 'For instance, you see somebody looking poetical, and you assume he is a poet. Do you know what the majority of poets look like? What a wild confusion was created by that coincidence of three good-looking aristocrats at the beginning of the nineteenth century: Byron and Goethe and Shelley! Believe me, in the common way, a man may write: 'Beauty has laid her flaming lips on mine,' or whatever that chap wrote, without being himself particularly beautiful. Besides, do you realize how *old* a man generally is by the time his fame has filled the world? Watts painted Swinburne with a halo of hair; but Swinburne was bald before most of his last American or Australian admirers had heard of his hyacinthine locks. So was D'Annunzio. As a fact, Romanes still has rather a fine head, as you will see if you look at it closely; he looks like an intellectual man; and he is. Unfortunately, like a good many other intellectual men, he's a fool. He's let himself go to seed with selfishness and fussing about his digestion. So that the ambitious American lady, who thought it would be like soaring to Olympus with the Nine Muses to elope with a poet, found that a day or so of it was about enough for her. So that when her husband came after her, and stormed the place, she was delighted to go back to him.'

'But her husband?' queried Rock. 'I am still rather puzzled about her husband.'

'Ah, you've been reading too many of your erotic modern novels,' said Father Brown; and partly closed his eyes in answer to the protesting glare of the other. 'I know a lot of stories start with a wildly beautiful woman wedded to some elderly swine in the stock market. But why? In that, as in most things, modern novels are the very reverse of modern. I don't say it never happens; but it hardly ever happens now except by her own fault. Girls nowadays marry whom they like; especially spoilt girls like Hypatia. And whom do they marry? A beautiful wealthy girl like that would have a ring of admirers; and whom would she choose? The chances are a hundred to one that she'd marry very young and choose the handsomest man she met at a dance or a tennis-party. Well, ordinary business men are sometimes handsome. A young god appeared (called Potter) and she wouldn't care if he was a broker or a burglar. But, given the environment, you will admit it's more likely he would be a broker; also, it's quite likely that he'd be called Potter. You see, you are so incurably romantic that your whole case was founded on the idea that a man looking like a young god, couldn't be called Potter. Believe me, names are not so appropriately distributed.'

'Well,' said the other, after a short pause, 'and what do you suppose happened after that?'

Father Brown got up rather abruptly from the seat in which he had collapsed; the candle-light threw the shadow of his short figure across the wall and ceiling, giving an odd impression that the balance of the room had been altered.

'Ah,' he muttered, 'that's the devil of it. That's the real devil. Much worse than the old Indian demons in this jungle. You thought I was only making out a case for the loose ways of these Latin Americans – well, the queer thing about you' – and he blinked owlishly at the other through his spectacles – 'the queerest thing about you is that in a way you're right.

'You say down with romance. I say I'd take my chance in fighting the genuine romances – all the more because they are precious few, outside the first fiery days of youth. I say – take away the Intellectual Friendships; take away the Platonic Unions; take away the Higher Laws of Self-fulfilment and the rest, and I'll risk the normal dangers of the job. Take away the love that isn't love, but only pride and vainglory and publicity and making a splash; and we'll take our chance of fighting the love that is love, when it has to be fought, as well as the love that is lust and lechery. Priests know young people will have passions, as doctors know they will have measles. But Hypatia Potter is forty if she is a day, and she cares no more for that little poet than if he were her publisher or her publicity man. That's just the point – he was her publicity man. It's your newspapers that have ruined her; it's living in the limelight; it's wanting to see herself in the headlines, even in a scandal if it were only sufficiently psychic and superior. It's wanting to be George Sand, her name immortally linked with Alfred de Musset. When her real romance of youth was over, it was the sin of middle age that got hold of her; the sin of intellectual ambition. She hasn't got any intellect to speak of; but you don't need any intellect to be an intellectual.'

'I should say she was pretty brainy in one sense,' observed Rock reflectively.

'Yes; in one sense,' said Father Brown. 'In only one sense. In a business sense. Not in any sense that has anything to do with these poor lounging Dagos down here. You curse the Film Stars and tell me you hate romance. Do you suppose the Film Star, who is married for the fifth time, is misled by any romance? Such people are very practical; more practical than you are. You say you admire the simple solid Business Man. Do you suppose that Rudel Romanes isn't a Business Man? Can't you see he knew, quite as well as she did, the advertising advantages of this last grand affair with a famous beauty. He also knew very well that his hold on it was pretty insecure; hence his fussing about and bribing servants to lock doors. But what I mean to say, first and last, is that there'd be a lot less scandal if people didn't idealize sin and pose as sinners. These poor Mexicans may seem sometimes to live like beasts, or rather sin like men; but they don't go in for Ideals. You must at least give them credit for that.'

He sat down again, as abruptly as he had risen, and laughed apologetically. 'Well, Mr Rock,' he said, 'that is my complete confession; the whole horrible story of how I helped a romantic elopement. You can do what you like with it.'

'In that case,' said Rock, rising, 'I will go to my room and make a few alterations in my report. But, first of all, I must ring up my paper and tell them I've been telling them a pack of lies.'

Not much more than half an hour had passed, between the time when Rock had telephoned to say the priest was helping the poet to run away with the lady, and the time when he telephoned to say that the priest had prevented the poet from doing precisely the same thing. But in that short interval of time was born and enlarged and scattered upon the winds the Scandal of Father Brown. The truth is still half an hour behind the slander; and nobody can be certain when or where it will catch up with it. The garrulity of pressmen and the eagerness of enemies had spread the first story through the city, even before it appeared in the first printed version. It was instantly corrected and contradicted by Rock himself, in a second message stating how the story had really ended; but it was by no means certain that the first story was killed. A positively incredible number of people seemed to have read the first issue of the paper and not the second. Again and again, in every corner of the world, like a flame bursting from blackened ashes, there would appear the old tale of the Brown Scandal, or Priest Ruins Potter Home. Tireless apologists of the Priest's party watched for it, and patiently tagged after it with contradictions and exposures and letters of protest. Sometimes the letters were published in the papers; and sometimes they were not. But still nobody knew how many people had heard the story without hearing the contradiction. It was possible to find whole blocks of blameless and innocent people who thought the Mexican Scandal was an ordinary recorded historical incident like the Gunpowder Plot. Then somebody would enlighten these simple people, only to discover that the old story had started afresh among a few quite educated people, who would seem the last people on earth to be duped by it. And so the two Father Browns chase each other round the world for ever; the first a shameless criminal fleeing from justice; the second a martyr broken by slander, in a halo of rehabilitation. But neither of them is very like the real Father Brown, who is not broken at all; but goes stumping with his stout umbrella through life, liking most of the people in it; accepting the world as his companion, but never as his judge.

2
The Quick One

The strange story of the incongruous strangers is still remembered along that strip of the Sussex coast, where the large and quiet hotel called the Maypole and Garland looks across its own gardens to the sea. Two quaintly assorted figures did, indeed, enter that quiet hotel on that sunny afternoon; one being conspicuous in the sunlight, and visible over the whole shore, by the fact of wearing a lustrous green turban, surrounding a brown face and a black beard; the other would have seemed to some even more wild and weird, by reason of his wearing a soft black clergyman's hat with a yellow moustache and yellow hair of leonine length. He at least had often been seen preaching on the sands or conducting Band of Hope services with a little wooden spade; only he had certainly never been seen going into the bar of an hotel. The arrival of these quaint companions was the climax of the story, but not the beginning of it; and, in order to make a rather mysterious story as clear as possible, it is better to begin at the beginning.

Half an hour before those two conspicuous figures entered the hotel, and were noticed by everybody, two other very inconspicuous figures had also entered it, and been noticed by nobody. One was a large man, and handsome in a heavy style, but he had a knack of taking up very little room, like a background; only an almost morbidly suspicious examination of his boots would have told anybody that he was an Inspector of Police in plain clothes; in very plain clothes. The other was a drab and insignificant little man, also in plain clothes, only that they happened to be clerical clothes; but nobody had ever seen *him* preaching on the sands.

These travellers also found themselves in a sort of large smoking-room with a bar, for a reason which determined all the events of that tragic afternoon. The truth is that the respectable hotel called the Maypole and Garland was being 'done-up'. Those who had liked it in the past were moved to say that it was being done down; or possibly done in. This was the opinion of the local grumbler, Mr Raggley, the eccentric old gentleman who drank cherry brandy in a corner and cursed. Anyhow, it was being carefully stripped of all the stray indications that it had once been an English inn; and being busily turned, yard by yard and room by room, into something resembling the sham palace of a Levantine usurer in an American film. It was, in short, being 'decorated'; but the only part where the decoration was complete, and where customers could yet be made comfortable, was this large room leading out of the hall. It had once been honourably known as a Bar Parlour and was now mysteriously known as a Saloon Lounge, and was newly 'decorated', in the manner of an Asiatic Divan. For Oriental ornament pervaded the new scheme; and where there had once been a gun hung on hooks, and sporting prints and a stuffed fish in a glass case, there were now festoons of Eastern drapery and trophies of scimitars, tulwars and yataghans, as if in unconscious preparation for the coming of the gentleman with the turban. The practical point was, however, that the few guests who did arrive had to be shepherded into this lounge, now swept and garnished, because all the more regular and refined parts of the hotel were still in a state of transition. Perhaps that was also the reason why even those few guests were somewhat neglected, the manager and others being occupied with explanations or exhortations elsewhere. Anyhow, the first two travellers who arrived had to kick their heels for some time unattended.

The bar was at the moment entirely empty, and the Inspector rang and rapped impatiently on the counter; but the little clergyman had already dropped into a lounge seat and seemed in no hurry for anything. Indeed his friend the policeman, turning his head, saw that the round face of the little cleric had gone quite blank, as it had a way of doing sometimes; he seemed to be staring through his moonlike spectacles at the newly decorated wall.

'I may as well offer you a penny for your thoughts,' said Inspector Greenwood, turning from the counter with a sigh, 'as nobody seems to want my pennies for anything else. This seems to be the only room in the house that isn't full of ladders and whitewash; and this is so empty that there isn't even a potboy to give me a pot of beer.'

'Oh . . . my thoughts are not worth a penny, let alone a pot of beer,' answered the cleric, wiping his spectacles, 'I don't know why . . . but I was thinking how easy it would be to commit a murder here.'

'It's all very well for you, Father Brown,' said the Inspector good-humouredly. 'You've had a lot more murders than your fair share; and we poor policemen sit starving all our lives, even for a little one. But why should you say . . . Oh I see, you're looking at all those Turkish daggers on the wall. There are plenty of things to commit a murder *with*, if that's what you mean. But not more than there are in any ordinary kitchen: carving-knives or pokers or what not. That isn't where the snag of a murder comes in.'

Father Brown seemed to recall his rambling thoughts in some bewilderment; and said that he supposed so.

'Murder is always easy,' said Inspector Greenwood. 'There can't possibly be anything more easy than murder. I could murder you at this minute – more easily than I can get a drink in this damned bar. The only difficulty is committing a murder without committing oneself as a murderer. It's this shyness about owning up to a murder; it's this silly modesty of murderers about their own masterpieces, that makes the trouble. They will stick to this extraordinary fixed idea of killing people without being found out; and that's what restrains them, even in a room full of daggers. Otherwise every cutler's shop would be piled with corpses. And that, by the way, explains the one kind of murder that really *can't* be prevented. Which is why, of course, we poor bobbies are always blamed for not preventing it. When a madman murders a King or a President, it can't be prevented. You can't make a King live in a coal-cellar, or carry about a President in a steel box. Anybody can murder him who does not mind being a murderer. That is where the madman is like the martyr – sort of beyond this world. A real fanatic can always kill anybody he likes.'

Before the priest could reply, a joyous band of bagmen rolled into the room like a shoal of porpoises; and the magnificent bellow of a big, beaming man, with an equally big and beaming tie-pin, brought the eager and obsequious manager running like a dog to the whistle, with a rapidity which the police in plain clothes had failed to inspire.

'I'm sure I'm very sorry, Mr Jukes,' said the manager, who wore a rather agitated smile and a wave or curl of very varnished hair across his forehead. 'We're rather understaffed at present; and I had to attend to something in the hotel, Mr Jukes.'

Mr Jukes was magnanimous, but in a noisy way; and ordered drinks all round, conceding one even to the almost cringing manager. Mr Jukes was a traveller for a very famous and fashionable wine and spirits firm; and may have conceived himself as lawfully the leader in such a place. Anyhow, he began a boisterous monologue, rather tending to tell the manager how to manage his hotel; and the others seemed to accept him as an authority. The policeman and the priest had retired to a low bench and small table in the background, from which they watched events, up to that rather remarkable moment when the policeman had very decisively to intervene.

For the next thing that happened, as already narrated, was the astonishing apparition of a brown Asiatic in a green turban, accompanied by the (if possible) more astonishing apparition of a Nonconformist minister; omens such as appear before a doom. In this case there was no doubt about evidence for the portent. A taciturn but observant boy cleaning the steps for the last hour (being a leisurely worker), the dark, fat, bulky bar attendant, even the diplomatic but distracted manager, all bore witness to the miracle.

The apparitions, as the sceptics say, were due to perfectly natural causes. The man with the mane of yellow hair and the semi-clerical clothes was not only familiar as a preacher on the sands, but as a propagandist throughout the modern world. He was no less a person than the Rev. David Pryce-Jones, whose far-resounding slogan was Prohibition and Purification for Our Land and the Britains Overseas. He was an excellent public speaker and organizer; and an idea had occurred to him that ought to have occurred to Prohibitionists long ago. It was the simple idea that, if Prohibition is right, some honour is due to the Prophet who was perhaps the first Prohibitionist. He had corresponded with the leaders of Mahommedan religious thought, and had finally induced a distinguished Moslem (one of whose names was Akbar and the rest an untranslatable ululation of Allah with attributes) to come and lecture in England on the ancient Moslem veto on wine. Neither of them certainly had been in a public-house bar before; but they had come there by the process already described; driven from the genteel tea-rooms, shepherded into the newly-decorated saloon.

Probably all would have been well, if the great Prohibitionist, in his innocence, had not advanced to the counter and asked for a glass of milk.

The commercial travellers, though a kindly race, emitted involuntary noises of pain; a murmur of suppressed jests was heard, as 'Shun the bowl,' or 'Better bring out the cow.' But the magnificent Mr Jukes, feeling it due to his wealth and tie-pin to produce more refined humour, fanned himself as one about to faint, and said pathetically: 'They know they can knock me down with a feather. They know a breath will blow me away. They know my doctor says I'm not to have these shocks. And they come and drink cold milk in cold blood, before my very eyes.'

The Rev. David Pryce-Jones, accustomed to deal with hecklers at public meetings, was so unwise as to venture on remonstrance and recrimination, in this very different and much more popular atmosphere. The Oriental total abstainer abstained from speech as well as spirits; and certainly gained in dignity by doing so. In fact, so far as he was concerned, the Moslem culture certainly scored a silent victory; he was obviously so much more of a gentleman than the commercial gentlemen, that a faint irritation began to arise against his aristocratic aloofness; and when Mr Pryce-Jones began to refer in argument to something of the kind, the tension became very acute indeed.

'I ask you, friends,' said Mr Pryce-Jones, with expansive platform gestures, 'why does our friend here set an example to us Christians in truly Christian self-control and brotherhood? Why does he stand here as a model of true Christianity, of real refinement, of genuine gentlemanly behaviour, amid all the quarrels and riots of such places as these? Because, whatever the doctrinal differences between us, at least in his soil the evil plant, the accursed hop or vine, has never –'

At this crucial moment of the controversy it was that John Raggley, the stormy petrel of a hundred storms of controversy, red-faced, white-haired, his antiquated top-hat on the back of his head, his stick swinging like a club, entered the house like an invading army.

John Raggley was generally regarded as a crank. He was the sort of man who writes letters to the newspaper, which generally do not appear in the newspaper; but which do appear afterwards as pamphlets, printed (or misprinted) at his own expense; and circulated to a hundred waste-paper baskets. He had quarrelled alike with the Tory squires and the

Radical County Councils; he hated Jews; and he distrusted nearly everything that is sold in shops, or even in hotels. But there was a backing of facts behind his fads; he knew the county in every corner and curious detail; and he was a sharp observer. Even the manager, a Mr Wills, had a shadowy respect for Mr Raggley, having a nose for the sort of lunacy allowed in the gentry; not indeed the prostrate reverence which he had for the jovial magnificence of Mr Jukes, who was really good for trade, but at least a disposition to avoid quarrelling with the old grumbler, partly perhaps out of fear of the old grumbler's tongue.

'And you will have your usual, Sir,' said Mr Wills, leaning and leering across the counter.

'It's the only decent stuff you've still got,' snorted Mr Raggley, slapping down his queer and antiquated hat. 'Damn it, I sometimes think the only English thing left in England is cherry brandy. Cherry brandy does taste of cherries. Can you find me any beer that tastes of hops, or any cider that tastes of apples, or any wine that has the remotest indication of being made out of grapes? There's an infernal swindle going on now in every inn in the country, that would have raised a revolution in any other country. I've found out a thing or two about it, I can tell you. You wait till I can get it printed, and people will sit up. If I could stop our people being poisoned with all this bad drink –'

Here again the Rev. David Pryce-Jones showed a certain failure in tact; though it was a virtue he almost worshipped. He was so unwise as to attempt to establish an alliance with Mr Raggley, by a fine confusion between the idea of bad drink and the idea that drink is bad. Once more he endeavoured to drag his stiff and stately Eastern friend into the argument, as a refined foreigner superior to our rough English ways. He was even so foolish as to talk of a broad theological outlook; and ultimately to mention the name of Mahomet, which was echoed in a sort of explosion.

'God damn your soul!' roared Mr Raggley, with a less broad theological outlook. 'Do you mean that Englishmen mustn't drink English beer, because wine was forbidden in a damned desert by that dirty old humbug Mahomet?'

In an instant, the Inspector of Police had reached the middle of the room with a stride. For, the instant before that, a remarkable change had taken place in the demeanour of the Oriental gentleman, who had hitherto stood perfectly still, with steady and shining eyes. He now proceeded, as his friend had said, to set an example in truly Christian self-control and brotherhood by reaching the wall with the bound of a tiger, tearing down one of the heavy knives hanging there and sending it smack like a stone from a sling, so that it stuck quivering in the wall exactly half an inch above Mr Raggley's ear. It would undoubtedly have stuck quivering in Mr Raggley, if Inspector Greenwood had not been just in time to jerk the arm and deflect the aim. Father Brown continued in his seat, watching the scene with screwed-up eyes and a screw of something almost like a smile at the corners of his mouth, as if he saw something beyond the mere momentary violence of the quarrel.

And then the quarrel took a curious turn; which may not be understood by everybody, until men like Mr John Raggley are better understood than they are. For the red-faced old fanatic was standing up and laughing uproariously as if it were the best joke he had ever heard. All his snapping vituperation and bitterness seemed to have gone out of him; and he regarded the other fanatic, who had just tried to murder him, with a sort of boisterous benevolence.

'Blast your eyes,' he said, 'you're the first man I've met in twenty years!'

'Do you charge this man, Sir?' said the Inspector, looking doubtful.

'Charge him, of course not,' said Raggley. 'I'd stand him a drink if he were allowed any drinks. I hadn't any business to insult his religion; and I wish to God all you skunks had the guts to kill a man, I won't say for insulting your religion, because you haven't got any, but for insulting anything – even your beer.'

'Now he's called us all skunks,' said Father Brown to Greenwood, 'peace and harmony seem to be restored. I wish that teetotal lecturer could get himself impaled on his friend's knife; it was he who made all the mischief.'

As he spoke, the odd groups in the room were already beginning to break up; it had been found possible to clear the commercial room for the commercial travellers, and they adjourned to it, the potboy carrying a new round of drinks after them on a tray. Father Brown stood for a moment gazing at the glasses left on the counter; recognizing at once the ill-omened glass of milk, and another which smelt of whisky; and then turned just in time to see the parting between those two quaint figures, fanatics of the East and West. Raggley was still ferociously genial; there was still something a little darkling and sinister about the Moslem, which was perhaps natural; but he bowed himself out with grave gestures of dignified reconciliation; and there was every indication that the trouble was really over.

Some importance, however, continued attached, in the mind of Father Brown at least, to the memory and interpretation of those last courteous salutes between the combatants. Because, curiously enough, when Father Brown came down very early next morning, to perform his religious duties in the neighbourhood, he found the long saloon bar, with its fantastic Asiatic decoration, filled with a dead white light of daybreak in which every detail was distinct; and one of the details was the dead body of John Raggley bent and crushed into a corner of the room, with the heavy-hilted crooked dagger rammed through his heart.

Father Brown went very softly upstairs again and summoned his friend the Inspector; and the two stood beside the corpse, in a house in which no one else was as yet stirring.

'We mustn't either assume or avoid the obvious,' said Greenwood after a silence, 'but it is well to remember, I think, what I was saying to you yesterday afternoon. It's rather odd, by the way, that I should have said it – yesterday afternoon.'

'I know,' said the priest, nodding with an owlish stare.

'I said,' observed Greenwood, 'that the one sort of murder we can't stop is murder by somebody like a religious fanatic. That brown fellow probably thinks that if he's hanged, he'll go straight to Paradise for defending the honour of the Prophet.'

'There is that, of course,' said Father Brown. 'It would be very reasonable, so to speak, of our Moslem friend to have stabbed him. And you may say we don't know of anybody else yet, who could at all reasonably have stabbed him. But . . . but I was thinking . . .' And his round face suddenly went blank again and all speech died on his lips.

'What's the matter now?' asked the other.

'Well, I know it sounds funny,' said Father Brown in a forlorn voice. 'But I was thinking . . . I was thinking, in a way, it doesn't much matter who stabbed him.'

'Is this the New Morality?' asked his friend. 'Or the old Casuistry, perhaps. Are the Jesuits really going in for murder?'

'I didn't say it didn't matter who murdered him,' said Father Brown. 'Of course the man who stabbed him might possibly be the man who murdered him. But it might be quite a different man. Anyhow, it was done at quite a different time. I suppose you'll want to work on the hilt for finger-prints; but don't take too much notice of them. I can imagine other reasons for other people sticking this knife in the poor old boy. Not very edifying reasons, of course, but quite distinct from the murder. You'll have to put some more knives into him, before you find out about that.'

'You mean –' began the other, watching him keenly.

'I mean the autopsy,' said the priest, 'to find the real cause of death.'

'You're quite right, I believe,' said the Inspector, 'about the stabbing, anyhow. We must wait for the doctor; but I'm pretty sure he'll say you're right. There isn't blood enough. This knife was stuck in the corpse when it had been cold for hours. But why?'

'Possibly to put the blame on the Mahommedan,' answered Father Brown. 'Pretty mean, I admit, but not necessarily murder. I fancy there are people in this place trying to keep secrets, who are not necessarily the murderers.'

'I haven't speculated on that line yet,' said Greenwood. 'What makes you think so?'

'What I said yesterday, when we first came into this horrible room. I said it would be easy to commit a murder here. But I wasn't thinking about all those stupid weapons, though you thought I was. About something quite different.'

For the next few hours the Inspector and his friend conducted a close and thorough investigation into the goings and comings of everybody for the last twenty-four hours, the way the drinks had been distributed, the glasses that were washed or unwashed, and every detail about every individual involved, or apparently not involved. One might have supposed they thought that thirty people had been poisoned, as well as one.

It seemed certain that nobody had entered the building except by the big entrance that adjoined the bar; all the others were blocked in one way or another by the repairs. A boy had been cleaning the steps outside this entrance; but he had nothing very clear to report. Until the amazing entry of the Turk in the Turban, with his teetotal lecturer, there did not seem to have been much custom of any kind, except for the commercial travellers who came in to take what they called 'quick ones'; and they seemed to have moved together, like Wordsworth's Cloud; there was a slight difference of opinion between the boy outside and the men inside about whether one of them had not been abnormally quick in obtaining a quick one, and come out on the doorstep by himself; but the manager and the barman had no memory of any such independent individual. The manager and the barman knew all the travellers quite well, and there was no doubt about their movements as a whole. They had stood at the bar chaffing and drinking; they had been involved, through their lordly leader, Mr Jukes, in a not very serious altercation with Mr Pryce-Jones; and they had witnessed the sudden and very serious altercation between Mr Akbar and Mr Raggley. Then they were told they could adjourn to the Commercial Room, and did so, their drinks being borne after them like a trophy.

'There's precious little to go on,' said Inspector Greenwood. 'Of course a lot of officious servants must do their duty as usual, and wash out all the glasses; including old Raggley's glass. If it weren't for everybody else's efficiency, we detectives might be quite efficient.'

'I know,' said Father Brown, and his mouth took on again the twisted smile. 'I sometimes think criminals invented hygiene. Or perhaps hygienic reformers invented crime; they look like it, some of them. Everybody talks about foul dens and filthy slums in which crime can run riot; but it's just the other way. They are called foul, not because crimes are committed, but because crimes are discovered. It's in the neat, spotless, clean and tidy places that crime can run riot; no mud to make footprints; no dregs to contain poison; kind servants washing out all traces of the murder; and the murderer killing and cremating six wives and all for want of a little Christian dirt. Perhaps I express myself with too much warmth – but look here. As it happens, I do remember one glass, which has doubtless been cleaned since, but I should like to know more about it.'

'Do you mean Raggley's glass?' asked Greenwood.

'No; I mean Nobody's glass,' replied the priest. 'It stood near that glass of milk and it still held an inch or two of whisky. Well, you and I had no whisky. I happen to remember that the manager, when treated by the jovial Jukes, had 'a drop of gin.' I hope you don't suggest that our Moslem was a whisky-drinker disguised in a green turban; or that the Rev. David Pryce-Jones managed to drink whisky and milk together, without noticing it.'

'Most of the commercial travellers took whisky,' said the Inspector. 'They generally do.'

'Yes; and they generally see they get it too,' answered Father Brown. 'In this case, they had it all carefully carted after them to their own room. But this glass was left behind.'

'An accident, I suppose,' said Greenwood, doubtfully. 'The man could easily get another in the Commercial Room afterwards.'

Father Brown shook his head. 'You've got to see people as they are. Now these sort of men – well, some call them vulgar and some common; but that's all likes and dislikes. I'd be content to say that they are mostly simple men. Lots of them very good men, very glad to go back to the missus and the kids; some of them might be blackguards; might have had several missuses; or even murdered several missuses. But most of them are simple men; and, mark you, just the least tiny little bit drunk. Not much; there's many a duke or don at Oxford drunker; but when that sort of man is at that stage of conviviality, he simply can't help noticing things, and noticing them very loud. Don't you observe that the least little incident jerks them into speech; if the beer froths over, they froth over with it, and have to say, "Whoa, Emma," or, "Doing me proud, aren't you?" Now I should say it's flatly impossible for five of these festive beings to sit round a table in the Commercial Room, and have only four glasses set before them, the fifth man being left out, without making a shout about it. Probably they would all make a shout about it. Certainly *he* would make a shout about it. He wouldn't wait, like an Englishman of another class, till he could get a drink quietly later. The air would resound with things like, "And what about little me?" or, "Here, George, have I joined the Band of Hope?" or, "Do you see any green in my turban, George?" But the barman heard no such complaints. I take it as certain that the glass of whisky left behind had been nearly emptied by somebody else; somebody we haven't thought about yet.'

'But can you think of any such person?' asked the other.

'It's because the manager and the barman won't hear of any such person, that you dismiss the one really independent piece of evidence; the evidence of that boy outside cleaning the steps. He says that a man, who may well have been a bagman, but who did not, in fact, stick to the other bagmen, went in and came out again almost immediately. The manager and the barman never saw him; or say they never saw him. But he got a glass of whisky from the bar somehow. Let us call him, for the sake of argument, The Quick One. Now you know I don't often interfere with your business, which I know you do better than I should do it, or should want to do it. I've never had anything to do with setting police machinery at work, or running down criminals, or anything like that. But, for the first time in my life, I want to do it now. I want you to find The Quick One; to follow The Quick One to the ends of the earth; to set the whole infernal official machinery at work like a drag-net across the nations, and jolly well recapture The Quick One. Because he is the man we want.'

Greenwood made a despairing gesture. 'Has he face or form or any visible quality except quickness?' he inquired.

'He was wearing a sort of Inverness cape,' said Father Brown, 'and he told the boy outside he must reach Edinburgh by next morning. That's all the boy outside remembers. But I know your organization has got on to people with less clue than that.'

'You seem very keen on this,' said the Inspector, a little puzzled.

The priest looked puzzled also, as if at his own thoughts; he sat with knotted brow and then said abruptly:

'You see, it's so easy to be misunderstood. All men matter. You matter. I matter. It's the hardest thing in theology to believe.'

The Inspector stared at him without comprehension; but he proceeded.

'We matter to God – God only knows why. But that's the only possible justification of the existence of policemen.' The policeman did not seem enlightened as to his own cosmic justification. 'Don't you see, the law really is right in a way, after all. If all men matter, all murders matter. That which He has so mysteriously created, we must not suffer to be mysteriously destroyed. But –'

He said the last word sharply, like one taking a new step in decision.

'*But* when once I step off that mystical level of equality, I don't see that most of your important murders are particularly important. You are always telling me that this case and that is important. As a plain, practical man of the world, I must realize that it is the Prime Minister who has been murdered. As a plain, practical man of the world, I don't think that the Prime Minister matters at all. As a mere matter of human importance, I should say he hardly exists at all. Do you suppose if he and the other public men were shot dead to-morrow, there wouldn't be other people to stand up and say that every avenue was being explored, or that the Government had the matter under the gravest consideration? The masters of the modern world don't matter. Even the real masters don't matter much. Hardly anybody you ever read about in a newspaper matters at all.'

He stood up, giving the table a small rap: one of his rare gestures; and his voice changed again.

'But Raggley did matter. He was one of a great line of some half a dozen men who might have saved England. They stand up stark and dark like disregarded sign-posts, down all that smooth descending road which has ended in this swamp of merely commercial collapse. Dean Swift and Dr Johnson and old William Cobbett; they had all without exception the name of being surly or savage, and they were all loved by their friends, and they all deserved to be. Didn't you see how that old man, with the heart of a lion, stood up and forgave his enemy as only fighters can forgive? He jolly well *did* do what that temperance lecturer talked about; he set an example to us Christians and was a model of Christianity. And when there is foul and secret murder of a man like that – then I do think it matters, matters so much that even the modern machinery of police will be a thing that any respectable person may make use of . . . Oh, don't mention it. And so, for once in a way, I really do want to make use of you.'

And so, for some stretch of those strange days and nights, we might almost say that the little figure of Father Brown drove before him into action all the armies and engines of the police forces of the Crown, as the little figure of Napoleon drove the batteries and the battle-lines of the vast strategy that covered Europe. Police stations and post offices worked all night; traffic was stopped, correspondence was intercepted, inquiries were made in a hundred places, in order to track the flying trail of that ghostly figure, without face or name, with an Inverness cape and an Edinburgh ticket.

Meanwhile, of course, the other lines of investigation were not neglected. The full report of the post-mortem had not yet come in; but
everybody seemed certain that it was a case of poisoning. This naturally
threw the primary suspicion upon the cherry brandy; and this again
naturally threw the primary suspicion on the hotel.

'Most probably on the manager of the hotel,' said Greenwood gruffly.
'He looks a nasty little worm to me. Of course it might be something to
do with some servant, like the barman; he seems rather a sulky specimen,
and Raggley might have cursed him a bit, having a flaming temper,
though he was generally generous enough afterwards. But, after all, as
I say, the primary responsibility, and therefore the primary suspicion,
rests on the manager.'

'Oh, I knew the primary suspicion would rest on the manager,' said
Father Brown. 'That was why I didn't suspect him. You see, I rather
fancied somebody else must have known that the primary suspicion
would rest on the manager; or the servants of the hotel. That is why I
said it would be easy to kill anybody in the hotel . . . But you'd better
go and have it out with him, I suppose.'

The Inspector went; but came back again after a surprisingly short
interview, and found his clerical friend turning over some papers that
seemed to be a sort of *dossier* of the stormy career of John Raggley.

'This is a rum go,' said the Inspector. 'I thought I should spend hours
cross-examining that slippery little toad there, for we haven't legally got
a thing against him. And instead of that, he went to pieces all at once,
and I really think he's told me all he knows in sheer funk.'

'I know,' said Father Brown. 'That's the way he went to pieces when
he found Raggley's corpse apparently poisoned in his hotel. That's why
he lost his head enough to do such a clumsy thing as decorate the corpse
with a Turkish knife, to put the blame on the nigger, as he would say.
There never is anything the matter with him but funk; he's the very last
man that ever would really stick a knife into a live person. I bet he had
to nerve himself to stick it into a dead one. But he's the very first person
to be frightened of being charged with what he didn't do; and to make
a fool of himself, as he did.'

'I suppose I must see the barman too,' observed Greenwood.

'I suppose so,' answered the other. 'I don't believe myself it was any
of the hotel people – well, because it was made to look as if it *must* be

the hotel people ... But look here, have you seen any of this stuff they've got together about Raggley? He had a jolly interesting life; I wonder whether anyone will write his biography.'

'I took a note of everything likely to affect an affair like this,' answered the official. 'He was a widower; but he did once have a row with a man about his wife; a Scotch land-agent then in these parts; and Raggley seems to have been pretty violent. They say he hated Scotchmen; perhaps that's the reason ... Oh, I know what you are smiling grimly about. A Scotchman ... Perhaps an Edinburgh man.'

'Perhaps,' said Father Brown. 'It's quite likely, though, that he did dislike Scotchmen, apart from private reasons. It's an odd thing, but all that tribe of Tory Radicals, or whatever you call them, who resisted the Whig mercantile movement, all of them did dislike Scotchmen. Cobbett did; Dr Johnson did; Swift described their accent in one of his deadliest passages; even Shakespeare has been accused of the prejudice. But the prejudices of great men generally have something to do with principles. And there was a reason, I fancy. The Scot came from a poor agricultural land, that became a rich industrial land. He was able and active; he thought he was bringing industrial civilization from the north; he simply didn't know that there had been for centuries a rural civilization in the south. His own grandfather's land was highly rural but not civilized ... Well, well; I suppose we can only wait for more news.'

'I hardly think you'll get the latest news out of Shakespeare and Dr Johnson,' grinned the police officer. 'What Shakespeare thought of Scotchmen isn't exactly evidence.'

Father Brown cocked an eyebrow, as if a new thought had surprised him. 'Why, now I come to think of it,' he said, 'there might be better evidence, even out of Shakespeare. He doesn't often mention Scotchmen. But he was rather fond of making fun of Welshmen.'

The Inspector was searching his friend's face; for he fancied he recognized an alertness behind its demure expression.

'By Jove,' he said. 'Nobody thought of turning the suspicions *that* way, anyhow.'

'Well,' said Father Brown, with broad-minded calm, 'you started by talking about fanatics; and how a fanatic could do anything. Well, I suppose we had the honour of entertaining, in this bar-parlour yesterday, about the biggest and loudest and most fat-headed fanatic in the modern world. If being a pig-headed idiot with one idea is the way to murder, I put in a claim for my reverend brother Pryce-Jones, the Prohibitionist, in preference to all the fakirs in Asia, and it's perfectly true, as I told you, that his horrible glass of milk was standing side by side on the counter with the mysterious glass of whisky.'

'Which you think was mixed up with the murder,' said Greenwood staring. 'Look here, I don't know whether you're really serious or not.'

Even as he was looking steadily in his friend's face, finding something still inscrutable in its expression, the telephone rang stridently behind the bar. Lifting the flap in the counter Inspector Greenwood passed rapidly inside, unhooked the receiver, listened for an instant, and then uttered a shout; not addressed to his interlocutor, but to the universe in general. Then he listened still more attentively and said explosively at intervals, 'Yes, yes . . . Come round at once; bring him round if possible . . . Good piece of work . . . Congratulate you.'

Then Inspector Greenwood came back into the outer lounge, like a man who has renewed his youth, sat down squarely on his seat, with his hands planted on his knees, stared at his friend, and said:

'Father Brown, I don't know how you do it. You seem to have known he was a murderer before anybody else knew he was a man. He was nobody; he was nothing; he was a slight confusion in the evidence; nobody in the hotel saw him; the boy on the steps could hardly swear to him; he was just a fine shade of doubt founded on an extra dirty glass. But we've got him, and he's the man we want.'

Father Brown had risen with the sense of the crisis, mechanically clutching the papers destined to be so valuable to the biographer of Mr Raggley; and stood staring at his friend. Perhaps this gesture jerked his friend's mind to fresh confirmations.

'Yes, we've got The Quick One. And very quick he was, like quicksilver, in making his get-away; we only just stopped him – off on a fishing trip to Orkney, he said. But he's the man, all right; he's the Scotch land agent who made love to Raggley's wife; he's the man who drank Scotch whisky in this bar and then took a train for Edinburgh. And nobody would have known it but for you.'

'Well, what I meant,' began Father Brown, in a rather dazed tone; and at that instant there was a rattle and rumble of heavy vehicles outside the hotel; and two or three other and subordinate policemen blocked the bar with their presence. One of them, invited by his superior to sit down, did so in an expansive manner, like one at once happy and fatigued; and he also regarded Father Brown with admiring eyes.

'Got the murderer, sir, oh yes,' he said; 'I know he's a murderer, 'cause he bally nearly murdered me. I've captured some tough characters before now; but never one like this – hit me in the stomach like the kick of a horse and nearly got away from five men. Oh, you've got a real killer this time, Inspector.'

'Where is he?' asked Father Brown, staring.

'Outside in the van, in handcuffs,' replied the policeman, 'and, if you're wise, you'll leave him there – for the present.'

Father Brown sank into a chair in a sort of soft collapse; and the papers he had been nervously clutching were shed around him, shooting and sliding about the floor like sheets of breaking snow. Not only his face, but his whole body, conveyed the impression of a punctured balloon.

'Oh . . . Oh,' he repeated, as if any further oath would be inadequate. 'Oh . . . I've done it again.'

'If you mean you've caught the criminal again,' began Greenwood. But his friend stopped him with a feeble explosion, like that of expiring soda-water.

'I mean,' said Father Brown, 'that it's always happening; and really, I don't know why. I always try to say what I mean. But everybody else means such a lot by what I say.'

'What in the world is the matter now?' cried Greenwood, suddenly exasperated.

'Well, I say things,' said Father Brown in a weak voice, which could alone convey the weakness of the words. 'I say things, but everybody seems to know they mean more than they say. Once I saw a broken mirror and said "Something has happened," and they all answered, "Yes, yes, as you truly say, two men wrestled and one ran into the garden," and so on. I don't understand it, "Something happened," and "Two men wrestled," don't seem to me at all the same; but I dare say I read old books of logic. Well, it's like that here. You seem to be all certain this man is a murderer. But I never said he was a murderer. I said he was the man we wanted. He is. I want him very much. I want him frightfully. I want him as the one thing we haven't got in the whole of this horrible case – a witness!'

They all stared at him, but in a frowning fashion, like men trying to follow a sharp new turn of the argument; and it was he who resumed the argument.

'From the first minute I entered that big empty bar or saloon, I knew that what was the matter with all this business was emptiness; solitude; too many chances for anybody to be alone. In a word, the absence of witnesses. All we knew was that when we came in, the manager and the barman were not in the bar. But when *were* they in the bar? What chance was there of making any sort of time-table of when anybody was anywhere? The whole thing was blank for want of witnesses. I rather fancy the barman or somebody was in the bar just before we came; and that's how the Scotchman got his Scotch whisky. He certainly didn't get it after we came. But we can't begin to inquire whether anybody in the hotel poisoned poor Raggley's cherry brandy, till we really know who was in the bar and when. Now I want you to do me another favour, in spite of this stupid muddle, which is probably all my fault. I want you to collect all the people involved in this room – I think they're all still available, unless the Asiatic has gone back to Asia – and then take the poor Scotchman out of his handcuffs, and bring him in here, and let him tell us who did serve him with whisky, and who was in the bar, and who else was in the room, and all the rest. He's the only man whose evidence can cover just that period when the crime was done. I don't see the slightest reason for doubting his word.'

'But look here,' said Greenwood. 'This brings it all back to the hotel authorities; and I thought you agreed that the manager isn't the murderer. Is it the barman, or what?'

'I don't know,' said the priest blankly. 'I don't know for certain even about the manager. I don't know anything about the barman. I fancy the manager might be a bit of a conspirator, even if he wasn't a murderer. But I do know there's one solitary witness on earth who may have seen something; and that's why I set all your police dogs on his trail to the ends of the earth.'

The mysterious Scotchman, when he finally appeared before the company thus assembled, was certainly a formidable figure; tall, with a hulking stride and a long sardonic hatchet face, with tufts of red hair;

and wearing not only an Inverness cape but a Glengarry bonnet. He might well be excused for a somewhat acrid attitude; but anybody could see he was of the sort to resist arrest, even with violence. It was not surprising that he had come to blows with a fighting fellow like Raggley. It was not even surprising that the police had been convinced, by the mere details of capture, that he was a tough and a typical killer. But he claimed to be a perfectly respectable farmer, in Aberdeenshire, his name being James Grant; and somehow not only Father Brown, but Inspector Greenwood, a shrewd man with a great deal of experience, was pretty soon convinced that the Scot's ferocity was the fury of innocence rather than guilt.

'Now what we want from you, Mr Grant,' said the Inspector gravely, dropping without further parley into tones of courtesy, 'is simply your evidence on one very important fact. I am greatly grieved at the mis-understanding by which you have suffered, but I am sure you wish to serve the ends of justice. I believe you came into this bar just after it opened, at half-past five, and were served with a glass of whisky. We are not certain what servant of the hotel, whether the barman or the manager or some subordinate, was in the bar at that time. Will you look round the room, and tell me whether the bar-attendant who served you is present here.'

'Aye, he's present,' said Mr Grant, grimly smiling, having swept the group with a shrewd glance. 'I'd know him anywhere; and ye'll agree he's big enough to be seen. Do ye have all your inn-servants as grand as yon?'

The Inspector's eye remained hard and steady, and his voice colour-less and continuous; the face of Father Brown was a blank; but on many other faces there was a cloud; the barman was not particularly big and not at all grand; and the manager was decidedly small.

'We only want the barman identified,' said the Inspector calmly, 'Of course we know him; but we should like you to verify it independently. You mean . . . ?' And he stopped suddenly.

'Weel, there he is plain enough,' said the Scotchman wearily; and made a gesture, and with that gesture the gigantic Jukes, the prince of commercial travellers, rose like a trumpeting elephant; and in a flash had three policemen fastened on him like hounds on a wild beast.

'Well, all that was simple enough,' said Father Brown to his friend afterwards. 'As I told you, the instant I entered the empty bar-room, my first thought was that, if the barman left the bar unguarded like that, there was nothing in the world to stop you or me, or anybody else lifting the flap and walking in, and putting poison in any of the bottles standing waiting for customers. Of course, a practical poisoner would probably do it as Jukes did, by substituting a poisoned bottle for the ordinary bottle; that could be done in a flash. It was easy enough for him, as he travelled in bottles, to carry a flask of cherry brandy prepared and of the same pattern. Of course, it requires one condition; but it's a fairly common condition. It would hardly do to start poisoning the beer or whisky that scores of people drink; it would cause a massacre. But when a man is well known as drinking only one special thing, like cherry brandy, that isn't very widely drunk, it's just like poisoning him in his own home. Only it's a jolly sight safer. For practically the whole suspicion instantly falls on the hotel, or somebody to do with the hotel; and there's no earthly argument to show that it was done by anyone out of a hundred customers that might come into the bar; even if people realized that a customer could do it. It was about as absolutely anonymous and irresponsible a murder as a man could commit.'

'And why exactly did the murderer commit it?' asked his friend.

Father Brown rose and gravely gathered the papers which he had previously scattered in a moment of distraction.

'May I recall your attention,' he said smiling, 'to the materials of the forthcoming Life and Letters of the Late John Raggley? Or, for that matter, to his own spoken words? He said in this very bar that he was going to expose a scandal about the management of hotels; and the scandal was the pretty common one of a corrupt agreement between hotel proprietors and a salesman who took and gave secret commissions, so that his business had a monopoly of all the drink sold in the place. It wasn't even an open slavery like an ordinary tied house; it was a swindle at the expense of everybody the manager was supposed to serve. It was a legal offence. So the ingenious Jukes, taking the first moment when the bar was empty, as it often was, stepped inside and made the exchange of bottles; unfortunately at that very moment a Scotchman in an Inverness cape came in harshly demanding whisky. Jukes saw his only chance was to pretend to be the barman and serve the customer. He was very much relieved that the customer was a Quick One.'

'I think you're rather a Quick One yourself,' observed Greenwood; 'if you say you smelt something at the start, in the mere air of an empty room. Did you suspect Jukes at all at the start?'

'Well, he sounded rather rich somehow,' answered Father Brown vaguely. 'You know when a man has a rich voice. And I did sort of ask myself why he should have such a disgustingly rich voice, when all those honest fellows were fairly poor. But I think I knew he was a sham when I saw that big shining breast-pin.'

'You mean because it was sham?' asked Greenwood doubtfully.

'Oh, no; because it was genuine,' said Father Brown.

3
The Blast of the Book

Professor Openshaw always lost his temper, with a loud bang, if anybody called him a Spiritualist; or a believer in Spiritualism. This, however, did not exhaust his explosive elements; for he also lost his temper if anybody called him a disbeliever in Spiritualism. It was his pride to have given his whole life to investigating Psychic Phenomena; it was also his pride never to have given a hint of whether he thought they were really psychic or merely phenomenal. He enjoyed nothing so much as to sit in a circle of devout Spiritualists and give devastating descriptions of how he had exposed medium after medium and detected fraud after fraud: for indeed he was a man of much detective talent and insight, when once he had fixed his eye on an object, and he always fixed his eye on a medium, as a highly suspicious object. There was a story of his having spotted the same Spiritualistic mountebank under three different disguises: dressed as a woman, a white-bearded old man, and a Brahmin of a rich chocolate brown. These recitals made the true believers rather restless, as indeed they were intended to do; but they could hardly complain, for no Spiritualist denies the existence of fraudulent mediums; only the Professor's flowing narrative might well seem to indicate that all mediums were fraudulent.

But woe to the simple-minded and innocent Materialist (and Materialists as a race are rather innocent and simple-minded) who, presuming on this narrative tendency, should advance the thesis that ghosts were against the laws of nature, or that such things were only old superstitions; or that it was all tosh, or, alternately, bunk. Him would the Professor, suddenly reversing all his scientific batteries, sweep from the field with a cannonade of unquestionable cases and unexplained phenomena, of which the wretched rationalist had never heard in his life, giving all the dates and details, stating all the attempted and abandoned natural explanations; stating everything, indeed, except whether he, John Oliver Openshaw, did or did not believe in Spirits; and that neither Spiritualist nor Materialist could ever boast of finding out.

Professor Openshaw, a lean figure with pale leonine hair and hypnotic blue eyes, stood exchanging a few words with Father Brown, who was a friend of his, on the steps outside the hotel where both had been breakfasting that morning and sleeping the night before. The Professor had come back rather late from one of his grand experiments, in general exasperation, and was still tingling with the fight that he always waged alone and against both sides.

'Oh, I don't mind you,' he said laughing. 'You don't believe in it even if it's true. But all these people are perpetually asking me what I'm trying to prove. They don't seem to understand that I'm a man of science. A man of science isn't trying to prove anything. He's trying to find out what will prove itself.'

'But he hasn't found out yet,' said Father Brown.

'Well, I have some little notions of my own, that are not quite so negative as most people think,' answered the Professor, after an instant of frowning silence; 'anyhow, I've begun to fancy that if there is something to be found, they're looking for it along the wrong line. It's all too theatrical; it's showing off, all their shiny ectoplasm and trumpets and voices and the rest; all on the model of old melodramas and mouldy historical novels about the Family Ghost. If they'd go to history instead of historical novels, I'm beginning to think they'd really find something. But not Apparitions.'

'After all,' said Father Brown, 'Apparitions are only Appearances. I suppose you'd say the Family Ghost is only keeping up appearances.'

The Professor's gaze, which had commonly a fine abstracted character, suddenly fixed and focussed itself as it did on a dubious medium. It had rather the air of a man screwing a strong magnifying-glass into his eye. Not that he thought the priest was in the least like a dubious medium; but he was startled into attention by his friend's thought following so closely on his own.

'Appearances!' he muttered, 'crikey, but it's odd you should say that just now. The more I learn, the more I fancy they lose by merely looking for appearances. Now if they'd look a little into Disappearances – '

'Yes,' said Father Brown, 'after all, the real fairy legends weren't so

331

very much about the appearance of famous fairies; calling up Titania or exhibiting Oberon by moonlight. But there were no end of legends about people *disappearing*, because they were stolen by the fairies. Are you on the track of Kilmeny or Thomas the Rhymer?'

'I'm on the track of ordinary modern people you've read of in the newspapers,' answered Openshaw. 'You may well stare; but that's my game just now; and I've been on it for a long time. Frankly, I think a lot of psychic appearances could be explained away. It's the disappearances I can't explain, unless they're psychic. These people in the newspapers who vanish and are never found – if you knew the details as I do . . . and now only this morning I got confirmation; an extraordinary letter from an old missionary, quite a respectable old boy. He's coming to see me at my office this morning. Perhaps you'd lunch with me or something; and I'd tell the results – in confidence.'

'Thanks; I will – unless,' said Father Brown modestly, 'the fairies have stolen me by then.'

With that they parted and Openshaw walked round the corner to a small office he rented in the neighbourhood; chiefly for the publication of a small periodical, of psychical and psychological notes of the driest and most agnostic sort. He had only one clerk, who sat at a desk in the outer office, totting up figures and facts for the purposes of the printed report; and the Professor paused to ask if Mr Pringle had called. The clerk answered mechanically in the negative and went on mechanically adding up figures; and the Professor turned towards the inner room that was his study. 'Oh, by the way, Berridge,' he added, without turning round, 'if Mr Pringle comes, send him straight in to me. You needn't interrupt your work; I rather want those notes finished to-night if possible. You might leave them on my desk to-morrow, if I am late.'

And he went into his private office, still brooding on the problem which the name of Pringle had raised; or rather, perhaps, had ratified and confirmed in his mind. Even the most perfectly balanced of agnostics is partially human; and it is possible that the missionary's letter seemed to have greater weight as promising to support his private and still tentative hypothesis. He sat down in his large and comfortable chair, opposite the engraving of Montaigne; and read once more the short letter from the Rev. Luke Pringle, making the appointment for that morning. No man knew better than Professor Openshaw the marks of the letter of the crank; the crowded details; the spidery handwriting; the unnecessary length and repetition. There were none of these things in this case; but a brief and businesslike typewritten statement that the writer had encountered some curious cases of Disappearance, which seemed to fall within the province of the Professor as a student of psychic problems. The Professor was favourably impressed; nor had he any unfavourable impression, in spite of a slight movement of surprise, when he looked up and saw that the Rev. Luke Pringle was already in the room.

'Your clerk told me I was to come straight in,' said Mr Pringle apologetically, but with a broad and rather agreeable grin. The grin was partly masked by masses of reddish-grey beard and whiskers; a perfect jungle of a beard, such as is sometimes grown by white men living in the jungles; but the eyes above the snub nose had nothing about them in the least wild or outlandish. Openshaw had instantly turned on them that concentrated spotlight or burning-glass of sceptical scrutiny which he turned on many men to see if they were mountebanks or maniacs; and, in this case, he had a rather unusual sense of reassurance. The wild beard might have belonged to a crank, but the eyes completely contradicted the beard; they were full of that quite frank and friendly laughter which is never found in the faces of those who are serious frauds or serious lunatics. He would have expected a man with those eyes to be a Philistine, a jolly sceptic, a man who shouted out shallow but hearty contempt for ghosts and spirits; but anyhow, no professional humbug could afford to look as frivolous as that. The man was buttoned up to the throat in a shabby old cape, and only his broad limp hat suggested the cleric; but missionaries from wild places do not always bother to dress like clerics.

'You probably think all this is another hoax, Professor,' said Mr Pringle, with a sort of abstract enjoyment, 'and I hope you will forgive my laughing at your very natural air of disapproval. All the same, I've got to tell my story to somebody who knows, because it's true. And, all joking apart, it's tragic as well as true. Well, to cut it short, I was missionary in Nya-Nya, a station in West Africa, in the thick of the forests, where almost the only other white man was the officer in command of the district, Captain Wales; and he and I grew rather thick. Not that he liked missions; he was, if I may say so, thick in many ways;

one of those square-headed, square-shouldered men of action who hardly need to think, let alone believe. That's what makes it all the queerer. One day he came back to his tent in the forest, after a short leave, and said he had gone through a jolly rum experience, and didn't know what to do about it. He was holding a rusty old book in a leather binding, and he put it down on a table beside his revolver and an old Arab sword he kept, probably as a curiosity. He said this book had belonged to a man on the boat he had just come off; and the man swore that nobody must open the book, or look inside it; or else they would be carried off by the devil, or disappear, or something. Wales said this was all nonsense, of course; and they had a quarrel; and the upshot seems to have been that this man, taunted with cowardice or super-stition, actually did look into the book; and instantly dropped it; walked to the side of the boat –'

'One moment,' said the Professor, who had made one or two notes. 'Before you tell me anything else. Did this man tell Wales where he had got the book, or who it originally belonged to?'

'Yes,' replied Pringle, now entirely grave. 'It seems he said he was bringing it back to Dr Hankey, the Oriental traveller now in England, to whom it originally belonged, and who had warned him of its strange properties. Well, Hankey is an able man and a rather crabbed and sneering sort of man; which makes it queerer still. But the point of Wales's story is much simpler. It is that the man who had looked into the book walked straight over the side of the ship, and was never seen again.'

'Do you believe it yourself?' asked Openshaw after a pause.

'Well, I do,' replied Pringle. 'I believe it for two reasons. First, that Wales was an entirely unimaginative man; and he added one touch that only an imaginative man could have added. He said that the man walked straight over the side on a still and calm day; but there was no splash.'

The Professor looked at his notes for some seconds in silence; and then said: 'And your other reason for believing it?'

'My other reason,' answered the Rev. Luke Pringle, 'is what I saw myself.'

There was another silence; until he continued in the same matter-of-fact way. Whatever he had, he had nothing of the eagerness with which the crank, or even the believer, tried to convince others.

'I told you that Wales put down the book on the table beside the sword. There was only one entrance to the tent; and it happened that I was standing in it, looking out into the forest, with my back to my companion. He was standing by the table grumbling and growling about the whole business; saying it was tomfoolery in the twentieth century to be frightened of opening a book; asking why the devil he shouldn't open it himself. Then some instinct stirred in me and I said that he had better not do that, it had better be returned to Dr Hankey. "What harm could it do?" he said restlessly. "What harm did it do?" I answered obstinately. "What happened to your friend on the boat?" He didn't answer, indeed I didn't know what he could answer; but I pressed my logical advantage in mere vanity. "If it comes to that," I said, "what is your version of what really happened on the boat?" Still he didn't answer; and I looked round and saw that he wasn't there.

'The tent was empty. The book was lying on the table; open, but on its face, as if he had turned it downwards. But the sword was lying on the ground near the other side of the tent; and the canvas of the tent showed a great slash, as if somebody had hacked his way out with the sword. The gash in the tent gaped at me; but showed only the dark glimmer of the forest outside. And when I went across and looked through the rent I could not be certain whether the tangle of the tall plants and the undergrowth had been bent or broken; at least not farther than a few feet. I have never seen or heard of Captain Wales from that day.

'I wrapped the book up in brown paper, taking good care not to look at it; and I brought it back to England, intending at first to return it to Dr Hankey. Then I saw some notes in your paper suggesting a hypothesis about such things; and I decided to stop on the way and put the matter before you; as you have a name for being balanced and having an open mind.'

Professor Openshaw laid down his pen and looked steadily at the man on the other side of the table; concentrating in that single stare all his long experience of many entirely different types of humbug, and even some eccentric and extraordinary types of honest men. In the ordinary way, he would have begun with the healthy hypothesis that the story was a pack of lies. On the whole he did incline to assume that it was a pack of lies. And yet he could not fit the man into his story; if

335

it were only that he could not see that sort of liar telling that sort of lie. The man was not trying to look honest on the surface, as most quacks and impostors do; somehow, it seemed all the other way; as if the man *was* honest, in spite of something else that was merely on the surface. He thought of a good man with one innocent delusion; but again the symptoms were not the same; there was even a sort of virile indifference; as if the man did not care much about his delusion, if it was a delusion.

'Mr Pringle,' he said sharply, like a barrister making a witness jump, 'where is this book of yours now?'

The grin reappeared on the bearded face which had grown grave during the recital.

'I left it outside,' said Mr Pringle. 'I mean in the outer office. It was a risk, perhaps; but the less risk of the two.'

'What do you mean?' demanded the Professor. 'Why didn't you bring it straight in here?'

'Because,' answered the missionary, 'I knew that as soon as you saw it, you'd open it – before you had heard the story. I thought it possible you might think twice about opening it – after you'd heard the story.'

Then after a silence he added: 'There was nobody out there but your clerk; and he looked a stolid steady-going specimen, immersed in business calculations.'

Openshaw laughed unaffectedly. 'Oh, Babbage,' he cried, 'your magic tomes are safe enough with him, I assure you. His name's Berridge – but I often call him Babbage; because he's so exactly like a Calculating Machine. No human being, if you can call him a human being, would be less likely to open other people's brown paper parcels. Well, we may as well go and bring it in now; though I assure you I will consider seriously the course to be taken with it. Indeed, I tell you frankly,' and he stared at the man again, 'that I'm not quite sure whether we ought to open it here and now, or send it to this Dr Hankey.'

The two had passed together out of the inner into the outer office; and even as they did so, Mr Pringle gave a cry and ran forward towards the clerk's desk. For the clerk's desk was there; but not the clerk. On the clerk's desk lay a faded old leather book, torn out of its brown-paper wrappings, and lying closed, but as if it had just been opened. The clerk's desk stood against the wide window that looked out into the street; and the window was shattered with a huge ragged hole in the glass; as if a human body had been shot through it into the world without. There was no other trace of Mr Berridge.

Both the two men left in the office stood as still as statues; and then it was the Professor who slowly came to life. He looked even more judicial than he had ever looked in his life, as he slowly turned and held out his hand to the missionary.

'Mr Pringle,' he said, 'I beg your pardon. I beg your pardon only for thoughts that I have had; and half-thoughts at that. But nobody could call himself a scientific man and not face a fact like this.'

'I suppose,' said Pringle doubtfully, 'that we ought to make some inquiries. Can you ring up his house and find out if he has gone home?'

'I don't know that he's on the telephone,' answered Openshaw, rather absently; 'he lives somewhere up Hampstead way, I think. But I suppose somebody will inquire here, if his friends or family miss him.'

'Could we furnish a description,' asked the other, 'if the police want it?'

'The police!' said the Professor, starting from his reverie. 'A description . . . Well, he looked awfully like everybody else, I'm afraid, except for goggles. One of those clean-shaven chaps. But the police . . . look here, what *are* we to do about this mad business?'

'I know what I ought to do,' said the Rev. Mr. Pringle firmly, 'I am going to take this book straight to the only original Dr Hankey, and ask him what the devil it's all about. He lives not very far from here, and I'll come straight back and tell you what he says.'

'Oh, very well,' said the Professor at last, as he sat down rather wearily; perhaps relieved for the moment to be rid of the responsibility. But long after the brisk and ringing footsteps of the little missionary had died away down the street, the Professor sat in the same posture, staring into vacancy like a man in a trance.

He was still in the same seat and almost in the same attitude, when the same brisk footsteps were heard on the pavement without and the missionary entered, this time, as a glance assured him, with empty hands.

'Dr Hankey,' said Pringle gravely, 'wants to keep the book for an hour and consider the point. Then he asks us both to call, and he will give us his decision. He specially desired, Professor, that you should accompany me on the second visit.'

Openshaw continued to stare in silence; then he said, suddenly:

'Who the devil is Dr Hankey?'

'You sound rather as if you meant he was the devil,' said Pringle, smiling, 'and I fancy some people have thought so. He had quite a reputation in your own line; but he gained it mostly in India, studying local magic and so on, so perhaps he's not so well known here. He is a yellow skinny little devil with a lame leg, and a doubtful temper; but he seems to have set up in an ordinary respectable practice in these parts, and I don't know anything definitely wrong about him – unless it's wrong to be the only person who can possibly know anything about all this crazy affair.'

Professor Openshaw rose heavily and went to the telephone; he rang up Father Brown, changing the luncheon engagement to a dinner, that he might hold himself free for the expedition to the house of the Anglo-Indian doctor; after that he sat down again, lit a cigar and sank once more into his own unfathomable thoughts.

Father Brown went round to the restaurant appointed for dinner, and kicked his heels for some time in a vestibule full of mirrors and palms in pots; he had been informed of Openshaw's afternoon engagement, and, as the evening closed in dark and stormy round the glass and the green plants, guessed that it had produced something unexpected and unduly prolonged. He even wondered for a moment whether the Professor would turn up at all; but when the Professor eventually did, it was clear that his own more general guesses had been justified. For it was a very wild-eyed and even wild-haired Professor who eventually drove back with Mr Pringle from the expedition to the North of London, where suburbs are still fringed with heathy wastes and scraps of common, looking more sombre under the rather thunderstorm sunset. Nevertheless, they had apparently found the house, standing a little apart though within hail of other houses; they had verified the brass-plate duly engraved: 'J. I. Hankey, MD, MRCS'. Only they did not find J. I. Hankey, MD, MRCS. They found only what a nightmare whisper had already subconsciously prepared them to find: a commonplace parlour with the accursed volume lying on the table, as if it had just been read; and beyond, a backdoor burst open and a faint trail of footsteps that ran a little way up so steep a garden-path that it seemed that no lame man could have run up so lightly. But it was a lame man who had run; for in those few steps there was the misshapen unequal mark of some sort of surgical boot; then two marks of that boot alone (as if the creature had hopped) and then nothing. There was nothing further to be learnt from Dr J. I. Hankey, except that he had made his decision. He had read the oracle and received the doom.

When the two came into the entrance under the palms, Pringle put the book down suddenly on a small table, as if it burned his fingers. The priest glanced at it curiously; there was only some rude lettering on the front with a couplet:

> They that looked into this book
> Them the Flying Terror took;

and underneath, as he afterwards discovered, similar warnings in Greek, Latin and French. The other two had turned away with a natural impulsion towards drinks, after their exhausion and bewilderment; and Openshaw had called to the waiter, who brought cocktails on a tray.

'You will dine with us, I hope,' said the Professor to the missionary; but Mr Pringle amiably shook his head.

'If you'll forgive me,' he said, 'I'm going off to wrestle with this book and this business by myself somewhere. I suppose I couldn't use your office for an hour or so?'

'I suppose – I'm afraid it's locked,' said Openshaw in some surprise.

'You forget there's a hole in the window.' The Rev. Luke Pringle gave the very broadest of all his broad grins and vanished into the darkness without.

'A rather odd fellow, that, after all,' said the Professor, frowning.

He was rather surprised to find Father Brown talking to the waiter who had brought the cocktails, apparently about the waiter's most private affairs; for there was some mention of a baby who was now out of danger. He commented on the fact with some surprise, wondering how the priest came to know the man; but the former only said, 'Oh, I dine here every two or three months, and I've talked to him now and then.'

The Professor, who himself dined there about five times a week, was conscious that he had never thought of talking to the man; but his thoughts were interrupted by a strident ringing and a summons to the telephone. The voice on the telephone said it was Pringle; it was rather a muffled voice, but it might well be muffled in all those bushes of beard and whisker. Its message was enough to establish identity.

'Professor,' said the voice, 'I can't stand it any longer. I'm going to look for myself. I'm speaking from your office and the book is in front of me. If anything happens to me, this is to say good-bye. No – it's no good trying to stop me. You wouldn't be in time anyhow. I'm opening the book now. I . . .'

Openshaw thought he heard something like a sort of thrilling or shivering yet almost soundless crash; then he shouted the name of Pringle again and again; but he heard no more. He hung up the receiver, and, restored to a superb academic calm, rather like the calm of despair, went back and quietly took his seat at the dinner-table. Then, as coolly as if he were describing the failure of some small silly trick at a séance, he told the priest every detail of this monstrous mystery.

'Five men have now vanished in this impossible way,' he said. 'Every one is extraordinary; and yet the one case I simply can't get over is my clerk, Berridge. It's just because he was the quietest creature that he's the queerest case.'

'Yes,' replied Father Brown, 'it was a queer thing for Berridge to do, anyway. He was awfully conscientious. He was always so jolly careful to keep all the office business separate from any fun of his own. Why, hardly anybody knew he was quite a humorist at home and –'

'Berridge!' cried the Professor. 'What on earth are you talking about? Did you know him?'

'Oh no,' said Father Brown carelessly, 'only as you say I know the waiter. I've often had to wait in your office, till you turned up; and of course I passed the time of day with poor Berridge. He was rather a card. I remember he once said he would like to collect valueless things, as collectors did the silly things they thought valuable. You know the old story about the woman who collected valueless things.'

'I'm not sure I know what you're talking about,' said Openshaw. 'But even if my clerk was eccentric (and I never knew a man I should have thought less so), it wouldn't explain what happened to him; and it certainly wouldn't explain the others.'

'What others?' asked the priest.

The Professor stared at him and spoke distinctly, as if to a child:

'My dear Father Brown, Five Men have disappeared.'

'My dear Professor Openshaw, no men have disappeared.'

Father Brown gazed back at his host with equal steadiness and spoke with equal distinctness. Nevertheless, the Professor required the words repeated, and they were repeated as distinctly.

'I say that no men have disappeared.'

After a moment's silence, he added, 'I suppose the hardest thing is to convince anybody that $0 + 0 + 0 = 0$. Men believe the oddest things if they are in a series; that is why Macbeth believed the three words of the three witches; though the first was something he knew himself; and the last something he could only bring about himself. But in your case the middle term is the weakest of all.'

'What do you mean?'

'You saw nobody vanish. You did not see the man vanish from the boat. You did not see the man vanish from the tent. All that rests on the word of Mr Pringle, which I will not discuss just now. But you'll admit this; you would never have taken his word yourself, *unless* you had seen it confirmed by your clerk's disappearance; just as Macbeth would never have believed he would be king, if he had not been confirmed in believing he would be Cawdor.'

'That may be true,' said the Professor, nodding slowly. 'But *when* it was confirmed, I knew it was the truth. You say I saw nothing myself. But I did; I saw my own clerk disappear. Berridge did disappear.'

'Berridge did not disappear,' said Father Brown. 'On the contrary.'

'What the devil do you mean by "on the contrary"?'

'I mean,' said Father Brown, 'that he never disappeared. He appeared.'

Openshaw stared across at his friend, but the eyes had already altered in his head, as they did when they concentrated on a new presentation of a problem. The priest went on:

'He appeared in your study, disguised in a bushy red beard and buttoned up in a clumsy cape, and announced himself as the Rev. Luke Pringle. And you had never noticed your own clerk enough to know him again, when he was in so rough-and-ready a disguise.'

'But surely,' began the Professor.

'Could you describe him for the police?' asked Father Brown. 'Not you. You probably knew he was clean-shaven and wore tinted glasses;

341

and merely taking off those glasses was a better disguise than putting on anything else. You had never seen his eyes any more than his soul; jolly laughing eyes. He had planted his absurd book and all the properties; then he calmly smashed the window, put on the beard and cape and walked into your study; knowing that you had never looked at him in your life.'

'But why should he play me such an insane trick?' demanded Openshaw.

'Why, *because* you had never looked at him in your life,' said Father Brown; and his hand slightly curled and clinched, as if he might have struck the table, if he had been given to gesture. 'You called him the Calculating Machine, because that was all you ever used him for. You never found out even what a stranger strolling into your office could find out, in five minutes' chat: that he was a character; that he was full of antics; that he had all sorts of views on you and your theories and your reputation for "spotting" people. Can't you understand his itching to prove that you couldn't spot your own clerk? He has nonsense notions of all sorts. About collecting useless things, for instance. Don't you know the story of the woman who bought the two most useless things: an old doctor's brass-plate and a wooden leg? With those your ingenious clerk created the character of the remarkable Dr Hankey; as easily as the visionary Captain Wales. Planting them in his own house –'

'Do you mean that place we visited beyond Hampstead was Berridge's own house?' asked Openshaw.

'Did *you* know his house – or even his address?' retorted the priest. 'Look here, don't think I'm speaking disrespectfully of you or your work. You are a great servant of truth and you know I could never be disrespectful to that. You've seen through a lot of liars, when you put your mind to it. But don't *only* look at liars. Do, just occasionally, look at honest men – like the waiter.'

'Where is Berridge now?' asked the Professor, after a long silence.

'I haven't the least doubt,' said Father Brown, 'that he is back in your office. In fact, he came back into your office at the exact moment when the Rev. Luke Pringle read the awful volume and faded into the void.'

There was another long silence and then Professor Openshaw laughed; with the laugh of a great man who is great enough to look small. Then he said abruptly:

'I suppose I do deserve it; for not noticing the nearest helpers I have. But you must admit the accumulation of incidents was rather formidable. Did you *never* feel just a momentary awe of the awful volume?'

'Oh, that,' said Father Brown. 'I opened it as soon as I saw it lying there. It's all blank pages. You see, I am not superstitious.'

4
The Green Man

A young man in knickerbockers, with an eager sanguine profile, was
playing golf against himself on the links that lay parallel to the sand and
sea, which were all growing grey with twilight. He was not carelessly
knocking a ball about, but rather practising particular strokes with a sort
of microscopic fury; like a neat and tidy whirlwind. He had learned many
games quickly but he had a disposition to learn them a little more quickly
than they can be learnt. He was rather prone to be a victim of those
remarkable invitations by which a man may learn the Violin in Six Lessons
– or acquire a perfect French accent by a Correspondence Course. He
lived in the breezy atmosphere of such hopeful advertisement and adventure. He was at present the private secretary of Admiral Sir Michael
Craven, who owned the big house behind the park abutting on the links.
He was ambitious, and had no intention of continuing indefinitely to be
private secretary to anybody. But he was also reasonable; and he knew
that the best way of ceasing to be a secretary was to be a good secretary.
Consequently he was a very good secretary; dealing with the ever-
accumulating arrears of the Admiral's correspondence with the same
swift centripetal concentration with which he addressed the golf-ball. He
had to struggle with the correspondence alone and at his own discretion
at present; for the Admiral had been with his ship for the last six months;
and, though now returning, was not expected for hours, or possibly days.

With an athletic stride, the young man, whose name was Harold
Harker, crested the rise of turf that was the rampart of the links and,
looking out across the sands to the sea, saw a strange sight. He did not
see it very clearly; for the dusk was darkening every minute under
stormy clouds; but it seemed to him, by a sort of momentary illusion,
like a dream of days long past or a drama played by ghosts, out of
another age in history.

The last of the sunset lay in long bars of copper and gold above the last dark strip of sea that seemed rather black than blue. But blacker still against this gleam in the west, there passed in sharp outline, like figures in a shadow pantomime, two men with three-cornered cocked hats and swords; as if they had just landed from one of the wooden ships of Nelson. It was not at all the sort of hallucination that would have come natural to Mr Harker, had he been prone to hallucinations. He was of the type that is at once sanguine and scientific; and would be more likely to fancy the flying-ships of the future than the fighting-ships of the past. He therefore very sensibly came to the conclusion that even a futurist can believe his eyes.

His illusion did not last more than a moment. On the second glance, what he saw was unusual but not incredible. The two men who were striding in single file across the sands, one some fifteen yards behind the other, were ordinary modern naval officers; but naval officers wearing that almost extravagant full-dress uniform which naval officers never do wear if they can possibly help it; only on great ceremonial occasions such as the visits of Royalty. In the man walking in front, who seemed more or less unconscious of the man walking behind, Harker recognized at once the high-bridged nose and spike-shaped beard of his own employer the Admiral. The other man following in his tracks he did not know. But he did know something about the circumstances connected with the ceremonial occasion. He knew that when the Admiral's ship put in at the adjacent port, it was to be formally visited by a Great Personage; which was enough, in that sense, to explain the officers being in full dress. But he did also know the officers; or at any rate the Admiral. And what could have possessed the Admiral to come on shore in that rig-out, when one could swear he would seize five minutes to change into mufti or at least into undress uniform, was more than his secretary could conceive. It seemed somehow to be the very last thing he would do. It was indeed to remain for many weeks one of the chief mysteries of this mysterious business. As it was, the outline of these fantastic court uniforms against the empty scenery, striped with dark sea and sand, had something suggestive of comic opera; and reminded the spectator of *Pinafore*.

The second figure was much more singular; somewhat singular in appearance, despite his correct lieutenant's uniform, and still more extraordinary in behaviour. He walked in a strangely irregular and uneasy manner; sometimes quickly and sometimes slowly; as if he could not make up his mind whether to overtake the Admiral or not. The Admiral was rather deaf and certainly heard no footsteps behind him on the yielding sand; but the footsteps behind him, if traced in the detective manner, would have given rise to twenty conjectures from a limp to a dance. The man's face was swarthy as well as darkened with shadow and every now and then the eyes in it shifted and shone, as if to accent his agitation. Once he began to run and then abruptly relapsed into a swaggering slowness and carelessness. Then he did something which Mr Harker could never have conceived any normal naval officer in His Britannic Majesty's Service doing, even in a lunatic asylum. He drew his sword.

It was at this bursting-point of the prodigy that the two passing figures disappeared behind a headland on the shore. The staring secretary had just time to notice the swarthy stranger, with a resumption of carelessness, knock off a head of sea-holly with his glittering blade. He seemed then to have abandoned all idea of catching the other man up. But Mr Harold Harker's face became very thoughtful indeed; and he stood there ruminating for some time before he gravely took himself inland, towards the road that ran past the gates of the great house and so by a long curve down to the sea.

It was up this curving road from the coast that the Admiral might be expected to come, considering the direction in which he had been walking, and making the natural assumption that he was bound for his own door. The path along the sands, under the links, turned inland just beyond the headland and solidifying itself into a road, returned towards Craven House. It was down this road, therefore, that the secretary darted, with characteristic impetuosity, to meet his patron returning home. But the patron was apparently not returning home. What was still more peculiar, the secretary was not returning home either; at least until many hours later; a delay quite long enough to arouse alarm and mystification at Craven House.

Behind the pillars and palms of that rather too palatial country house, indeed, there was expectancy gradually changing to uneasiness. Gryce the butler, a big bilious man abnormally silent below as well as above stairs, showed a certain restlessness as he moved about the main front-hall and occasionally looked out of the side windows of the porch, on the white road that swept towards the sea. The Admiral's sister Marion, who kept house for him, had her brother's high nose with a more sniffy expression; she was voluble, rather rambling, not without humour, and capable of sudden emphasis as shrill as a cockatoo. The Admiral's daughter Olive was dark, dreamy, and as a rule abstractedly silent, perhaps melancholy; so that her aunt generally conducted most of the conversation, and that without reluctance. But the girl also had a gift of sudden laughter that was very engaging.

'I can't think why they're not here already,' said the elder lady. 'The postman distinctly told me he'd seen the Admiral coming along the beach; along with that dreadful creature Rook. Why in the world they call him Lieutenant Rook –'

'Perhaps,' suggested the melancholy young lady, with a momentary brightness, 'perhaps they call him Lieutenant because he is a Lieutenant.'

'I can't think why the Admiral keeps him,' snorted her aunt, as if she were talking of a housemaid. She was very proud of her brother and always called him the Admiral; but her notions of a commission in the Senior Service were inexact.

'Well, Roger Rook is sulky and unsociable and all that,' replied Olive, 'but of course that wouldn't prevent him being a capable sailor.'

'Sailor!' cried her aunt with one of her rather startling cockatoo notes, 'he isn't my notion of a sailor. The Lass that Loved a Sailor, as they used to sing when I was young . . . Just think of it! He's not gay and free and whatsitsname. He doesn't sing shanties or dance a hornpipe.'

'Well,' observed her niece with gravity. 'The Admiral doesn't very often dance a hornpipe.'

'Oh, you know what I mean – he isn't bright or breezy or anything,' replied the old lady. 'Why, that secretary fellow could do better than that.'

Olive's rather tragic face was transfigured by one of her good and rejuvenating waves of laughter.

'I'm sure Mr Harker would dance a hornpipe for you,' she said, 'and say he had learnt it in half an hour from the book of instructions. He's always learning things of that sort.'

She stopped laughing suddenly and looked at her aunt's rather strained face.

'I can't think why Mr Harker doesn't come,' she added.

'I don't care about Mr Harker,' replied the aunt, and rose and looked out of the window.

The evening light had long turned from yellow to grey and was now turning almost to white under the widening moonlight, over the large flat landscape by the coast; unbroken by any features save a clump of sea-twisted trees round a pool and beyond, rather gaunt and dark against the horizon, the shabby fishermen's tavern on the shore that bore the name of the Green Man. And all that road and landscape was empty of any living thing. Nobody had seen the figure in the cocked hat that had been observed, earlier in the evening, walking by the sea; or the other and stranger figure that had been seen trailing after him. Nobody had even seen the secretary who saw them.

It was after midnight when the secretary at last burst in and aroused the household; and his face, white as a ghost, looked all the paler against the background of the stolid face and figure of a big Inspector of Police. Somehow that red, heavy, indifferent face looked, even more than the white and harassed one, like a mask of doom. The news was broken to the two women with such consideration or concealments as were possible. But the news was that the body of Admiral Craven had been eventually fished out of the foul weeds and scum of the pool under the trees; and that he was drowned and dead.

Anybody acquainted with Mr Harold Harker, secretary, will realize that, whatever his agitation, he was by morning in a mood to be tremendously on the spot. He hustled the Inspector, whom he had met the night before on the road down by the Green Man, into another room for private and practical consultation. He questioned the Inspector rather as the Inspector might have questioned a yokel. But Inspector Burns was a stolid character; and was either too stupid or too clever to resent such trifles. It soon began to look as if he were by no means so stupid as he looked; for he disposed of Harker's eager questions in a manner that was slow but methodical and rational.

'Well,' said Harker (his head full of many manuals with titles like 'Be a Detective in Ten Days'). 'Well, it's the old triangle, I suppose. Accident, Suicide or Murder.'

'I don't see how it could be accident,' answered the policeman. 'It wasn't even dark yet and the pool's fifty yards from the straight road that he knew like his own doorstep. He'd no more have got into that pond than he'd go and carefully lie down in a puddle in the street. As for suicide, it's rather a responsibility to suggest it, and rather improbable too. The Admiral was a pretty spry and successful man and frightfully rich, nearly a millionaire in fact; though of course that doesn't prove anything. He seemed to be pretty normal and comfortable in his private life too; he's the last man I should suspect of drowning himself.'

'So that we come,' said the secretary, lowering his voice with the thrill, 'I suppose we come to the third possibility.'

'We won't be in too much of a hurry about that,' said the Inspector to the annoyance of Harker, who was in a hurry about everything. 'But naturally there are one or two things one would like to know. One would like to know about his property, for instance. Do you know who's likely to come in for it? You're his private secretary; do you know anything about his will?'

'I'm not so private a secretary as all that,' answered the young man. 'His solicitors are Messrs Willis, Hardman and Dyke, over in Suttford High Street; and I believe the will is in their custody.'

'Well, I'd better get round and see them pretty soon,' said the Inspector.

'Let's get round and see them at once,' said the impatient secretary.

He took a turn or two restlessly up and down the room and then exploded in a fresh place.

'What have you done about the body, Inspector?' he asked.

'Dr Straker is examining it now at the Police Station. His report ought to be ready in an hour or so.'

'It can't be ready too soon,' said Harker. 'It would save time if we could meet him at the lawyer's.' Then he stopped and his impetuous tone changed abruptly to one of some embarrassment.

'Look here,' he said, 'I want . . . we want to consider the young lady, the poor Admiral's daughter, as much as possible just now. She's got a notion that may be all nonsense; but I wouldn't like to disappoint her. There's some friend of hers she wants to consult, staying in the town at present. Man of the name of Brown; priest or parson of some sort; she's given me his address. I don't take much stock in priests or parsons, but –'

The Inspector nodded. 'I don't take any stock in priests or parsons;

349

but I take a lot of stock in Father Brown,' he said. 'I happened to have to do with him in a queer sort of society jewel case. He ought to have been a policeman instead of a parson.'

'Oh, all right,' said the breathless secretary as he vanished from the room. 'Let him come to the lawyer's too.'

Thus it happened that, when they hurried across to the neighbouring town to meet Dr Straker at the solicitor's office, they found Father Brown already seated there, with his hands folded on his heavy umbrella, chatting pleasantly to the only available member of the firm. Dr Straker also had arrived, but apparently only at that moment, as he was carefully placing his gloves in his top-hat and his top-hat on a side-table. And the mild and beaming expression of the priest's moonlike face and spectacles, together with the silent chuckles of the jolly old grizzled lawyer, to whom he was talking, were enough to show that the doctor had not yet opened his mouth to bring the news of death.

'A beautiful morning after all,' Father Brown was saying. 'That storm seems to have passed over us. There were some big black clouds, but I notice that not a drop of rain fell.'

'Not a drop,' agreed the solicitor toying with a pen; he was the third partner, Mr Dyke; 'there's not a cloud in the sky now. It's the sort of day for a holiday.' Then he realized the newcomers and looked up, laying down the pen and rising. 'Ah, Mr Harker, how are you? I hear the Admiral is expected home soon.' Then Harker spoke, and his voice rang hollow in the room.

'I am sorry to say we are the bearers of bad news. Admiral Craven was drowned before reaching home.'

There was a change in the very air of the still office, though not in the attitudes of the motionless figures; both were staring at the speaker as if a joke had been frozen on their lips. Both repeated the word 'drowned' and looked at each other, and then again at their informant. Then there was a small hubbub of questions.

'When did this happen?' asked the priest.

'Where was he found?' asked the lawyer.

'He was found,' said the Inspector, 'in that pool by the coast, not far from the Green Man, and dragged out all covered with green scum and weeds so as to be almost unrecognizable. But Dr Straker here has – What is the matter, Father Brown? Are you ill?'

'The Green Man,' said Father Brown with a shudder. 'I'm so sorry . . . I beg your pardon for being upset.'

'Upset by what?' asked the staring officer.

'By his being covered with green scum, I suppose,' said the priest, with a rather shaky laugh. Then he added rather more firmly, 'I thought it might have been seaweed.'

By this time everybody was looking at the priest, with a not unnatural suspicion that he was mad; and yet the next crucial surprise was not to come from him. After a dead silence, it was the doctor who spoke.

Dr Straker was a remarkable man, even to look at. He was very tall and angular, formal and professional in his dress; yet retaining a fashion that has hardly been known since Mid-Victorian times. Though comparatively young, he wore his brown beard very long and spreading over his waistcoat; in contrast with it, his features, which were both harsh and handsome, looked singularly pale. His good looks were also diminished by something in his deep eyes that was not squinting, but like the shadow of a squint. Everybody noticed these things about him, because the moment he spoke, he gave forth an indescribable air of authority. But all he said was:

'There is one more thing to be said, if you come to details, about Admiral Craven being drowned.' Then he added reflectively, 'Admiral Craven was not drowned.'

The Inspector turned with quite a new promptitude and shot a question at him.

'I have just examined the body,' said Dr Straker, 'the cause of death was a stab through the heart with some pointed blade like a stiletto. It was after death, and even some little time after, that the body was hidden in the pool.'

Father Brown was regarding Dr Straker with a very lively eye, such as he seldom turned upon anybody; and when the group in the office began to break up, he managed to attach himself to the medical man for a little further conversation, as they went back down the street. There had not been very much else to detain them except the rather formal question of the will. The impatience of the young secretary had been somewhat tried by the professional etiquette of the old lawyer. But the latter was ultimately induced, rather by the tact of the priest than the authority of the policeman, to refrain from making a mystery

351

where there was no mystery at all. Mr Dyke admitted, with a smile, that the Admiral's will was a very normal and ordinary document, leaving everything to his only child Olive; and that there really was no particular reason for concealing the fact.

The doctor and the priest walked slowly down the street that struck out of the town in the direction of Craven House. Harker had plunged on ahead of them with all his native eagerness to get somewhere; but the two behind seemed more interested in their discussion than their direction. It was in rather an enigmatic tone that the tall doctor said to the short cleric beside him:

'Well, Father Brown, what do you think of a thing like this?'

Father Brown looked at him rather intently for an instant and then said: 'Well, I've begun to think of one or two things; but my chief difficulty is that I only knew the Admiral slightly; though I've seen something of his daughter.'

'The Admiral,' said the doctor with a grim immobility of feature, 'was the sort of man of whom it is said that he had not an enemy in the world.'

'I suppose you mean,' answered the priest, 'that there's something else that will not be said.'

'Oh, it's no affair of mine,' said Straker hastily but rather harshly. 'He had his moods, I suppose. He once threatened me with a legal action about an operation; but I think he thought better of it. I can imagine his being rather rough with a subordinate.'

Father Brown's eyes were fixed on the figure of the secretary striding far ahead; and as he gazed he realized the special cause of his hurry. Some fifty yards farther ahead the Admiral's daughter was dawdling along the road towards the Admiral's house. The secretary soon came abreast of her; and for the remainder of the time Father Brown watched the silent drama of two human backs as they diminished into the distance. The secretary was evidently very much excited about something; but if the priest guessed what it was, he kept it to himself. When he came to the corner leading to the doctor's house, he only said briefly: 'I don't know if you have anything more to tell us.'

'Why should I?' answered the doctor very abruptly; and striding off, left it uncertain whether he was asking why he should have anything to tell, or why he should tell it.

Father Brown went stumping on alone, in the track of the two young people; but when he came to the entrance and avenues of the Admiral's park, he was arrested by the action of the girl, who turned suddenly and came straight towards him; her face unusually pale and her eyes bright with some new and as yet nameless emotion.

'Father Brown,' she said in a low voice. 'I must talk to you as soon as possible. You must listen to me, I can't see any other way out.'

'Why certainly,' he replied, as coolly as if a gutter-boy had asked him the time. 'Where shall we go and talk?'

The girl led him at random to one of the rather tumbledown arbours in the grounds; and they sat down behind a screen of large ragged leaves. She began instantly, as if she must relieve her feelings or faint.

'Harold Harker,' she said, 'has been talking to me about things. Terrible things.'

The priest nodded and the girl went on hastily. 'About Roger Rook. Do you know about Roger?'

'I've been told,' he answered, 'that his fellow-seamen call him The Jolly Roger, because he is never jolly; and looks like the pirate's skull and crossbones.'

'He was not always like that,' said Olive in a low voice. 'Something very queer must have happened to him. I knew him well when we were children; we used to play over there on the sands. He was harum-scarum and always talking about being a pirate; I dare say he was the sort they say might take to crime through reading shockers; but there was something poetical in his way of being piratical. He really was a Jolly Roger then. I suppose he was the last boy who kept up the old legend of really running away to sea; and at last his family had to agree to his joining the Navy. Well . . .'

'Yes,' said Father Brown patiently.

'Well,' she admitted, caught in one of her rare moments of mirth, 'I suppose poor Roger found it disappointing. Naval officers so seldom carry knives in their teeth or wave bloody cutlasses and black flags. But that doesn't explain the change in him. He just stiffened; grew dull and dumb, like a dead man walking about. He always avoids me; but that doesn't matter. I supposed some great grief that's no business of mine had broken him up. And now – well, if what Harold says is true, the grief is neither more nor less than going mad; or being possessed of a devil.'

'And what does Harold say?' asked the priest.

'It's so awful I can hardly say it,' she answered. 'He swears he saw Roger creeping behind my father that night; hesitating and then drawing his sword . . . and the doctor says father was stabbed with a steel point . . . I *can't* believe Roger Rook had anything to do with it. His sulks and my father's temper sometimes led to quarrels; but what are quarrels? I can't exactly say I'm standing up for an old friend; because he isn't even friendly. But you can't help feeling sure of some things, even about an old acquaintance. And yet Harold swears that he –'

'Harold seems to swear a great deal,' said Father Brown.

There was a sudden silence; after which she said in a different tone:

'Well, he does swear other things too. Harold Harker proposed to me just now.'

'Am I to congratulate you, or rather him?' inquired her companion.

'I told him he must wait. He isn't good at waiting.' She was caught again in a ripple of her incongruous sense of the comic: 'He said I was his ideal and his ambition and so on. He has lived in the States; but somehow I never remember it when he is talking about dollars; only when he is talking about ideals.'

'And I suppose,' said Father Brown very softly, 'that it is because you have to decide about Harold that you want to know the truth about Roger.'

She stiffened and frowned, and then equally abruptly smiled, saying: 'Oh, you know too much.'

'I know very little, especially in this affair,' said the priest gravely. 'I only know who murdered your father.' She started up and stood staring down at him stricken white. Father Brown made a wry face as he went on: 'I made a fool of myself when I first realized it; when they'd just been asking where he was found, and went on talking about green scum and the Green Man.'

Then he also rose; clutching his clumsy umbrella with a new resolution, he addressed the girl with a new gravity.

'There is something else that I know, which is the key to all these riddles of yours; but I won't tell you yet. I suppose it's bad news; but it's nothing like so bad as the things you have been fancying.' He buttoned up his coat and turned towards the gate. 'I'm going to see this Mr Rook of yours. In a shed by the shore, near where Mr Harker saw

him walking. I rather think he lives there.' And he went bustling off in
the direction of the beach.

Olive was an imaginative person; perhaps too imaginative to be safely
left to brood over such hints as her friend had thrown out; but he was
in rather a hurry to find the best relief for her broodings. The mysterious
connexion between Father Brown's first shock of enlightenment and
the chance language about the pool and the inn, hag-rode her fancy in
a hundred forms of ugly symbolism. The Green Man became a ghost
trailing loathsome weeds and walking the countryside under the moon;
the sign of the Green Man became a human figure hanging as from a
gibbet; and the tarn itself became a tavern, a dark subaqueous tavern
for the dead sailors. And yet he had taken the most rapid method to
overthrow all such nightmares, with a burst of blinding daylight which
seemed more mysterious than the night.

For before the sun had set, something had come back into her life
that turned her whole world topsy-turvy once more; something she had
hardly known that she desired until it was abruptly granted; something
that was, like a dream, old and familiar, and yet remained incomprehensible and incredible. For Roger Rook had come striding across the
sands, and even when he was a dot in the distance, she knew he was
transfigured; and as he came nearer and nearer, she saw that his dark
face was alive with laughter and exultation. He came straight towards
her, as if they had never parted, and seized her shoulders saying: 'Now
I can look after you, thank God.'

She hardly knew what she answered; but she heard herself questioning rather wildly why he seemed so changed and so happy.

'Because I am happy,' he answered. 'I have heard the bad news.'

All parties concerned, including some who seemed rather unconcerned,
found themselves assembled on the garden path leading to Craven
House, to hear the formality, now truly formal, of the lawyer's reading
of the will; and the probable, and more practical, sequel of the lawyer's
advice upon the crisis. Besides the grey-haired solicitor himself, armed
with the testamentary document, there was the Inspector armed with
more direct authority touching the crime, and Lieutenant Rook in
undisguised attendance on the lady; some were rather mystified on
seeing the tall figure of the doctor, some smiled a little on seeing the

dumpy figure of the priest. Mr Harker, that Flying Mercury, had shot down to the lodge-gates to meet them, led them back on to the lawn, and then dashed ahead of them again to prepare their reception. He said he would be back in a jiffy; and anyone observing his piston-rod of energy could well believe it; but, for the moment, they were left rather stranded on the lawn outside the house.

'Reminds me of somebody making runs at cricket,' said the Lieutenant.

'That young man,' said the lawyer, 'is rather annoyed that the law cannot move quite so quickly as he does. Fortunately Miss Craven understands our professional difficulties and delays. She has kindly assured me that she still has confidence in my slowness.'

'I wish,' said the doctor, suddenly, 'that I had as much confidence in his quickness.'

'Why, what do you mean?' asked Rook, knitting his brows; 'do you mean that Harker is too quick?'

'Too quick and too slow,' said Dr Straker, in his rather cryptic fashion. 'I know one occasion at least when he was not so very quick. Why was he hanging about half the night by the pond and the Green Man, before the Inspector came down and found the body? Why did he meet the Inspector? Why should he expect to meet the Inspector outside the Green Man?'

'I don't understand you,' said Rook. 'Do you mean that Harker wasn't telling the truth?'

Dr Straker was silent. The grizzled lawyer laughed with grim good humour.

'I have nothing more serious to say against the young man,' he said, 'than that he made a prompt and praiseworthy attempt to teach me my own business.'

'For that matter, he made an attempt to teach me mine,' said the Inspector, who had just joined the group in front. 'But that doesn't matter. If Dr Straker means anything by his hints, they do matter. I must ask you to speak plainly, doctor. It may be my duty to question him at once.'

'Well, here he comes,' said Rook, as the alert figure of the secretary appeared once more in the doorway.

At this point Father Brown, who had remained silent and inconspicuous at the tail of the procession, astonished everybody very much, perhaps especially those who knew him. He not only walked rapidly to the front, but turned facing the whole group with an arresting and almost threatening expression, like a sergeant bringing soldiers to the halt.

'Stop!' he said almost sternly. 'I apologize to everybody; but it's absolutely necessary that I should see Mr Harker first. I've got to tell him something I know; and I don't think anybody else knows; something he's got to hear. It may save a very tragic misunderstanding with somebody later on.'

'What on earth do you mean?' asked old Dyke the lawyer.

'I mean the bad news,' said Father Brown.

'Here, I say,' began the Inspector indignantly; and then suddenly caught the priest's eye and remembered strange things he had seen in other days. 'Well, if it were anyone in the world but you I should say of all the infernal cheek –'

But Father Brown was already out of hearing, and a moment afterwards was plunged in talk with Harker in the porch. They walked to and fro together for a few paces and then disappeared into the dark interior. It was about twelve minutes afterwards that Father Brown came out alone.

To their surprise he showed no disposition to re-enter the house, now that the whole company were at last about to enter it. He threw himself down on the rather rickety seat in the leafy arbour, and as the procession disappeared through the doorway, lit a pipe and proceeded to stare vacantly at the long ragged leaves about his head and to listen to the birds. There was no man who had a more hearty and enduring appetite for doing nothing.

He was apparently in a cloud of smoke and a dream of abstraction, when the front doors were once more flung open and two or three figures came out helter-skelter, running towards him, the daughter of the house and her young admirer Mr Rook being easily winners in the race. Their faces were alight with astonishment; and the face of Inspector Burns, who advanced more heavily behind them, like an elephant shaking the garden, was inflamed with some indignation as well.

'What *can* all this mean?' cried Olive, as she came panting to a halt. 'He's gone!'

'Bolted!' said the Lieutenant explosively. 'Harker's just managed to pack a a suitcase and bolted! Gone clean out of the back door and over the garden-wall to God knows where. What *did* you say to him?'

'Don't be silly!' said Olive, with a more worried expression. 'Of course you told him you'd found him out, and now he's gone. I never could have believed he was wicked like that!'

'Well!' gasped the Inspector, bursting into their midst. 'What have you done now? What have you let me down like this for?'

'Well,' repeated Father Brown, 'what have I done?'

'You have let a murderer escape,' cried Burns, with a decision that was like a thunderclap in the quiet garden; 'you have *helped* a murderer to escape. Like a fool I let you warn him; and now he is miles away.'

'I have helped a few murderers in my time, it is true,' said Father Brown; then he added, in careful distinction, 'not, you will understand, helped them to commit the murder.'

'But you knew all the time,' insisted Olive. 'You guessed from the first that it must be he. That's what you meant about being upset by the business of finding the body. That's what the doctor meant by saying my father might be disliked by a subordinate.'

'That's what I complain of,' said the official indignantly. 'You knew even then that he was the –'

'You knew even then,' insisted Olive, 'that the murderer was –'

Father Brown nodded gravely. 'Yes,' he said. 'I knew even then that the murderer was old Dyke.'

'Was *who*?' repeated the Inspector and stopped amid a dead silence; punctuated only by the occasional pipe of birds.

'I mean Mr Dyke, the solicitor,' explained Father Brown, like one explaining something elementary to an infant class. 'That gentleman with grey hair who's supposed to be going to read the will.'

They all stood like statues staring at him, as he carefully filled his pipe again and struck a match. At last Burns rallied his vocal powers to break the strangling silence with an effort resembling violence.

'But, in the name of heaven, *why*?'

'Ah, why?' said the priest and rose thoughtfully, puffing at his pipe. 'As to why he did it . . . Well, I suppose the time has come to tell you, or those of you who don't know, the fact that is the key of all this business. It's a great calamity; and it's a great crime; but it's not the murder of Admiral Craven.'

He looked Olive full in the face and said very seriously:

'I tell you the bad news bluntly and in few words; because I think you are brave enough, and perhaps happy enough, to take it well. You have the chance, and I think the power, to be something like a great woman. You are not a great heiress.'

Amid the silence that followed it was he who resumed his explanation.

'Most of your father's money, I am sorry to say, has gone. It went by the financial dexterity of the grey-haired gentleman named Dyke, who is (I grieve to say) a swindler. Admiral Craven was murdered to silence him about the way in which he was swindled. The fact that he was ruined and you were disinherited is the single simple clue, not only to the murder, but to all the other mysteries in this business.' He took a puff or two and then continued.

'I told Mr Rook you were disinherited and he rushed back to help you. Mr Rook is a rather remarkable person.'

'Oh, chuck it,' said Mr Rook with a hostile air.

'Mr Rook is a monster,' said Father Brown with scientific calm. 'He is an anachronism, an atavism, a brute survival of the Stone Age. If there was one barbarous superstition we all supposed to be utterly extinct and dead in these days, it was that notion about honour and independence. But then I get mixed up with so many dead superstitions. Mr Rook is an extinct animal. He is a plesiosaurus. He did not want to live on his wife or have a wife who could call him a fortune-hunter. Therefore he sulked in a grotesque manner and only came to life again when I brought him the good news that you were ruined. He wanted to work for his wife and not be kept by her. Disgusting, isn't it? Let us turn to the brighter topic of Mr Harker.

'I told Mr Harker you were disinherited and he rushed away in a sort of panic. Do not be too hard on Mr Harker. He really had better as well as worse enthusiasms; but he had them all mixed up. There is no harm in having ambitions; but he had ambitions and called them ideals. The old sense of honour taught men to suspect success; to say, 'This is a benefit; it may be a bribe.' The new nine-times-accursed nonsense about Making Good teaches men to identify being good with making money. That was all that was the matter with him; in every other way he was a thoroughly good fellow, and there are thousands like him. Gazing at the stars and rising in the world were all Uplift. Marrying a good wife and marrying a rich wife were all Making Good. But he was not a cynical scoundrel; or he would simply have come back and jilted or cut you as the case might be. He could not face you; while you were there, half of his broken ideal was left.

'I did not tell the Admiral; but somebody did. Word came to him somehow, during the last grand parade on board, that his friend the family lawyer had betrayed him. He was in such a towering passion that he did what he could never have done in his senses; came straight on shore in his cocked hat and gold lace to catch the criminal; he wired to the police station, and that was why the Inspector was wandering round the Green Man. Lieutenant Rook followed him on shore because he suspected some family trouble and had half a hope he might help and put himself right. Hence his hesitating behaviour. As for his drawing his sword when he dropped behind and thought he was alone, well that's a matter of imagination. He was a romantic person who had dreamed of swords and run away to sea; and found himself in a service where he wasn't even allowed to wear a sword except about once in three years. He thought he was quite alone on the sands where he played as a boy. If you don't understand what he did, I can only say, like Stevenson, "you will never be a pirate." Also you will never be a poet; and you have never been a boy.'

'I never have,' answered Olive gravely, 'and yet I think I understand.'

'Almost every man,' continued the priest musing, 'will play with anything shaped like a sword or dagger, even if it is a paper-knife. That is why I thought it so odd when the lawyer didn't.'

'What do you mean?' asked Burns, 'didn't what?'

'Why, didn't you notice,' answered Brown, 'at that first meeting in the office, the lawyer played with a pen and not with a paper-knife; though he had a beautiful bright steel paper-knife in the pattern of a stiletto? The pens were dusty and splashed with ink; but the knife had just been cleaned. But he did not play with it. There are limits to the irony of assassins.'

After a silence the Inspector said, like one waking from a dream: 'Look here . . . I don't know whether I'm on my head or my heels; I don't know whether you think you've got to the end; but I haven't got to the beginning. Where do you get all this lawyer stuff from? What started you out on that trail?'

Father Brown laughed curtly and without mirth.

'The murderer made a slip at the start,' he said, 'and I can't think why nobody else noticed it. When you brought the first news of the death to the solicitor's office, nobody was supposed to know anything there, except that the Admiral was expected home. When you said he was drowned, I asked when it happened and Mr Dyke asked where the corpse was found.'

He paused a moment to knock out his pipe and resumed reflectively:

'Now when you are simply told of a seaman, returning from the sea, that he has been drowned, it is natural to assume that he has been drowned at sea. At any rate, to allow that he may have been drowned at sea. If he had been washed overboard, or gone down with his ship, or had his body "committed to the deep", there would be no reason to expect his body to be found at all. The moment that man asked where it was found, I was sure he knew where it was found. Because he had put it there. Nobody but the murderer need have thought of anything so unlikely as a seaman being drowned in a land-locked pool a few hundred yards from the sea. That is why I suddenly felt sick and turned green, I dare say; as green as the Green Man. I never *can* get used to finding myself suddenly sitting beside a murderer. So I had to turn it off by talking in parables; but the parable meant something, after all. I said that the body was covered with green scum, but it might just as well have been seaweed.'

It is fortunate that tragedy can never kill comedy and that the two can run side by side; and that while the only acting partner of the business of Messrs. Willis, Hardman and Dyke blew his brains out when the Inspector entered the house to arrest him, Olive and Roger were calling to each other across the sands at evening, as they did when they were children together.

5
The Crime of the Communist

Three men came out from under the low-browed Tudor arch in the mellow façade of Mandeville College, into the strong evening sunlight of a summer day which seemed as if it would never end; and in that sunlight they saw something that blasted like lightning; well fitted to be the shock of their lives.

Even before they had realized anything in the way of a catastrophe, they were conscious of a contrast. They themselves, in a curious quiet way, were quite harmonious with their surroundings. Though the Tudor arches that ran like a cloister round the College gardens had been built four hundred years ago, at that moment when the Gothic fell from heaven and bowed, or almost crouched, over the cosier chambers of Humanism and the Revival of Learning – though they themselves were in modern clothes (that is in clothes whose ugliness would have amazed any of the four centuries) yet something in the spirit of the place made them all at one. The gardens had been tended so carefully as to achieve the final triumph of looking careless; the very flowers seemed beautiful by accident, like elegant weeds; and the modern costumes had at least any picturesqueness that can be produced by being untidy. The first of the three, a tall, bald, bearded maypole of a man, was a familiar figure in the Quad in cap and gown; the gown slipped off one of his sloping shoulders. The second was very square-shouldered, short and compact, with a rather jolly grin, commonly clad in a jacket, with his gown over his arm. The third was even shorter and much shabbier, in black clerical clothes. But they all seemed suitable to Mandeville College; and the indescribable atmosphere of the two ancient and unique Universities of England. They fitted into it and they faded into it; which is there regarded as most fitting.

The two men seated on garden chairs by a little table were a sort of brilliant blot on this grey-green landscape. They were clad mostly in black and yet they glittered from head to heel, from their burnished top hats to their perfectly polished boots. It was dimly felt as an outrage that anybody should be so well dressed in the well-bred freedom of Mandeville College. The only excuse was that they were foreigners. One was an American, a millionaire named Hake, dressed in the spotlessly and sparklingly gentlemanly manner known only to the rich of New York. The other, who added to all these things the outrage of an astrakhan overcoat (to say nothing of a pair of florid whiskers), was a German Count of great wealth, the shortest part of whose name was Von Zimmern. The mystery of this story, however, is not the mystery of why they were there. They were there for the reason that commonly explains the meeting of incongruous things; they proposed to give the College some money. They had come in support of a plan supported by several financiers and magnates of many countries, for founding a new Chair of Economics at Mandeville College. They had inspected the College with that tireless conscientious sightseeing of which no sons of Eve are capable except the American and the German. And now they were resting from their labours and looking solemnly at the College gardens. So far so good.

The three other men, who had already met them, passed with a vague salutation; but one of them stopped; the smallest of the three, in the black clerical clothes.

'I say,' he said, with rather the air of a frightened rabbit, 'I don't like the look of those men.'

'Good God! Who could?' ejaculated the tall man, who happened to be the Master of Mandeville. 'At least we have some rich men who don't go about dressed up like tailors' dummies.'

'Yes,' hissed the little cleric, 'that's what I mean. Like tailors' dummies.'

'Why, what do you mean?' asked the shorter of the other men, sharply.

'I mean they're like horrible waxworks,' said the cleric in a faint voice. 'I mean they don't move. Why don't they move?'

Suddenly starting out of his dim retirement, he darted across the garden and touched the German Baron on the elbow. The German Baron fell over, chair and all, and the trousered legs that stuck up in the air were as stiff as the legs of the chair.

Mr Gideon P. Hake continued to gaze at the College gardens with glassy eyes; but the parallel of a waxwork confirmed the impression that they were like eyes made of glass. Somehow the rich sunlight and the coloured garden increased the creepy impression of a stiffly dressed doll; a marionette on an Italian stage. The small man in black, who was a priest named Brown, tentatively touched the millionaire on the shoulder, and the millionaire fell sideways, but horribly all of a piece, like something carved in wood.

'*Rigor mortis*,' said Father Brown, 'and so soon. But it does vary a good deal.'

The reason the first three men had joined the other two men so late (not to say too late) will best be understood by noting what had happened just inside the building, behind the Tudor archway, but a short time before they came out. They had all dined together in Hall, at the High Table; but the two foreign philanthropists, slaves of duty in the matter of seeing everything, had solemnly gone back to the chapel, of which one cloister and a staircase remained unexamined; promising to rejoin the rest in the garden, to examine as earnestly the College cigars. The rest, in a more reverent and right-minded spirit, had adjourned as usual to the long narrow oak table, round which the after-dinner wine had circulated, for all anybody knew, ever since the College had been founded in the Middle Ages by Sir John Mandeville, for the encouragement of telling stories. The Master, with the big fair beard and the bald brow, took the head of the table, and the squat man in the square jacket sat on his left; for he was the Bursar or business man of the College. Next to him, on that side of the table, sat a queer-looking man with what could only be called a crooked face; for its dark tufts of moustache and eyebrow, slanting at contrary angles, made a sort of zig-zag, as if half his face were puckered or paralysed. His name was Byles; he was the lecturer in Roman History, and his political opinions were founded on those of Coriolanus, not to mention Tarquinius Superbus. This tart Toryism, and rabidly reactionary view of all current problems, was not altogether unknown among the more old-fashioned sort of dons; but in the case of Byles there was a suggestion that it was a result rather than a cause of his acerbity. More than one sharp observer had received the impression that there was something really wrong with Byles; that some secret or some great misfortune had embittered him; as if that half-withered face had really been blasted like a storm-stricken tree.

Beyond him again sat Father Brown and at the end of the table a Professor of Chemistry, large and blond and bland, with eyes that were sleepy and perhaps a little sly. It was well known that this natural philosopher regarded the other philosophers, of a more classical tradition, very much as old fogies. On the other side of the table, opposite Father Brown, was a very swarthy and silent young man, with a black pointed beard, introduced because somebody had insisted on having a Chair of Persian; opposite the sinister Byles was a very mild-looking little Chaplain, with a head like an egg. Opposite the Bursar, and at the right hand of the Master, was an empty chair; and there were many there who were glad to see it empty.

'I don't know whether Craken is coming,' said the Master, not without a nervous glance at the chair, which contrasted with the usual languid freedom of his demeanour. 'I believe in giving people a lot of rope myself; but I confess I've reached the point of being glad when he is here, merely because he isn't anywhere else.'

'Never know what he'll be up to next,' said the Bursar cheerfully, 'especially when he's instructing the young.'

'A brilliant fellow, but fiery of course,' said the Master, with a rather abrupt relapse into reserve.

'Fireworks are fiery, and also brilliant,' growled old Byles, 'but I don't want to be burned in my bed so that Craken can figure as a real Guy Fawkes.'

'Do you really *think* he would join a physical force revolution, if there were one,' asked the Bursar smiling.

'Well, *he* thinks he would,' said Byles sharply. 'Told a whole hall full of undergraduates the other day that nothing now could avert the Class War turning into a real war, with killing in the streets of the town; and it didn't matter, so long as it ended in Communism and the victory of the working-class.'

'The Class War,' mused the Master, with a sort of distaste mellowed by distance; for he had known William Morris long ago and been familiar enough with the more artistic and leisurely Socialists. 'I never can understand all this about the Class War. When I was young, Socialism was supposed to mean saying that there are no classes.'

''Nother way of saying that Socialists are no class,' said Byles with sour relish.

365

'Of course, you'd be more against them than I should,' said the Master thoughtfully, 'but I suppose my Socialism is almost as old-fashioned as your Toryism. Wonder what our young friends really think. What do you think, Baker?' he said abruptly to the Bursar on his left.

'Oh, I *don't* think, as the vulgar saying is,' said the Bursar laughing. 'You must remember I'm a very vulgar person. I'm not a thinker. I'm only a business man; and as a business man I think it's all bosh. You can't make men equal and it's damned bad business to pay them equal; especially a lot of them not worth paying for at all. Whatever it is, you've got to take the practical way out, because it's the only way out. It's not our fault if nature made everything a scramble.'

'I agree with you there,' said the Professor of Chemistry, speaking with a lisp that seemed childish in so large a man. 'Communism pretends to be oh so modern; but it is not. Throw-back to the superstitions of monks and primitive tribes. A scientific government, with a really ethical responsibility to posterity, would be always looking for the line of promise and progress; not levelling and flattening it all back into the mud again. Socialism is sentimentalism; and more dangerous than a pestilence, for in that at least the fittest would survive.'

The Master smiled a little sadly. 'You know you and I will never feel quite the same about differences of opinion. Didn't somebody say up here, about walking with a friend by the river. "Not differing much, except in opinion." Isn't that the motto of a university? To have hundreds of opinions and not be opinionated. If people fall here, it's by what they are, not what they think. Perhaps I'm a relic of the eighteenth century; but I incline to the old sentimental heresy, "For forms of faith let graceless zealots fight; he can't be wrong whose life is in the right." What do you think about that, Father Brown?'

He glanced a little mischievously across at the priest and was mildly startled. For he had always found the priest very cheerful and amiable and easy to get on with; and his round face was mostly solid with good humour. But for some reason the priest's face at this moment was knotted with a frown much more sombre than any the company had ever seen on it; so that for an instant that commonplace countenance actually looked darker and more ominous than the haggard face of Byles. An instant later the cloud seemed to have passed; but Father Brown still spoke with a certain sobriety and firmness.

'I don't believe in that, anyhow,' he said shortly. 'How can his life be in the right, if his whole view of life is wrong? That's a modern muddle that arose because people didn't know how much views of life can differ. Baptists and Methodists knew they didn't differ very much in morality; but then they didn't differ very much in religion or philosophy. It's quite different when you pass from the Baptists to the Anabaptists; or from the Theosophists to the Thugs. Heresy always does affect morality, if it's heretical enough. I suppose a man may honestly believe that thieving isn't wrong. But what's the good of saying that he honestly believes in dishonesty?'

'Damned good,' said Byles with a ferocious contortion of feature, believed by many to be meant for a friendly smile. 'And that's why I object to having a Chair of Theoretical Thieving in this College.'

'Well, you're all very down on Communism, of course,' said the Master, with a sigh. 'But do you really think there's so much of it to be down on? Are any of your heresies really big enough to be dangerous?'

'I think they have grown so big,' said Father Brown gravely, 'that in some circles they are already taken for granted. They are actually unconscious. That is, without conscience.'

'And the end of it,' said Byles, 'will be the ruin of this country.'

'The end will be something worse,' said Father Brown.

A shadow shot or slid rapidly along the panelled wall opposite, as swiftly followed by the figure that had flung it; a tall but stooping figure with a vague outline like a bird of prey; accentuated by the fact that its sudden appearance and swift passage were like those of a bird startled and flying from a bush. It was only the figure of a long-limbed, high-shouldered man with long drooping moustaches, in fact, familiar enough to them all; but something in the twilight and candlelight and the flying and streaking shadow connected it strangely with the priest's unconscious words of omen; for all the world, as if those words had indeed been an augury, in the old Roman sense; and the sign of it the flight of a bird. Perhaps Mr Byles might have given a lecture on such Roman augury; and especially on that bird of ill-omen.

The tall man shot along the wall like his own shadow until he sank into the empty chair on the Master's right, and looked across at the Bursar and the rest with hollow and cavernous eyes. His hanging hair and moustache were quite fair, but his eyes were so deep-set that they might have been black. Everyone knew, or could guess, who the newcomer was; but an incident instantly followed that sufficiently illuminated the situation. The Professor of Roman History rose stiffly to his feet and stalked out of the room, indicating with little *finesse* his feelings about sitting at the same table with the Professor of Theoretical Thieving, otherwise the Communist, Mr Craken.

The Master of Mandeville covered the awkward situation with nervous grace. 'I was defending you, or some aspects of you, my dear Craken,' he said smiling, 'though I am sure you would find me quite indefensible. After all, I can't forget that the old Socialist friends of my youth had a very fine ideal of fraternity and comradeship. William Morris put it all in a sentence, "Fellowship is heaven; and lack of fellowship is hell."'

'Dons as Democrats; see headline,' said Mr Craken rather disagreeably. 'And is Hard-Case Hake going to dedicate the new Commercial Chair to the memory of William Morris?'

'Well,' said the Master, still maintaining a desperate geniality, 'I hope we may say, in a sense, that all our Chairs are Chairs of good-fellowship.'

'Yes; that's the academic version of the Morris maxim,' growled Craken. '"A Fellowship is heaven; and lack of a Fellowship is hell."'

'Don't be so cross, Craken,' interposed the Bursar briskly. 'Take some port. Tenby, pass the port to Mr Craken.'

'Oh well, I'll have a glass,' said the Communist Professor a little less ungraciously. 'I really came down here to have a smoke in the garden. Then I looked out of the window and saw your two precious millionaires were actually blooming in the garden; fresh, innocent buds. After all, it might be worth while to give them a bit of my mind.'

The Master had risen under cover of his last conventional cordiality, and was only too glad to leave the Bursar to do his best with the Wild Man. Others had risen, and the groups at the table had begun to break up; and the Bursar and Mr Craken were left more or less alone at the end of the long table. Only Father Brown continued to sit staring into vacancy with a rather cloudy expression.

'Oh, as to that,' said the Bursar. 'I'm pretty tired of them myself, to tell the truth; I've been with them the best part of a day going into facts and figures and all the business of this new Professorship. But look here, Craken,' and he leaned across the table and spoke with a sort of soft emphasis, 'you really needn't cut up so rough about this new Professorship. It doesn't really interfere with your subject. You're the only Professor of Political Economy at Mandeville and, though I don't pretend to agree with your notions, everybody knows you've got a European reputation. This is a special subject they call Applied Economics. Well, even to-day, as I told you, I've had a hell of a lot of Applied Economics. In other words, I've had to talk business with two business men. Would you particularly want to do that? Would you envy it? Would you stand it? Isn't that evidence enough that there is a separate subject and may well be a separate Chair?'

'Good God,' cried Craken with the intense invocation of the atheist. 'Do you think I don't want to apply Economics? Only, when we apply it, you call it red ruin and anarchy; and when you apply it, I take the liberty of calling it exploitation. If only you fellows would apply Economics, it's just possible that people might get something to eat. We are the practical people; and that's why you're afraid of us. That's why you have to get two greasy Capitalists to start another Lectureship; just because I've let the cat out of the bag.'

'Rather a wild cat, wasn't it,' said the Bursar smiling, 'that you let out of the bag?'

'And rather a gold-bag, wasn't it,' said Craken, 'that you are tying the cat up in again?'

'Well, I don't suppose we shall ever agree about all that,' said the other. 'But those fellows have come out of their chapel into the garden; and if you want to have your smoke there, you'd better come.' He watched with some amusement his companion fumbling in all his pockets till he produced a pipe, and then, gazing at it with an abstracted air, Craken rose to his feet, but even in doing so, seemed to be feeling all over himself again. Mr Baker the Bursar ended the controversy with a happy laugh of reconciliation. 'You are the practical people, and you will blow up the town with dynamite. Only you'll probably forget the dynamite, as I bet you've forgotten the tobacco. Never mind, take a fill of mine. Matches?' He threw a tobacco pouch and its accessories across the table; to be caught by Mr Craken with that dexterity never forgotten by a cricketer, even when he adopts opinions generally regarded as not cricket. The two men rose together; but Baker could not forbear remarking, 'Are you really the only practical people? Isn't there anything to be said for the Applied Economics, that remembers to carry a tobacco pouch as well as a pipe?'

Craken looked at him with smouldering eyes; and said at last, after slowly draining the last of his wine:

'Let's say there's another sort of practicality. I dare say I do forget details and so on. What I want you to understand is this' – he automatically returned the pouch; but his eyes were far away and jet-burning, almost terrible – 'because the inside of our intellect has changed, because we really have a new idea of right, we shall do things you think really wrong. And they will be very practical.'

'Yes,' said Father Brown, suddenly coming out of his trance. 'That's exactly what I said.'

He looked across at Craken with a glassy and rather ghastly smile, saying: 'Mr Craken and I are in complete agreement.'

'Well,' said Baker, 'Craken is going out to smoke a pipe with the plutocrats; but I doubt whether it will be a pipe of peace.'

He turned rather abruptly and called to an aged attendant in the background. Mandeville was one of the last of the very old-fashioned Colleges; and even Craken was one of the first of the Communists; before the Bolshevism of to-day. 'That reminds me,' the Bursar was saying, 'as you won't hand round your peace pipe, we must send out the cigars to our distinguished guests. If they're smokers they must be longing for a smoke; for they've been nosing about in the chapel since feeding-time.'

Craken exploded with a savage and jarring laugh. 'Oh, I'll take them their cigars,' he said. 'I'm only a proletarian.'

Baker and Brown and the attendant were all witnesses to the fact that the Communist strode furiously into the garden to confront the millionaires; but nothing more was seen or heard of them until, as is already recorded, Father Brown found them dead in their chairs.

It was agreed that the Master and the priest should remain to guard the scene of tragedy, while the Bursar, younger and more rapid in his movements, ran off to fetch doctors and policemen. Father Brown approached the table on which one of the cigars had burned itself away all but an inch or two; the other had dropped from the hand and been dashed out into dying sparks on the crazy-pavement. The Master of Mandeville sat down rather shakily on a sufficiently distant seat and buried his bald brow in his hands. Then he looked up at first rather wearily; and then he looked very startled indeed and broke the stillness of the garden with a word like a small explosion of horror.

There was a certain quality about Father Brown which might some-times be called blood-curdling. He always thought about what he was doing and never about whether it was done; he would do the most ugly or horrible or undignified or dirty things as calmly as a surgeon. There was a certain blank, in his simple mind, of all those things commonly associated with being superstitious or sentimental. He sat down on the chair from which the corpse had fallen, picked up the cigar the corpse had partially smoked, carefully detached the ash, examined the butt-end and then stuck it in his mouth and lit it. It looked like some obscene and grotesque antic in derision of the dead; and it seemed to him to be the most ordinary common sense. A cloud floated upwards like the smoke of some savage sacrifice and idolatry; but to Father Brown it appeared a perfectly self-evident fact that the only way to find out what a cigar is like is to smoke it. Nor did it lessen the horror for his old friend, the Master of Mandeville, to have a dim but shrewd guess that Father Brown was, upon the possibilities of the case, risking his own life.

'No; I think that's all right,' said the priest, putting the stump down again. 'Jolly good cigars. Your cigars. Not American or German. I don't think there's anything odd about the cigar itself; but they'd better take care of the ashes. These men were poisoned somehow with the sort of stuff that stiffens the body quickly . . . By the way, there goes somebody who knows more about it than we do.'

The Master sat up with a curiously uncomfortable jolt; for indeed the large shadow which had fallen across the pathway preceded a figure which, however heavy, was almost as soft-footed as a shadow. Professor Wadham, eminent occupant of the Chair of Chemistry, always moved very quietly in spite of his size, and there was nothing odd about his strolling in the garden; yet there seemed something unnaturally neat in his appearing at the exact moment when chemistry was mentioned.

Professor Wadham prided himself on his quietude; some would say his insensibility. He did not turn a hair on his flattened flaxen head, but stood looking down at the dead men with a shade of something like indifference on his large froglike face. Only when he looked at the cigar-ash, which the priest had preserved, he touched it with one finger; then he seemed to stand even stiller than before; but in the shadow of his face his eyes for an instant seemed to shoot out telescopically like one of his own microscopes. He had certainly realized or recognized something; but he said nothing.

'I don't know where anyone is to begin in this business,' said the Master.

'I should begin,' said Father Brown, 'by asking where these unfortunate men had been most of the time to-day.'

'They were messing about in my laboratory for a good time,' said Wadham, speaking for the first time. 'Baker often comes up to have a chat, and this time he brought his two patrons to inspect my department. But I think they went everywhere; real tourists. I know they went to the chapel and even into the tunnel under the crypt, where you have to light candles; instead of digesting their food like sane men. Baker seems to have taken them everywhere.'

'Were they interested in anything particular in your department?' asked the priest. 'What were you doing there just then?'

The Professor of Chemistry murmured a chemical formula beginning with 'sulphate', and ending with something that sounded like 'silentium'; unintelligible to both his hearers. He then wandered wearily away and sat on a remote bench in the sun, closing his eyes, but turning up his large face with heavy forbearance.

At this point, by a sharp contrast, the lawns were crossed by a brisk figure travelling as rapidly and as straight as a bullet; and Father Brown recognized the neat black clothes and shrewd doglike face of a police surgeon whom he had met in the poorer parts of the town. He was the first to arrive of the official contingent.

'Look here,' said the Master to the priest, before the doctor was within earshot, 'I must know something. Did you mean what you said about Communism being a real danger and leading to crime?'

'Yes,' said Father Brown smiling rather grimly, 'I have really noticed the spread of some Communist ways and influences; and, in one sense, this is a Communist crime.'

'Thank you,' said the Master. 'Then I must go off and see to something at once. Tell the authorities I'll be back in ten minutes.'

The Master had vanished into one of the Tudor archways at just about the moment when the police-doctor had reached the table and cheerfully recognized Father Brown. On the latter's suggestion that they should sit down at the tragic table, Dr Blake threw one sharp and doubtful glance at the big, bland and seemingly somnolent chemist, who occupied a more remote seat. He was duly informed of the Professor's identity, and what had so far been gathered of the Professor's evidence; and listened to it silently while conducting a preliminary examination of the dead bodies. Naturally, he seemed more concentrated on the actual corpses than on the hearsay evidence, until one detail suddenly distracted him entirely from the science of anatomy.

'What did the Professor say he was working at?' he inquired.

Father Brown patiently repeated the chemical formula he did not understand.

'What?' snapped Dr Blake, like a pistol-shot. 'Gosh! This is pretty frightful!'

'Because it's poison?' inquired Father Brown.

'Because it's piffle,' replied Dr Blake. 'It's simply nonsense. The Professor is quite a famous chemist. Why is a famous chemist deliberately talking nonsense?'

'Well, I think I know that one,' answered Father Brown mildly. 'He is talking nonsense, because he is telling lies. He is concealing something; and he wanted specially to conceal it from these two men and their representatives.'

The doctor lifted his eyes from the two men and looked across at the almost unnaturally immobile figure of the great chemist. He might almost have been asleep; a garden butterfly had settled upon him and seemed to turn his stillness into that of a stone idol. The large folds of his froglike face reminded the doctor of the hanging skins of a rhinoceros.

'Yes,' said Father Brown, in a very low voice. 'He is a wicked man.'

'God damn it all!' cried the doctor, suddenly moved to his very depths. 'Do you mean that a great scientific man like that deals in murder?'

'Fastidious critics would have complained of his dealing in murder,' said the priest dispassionately. 'I don't say I'm very fond of people dealing in murder in that way myself. But what's much more to the point – I'm sure that *these* poor fellows were among his fastidious critics.'

'You mean they found his secret and he silenced them?' said Blake frowning. 'But what in hell was his secret? How could a man murder on a large scale in a place like this?'

'I have told you his secret,' said the priest. 'It is a secret of the soul. He is a bad man. For heaven's sake don't fancy I say that because he and I are of opposite schools or traditions. I have a crowd of scientific friends; and most of them are heroically disinterested. Even of the most sceptical, I would only say they are rather irrationally disinterested. But now and then you do get a man who is a materialist, in the sense of a beast. I repeat he's a bad man. Much worse than –' And Father Brown seemed to hesitate for a word.

'You mean much worse than the Communist?' suggested the other.

'No; I mean much worse than the murderer,' said Father Brown.

He got to his feet in an abstracted manner; and hardly realized that his companion was staring at him.

'But didn't you mean,' asked Blake at last, 'that this Wadham is the murderer?'

'Oh, no,' said Father Brown more cheerfully. 'The murderer is a much more sympathetic and understandable person. He at least was desperate; and had the excuses of sudden rage and despair.'

'Why,' cried the doctor, 'do you mean it was the Communist after all?'

It was at this very moment, appropriately enough, that the police officials appeared with an announcement that seemed to conclude the case in a most decisive and satisfactory manner. They had been somewhat delayed in reaching the scene of the crime, by the simple fact that they had already captured the criminal. Indeed, they had captured him almost at the gates of their own official residence. They had already had reason to suspect the activities of Craken the Communist during various disorders in the town; when they heard of the outrage they felt it safe to arrest him; and found the arrest thoroughly justified. For, as Inspector Cook radiantly explained to dons and doctors on the lawn of Mandeville garden, no sooner was the notorious Communist searched than it was found that he was actually carrying a box of poisoned matches.

The moment Father Brown heard the word 'matches', he jumped from his seat as if a match had been lighted under him.

374

'Ah,' he cried, with a sort of universal radiance, 'and now it's all clear.'

'What do you mean by all clear?' demanded the Master of Mandeville, who had returned in all the pomp of his own officialism to match the pomp of the police officials now occupying the College like a victorious army. 'Do you mean you are convinced now that the case against Craken is clear?'

'I mean that Craken is cleared,' said Father Brown firmly, 'and the case against Craken is cleared away. Do you really believe Craken is the kind of man who would go about poisoning people with matches?'

'That's all very well,' replied the Master, with the troubled expression he had never lost since the first sensation occurred. 'But it was you yourself who said that fanatics with false principles may do wicked things. For that matter, it was you yourself who said that Communism is cropping up everywhere and Communistic habits spreading.'

Father Brown laughed in a rather shamefaced manner.

'As to the last point,' he said, 'I suppose I owe you all an apology. I seem to be always making a mess of things with my silly little jokes.'

'Jokes!' repeated the Master, staring rather indignantly.

'Well,' explained the priest, rubbing his head. 'When I talked about a Communist habit spreading, I only meant a habit I happen to have noticed about two or three times even to-day. It is a Communist habit by no means confined to Communists. It is the extraordinary habit of so many men, especially Englishmen, of putting other people's matchboxes in their pockets without remembering to return them. Of course, it seems an awfully silly little trifle to talk about. But it does happen to be the way the crime was committed.'

'It sounds to me quite crazy,' said the doctor.

'Well, if almost any man may forget to return matches, you can bet your boots that Craken would forget to return them. So the poisoner who had prepared the matches got rid of them on to Craken, by the simple process of lending them and not getting them back. A really admirable way of shedding responsibility; because Craken himself would be perfectly unable to imagine where he had got them from. But when he used them quite innocently to light the cigars he offered to our two visitors, he was caught in an obvious trap; one of those too obvious traps. He was the bold bad Revolutionist murdering two millionaires.'

'Well, who else would want to murder them?' growled the doctor.

'Ah, who indeed?' replied the priest; and his voice changed to much greater gravity. 'There we come to the other thing I told you; and that, let me tell you, was not a joke. I told you that heresies and false doctrines had become common and conversational; that everybody was used to them; that nobody really noticed them. Did you think I meant *Communism* when I said that? Why, it was just the other way. You were all as nervous as cats about Communism; and you watched Craken like a wolf. Of course, Communism is a heresy; but it isn't a heresy that you people take for granted. It is Capitalism you take for granted; or rather the vices of Capitalism disguised as a dead Darwinism. Do you recall what you were all saying in the Common Room, about life being only a scramble, and nature demanding the survival of the fittest, and how it doesn't matter whether the poor are paid justly or not? Why *that* is the heresy that you have grown accustomed to, my friends; and it's every bit as much a heresy as Communism. That's the anti-Christian morality or immorality that you take quite naturally. And that's the immorality that has made a man a murderer to-day.'

'What man?' cried the Master, and his voice cracked with a sudden weakness.

'Let me approach it another way,' said the priest placidly. 'You all talk as if Craken ran away; but he didn't. When the two men toppled over, he ran down the street, summoned the doctor merely by shouting through the window, and shortly afterwards was trying to summon the police. That was how he was arrested. But doesn't it strike you, now one comes to think of it, that Mr Baker the Bursar is rather a long time looking for the police?'

'What is he doing then?' asked the Master sharply.

'I fancy he's destroying papers, or perhaps ransacking these men's rooms to see they haven't left us a letter. Or it may have something to do with our friend Wadham. Where does he come in? That is really very simple and a sort of joke too. Mr Wadham is experimenting in poisons for the next war; and has something of which a whiff of flame will stiffen a man dead. Of course, he had nothing to do with killing these men; but he did conceal his chemical secret for a very simple reason. One of them was a Puritan Yankee and the other a cosmopolitan Jew; and those two types are often fanatical Pacifists. They would have called it planning murder and probably refused to help the College. But Baker was a friend of Wadham and it was easy for him to dip matches in the new material.'

Another peculiarity of the little priest was that his mind was all of a piece, and he was unconscious of many incongruities; he would change the note of his talk from something quite public to something quite private, without any particular embarrassment. On this occasion, he made most of the company stare with mystification, by beginning to talk to one person when he had just been talking to ten; quite indifferent to the fact that only the one could have any notion of what he was talking about.

'I'm sorry if I misled you, doctor, by that maundering metaphysical digression on the man of sin,' he said apologetically. 'Of course it had nothing to do with the murder; but the truth is I'd forgotten all about the murder for the moment. I'd forgotten everything, you see, but a sort of vision of that fellow, with his vast unhuman face, squatting among the flowers like some blind monster of the Stone Age. And I was thinking that some men are pretty monstrous, like men of stone; but it was all irrelevant. Being bad inside has very little to do with committing crimes outside. The worst criminals have committed no crimes. The practical point is why did the practical criminal commit this crime. Why did Baker the Bursar want to kill these men? That's all that concerns us now. The answer is the answer to the question I've asked twice. Where were these men most of the time, apart from nosing in chapels or laboratories? By the Bursar's own account, they were talking business with the Bursar.

'Now, with all respect to the dead, I do not exactly grovel before the intellect of these two financiers. Their views on economics and ethics were heathen and heartless. Their views on Peace were tosh. Their views on Port were even more deplorable. But one thing they did understand; and that was business. And it took them a remarkably short time to discover that the business man in charge of the funds of this College was a swindler. Or shall I say, a true follower of the doctrine of the unlimited struggle for life and the survival of the fittest.'

'You mean they were going to expose him and he killed them before they could speak,' said the doctor frowning. 'There are a lot of details I don't understand.'

377

'There are some details I'm not sure of myself,' said the priest frankly. 'I suspect all that business of candles underground had something to do with abstracting the millionaires' own matches, or perhaps making sure they had no matches. But I'm sure of the main gesture, the gay and careless gesture of Baker tossing his matches to the careless Craken. That gesture was the murderous blow.'

'There's one thing I don't understand,' said the Inspector. 'How did Baker know that Craken wouldn't light up himself then and there at the table and become an unwanted corpse?'

The face of Father Brown became almost heavy with reproach; and his voice had a sort of mournful yet generous warmth in it.

'Well, hang it all,' he said, 'he was only an atheist.'

'I'm afraid I don't know what you mean,' said the Inspector, politely.

'He only wanted to abolish God,' explained Father Brown in a temperate and reasonable tone. 'He only wanted to destroy the Ten Commandments and root up all the religion and civilization that had made him, and wash out all the common sense of ownership and honesty; and let his culture and his country be flattened out by savages from the ends of the earth. That's all he wanted. You have no right to accuse him of anything beyond that. Hang it all, everybody draws the line somewhere! And you come here and calmly suggest that a Mandeville Man of the old generation (for Craken was of the old generation, whatever his views) would have begun to smoke, or even strike a match, while he was still drinking the College Port, of the vintage of '08 – no, no; men are not so utterly without laws and limits as all that! I was there; I saw him; he had not finished his wine, and you ask me why he did not *smoke*! No such anarchic question has ever shaken the arches of Mandeville College ... Funny place, Mandeville College. Funny place, Oxford. Funny place, England.'

'But you haven't anything particular to do with Oxford?' asked the doctor curiously.

'I have to do with England,' said Father Brown. 'I come from there. And the funniest thing of all is that even if you love it and belong to it, you still can't make head or tail of it.'

6

The Point of a Pin

Father Brown always declared that he solved this problem in his sleep. And this was true, though in rather an odd fashion; because it occurred at a time when his sleep was rather disturbed. It was disturbed very early in the morning by the hammering that began in the huge building, or half-building, that was in process of erection opposite to his rooms; a colossal pile of flats still mostly covered with scaffolding and with boards announcing Messrs. Swindon & Sand as the builders and owners. The hammering was renewed at regular intervals and was easily recognizable: because Messrs. Swindon & Sand specialized in some new American system of cement flooring which, in spite of its subsequent smoothness, solidity, impenetrability and permanent comfort (as described in the advertisements), had to be clamped down at certain points with heavy tools. Father Brown endeavoured, however, to extract exiguous comfort from it; saying that it always woke him up in time for the very earliest Mass, and was therefore something almost in the nature of a carillon. After all, he said, it was almost as poetic that Christians should be awakened by hammers as by bells. As a fact, however, the building operations were a little on his nerves, for another reason. For there was hanging like a cloud over the half-built skyscraper the possibility of a Labour crisis, which the newspapers doggedly insisted on describing as a Strike. As a matter of fact, if ever it happened, it would be a Lock-out. But he worried a good deal about whether it would happen. And it might be questioned whether hammering is more of a strain on the attention because it may go on for ever, or because it may stop at any minute.

'As a mere matter of taste and fancy,' said Father Brown, staring up at the edifice with his owlish spectacles, 'I rather wish it would stop. I wish all houses would stop while they still have the scaffolding up. It seems almost a pity that houses are ever finished. They look so fresh and hopeful with all that fairy filigree of white wood, all light and bright in the sun; and a man so often only finishes a house by turning it into a tomb.'

As he turned away from the object of his scrutiny, he nearly ran into a man who had just darted across the road towards him. It was a man whom he knew slightly, but sufficiently to regard him (in the circumstances) as something of a bird of ill-omen. Mr Mastyk was a squat man with a square head that looked hardly European, dressed with a heavy dandyism that seemed rather too consciously Europeanized. But Brown had seen him lately talking to young Sand of the building firm; and he did not like it. This man Mastyk was the head of an organization rather new in English industrial politics; produced by extremes at both ends; a definite army of non-Union and largely alien labour hired out in gangs to various firms; and he was obviously hovering about in the hope of hiring it out to this one. In short, he might negotiate some way of out-manoeuvring the Trade Union and flooding the works with blacklegs. Father Brown had been drawn into some of the debates, being in some sense called in on both sides. And as the Capitalists all reported that, to their positive knowledge, he was a Bolshevist; and as the Bolshevists all testified that he was a reactionary rigidly attached to *bourgeois* ideologies, it may be inferred that he talked a certain amount of sense without any appreciable effect on anybody. The news brought by Mr Mastyk, however, was calculated to jerk everybody out of the ordinary rut of the dispute.

'They want you to go over there at once,' said Mr Mastyk, in awkwardly accented English. 'There is a threat to murder.'

Father Brown followed his guide in silence up several stairways and ladders to a platform of the unfinished building, on which were grouped the more or less familiar figures of the heads of the building business. They included even what had once been the head of it; though the head had been for some time rather a head in the clouds. It was at least a head in a coronet, that hid it from human sight like a cloud. Lord Stanes, in other words, had not only retired from the business but been caught up into the House of Lords and disappeared. His rare reappearances were languid and somewhat dreary; but this one, in conjunction with that of Mastyk, seemed none the less menacing. Lord Stanes was a lean, long-headed, hollow-eyed man with very faint fair hair fading into baldness; and he was the most evasive person the priest had ever met. He was unrivalled in the true Oxford talent of saying, 'No doubt you're right,' so as to sound like, 'No doubt you think you're right,' or of merely remarking, 'You think so?' so as to imply the acid addition. 'You would.' But Father Brown fancied that the man was not merely bored but faintly embittered, though whether at being called down from Olympus to control such trade squabbles, or merely at not being really any longer in control of them, it was difficult to guess.

On the whole, Father Brown rather preferred the more *bourgeois* group of partners, Sir Hubert Sand and his nephew Henry; though he doubted privately whether they really had very many ideologies. True, Sir Hubert Sand had obtained considerable celebrity in the newspapers; both as a patron of sport and as a patriot in many crises during and after the Great War. He had won notable distinction in France, for a man of his years, and had afterwards been featured as a triumphant captain of industry overcoming difficulties among the munition-workers. He had been called a Strong Man; but that was not his fault. He was in fact a heavy, hearty Englishman; a great swimmer; a good squire; an admirable amateur colonel. Indeed, something that can only be called a military make-up pervaded his appearance. He was growing stout, but he kept his shoulders set back; his curly hair and moustache were still brown while the colours of his face were already somewhat withered and faded. His nephew was a burly youth of the pushing, or rather shouldering, sort with a relatively small head thrust out on a thick neck, as if he went at things with his head down; a gesture somehow rendered rather quaint and boyish by the pince-nez that were balanced on his pugnacious pug nose.

Father Brown had looked at all these things before; and at that moment everybody was looking at something entirely new. In the centre of the wood-work there was nailed up a large loose flapping piece of paper on which something was scrawled in crude and almost crazy capital letters, as if the writer were either almost illiterate or were affecting or parodying illiteracy. The words actually ran: 'The Council of the Workers warns Hubert Sand that he will lower wages and lock out workmen at his peril. If the notices go out to-morrow, he will be dead by the justice of the people.'

Lord Stanes was just stepping back from his examination of the paper, and, looking across at his partner, he said with rather a curious intonation:

'Well, it's you they want to murder. Evidently I'm not considered worth murdering.'

One of those still electric shocks of fancy that sometimes thrilled Father Brown's mind in an almost meaningless way shot through him at that particular instant. He had a queer notion that the man who was speaking could not now be murdered, because he was already dead. It was, he cheerfully admitted, a perfectly senseless idea. But there was something that always gave him the creeps about the cold disenchanted detachment of the noble senior partner; about his cadaverous colour and inhospitable eyes. 'The fellow,' he thought in the same perverse mood, 'has green eyes and looks as if he had green blood.'

Anyhow, it was certain that Sir Hubert Sand had not got green blood. His blood, which was red enough in every sense, was creeping up into his withered or weather-beaten cheeks with all the warm fullness of life that belongs to the natural and innocent indignation of the good-natured.

'In all my life,' he said, in a strong voice and yet shakily, 'I have never had such a thing said or done about me. I may have differed –'

'We can none of us differ about this,' struck in his nephew impetuously. 'I've tried to get on with them, but this is a bit too thick.'

'You don't really think,' began Father Brown, 'that your workmen –'

'I say we may have differed,' said old Sand, still a little tremulously, 'God knows I never liked the idea of threatening English workmen with cheaper labour –'

'We none of us liked it,' said the young man, 'but if I know you, uncle, this has about settled it.'

Then after a pause he added, 'I suppose, as you say; we did disagree about details; but as to real policy –'

'My dear fellow,' said his uncle, comfortably. 'I hoped there would never be any real disagreement.' From which anybody who understands the English nation may rightly infer that there had been very considerable disagreement. Indeed the uncle and nephew differed almost as much as an Englishman and an American. The uncle had the English ideal of getting outside the business, and setting up a sort of an alibi as a country gentleman. The nephew had the American ideal of getting inside the business; of getting inside the very mechanism like a mechanic. And, indeed, he had worked with most of the mechanics and was familiar with most of the processes and tricks of the trade. And he was American again, in the fact that he did this partly as an employer to keep his men up to the mark, but in some vague way also as an equal, or at least with a pride in showing himself also as a worker. For this reason he had often appeared almost as a representative of the workers, on technical points which were a hundred miles away from his uncle's popular eminence in politics or sport. The memory of those many occasions, when young Henry had practically come out of the workshop in his shirt-sleeves, to demand some concession about the conditions of the work, lent a peculiar force and even violence to his present reaction the other way.

'Well, they've damned well locked themselves out this time,' he cried. 'After a threat like that there's simply nothing left but to defy them. There's nothing left but to sack them all now; instanter; on the spot. Otherwise we'll be the laughing-stock of the world.'

Old Sand frowned with equal indignation, but began slowly: 'I shall be very much criticized – '

'Criticized!' cried the young man shrilly. 'Criticized if you defy a threat of murder! Have you any notion how you'll be criticized if you don't defy it? Won't you enjoy the headlines? "Great Capitalist Terrorized" – "Employer Yields to Murder Threat."'

'Particularly,' said Lord Stanes, with something faintly unpleasant in his tone. 'Particularly when he has been in so many headlines already as "The Strong Man of Steel-Building".'

Sand had gone very red again and his voice came thickly from under his thick moustache. 'Of course you're right there. If these brutes think I'm afraid – '

At this point there was an interruption in the conversation of the group; and a slim young man came towards them swiftly. The first notable thing about him was that he was one of those whom men, and women too, think are just a little too nice-looking to look nice. He had beautiful dark curly hair and a silken moustache and he spoke like a gentleman, but with almost too refined and exactly modulated an accent. Father Brown knew him at once as Rupert Rae, the secretary of Sir

Hubert, whom he had often seen pottering about in Sir Hubert's house; but never with such impatience in his movements or such a wrinkle on his brow.

'I'm sorry, sir,' he said to his employer, 'but there's a man been hanging about over there. I've done my best to get rid of him. He's only got a letter, but he swears he must give it to you personally.'

'You mean he went first to my house?' said Sand, glancing swiftly at his secretary. 'I suppose you've been there all the morning.'

'Yes, sir,' said Mr Rupert Rae.

There was a short silence; and then Sir Hubert Sand curtly intimated that the man had better be brought along; and the man duly appeared.

Nobody, not even the least fastidious lady, would have said that the newcomer was too nice-looking. He had very large ears and a face like a frog, and he stared before him with an almost ghastly fixity, which Father Brown attributed to his having a glass eye. In fact, his fancy was tempted to equip the man with two glass eyes; with so glassy a stare did he contemplate the company. But the priest's experience, as distinct from his fancy, was able to suggest several natural causes for that unnatural waxwork glare; one of them being an abuse of the divine gift of fermented liquor. The man was short and shabby and carried a large bowler hat in one hand and a large sealed letter in the other.

Sir Hubert Sand looked at him; and then said quietly enough, but in a voice that somehow seemed curiously small, coming out of the fullness of his bodily presence: 'Oh – it's you.'

He held out his hand for the letter; and then looked around apologetically, with poised finger, before ripping it open and reading it. When he had read it, he stuffed it into his inside pocket and said hastily and a little harshly:

'Well, I suppose all this business is over, as you say. No more negotiations possible now; we couldn't pay the wages they want anyhow. But I shall want to see you again, Henry, about – about winding things up generally.'

'All right,' said Henry, a little sulkily perhaps, as if he would have preferred to wind them up by himself. 'I shall be up in number 188 after lunch; got to know how far they've got up there.'

The man with the glass eye, if it was a glass eye, stumped stiffly away; and the eye of Father Brown (which was by no means a glass eye) followed him thoughtfully as he threaded his way through the ladders and disappeared into the street.

It was on the following morning that Father Brown had the unusual experience of over-sleeping himself; or at least of starting from sleep with a subjective conviction that he must be late. This was partly due to his remembering, as a man may remember a dream, the fact of having been half-awakened at a more regular hour and fallen asleep again; a common enough occurrence with most of us, but a very uncommon occurrence with Father Brown. And he was afterwards oddly convinced, with that mystic side of him which was normally turned away from the world, that in that detached dark islet of dreamland, between the two wakings, there lay like buried treasure the truth of this tale.

As it was, he jumped up with great promptitude, plunged into his clothes, seized his big knobby umbrella and bustled out into the street, where the bleak white morning was breaking like splintered ice about the huge black building facing him. He was surprised to find that the streets shone almost empty in the cold crystalline light; the very look of it told him it could hardly be so late as he had feared. Then suddenly the stillness was cloven by the arrowlike swiftness of a long grey car which halted before the big deserted flats. Lord Stanes unfolded himself from within and approached the door, carrying (rather languidly) two large suitcases. At the same moment the door opened, and somebody seemed to step back instead of stepping out into the street. Stanes called twice to the man within, before that person seemed to complete his original gesture by coming out on to the doorstep; then the two held a brief colloquy, ending in the nobleman carrying his suitcases upstairs, and the other coming out into full daylight and revealing the heavy shoulders and peering head of young Henry Sand.

Father Brown made no more of this rather odd meeting, until two days later the young man drove up in his own car, and implored the priest to enter it. 'Something awful has happened,' he said, 'and I'd rather talk to you than Stanes. You know Stanes arrived the other day with some mad idea of camping in one of the flats that's just finished. That's why I had to go there early and open the door to him. But all that will keep. I want you to come up to my uncle's place at once.'

'Is he ill?' inquired the priest quickly.

'I think he's dead,' answered the nephew.

'What do you mean by saying you think he's dead?' asked Father Brown a little briskly. 'Have you got a doctor?'

'No,' answered the other. 'I haven't got a doctor or a patient either . . . It's no good calling in doctors to examine the body; because the body has run away. But I'm afraid I know where it has run to . . . the truth is – we kept it dark for two days; but he's disappeared.'

'Wouldn't it be better,' said Father Brown mildly, 'if you told me what has really happened from the beginning?'

'I know,' answered Henry Sand; 'it's an infernal shame to talk flippantly like this about the poor old boy; but people get like that when they're rattled. I'm not much good at hiding things; the long and the short of it is – well, I won't tell you the long of it now. It's what some people would call rather a long shot; shooting suspicions at random and so on. But the short of it is that my unfortunate uncle has committed suicide.'

They were by this time skimming along in the car through the last fringes of the town and the first fringes of the forest and park beyond it; the lodge gates of Sir Hubert Sand's small estate were about half a mile farther on amid the thickening throng of the beeches. The estate consisted chiefly of a small park and a large ornamental garden, which descended in terraces of a certain classical pomp to the very edge of the chief river of the district. As soon as they arrived at the house, Henry took the priest somewhat hastily through the old Georgian rooms and out upon the other side; where they silently descended the slope, a rather steep slope embanked with flowers, from which they could see the pale river spread out before them almost as flat as in a bird's-eye view. They were just turning the corner of the path under an enormous classical urn crowned with a somewhat incongruous garland of geraniums, when Father Brown saw a movement in the bushes and thin trees just below him, that seemed as swift as a movement of startled birds.

In the tangle of thin trees by the river two figures seemed to divide or scatter; one of them glided swiftly into the shadows and the other came forward to face them; bringing them to a halt and an abrupt and rather unaccountable silence. Then Henry Sand said in his heavy way: 'I think you know Father Brown . . . Lady Sand.'

Father Brown did know her; but at that moment he might almost have said that he did not know her. The pallor and constriction of her face was like a mask of tragedy; she was much younger than her husband, but at that moment she looked somehow older than everything in that old house and garden. And the priest remembered, with a subconscious thrill, that she was indeed older in type and lineage and was the true possessor of the place. For her own family had owned it as impoverished aristocrats, before she had restored its fortunes by marrying a successful business man. As she stood there, she might have been a family picture, or even a family ghost. Her pale face was of that pointed yet oval type seen in some old pictures of Mary Queen of Scots; and its expression seemed almost to go beyond the natural unnaturalness of a situation, in which her husband had vanished under suspicion of suicide. Father Brown, with the same subconscious movement of the mind, wondered who it was with whom she had been talking among the trees.

'I suppose you know all this dreadful news,' she said, with a comfortless composure. 'Poor Hubert must have broken down under all this revolutionary persecution, and been just maddened into taking his own life. I don't know whether you can do anything; or whether these horrible Bolsheviks can be made responsible for hounding him to death.'

'I am terribly distressed, Lady Sand,' said Father Brown. 'And still, I must own, a little bewildered. You speak of persecution; do you think that anybody could hound him to death merely by pinning up that paper on the wall?'

'I fancy,' answered the lady, with a darkening brow, 'that there were other persecutions besides the paper.'

'It shows what mistakes one may make,' said the priest sadly. 'I never should have thought he would be so illogical as to die in order to avoid death.'

'I know,' she answered, gazing at him gravely. 'I should never have believed it, if it hadn't been written with his own hand.'

'What?' cried Father Brown, with a little jump like a rabbit that has been shot at.

'Yes,' said Lady Sand calmly. 'He left a confession of suicide; so I fear there is no doubt about it.' And she passed on up the slope alone, with all the inviolable isolation of the family ghost.

The spectacles of Father Brown were turned in mute inquiry to the eyeglasses of Mr Henry Sand. And the latter gentleman, after an instant's hesitation, spoke again in his rather blind and plunging fashion: 'Yes, you see, it seems pretty clear now what he did. He was always a great swimmer and used to come down in his dressing-gown every morning for a dip in the river. Well, he came down as usual, and left his dressing-gown on the bank; it's lying there still. But he also left a message saying he was going for his last swim and then death, or something like that.'

'Where did he leave the message?' asked Father Brown.

'He scrawled it on that tree there, overhanging the water, I suppose the last thing he took hold of; just below where the dressing-gown's lying. Come and see for yourself.'

Father Brown ran down the last short slope to the shore and peered under the hanging tree, whose plumes were almost dipping in the stream. Sure enough, he saw on the smooth bark the words scratched conspicuously and unmistakably: 'One more swim and then drowning. Good-bye. Hubert Sand.' Father Brown's gaze travelled slowly up the bank till it rested on a gorgeous rag of raiment, all red and yellow with gilded tassels. It was the dressing-gown and the priest picked it up and began to turn it over. Almost as he did so he was conscious that a figure had flashed across the field of vision; a tall dark figure that slipped from one clump of trees to another, as if following the trail of the vanishing lady. He had little doubt that it was the companion from whom she had lately parted. He had still less doubt that it was the dead man's secretary, Mr Rupert Rae.

'Of course, it might be a final after-thought to leave the message,' said Father Brown, without looking up, his eye riveted on the red and gold garment. 'We've all heard of love-messages written on trees; and I suppose there might be death-messages written on trees too.'

'Well, he wouldn't have anything in the pockets of his dressing-gown, I suppose,' said young Sand. 'And a man might naturally scratch his message on a tree if he had no pens, ink or paper.'

'Sounds like French exercises,' said the priest dismally. 'But I wasn't thinking of that.' Then, after a silence, he said in a rather altered voice: 'To tell the truth, I was thinking whether a man might not naturally scratch his message on a tree, even if he had stacks of pens, and quarts of ink, and reams of paper.'

Henry was looking at him with a rather startled air, his eyeglasses crooked on his pug nose. 'And what do you mean by that?' he asked sharply.

'Well,' said Father Brown slowly, 'I don't exactly mean that postmen will carry letters in the form of logs, or that you will ever drop a line to a friend by putting a postage stamp on a pine tree. It would have to be a particular sort of position – in fact, it would have to be a particular sort of person, who really preferred this sort of arboreal correspondence. But, given the position and the person, I repeat what I said. He would still write on a tree, as the song says, if all the world were paper and all the sea were ink; if that river flowed with everlasting ink or all these woods were a forest of quills and fountain-pens.'

It was evident that Sand felt something creepy about the priest's fanciful imagery; whether because he found it incomprehensible or because he was beginning to comprehend.

'You see,' said Father Brown, turning the dressing-gown over slowly as he spoke, 'a man isn't expected to write his very best handwriting when he chips it on a tree. And if the man were not the man, if I make myself clear – Hullo!'

He was looking down at the red dressing-gown, and it seemed for the moment as if some of the red had come off on his finger; but both the faces turned towards it were already a shade paler.

'Blood!' said Father Brown; and for the instant there was a deadly stillness save for the melodious noises of the river.

Henry Sand cleared his throat and nose with noises that were by no means melodious. Then he said rather hoarsely: 'Whose blood?'

'Oh, mine,' said Father Brown; but he did not smile.

A moment after he said: 'There was a pin in this thing and I pricked myself. But I don't think you quite appreciate the point . . . the point of the pin, I do'; and he sucked his finger like a child.

'You see,' he said after another silence, 'the gown was folded up and pinned together; nobody could have unfolded it – at least without scratching himself. In plain words, Hubert Sand never *wore* this dressing-gown. Any more than Hubert Sand ever wrote on that tree. Or drowned himself in that river.'

The pince-nez tilted on Henry's inquiring nose fell off with a click; but he was otherwise motionless, as if rigid with surprise.

'Which brings us back,' went on Father Brown cheerfully, 'to somebody's taste for writing his private correspondence on trees, like Hiawatha and his picture-writing. Sand had all the time there was, before
drowning himself. Why didn't he leave a note for his wife like a sane
man? Or, shall we say . . . Why didn't the Other Man leave a note for
the wife like a sane man? Because he would have had to forge the
husband's handwriting; always a tricky thing now that experts are so
nosey about it. But nobody can be expected to imitate even his own
handwriting, let alone somebody else's, when he carves capital letters
in the bark of a tree. This is not a suicide, Mr Sand. If it's anything at
all, it's a murder.'

The bracken and bushes of the undergrowth snapped and crackled
as the big young man rose out of them like a leviathan, and stood
lowering, with his thick neck thrust forward.

'I'm no good at hiding things,' he said, 'and I half-suspected something
like this – expected it, you might say, for a long time. To tell the truth,
I could hardly be civil to the fellow – to either of them, for that matter.'

'What exactly do you mean?' asked the priest, looking him gravely
full in the face.

'I mean,' said Henry Sand, 'that you have shown me the murder and
I think I could show you the murderers.'

Father Brown was silent and the other went on rather jerkily.

'You said people sometimes wrote love-messages on trees. Well, as a
fact, there are some of them on that tree; there are two sorts of
monograms twisted together up there under the leaves – I suppose you
know that Lady Sand was the heiress of this place long before she
married; and she knew that damned dandy of a secretary even in those
days. I guess they used to meet here and write their vows upon the
trysting-tree. They seem to have used the trysting-tree for another
purpose later on. Sentiment, no doubt, or economy.'

'They must be very horrible people,' said Father Brown.

'Haven't there been any horrible people in history or the police-
news?' demanded Sand with some excitement. 'Haven't there been
lovers who made love seem more horrible than hate? Don't you know
about Bothwell and all the bloody legends of such lovers?'

'I know the legend of Bothwell,' answered the priest. 'I also know it
to be quite legendary. But of course it's true that husbands have been

sometimes put away like that. By the way, where was he put away? I
mean, where did they hide the body?'

'I suppose they drowned him, or threw him in the water when he was
dead,' snorted the young man impatiently.

Father Brown blinked thoughtfully and then said: 'A river is a good
place to hide an imaginary body. It's a rotten bad place to hide a real
one. I mean, it's easy to *say* you've thrown it in, because it *might* be
washed away to sea. But if you really did throw it in, it's about a hundred
to one it wouldn't; the chances of it going ashore somewhere are
enormous. I think they must have had a better scheme for hiding the
body than that – or the body would have been found by now. And if
there were any marks of violence –'

'Oh, bother hiding the body,' said Henry, with some irritation; 'haven't
we witness enough in the writing on their own devilish tree?'

'The body is the chief witness in every murder,' answered the other.
'The hiding of the body, nine times out of ten, is the practical problem
to be solved.'

There was a silence; and Father Brown continued to turn over the
red dressing-gown and spread it out on the shining grass of the sunny
shore; he did not look up. But, for some time past he had been conscious
that the whole landscape had been changed for him by the presence of
a third party; standing as still as a statue in the garden.

'By the way,' he said, lowering his voice, 'how do you explain that
little guy with the glass eye, who brought your poor uncle a letter
yesterday? It seemed to me he was entirely altered by reading it; that's
why I wasn't surprised at the suicide, when I thought it was a suicide.
That chap was a rather low-down private detective, or I'm much
mistaken.'

'Why,' said Henry in a hesitating manner, 'why, he might have been
– husbands do sometimes put on detectives in domestic tragedies like
this, don't they? I suppose he'd got the proofs of their intrigue; and so
they –'

'I shouldn't talk too loud,' said Father Brown, 'because your detective
is detecting us at this moment, from about a yard beyond those bushes.'

They looked up, and sure enough the goblin with the glass eye was
fixing them with that disagreeable optic, looking all the more grotesque
for standing among the white and waxen blooms of the classical garden.

Henry Sand scrambled to his feet again with a rapidity that seemed breathless for one of his bulk, and asked the man very angrily and abruptly what he was doing, at the same time telling him to clear out at once.

'Lord Stanes,' said the goblin of the garden, 'would be much obliged if Father Brown would come up to the house and speak to him.'

Henry Sand turned away furiously; but the priest put down his fury to the dislike that was known to exist between him and the nobleman in question. As they mounted the slope, Father Brown paused a moment as if tracing patterns on the smooth tree-trunk, glanced upwards once at the darker and more hidden hieroglyph said to be a record of romance; and then stared at the wider and more sprawling letters of the confession, or supposed confession of suicide.

'Do those letters remind you of anything?' he asked. And when his sulky companion shook his head, he added:

'They remind me of the writing on that placard that threatened him with the vengeance of the strikers.'

'This is the hardest riddle and the queerest tale I have ever tackled,' said Father Brown, a month later, as he sat opposite Lord Stanes in the recently furnished apartment of No. 188, the end flat which was the last to be finished before the interregnum of the industrial dispute and the transfer of work from the Trade Union. It was comfortably furnished; and Lord Stanes was presiding over grog and cigars, when the priest made his confession with a grimace. Lord Stanes had become rather surprisingly friendly, in a cool and casual way.

'I know that is saying a good deal, with your record,' said Stanes, 'but certainly the detectives, including our seductive friend with the glass eye, don't seem at all able to see the solution.'

Father Brown laid down his cigar and said carefully:

'It isn't that they can't see the solution. It is that they can't see the problem.'

'Indeed,' said the other, 'perhaps I can't see the problem either.'

'The problem is unlike all other problems, for this reason,' said Father Brown. 'It seems as if the criminal deliberately did two different things, either of which might have been successful; but which, when done together, could only defeat each other. I am assuming, what I firmly

believe, that the same murderer pinned up the proclamation threatening
a sort of Bolshevik murder, and also wrote on the tree confessing to an
ordinary suicide. Now you may say it is after all possible that the
proclamation was a proletarian proclamation; that some extremist workmen wanted to kill their employer, and killed him. Even if that were
true, it would still stick at the mystery of why they left, or why anybody
left, a contrary trail of private self-destruction. But it certainly isn't true.
None of these workmen, however bitter, would have done a thing like
that. I know them pretty well; I know their leaders quite well. To suppose
that people like Tom Bruce or Hogan would assassinate somebody they
could go for in the newspapers, and damage in all sorts of different
ways, is the sort of psychology that sensible people call lunacy. No;
there was somebody, who was not an indignant workman, who first
played the part of an indignant workman, and then played the part of a
suicidal employer. But, in the name of wonder, why? If he thought he
could pass it off smoothly as a suicide, why did he first spoil it all by
publishing a threat of murder? You might say it was an after-thought to
fix up the suicide story, as less provocative than the murder story. But
it wasn't less provocative *after* the murder story. He must have known
he had already turned our thoughts towards murder, when it should
have been his whole object to keep our thoughts away from it. If it was
an after-thought, it was the after-thought of a very thoughtless person.
And I have a notion that this assassin is a very thoughtful person. Can
you make anything of it?'

'No; but I see what you mean,' said Stanes, 'by saying that I didn't
even see the problem. It isn't merely who killed Sand; it's why anybody
should accuse somebody else of killing Sand and then accuse Sand of
killing himself.'

Father Brown's face was knotted and the cigar was clenched in his
teeth; the end of it glowed and darkened rhythmically like the signal of
some burning pulse of the brain. Then he spoke as if to himself:

'We've got to follow very closely and very clearly. It's like separating
threads of thought from each other; something like this. Because the
murder charge really rather spoilt the suicide charge, he wouldn't
normally have made the murder charge. But he did make it; so he had
some other reason for making it. It was so strong a reason that perhaps
it reconciled him even to weakening his other line of defence: that it

393

was a suicide. In other words, the murder charge wasn't really a murder charge. I mean he wasn't using it as a murder charge; he wasn't doing it so as to shift to somebody else the guilt of murder; he was doing it for some other extraordinary reason of his own. His plan had to contain a proclamation that Sand would be murdered; whether it threw suspicion on other people or not. Somehow or other the mere proclamation itself was necessary. But why?'

He smoked and smouldered away with the same volcanic concentration for five minutes before he spoke again.

'What could a murderous proclamation do, besides suggesting that the strikers were the murderers? What *did* it do? One thing is obvious; it inevitably did the opposite of what it said. It told Sand not to lock out his men; and it was perhaps the only thing in the world that would really have made him do it. You've got to think of the sort of man and the sort of reputation. When a man has been called a Strong Man in our silly sensational newspapers, when he is fondly regarded as a Sportsman by all the most distinguished asses in England, he simply can't back down because he is threatened with a pistol. It would be like walking about at Ascot with a white feather stuck in his absurd white hat. It would break the inner idol or ideal of oneself, which every man not a downright dastard does really prefer to life. And Sand wasn't a dastard; he was courageous; he was also impulsive. It acted instantly like a charm; his nephew, who had been more or less mixed up with the workmen, cried out instantly that the threat must be absolutely and instantly defied.'

'Yes,' said Lord Stanes, 'I noticed that.' They looked at each other for an instant, and then Stanes added carelessly: 'So you think the thing the criminal really wanted was –'

'The Lock-out!' cried the priest energetically. 'The Strike or whatever you call it; the cessation of work, anyhow. He wanted the work to stop at once; perhaps the black-legs to come in at once; certainly the Trade Unionists to go out at once. That is what he really wanted; God knows why. And he brought that off, I think, really without bothering much about its other implication of the existence of Bolshevist assassins. But then . . . then I think something went wrong. I'm only guessing and groping very slowly here; but the only explanation I can think of is that something began to draw attention to the real seat of the trouble; to the reason, whatever it was, of his wanting to bring the building to a halt.

And then belatedly, desperately, and rather inconsistently, he tried to lay the other trail that led to the river, simply and solely because it led away from the flats.'

He looked up through his moonlike spectacles, absorbing all the quality of the background and furniture; the restrained luxury of a quiet man of the world; and contrasting it with the two suitcases with which its occupant had arrived so recently in a newly-finished and quite unfurnished flat. Then he said rather abruptly:

'In short, the murderer was frightened of something or somebody in the flats. By the way, why did *you* come to live in the flats? . . . Also by the way, young Henry told me you made an early appointment with him when you moved in. Is that true?'

'Not in the least,' said Stanes, 'I got the key from his uncle the night before. I've no notion why Henry came here that morning.'

'Ah,' said Father Brown, 'then I think I have some notion of why he came . . . I *thought* you startled him by coming in just when he was coming out.'

'And yet,' said Stanes, looking across with a glitter in his grey-green eyes, 'you do rather think that I also am a mystery.'

'I think you are two mysteries,' said Father Brown. 'The first is why you originally retired from Sand's business. The second is why you have since come back to live in Sand's buildings.'

Stanes smoked reflectively, knocked out his ash, and rang a bell on the table before him. 'If you'll excuse me,' he said, 'I will summon two more to the council. Jackson, the little detective you know of, will answer the bell; and I've asked Henry Sand to come in a little later.'

Father Brown rose from his seat, walked across the room and looked down frowning into the fire-place.

'Meanwhile,' continued Stanes, 'I don't mind answering both your questions. I left the Sand business because I was sure there was some hanky-panky in it and somebody was pinching all the money. I came back to it, and took this flat, because I wanted to watch for the real truth about old Sand's death – on the spot.'

Father Brown faced round as the detective entered the room; he stood staring at the hearthrug and repeated: 'On the spot.'

'Mr Jackson will tell you,' said Stanes, 'that Sir Hubert commissioned him to find out who was the thief robbing the firm; and he brought a note of his discoveries the day before old Hubert disappeared.'

'Yes,' said Father Brown, 'and I know now where he disappeared to. I know where the body is.'

'Do you mean – ?' began his host hastily.

'It is here,' said Father Brown, and stamped on the hearthrug. 'Here, under the elegant Persian rug in this cosy and comfortable room.'

'Where in the world did you find that?'

'I've just remembered,' said Father Brown, 'that I found it in my sleep.'

He closed his eyes as if trying to picture a dream, and went on dreamily:

'This is a murder story turning on the problem of How to Hide the Body; and I found it in my sleep. I was always woken up every morning by hammering from this building. On that morning I half-woke up, went to sleep again and woke once more, expecting to find it late; but it wasn't. Why? Because there *had* been hammering that morning, though all the usual work had stopped; short, hurried hammering in the small hours before dawn. Automatically a man sleeping stirs at such a familiar sound. But he goes to sleep again, because the usual sound is not at the usual hour. Now why did a certain secret criminal want all the work to cease suddenly; and only new workers come in? Because, if the old workers had come in next day, they would have found a new piece of work done in the night. The old workers would have known where they left off; and they would have found the whole flooring of this room already nailed down. Nailed down by a man who knew how to do it; having mixed a good deal with the workmen and learned their ways.'

As he spoke, the door was pushed open and a head poked in with a thrusting motion; a small head at the end of a thick neck and a face that blinked at them through glasses.

'Henry Sand said,' observed Father Brown, staring at the ceiling, 'that he was no good at hiding things. But I think he did himself an injustice.'

Henry Sand turned and moved swiftly away down the corridor.

'He not only hid his thefts from the firm quite successfully for years,' went on the priest with an air of abstraction, 'but when his uncle discovered them, he hid his uncle's corpse in an entirely new and original manner.'

At the same instant Stanes again rang a bell, with a long strident steady ringing; and the little man with the glass eye was propelled or shot along the corridor after the fugitive, with something of the rotatory motion of a mechanical figure in a zoetrope. At the same moment, Father Brown looked out of the window, leaning over a small balcony, and saw five or six men start from behind bushes and railings in the street below and spread out equally mechanically like a fan or net; opening out after the fugitive who had shot like a bullet out of the front door. Father Brown saw only the pattern of the story; which had never strayed from that room; where Henry had strangled Hubert and hid his body under impenetrable flooring, stopping the whole work on the building to do it. A pin-prick had started his own suspicions; but only to tell him he had been led down the long loop of a lie. The point of the pin was that it was pointless.

He fancied he understood Stanes at last, and he liked to collect queer people who were difficult to understand. He realized that this tired gentleman, whom he had once accused of having green blood, had indeed a sort of cold green flame of conscientiousness or conventional honour, that had made him first shift out of a shady business, and then feel ashamed of having shifted it on to others; and come back as a bored laborious detective; pitching his camp on the very spot where the corpse had been buried; so that the murderer, finding him sniffing so near the corpse, had wildly staged the alternative drama of the dressing-gown and the drowned man. All that was plain enough, but, before he withdrew his head from the night air and the stars, Father Brown threw one glance upwards at the vast black bulk of the cyclopean building heaved far up into the night, and remembered Egypt and Babylon, and all that is at once eternal and ephemeral in the work of man.

'I was right in what I said first of all,' he said. 'It reminds one of Coppée's poem about the Pharaoh and the Pyramid. This house is supposed to be a hundred houses; and yet the whole mountain of building is only one man's tomb.'